Enjoy!

Kristine Cayne

HER TWO MEN
In London

Dear Sharon,

I hope you enjoy the series!

Dena Delamar

What Readers Are Saying

Praise for Dana Delamar

"This story truly exceeded my expectations. *Revenge* is action packed, and when the pace picks up, it does not slow down.... I cannot wait to read the next book."

—*The Romance Reviews (TRR)* site, 5 stars, Top Pick

"A taut thrilling romance of moral ambiguity... The thrills are intense and the suspense is strong, as the main characters struggle to determine who they can trust."—Kerry L. Reis, Amazon reviewer

"5 stars = I freaking LOVED this book!!! Holy moly! I thought *Malavita* was good, but Ms. Delamar blew it out of the water with *Revenge*.... I look forward to reading *Retribution* to find out where the story goes from here."—Angela S. Goodrich, *Crystal's Many Reviewers*

"Wow where to start with this review. This book had me completely gripped from start to finish; I wasn't able to put it down until I'd read right to the last page.... Definitely a book I would read again."—Amazon UK reader review

Praise for Kristine Cayne

"I loved this book... The story of Chad and Hollywood is so deep and intense... a total gut wrenching and emotional book... it made me cry... made me laugh... it was packed full of everything a book needs.... One of the best M/M books I have read."

—Diane, *For the Love of Pimping* blog, on *Lover on Top*

"WOW!! This book is going to be one of the best I've read this year. It was flawless in my opinion. [...] I went through so many emotions reading this story but I couldn't turn the page fast enough."

—Kathy, *KathyMac Reviews* blog, on *Lover on Top*

"Stock up on ice cubes because this is definitely one sizzling debut.... As rich as a white chocolate cheesecake, Cayne's entrance into the suspense genre is invigorating, explosive and simply intoxicating...."

—*RT Book Reviews*, 4½ stars, Top Pick! on *Deadly Obsession*

The Total Indulgence Series

Her Two Men in London (Book One)

Her Two Men in Tahiti (Book Two) – coming 2018

Her Two Men in Sonoma (Book Three) – coming 2018

Her Two Men In London

TOTAL INDULGENCE, BOOK 1

DANA DELAMAR
KRISTINE CAYNE

Three Orcas Press

ISBN (print): 1-949071-01-4
ISBN-13 (print): 978-1-949071-01-6
ISBN (ebook): 1-949071-00-6
ISBN-13 (ebook): 978-1-949071-00-9

Publisher's Note: This is a work of fiction. Names, characters, places, and incidents either are the product of the author's imagination or are used fictitiously, and any resemblance to actual persons, living or dead, business establishments, events, or locales is entirely coincidental.

Cover artwork & series logo design
© 2018 L.J. Anderson of Mayhem Cover Creations
mayhemcovercreations.com

Cover photo: © The Killion Group Inc.

Dana Delamar author image courtesy of LGImages

Editing, proofreading, and print formatting:
By Your Side Self-Publishing
www.ByYourSideSelfPub.com

ACKNOWLEDGMENTS

Many thanks to our husbands for putting up with our shenanigans and feeding us when we're hungry. We love you!

And many thanks to our readers for encouraging our craziness!

Chapter 1

RILEY

Sometimes I couldn't believe it had all started with a blow job. The blow job that had gotten me fired, put me on the front page of my hometown newspaper, and eventually led to my writing a blockbuster erotic romance series that had sold to Hollywood and made me a millionaire.

A millionaire who was close to broke and was probably going to have to declare bankruptcy. Because I couldn't seem to write about blow jobs, or any other kind of sex, anymore.

I could try to blame her, Amber Rose McCallan, the girl who'd given me the blow job in my office when she'd been a nineteen-year-old co-ed and I'd been a twenty-six-year-old college professor who should have known better. But that would be taking the easy way out. It wasn't Amber's fault, not entirely.

Yes, Amber, the inspiration behind my best-selling trilogy, "The Temptation of Amber Rose," had left me eight months ago for Holden Wilder, the actor playing me in the movies. And she'd pranced off with a big fat check after suing me for palimony.

But I was the idiot who'd lied to my publisher, Exotica Press, who had me under contract. A seven-figure contract, with a mid-six-figure advance on my next book.

The book I'd supposedly been writing during the last six months.

The book I hadn't even started. Because I couldn't.

The book I was supposed to deliver to my editor today.

And now here I was, standing outside Exotica, about to face my doom.

Rubbing at the ache in my chest, I pushed through the etched glass doors of Exotica's Brooklyn office and strode up to the receptionist. I'd barely opened my mouth before she shoved a copy of my first book, *Amber Falls*, at me along with a pen. "Oh my God, it's you!" she squealed. "Riley Kendrick!"

I almost laughed. The girl was a pretty blonde with curly hair. I picked up the pen she'd shoved at me. "Who should I make this out to?"

She pointed to the tag on her chest, practically poking my eyes out with her double D's. "Jenna."

My dick should have perked up at the sight, but it merely yawned. Yep, I'd had my hands on more than enough fake boobs in Hollywood. I began signing the book. "You're new here."

"Started this week."

Normally I'd have flirted with her, but no more delays. I pulled in a deep breath, trying to slow my quickening pulse. "Can you tell Nora Delaney I'm here?"

"Oh yes. Gosh! Sorry! I just don't meet celebrities every day."

I handed the book back to her as she buzzed my editor. It was nice being recognized by fans, but I wished now that I'd used a pen name so I could pretend it was all happening to someone else.

Someone whose face hadn't been plastered all over every tabloid, gossip website, and entertainment news TV show.

Someone who could fucking write, rain or shine. Heartbreak or joy. Hell or heaven.

But I wasn't that person.

Instead of a book draft, all I had on me was an empty USB drive. And a belly full of nerves. If Nora demanded that I return the advance, I'd be screwed. Good and hard, with no lube, fuck you very much.

I'd spent it. Every dime. Well, most of it had ended up in Amber's pocket, actually.

She got to swan around Hollywood and act injured.

I got to *be* injured, and wander the streets of the quiet Vermont neighborhood I'd grown up in. Probably where I'd die too, like my parents, whose old house I was living in.

When you had it all and lost it all at twenty-eight, where did you go from there?

Nora sauntered out of her office, her reading glasses perched atop the tight bun on her head. Her strand of pearls and sweater set looked like something out of the 50s, except with a modern twist, and it was a look she pulled off well. Sexy Librarian. Probably my favorite look after Sex-Starved Co-Ed.

If I coaxed Nora into bending over her desk so I could give her something she wouldn't forget, would she forgive me for arriving empty-handed?

Probably not, but the fucking might be fun. Until she kneed me in the balls.

Nora greeted me with a big smile. "So good to see you, Riley." She gave me a loose hug and an air kiss on both cheeks. "Coffee, tea, water?"

"Sorry I'm late. Tea will be fine."

Nora nodded to Jenna, who practically jumped out of her chair.

I followed Nora into her office, accepted a steaming mug from Jenna, and contemplated what to say. Not that I hadn't rehearsed it a million times already. I could tell her I'd started the book, but that was only technically true.

I'd started dozens of new books and tossed them all out.

"So," Nora said, eyeing me as I blew on my tea. "Is it done?"

I took a sip to delay the inevitable. Then I set my cup on the edge of her desk and crossed my legs, taking hold of the ankle lying on my right knee as if it were a lifeline.

Somehow I met her expectant gaze. I swallowed hard. Honesty was the best policy, right? "Nora, I've tried. I really have. It's all shit. Everything I write is shit."

A crease developed between her perfectly plucked eyebrows. "But you have something? I'm sure it's not shit, Riley. You're just worried that it won't be a big success."

I shook my head slowly. "While that's true, that's not the problem."

Nora clasped her hands together and leaned forward. "Then what is the problem?"

I slumped back in the chair, unable to hold her eyes any longer. A lump crowded my throat, and when I opened my mouth to speak, the words seemed stuck, unwilling to spill forth. Taking a deep breath, I prayed my voice would be steady, but the damn thing cracked when I finally forced the truth out.

"I can't write without her."

Nora said nothing for a minute. When she finally smiled, it was tight. "So you're telling me you're Austin Powers and Amber has stolen your mojo?"

I couldn't help a weak laugh, then when I saw she wasn't smiling, I sobered and spread my hands. "I've got nothing. Not a word."

Nora crossed her arms and sat back. "You're *not* doing this to me, Riley. You're not."

I hated making her worry. "I'm afraid I am. My muse has left me."

"Your muse took up residence in Amber's pussy? Is that it? Because if not, you still have everything it takes to be Riley Kendrick."

I groaned. "I've come to hate that name."

"Well, you're stuck with it." Nora gave me a considering look. "So you need a new muse, is that it?"

"Or something. The Amber books just poured out. Now the words won't come."

Nora pulled her reading glasses off her head and played with them. "I assume you've seen the papers." She said the words softly, but they were a blow nevertheless. A reminder. "They're engaged."

"Yes." A year ago, three Hollywood studios had been in a bidding war for the rights to the trilogy. Amber and I had been the toast of the town—partying with the who's who of the silver screen, living a life neither of us had ever imagined. A life full of late nights, drugs, booze, and sex—more sex than we could handle.

Apparently.

I'd always had an open mind about sex—nothing was off the books. When Amber wanted to have a threesome with Holden Wilder, the handsome actor cast in the lead role of Riley, I hadn't objected. As long as I was a part of it, I'd said yes to anything and everything Amber wanted. And truth be told, I'd fallen for Holden too.

Hook, line, and big fat sinker. I had been on top of the world; I'd had it bad for both of them.

But Amber and Holden were with each other now, and they didn't need me.

No one did.

Except for Exotica. They needed me to write their next big hit.

And then there was Carter Templeton, the guy I'd been fucking these last three months. But fucking was all it was. Right?

That's all I'd meant to Amber. And Holden.

After a pause, Nora said, "So Amber's not coming back. And Exotica can't afford to give you a half-million-dollar advance and not get a book in return."

"I know." I rubbed at the stubble on my jaw, the hairs rasping against my skin.

"Can you repay the advance?" Again Nora's voice was gentle, even though the words eviscerated me.

"Nope." Too bad the tea I was holding wasn't something stronger. Something with a sky-high alcohol content. The last time I'd seen Amber, she'd complained that the palimony check was too small. "You owe me, Riley Kendrick," she'd said, her pretty face flushed a deep pink, her hands shaking. "I made you who you are!"

I didn't disagree. My obsession with Amber had upended my life—gotten me fired from my first teaching job and launched my new career.

And left me heartbroken in the end.

Nora leaned forward, her eyes locked on mine. "Then what's it going to take to get you writing again?"

"I need a new muse."

"What you need is to get out of the damn house more often. You need a change of scenery."

I scrubbed both hands through my hair, then nodded. "Perhaps you're right."

"Of course I am."

"Or maybe I need to sign up for Tinder."

Nora made a face. "Look, if all you need is some inspiration, I'm sure Jenna could help in that department."

I laughed. "She's cute."

"She adores you. How about that dynamic for a change?"

"Being the object of someone's desire? Hmm..."

Could work. Except I didn't want the endless moaning when we broke up. Jenna looked like she could pull off Sexy Stalker in a heartbeat.

And then there was Carter to consider. We'd done a number of threesomes with women, but we'd never discussed adding a third to whatever we had. Which we also hadn't defined.

Which was how I wanted it. No strings, no attachments. No way to be hurt.

"Did you have someone in mind?" Nora asked.

"No. No one and nothing has inspired me. The only thing I've liked in months is *Outlander*."

"So write Scottish Highland historicals. Just keep them sexy."

"I know fuck-all about Scotland."

"Then go. Write it off as research, but go." She rummaged around her desk, picking up papers, then setting them down before extracting something from a pile. "Or do this." She pressed a red brochure in my hand.

Romance Writers' Jolly Old England Writing Retreat
Want to explore England and Scotland from a local point of view?
Need more settings for your historical romance? We'll show you plenty!
Stuck? We'll get you going again.
Need inspiration? We'll get you fired up!

Could something like this work? The pictures looked inviting. Was I really cut out to write historicals though?

"I don't know, Nora."

"You've got to do something."

"True." There were certainly worse ways to spend my time. Such as cooped up in my house sniffing Amber's clothes and hoping she'd come running back to me. That wasn't going to happen. Not now. Not ever.

And it really wasn't fair to Carter. I had to get out of this funk. And then maybe I could figure out if we actually had something, or if it was just sex.

Maybe Nora was right, and a trip was exactly what I needed to clear my head and jump-start the words again. I met her eyes. "I'll do it. How long can you give me to turn in a draft?"

"Three months."

I looked at the brochure. The trip started in three days and ended two days before the press junket for the first movie. Maybe the stars were aligning.

Now I just had to hope my muse would come back. Amber had taken so much from me, but Nora was right. I was Riley fucking Kendrick.

Fuck Amber, and fuck her magic pussy. I could write without her.

I had to.

PAIGE

I'd already ended the call, but I couldn't seem to put down the phone. Looking around at the travel posters in my office at Total Indulgence Tours, I shook my head and swore. "Shit!" This wasn't good. This wasn't good at all.

My boss, Arianna Rodriguez, poked her head into my office, her eyebrows raised. "What's up? The Paige Sutherland I know doesn't swear unless the world's coming to an end."

Finally releasing the receiver, I slowly turned to face Ari. "Sara fell walking down the stairs from her apartment. She's got a broken leg. There's no way she's going to be able to guide the Jolly Old England romance writing retreat."

Arianna frowned. "That does merit a 'shit' then."

"Do we have anyone who can take it?" I pressed a hand to my stomach, my mind adding up the consequences if we had to cancel the tour at the last minute.

Arianna tapped a French-manicured finger against her lips, then shook her head. "We could try looking for a sub, but with less than two days, I don't see how we'll find someone."

"I just filled the last slot too." And it was a male writer. One with a deep, velvety voice that made me wonder what he looked like.

With a clap of her hands, Arianna's expression lightened. "You, *chica*!

You could do it. You put the whole thing together. You know all the contacts. And you could *definitely* use a vacation."

"Guiding a tour isn't a vacation."

"For you, it would be. You never go anywhere. And that's kind of ridiculous, considering where you work." Arianna perched her perky butt on my desk. "Maybe you'll meet a hot Englishman. Or maybe a Scot." Arianna fanned her cheeks. "Wouldn't you love that brogue purring in your ears?"

I rolled my eyes. Yeah. That was *so* not going to happen. What hunky Scot would want a thirty-seven-year-old single mom whose daughter had Down syndrome?

Not that I could leave Emma alone anyway. "I can't, Ari. And you know why."

Arianna placed a hand over mine and squeezed. "It's time to let Emma spread her wings. She *is* eighteen."

"With the reasoning ability of a twelve-year-old." A twelve-year-old who was boy crazy. Emma had been begging me to let her move into an adult group home, but that was a surefire recipe for disaster. I didn't want my disabled daughter repeating my mistake and getting pregnant at eighteen. Especially since Emma could never care for a child on her own.

I looked up at my beautiful boss. Arianna didn't have kids. At twenty-eight, Ari didn't have a clue about how tough it was to raise a child, much less one with Down syndrome. A child who would forever be a child. "Anything could happen to Emma. She's so trusting."

"You can't be there for her forever. Someday you have to let go. Why not use this as a trial? It's only three weeks."

"She could get pregnant in three weeks."

"So put her on birth control."

"That won't stop her from getting abused."

"I'm sure the home has people watching out for the residents."

My mouth went dry. No one would watch over my baby as well as I could.

Arianna gave my hand another squeeze. "She's been doing great at her job, hasn't she?"

"Yes." The job at the coffeehouse was something else Arianna had talked me into. I'd been struggling to cover Emma's daycare now that she was finished with school. But ever since Emma had had a job to go to, my money worries had abated.

But a group home… "I just don't know. What if something happens?"

"You've had the talk, right?"

"Yes, but it's hard to know how much she really understands. Sometimes Emma surprises me, but it's not always in a good way."

"I'll check on her. Every day." Arianna crossed herself. "I swear it on my *abuelita*'s grave."

I laughed. "Both of your grandmothers are still alive!"

Ari gave me a wink. "You know what I mean. I know Emma is your whole life." She said the words softly. "But she can't be your whole life forever. It's not healthy." She motioned to the neat stacks of paper on my desk. "All you do is work and take care of her. Don't get me wrong—Daniel, Javier, and I really appreciate all the hours you put in, but we're worried about you too. You've been here five years now. And you've never taken a day off unless you were sick."

I looked away from the concern in Arianna's eyes. It was true. I was tired, the kind of bone-deep tired that went beyond mere exhaustion. I was close to burnout.

And while this trip wouldn't exactly be a vacation, it would be a change of pace and a change of scenery. And I'd get to visit all the places I'd longed to see. I'd spent my whole life in Miami. Rather ironic for someone who worked at one of the most exclusive tour companies in the world. It was high time I saw some of it.

"You'll check on her every day? You swear it?"

A wide smile broke across Arianna's face, her perfect white teeth contrasting nicely with her light tan complexion. "I swear it, *chica*."

I took a deep breath. A thrill raced through me. I was going to do it. I was going to get out there and live for once.

Even if it was for only three weeks.

Arianna flipped her shiny black hair over her shoulders. "Just promise me you'll get laid. And tell me all the details."

Heat flooded my cheeks. "You have no idea how long it's been since I've had sex."

"Don't tell me it's been eighteen years."

The heat spread down my neck until my whole face and chest felt like they were burning. "It hasn't been quite that long, but not since I started here."

Arianna's jaw dropped open, her rosy lips forming a perfect O. She shook her head. "¡*Ay, chica*! You're probably a virgin all over again by now!"

I pressed my hands to my flaming cheeks. "That's what I'm afraid of."

"It's like riding a bike, right?"

"Haven't done that in ages either. I'd probably fall off if I tried."

Arianna leaned forward, grinning like a loon. "Then let him get on top!"

I started to giggle. "It's that easy?"

"Yes, it's that easy. But maybe for you…" Arianna paused, looking me over. "I'd suggest having a few drinks to loosen up first."

I groaned. "When did I become so hopeless?"

"About the time you forgot that you have a great rack and a tight ass." I opened my mouth to protest, but Arianna wagged a finger in my face. "And before you object, I can say those things even though I'm your boss. *I'm* not trying to take advantage of your God-given assets. I'm trying to get *you* to take advantage of them. Outside the workplace, of course."

Ari was right; I did need to get laid. It would be the second item on my bucket list. Right after seeing the house Jane Austen had lived in.

No need to tell Ari that though. She'd just tell me my priorities were all screwed up.

And maybe they were.

Ari gave me a wave and sashayed out the door, her form-fitting fuchsia dress highlighting every luscious curve. Men chased Arianna Rodriguez like they'd never seen a woman before.

When was the last time a man had looked at me that way?

Probably the night I'd gotten pregnant.

I pressed a hand to my belly. I'd better stop at the drugstore on my way home and stock up on condoms.

I had some living to do, but this time I wasn't going to make any mistakes.

CARTER

Someday I should say no to the booty calls. But damn it, I had it bad for Riley Kendrick, and all I could do was say *yes, yes, yes. Please God yes.*

All in the hope that someday he would ask for more.

Standing on the front porch of Riley's house, I leaned against the frame of the door he had just opened to me, my eyes raking up and down his tall, lithe body. The three months we'd been seeing each other—if you could call it that—had led to some of the best sex I'd ever had. Riley was adventurous, and he'd introduced me to threesomes. Not that sex wasn't good when it was only the two of us, but he really seemed to light up when a woman was added into the mix.

The thought had me frowning. Was that what was holding him back, because something definitely was. Did he want to be in a relationship with a woman instead of with me—another man? Shit.

Riley focused in on my frown, and I forced myself to smile. "Hey, sexy." I stepped forward, my hand cupping the back of his neck, pulling him in, as I inhaled the spicy, woody scent of expensive cologne deep into my lungs, a holdover from his Hollywood days no doubt. The fragrance always reminded me of what a catch Riley was. Sure, he wasn't topping the Who's Who charts anymore, but that would all change once his new movie was released. Even now, he was often recognized by the thousands of fans who followed him on social media, eagerly awaiting word of his next novel, his next guest appearance, his next book signing.

My lips met his in an impassioned kiss. When I stroked my tongue over that plump bottom lip I'd never get enough of, my cock filled, lengthened, hardened. "What the hell is it about you?" I whispered, before plunging into his mouth.

Riley's fingers dug into my arms, then slid inside the back of my jeans to grasp my ass in a firm grip. His low moan sent shivers racing up my spine. Unable to wait another moment, I pinned him against the entrance hall wall and pressed our hips together. I needed more. Needed to feel our bare cocks sliding against each other. Needed to sink my dick into his tight ass.

And I needed it now.

I quickly dealt with the open front door, then I advanced on him. I pushed my hands under his shirt, lifting it over his head, and latched onto a dark nipple as soon as one became visible. Riley's hips jerked against my own, and he pressed his chest against my hungry lips.

"Oh fuck. Don't stop," Riley pleaded. He fumbled with the tab of my jeans, then the zipper.

"Never." I shifted to his other nipple while pinching the first with just the amount of pressure that would drive him crazy.

Riley managed to free us both of our pants and underwear, and it wasn't until he tugged off my shirt that I stopped torturing his now-reddened nipples. They'd be ripe for the plucking when the time came.

I threaded my fingers through Riley's almost-black hair, capturing his head between my hands. Over the past few days, he'd stopped shaving, and he already had a half inch of scruff on his cheeks and chin. It made him look a little older, a little rougher, and the feel of it scraping my own smooth cheeks had my cock straining and leaking pre-cum.

He was dark everywhere that I was light. Even his eyes were brown where mine were blue. And I loved the contrast between us.

"Christ," I said on a moan, my chest heaving as I tried to catch my breath. "You're so damn sexy. I could come just looking at you."

Riley broke into a wide grin, the same one I had seen in numerous photos of him and his ex, Amber, in Hollywood rags at the grocery store checkout. It was a beautiful smile. And it was utterly fake.

"Rye." I stroked his jaw. "Did I say something wrong?"

His gaze dropped to the carpet and his lips drew into a thin line. He shrugged before taking my hand. "Not at all." Pressing his lips to our joined fingers, he turned and pulled me farther into the secluded, newly renovated house on the shores of Lake Champlain. "Let's go to bed. I've got plans for us tonight." He shot me a sassy wink over his shoulder.

But I wasn't fooled. I'd let it slide for now, but I'd make sure he told me tomorrow. If something was bothering him, whether it was something I had done or not, I wanted to know what it was. Three months was long enough for me to learn that Riley had a problem expressing himself. He would keep things bottled up until they exploded out of him and photos of the resulting disaster ended up splashed all over social media.

Riley opened the door to his bedroom and ushered me in. Taking his arm, I spun him around so his back was to my front, and my cock was nestled between his butt cheeks.

"So"—I kissed his neck, nibbling the tight tendons when he tilted his head to the side—"tell me about these plans."

Riley's body stiffened. "Plans?"

Something was definitely up. I tightened my arms around his waist, gently rolling my hips so my cock slid in that tight valley. "Yeah, you said you had plans for us tonight. I hope they involve you, me, and some sticky chocolate syrup."

Laughing, he pushed his ass against my aching cock. "Oh, there'll be something sticky all right, but I can't guarantee it'll be chocolate."

I reached down and gripped his long, hard erection, stroking it from the base to the tip. I loved the look and heft of Riley's cock, thick and with just the right curve to peg my prostate with every thrust. I usually topped, since he seemed to prefer to bottom, but the occasional times we'd switched things up, I'd been on cloud nine.

"Maybe you had some cream in mind instead?"

Groaning, he thrust into my fist. "Yeah, something like that. Now fuck me, you sadistic bastard."

I shoved him toward the bed so he landed with his hands on the mattress. "Stay like that."

Riley's only response was to widen his stance and arch his back as he wiggled his ass invitingly. I grabbed a condom and the lube from the nightstand and closed the distance between us.

With trembling fingers, I leaned forward and teased the lube along the edges of his sensitive hole, reveling in his answering moans.

"Oh God, oh God." Riley pushed back, impaling himself on my fingers. I shivered, imagining myself buried balls deep in all that heat and tightness. I grasped his ass more firmly and plunged my fingers into that delicious hole, over and over. We were both trembling. Riley's thighs quivered and shook. The scent of sweat and sex filled my nostrils, and my hips bucked involuntarily.

Shit. "If I don't get inside you right now, this will be over before it starts."

He pressed his head against his forearms on the bed, his gorgeous ass up in the air. "Hurry the hell up, then. I need to feel you inside me. Need you fill me up."

Moments later, appropriately gloved up, I slathered lube onto my throbbing cock and applied some more to Riley's flexing hole. I pressed a few fingers back inside, scissoring them to stretch him a little more. I didn't want him hurting.

"Enough with the damn prep," he yelled. "Fuck me now."

Grinning, I stood behind him and slowly eased my cock where we both wanted it to go. I ran my hands up and down his smooth back, letting him adjust to my invasion.

"You're so damn hot and tight, Rye. Nothing feels as good as being inside you."

"Hey, Chatty Cathy." He shot me a narrowed glare over his shoulder. "Less talking, more fucking."

I bit back a laugh. "Anything for my man."

And there it was again, that fake grin and pained look. Fuck. Desperate to salvage the moment, I gripped his hips. "Hang on, dude. Things are about to get nasty."

Like a jackhammer, I rammed into his ass, deep strokes, shallow strokes, slow, fast. Anything to keep us both on the edge for as long as I could.

"That's it. Fuck me. Harder. Oh fuck. Yeah." He moaned long and loud as I hit his prostate. "Oh yeah. Like that."

I closed my eyes so the sight of Riley at his loudest and dirtiest didn't toss me over the precipice. I loved seeing him come undone, but if I'd learned anything about the man during our short acquaintance, it was that everything, especially sex, had to be on his terms.

Taking a deep breath, I slowed my thrusts a bit. His growl had my lids snapping open. Riley's lips were pulled back, baring his teeth. "Stop on penalty of death, you sexy motherfucker."

"Wasn't stopping," I said between pants. "Just catching my breath."

"Breathe later." And with that, he jerked his hips forward, forcing me to pull out. With a twist of his shoulders, he fell onto his back on the bed and held his legs up at the knees, leaving himself spread wide and exposed.

How could I argue with an offer like that?

"Jesus, Rye." The things the guy did. Just when I feared he was pulling away, he did something like this. Made himself vulnerable in a way I couldn't. Made me fall a little more. "Goddamn you." He was going to break my fucking heart and there wasn't a damned thing I could do about it.

Except, maybe, make Riley fall for me too.

Positioning myself over him, I entered him as our mouths met in an intense kiss that had butterflies taking off in the pit of my stomach.

Despite his urgings, I slowed things down, pressing into him with long, smooth strokes that brushed his prostate with each roll of my hips.

Riley's fingers curled over my shoulders, digging in. I'd have marks in the morning. He arched his back and stared into my eyes. "Oh God, Carter. I'm coming."

"Yes. I want to see you come so fucking bad." Not so gently, I tweaked his roughened nipple and swallowed his cries with a scorching kiss. I poured all my emotions into it, hoping beyond hope that he would sense the change. Would accept it and reciprocate. Maybe not today, but someday soon.

My heart full, I pushed into his ass as deep as I could, before finally letting my climax wash over me in wave after wave. For several moments, I lay still, panting against his neck, the evidence of Riley's pleasure cooling against his abdomen. His heart beat steadily, lulling me into a world of possibilities.

A world that splintered into a million shards with Riley's next words.

"I'm leaving for Europe in the morning."

Chapter 2

RILEY

"What the fuck, Riley?" Carter asked. "You're leaving? Tomorrow?"

Shit. This was not how this evening was supposed to go. He left the bed, but instead of walking away, he folded his arms across his chest and stared down at me as I lay there, unsure what to say, my own cum drying on my stomach.

"Speak," Carter said, his blue eyes darkening.

I sat up. I was a fucking mess, I wanted a shower, I needed to pack… I wanted to do anything but have this conversation. "There's no need to get wound up. I'm going on a writers' retreat. It's in the UK."

"The UK?"

"Yeah." I leaned over and pawed through the messy stack of books and papers on my nightstand and pulled out the red brochure. "Here."

Carter took it and scanned the pages. Then he folded it shut, his fingers tightening on the stiff paper until it was helplessly bent. "You're running away."

I swallowed hard and stared at the hardwood floor. Was I? "I need to get away for a while. But I'm coming back."

"Are you? Are you coming back to me? To whatever it is we have?"

Fuck. I ran my hands through my hair. I'd thought a guy would be easier—less pressure to define everything, just have a good time, keep things casual… But here we were, three months in, having "the" conversation. "I'm coming back, Carter. That's all I know right now."

A muscle ticked in his jaw. "You've been acting weird tonight. Something's wrong."

"Nothing's wrong," I lied, something I'd gotten alarmingly good at recently. Deny, deny, deny. God, I needed a drink, a line of blow, a hot body to plow into…

"Don't try to bullshit me. I know you well enough to tell when you're lying." Before I could formulate a reply, he continued. "Am I not enough for you? Do you want a woman instead? Is that what will make you happy?"

A knot formed in my gut. I'd been avoiding thinking about it. What did I need long-term? The happiest I'd ever been was with Amber and Holden, those brief few months when we'd been a trio, the three of us fucking like rabbits, waking up in each other's arms, one big happy tangle. I'd written the third book of the trilogy in a joyous rush, the words pouring out, my heart so full it had felt like it would burst. And then it was all over, almost as soon as the ink had dried on the newly printed books.

I'd caught Amber and Holden sneaking off together, lying about the fact that they were shutting me out, that they were done with me like so much used tissue.

"Your silence speaks volumes, Riley," Carter said, his tone cutting.

I could come just looking at you, he'd said earlier. The words were so close to something Amber had said to me once. Amber, who hadn't meant a fucking word of the declarations of love she'd whispered in my ear. And Holden? He'd lied too. But then, he was an actor, so what else did I expect?

I looked up at Carter. "You think you want more with me, right?"

"Yeah. At least I did. Now I'm not so sure."

"Well, I'm not sure about anything. I used to be. But the last year taught me that I don't know shit. And things that seem solid might be illusions."

"I'm not Amber. Or Holden."

"I know that."

"Do you?"

I met his eyes. "I want to trust you. I do. But I'm not sure I can even trust myself."

Carter looked away. "Am I just pissing away some time here, or do I have a chance with you?" His voice came out thick, raw.

Goddammit. I didn't want to hurt him. "I'm not leaving you."

"Not yet."

"Fuck." I rose and stepped toward him. "I don't know what I want. I don't know if I need a woman to be happy. Or a man. Or both. I do know that I really like you, and I like what we have together. But I also know something's not working for me, not entirely." I paused. "I can't write."

Carter's brow furrowed. "Weren't you supposed to deliver your next book today?"

I nodded. "I've got nothing. And I owe Exotica a six-figure advance if I don't deliver a draft in three months."

He whistled. "Shit."

I almost smiled. "So now you know what's wrong."

He touched my cheek, his fingers rasping on my stubble. "Is that all?"

"I have to figure this out. If I can't write, and I can't teach, what the fuck am I going to do?"

His hand cupped the base of my skull, its warmth seeping into my skin. It would be so easy to lean on him, to just let myself fall, to stop trying. "You're not alone in all this, you know. I've got the summer off. I could go with you."

Heat rose to my cheeks. Should I tell him the truth? That I'd signed up for the retreat using his name? "I really need to do this on my own. This has nothing to do with you. With us."

His gaze narrowed. "Be honest with me. Are we breaking up?"

"Think of this as a hiatus. A little time apart to see where we stand."

"I don't want this to be casual anymore." He squeezed the nape of my neck, the touch gentle but firm. "I'm falling for you, Rye. Hard."

I sucked in a breath. I owed him the truth. "I want to say the same, but I'm a fucking mess inside. I don't want to mislead you. I don't want this to be the end, but I need some time to figure things out, and if you can't give me that space, then maybe this isn't going to work."

He said nothing for a moment, then he sighed. "This have anything to do with their engagement announcement?"

"Maybe. Probably." I closed my eyes. Fuck. Was I always going to feel this black hole where my heart used to be?

"I'm sorry." Carter pulled me into his arms. "I'm an asshole for bringing this up now."

I relaxed into his embrace. "No. You're not." I smiled and nipped at his ear. "The timing is a bit shitty maybe."

"Maybe?" He shook his head and kissed my neck. Then he pulled back and looked me in the eyes. "You really just want time to figure things out?"

"I do."

"So by 'figure things out,' do you mean you're going to fuck around?"

He wouldn't like the truth, but I couldn't lie about this. "We've never said we were exclusive. So if the occasion presents itself, sure. I have to find my muse."

"What the fuck does that mean?"

"Writing and sex are connected for me. You've read the books, right?"

"No. I'm probably the last person on the planet who hasn't, but why would I need to read about Riley Kendrick when I have him in the flesh?"

I smiled. God, he could be so fucking endearing sometimes. Any normal human being would have at least skimmed the novels out of curiosity, if nothing else. "Read the books, and then you'll understand me a lot better. We can talk when you're done."

"I'm not sure I can take reading about you with someone else."

"It'll explain a lot to you. Things I can't talk about now. But I did write about it. It's all there."

"Okay." He held my gaze. "You'll come back to me?"

I took a deep breath. "I will. I promise."

But would I come back the same person? That I didn't know. I hoped not. I hoped I'd come back as someone steadier, less fucked up. Someone who could work again. Someone whole.

PAIGE

My heart pounded with excitement and more than a touch of nerves as I stepped off the elevator and into the beautifully appointed mezzanine above the impressive lobby of the Grosvenor Hotel in London. I'd never stayed at such a fancy place before and certainly never as a representative of Total Indulgence Tours, responsible for the pleasure and well-being of thirty authors and their entourage.

After taking a deep calming breath, I placed my hand on the stone railing and descended the burgundy-carpeted grand staircase into the lobby proper. I stopped for a moment to admire the gorgeous crystal chandelier above me as I stood on an immense Persian carpet, all decorated in shades of white and wine, then I proceeded on toward the concierge's desk to inquire about my event.

"Hello. I'm Paige Sutherland. Is everything ready for the Total Indulgence welcome tea?"

The concierge, a small, narrow-faced man, nodded. "Of course, ma'am. The Victorian Lounge is just down this hallway." He snapped his fingers at a young woman working a few feet away. "Darla, please accompany Ms. Sutherland to the Victorian Lounge and ensure that everything is running smoothly for her group's afternoon tea."

She stepped out from behind the high desk. "Right this way, ma'am."

A few minutes later, I was led into a bright, high-ceilinged room. An entire wall consisted of enormous windows, through which streamed the warm afternoon light. The tea room was meticulously decorated in tones of yellow and purple, transporting me back to Victorian times.

I sighed with pleasure as I looked around the room, taking in the couches and chairs arranged around tables suitable for groups of two or four.

Darla walked over to the first section closest to one of the large windows. "This area has been reserved for your group."

Each table was set with a white porcelain tea service and silverware, along with a three-tiered platter of tea cakes, mini fruit scones, preserves, clotted cream, and traditional finger sandwiches. "Oh, it all looks so perfect." I turned to Darla. "Please thank the staff for me."

"It's our pleasure. We're quite proud of our Victorian tea room. Did you know that it commemorates powerful women from the era?" She indicated the various portraits adorning the walls. "Here you have Nancy Astor, our first female member of Parliament. And this is Lillie Langtry, a famous actress at the time."

I pointed to another portrait. "Who is this?"

"Oh!" Darla tittered, covering her mouth. "That's Cora Pearl, the Parisian courtesan, one of our most famous guests. We have an entire suite dedicated to her."

"A French boudoir? Now that's something this group would love to see."

"I'll try to get that sorted," Darla said with a wink. She pointed to a discreet phone on the wall. "Dial nine if you require assistance."

Left on my own, I stepped up to a large window and stared out at the beautiful city beyond. I'd never been to London before, and I couldn't wait to begin exploring. Tomorrow we'd be visiting the British Museum, and I'd get to check another item off my bucket list.

I glanced at my watch. Hmmm… people would start arriving soon. I extracted the list of participants and a pen from my shoulder bag, then looked around for somewhere to stand and something to write on. Oh, right. Digging into my shoulder bag once again, I pulled out my current read, a copy of Riley Kendrick's *Amber's Fall.* Although it was quite a spicy book and the cover rather sexy, no one would see it with the list on top of it.

A couple arrived, so I hurried back to the entrance to greet them. I recognized this author on sight. Smiling brightly, I held out my hand. "Good afternoon, Mrs. Clark. I'm Paige Sutherland with Total Indulgence Tours. I'll be your guide for the next three weeks."

"It's a pleasure to meet you, dear. Call me Marietta. This is my husband, Tom."

We shook hands, and I pointed out the reserved tables. "Please, make yourselves comfortable and enjoy your Victorian Tea."

The lounge filled up over the following quarter hour. Of the thirty authors registered, twenty-seven were women from twenty-one to eighty, and all were thrilled to be participating in such a unique trip. I didn't tell them, but it filled my heart with pride since this was a tour I'd designed from start to finish.

Of the remaining three authors, all male, one, David Laughton, was married and part of a husband and wife writing duo. The other, Kenji Tamashiro, was quite clearly batting for the other team. It seemed my prospects for a bed partner among the authors were nil. A couple of waiters entered, carrying additional platters and teapots. I eyed them critically and groaned internally. One was too thin, the other too stocky.

Beggars can't be choosers, a voice echoed in my mind.

"Shut up, Ari," I muttered under my breath.

"Excuse me?"

The voice, rich, melodious, American, and definitely very male, made me snap my head up and spin around. In front of me stood a truly gorgeous, if understated, man. He had a dark beard, black glasses, and an amused smile that lit up the room. "My name isn't Ari, and I haven't said a word." He raised two fingers. "Scout's honor."

Heat flooded my chest, quickly rising to encompass my neck and cheeks. I clapped a hand over my mouth as my eyes remained glued on the man's humor-filled expression. If a genie were to suddenly offer me one wish, I'd wish to disappear.

Sure you would.

Okay, okay. If I could have any wish in the world, I'd wish for this man in my bed.

Go get him, girl!

Oh God. Ari and her silly ideas had turned me into a hormonally-imbalanced teenage girl. That was the only excuse for my complete lack of professionalism. I held out my hand, and rattled off my spiel. "Welcome. I'm Paige Sutherland with Total Indulgence Tours. I'll be your tour guide for the next three weeks. And you are?"

Only one name remained unchecked on my list, and this man's voice matched the one that had intruded on my thoughts too many times since he'd called to book his trip. It wouldn't do for me to make assumptions though. I doubted it, but he could be some lonely soul who'd wandered into the lounge by accident. In which case, my hopes of a vacation fling would be completely dashed.

He took my hand in his and brought it to his mouth, pressing a soft kiss against my knuckles. "Carter Templeton." As he spoke, his lips tightened ever so slightly before once again relaxing into a grin.

A grin that made butterflies swoop around my belly.

Taking a step inside the room, I indicated the food and tea. "Help yourself, Mr. Templeton."

"Carter, please."

I swallowed, my mouth suddenly dry. "Of course, Carter. Since you're the last to arrive, I'll give you a few moments to settle in, then I'll explain the tour to everyone and hand out our updated itinerary." I tried to tug my hand out of his, but he seemed determined not to let it go. "Is there something else I can do for you?"

His gaze lingered over my body before settling on my lips. "Oh, I can think of a few things, Ms. Sutherland."

"Paige," I said, a little too breathily for my liking.

He licked his full bottom lip. "Paige."

It should have been ridiculous. A caricature of seduction. Instead, the way he said my name, rolling it off his tongue as though he were relishing a deep dark chocolate, had my belly squeezing. Was this what it felt like to be the sole focus of a man's desire?

Oh, get over yourself, Paige.

He was definitely too young for me, despite the corduroy jacket with leather patches at the elbows. His professorial attire fit him well, but somehow it didn't suit him. Perhaps he was something of a method author, one who had to become a character in order to write him. I gave a sharp jerk and pulled my hand free.

Undeterred, he ran his fingers down my arm. I shivered and plastered my copy of *Amber's Fall* against my chest to hide the fact that my nipples had to be poking holes through my blouse. Good Lord, the man was potent.

"I don't know anyone here," he said, still staring at me.

How would he know? He hadn't even glanced at the other participants. Still, this was where my experience came in handy. Taking his arm, I led him into the room, glad to once again be in control of the situation. "In that case, let me introduce you to the others." And as he rested his warm hand at the small of my back, I did my best not to swallow my tongue, although a squeak might have escaped my gasping lips.

I clutched my book and participant list tightly in my fist and waved them in front of my face in a futile attempt to cool the longing searing a path through my veins.

Things were definitely looking up.

I just might get to have that vacation fling after all.

RILEY

With a strange bubbling in my chest like someone had filled me with helium during the night, I entered the Grosvenor Arms restaurant at an ungodly early hour, my feet practically hovering over the thick carpet. The group was gathering for a quick breakfast before our introductory tour of London, including a visit to the British Museum later in the day. I'd been to London before on a book tour, but I'd barely seen any of it. It would be nice to get a chance to explore.

I scanned the restaurant, looking for the woman I'd also like to explore. My eyes zeroed in on Paige Sutherland sitting at a table for two near a window. Had she chosen that table with me in mind? She was reading, and even from a distance, I recognized the book. *Amber's Conquest*, book two of my trilogy. Last night, she'd been clutching *Amber's Fall* to her perky chest. Shit, Paige read fast. My lips curved into a smile. Must mean she liked what she was reading.

I headed directly for her table, my stomach flipping with nerves. Would she recognize me today? My picture was in the back of the book. Granted, it was black and white, and I was clean-shaven and wearing contacts in the picture, my hair shorter than it was now. But did I really think my Clark Kent-ish "professor" disguise would hold?

I paused at the empty chair across from her. "May I join you?"

She looked up at me, her eyes sparkling and her cheeks flushing a pretty pink. God she was gorgeous. All blonde perfection, like Carter. Except so very feminine. "Please do," she said, her voice like music in my ears.

What would she sound like, moaning my name?

I took the seat and smiled as she set the book aside. "Looks like you're enjoying the series," I said. *Jesus, Kendrick, angling for a compliment much?*

She blushed deeper and bit her bottom lip. *Fuck me.* If she kept doing that, I was done for.

"It's really… good," she said.

I laughed. "I think you meant something else."

"You've read them, then?"

"Of course. Who hasn't?"

"Then, you know what's in them…" Her voice trailed off and she covered her eyes for a second.

"I know. And I enjoyed every minute of it."

She laughed and met my gaze. "You seem determined to keep me off-balance, Mr. Templeton."

Fuck. Why had I used Carter's name again? I'd love to hear "Riley" coming out of those seashell-pink lips. "Call me Carter. Please."

"I'm still learning everyone's name," she said.

"Ouch. Forgotten so soon?" My mojo was off in more ways than one.

"Oh I didn't mean you. Your name, I remembered." She looked down and tucked a strand of hair behind her ear.

I couldn't help grinning at her. "Thank you for propping up my fragile male ego."

The waiter came over and asked for my order. I hadn't even looked at the menu. "I'll have what she's having."

"Muesli and yogurt?" the waiter said.

I made a face. "Um, how about sausage, eggs, something like that?"

Paige laughed, a gentle tinkling in my ears. I could get addicted to that sound.

"Righto," the waiter said. "Coffee or tea?"

"Coffee. Cream and sugar."

"Is there any other way?" the waiter asked, a teasing lilt in his voice. I finally looked at the guy, catching something in his tone, a tendril of interest. He was cute, and normally I would've flirted shamelessly with him, but there was only one person I wanted at the moment. And she was sitting right across from me.

"A man after my own heart," I said, with just enough eye contact to say I was appreciative, but not on the market.

The waiter smiled, his gaze flicking to Paige, then back to me, before he turned to her. "Something else for you, ma'am?"

"No, thank you."

The waiter left and Paige gave me an assessing look. "I think he was flirting with you."

I held her gaze. "He was."

"And I think you weren't immune."

My grin widened. "I wasn't."

"But…" She trailed off again.

"But?"

"I thought"—she motioned between us—"maybe you were…"

"I was. And I am. Most definitely."

"Oh." I saw her doing the math.

"Does that bother you?" I asked.

"No. I'm just surprised."

"There are advantages," I said, and motioned to the book.

"You mean the… threesomes?" she asked, her voice dropping on the last word, as if it were too scandalous to say aloud.

"Amber certainly seemed to be enjoying them, don't you think?"

She fanned her cheeks and laughed. "That's one way to put it." She took a sip from her teacup. "How do we keep ending up talking about sex?"

"You inspire me," I said. It was true. I'd dreamed of her last night, coming apart under my tongue. I'd had to rub one out in the shower before breakfast just thinking about it. The images I'd conjured up cycled through my mind again. Paige trembling, her thighs quaking, her hands in my hair, her voice hoarse from moaning my name… Fuck. Now I was hard again. I shifted in my seat, trying to subtly adjust myself in my slacks to take the pressure off my burgeoning cock.

Her cell phone rang. She glanced at the display. "It's my boss. I have to take this. Excuse me," she said and hurried off to the lobby. I followed her with my eyes. Paige Sutherland had one fine ass under that tight skirt.

Not helping with the inconvenient erection, Kendrick.

The waiter came back with a plate brimming with sausage, bacon, and eggs, with some fried potatoes on the side. He also handed me a copy of the *Daily Mail.*

"Perfect," I said.

"Indeed," the waiter said, looking me up and down. "I'm Gerry, if you need anything."

"Thanks, Gerry," I said.

Gerry jotted something on a notepad, then handed it to me. "Just in case."

I took the paper and saw the number written on it. "I'm flattered."

"Call me, and I will be too."

I pocketed the number and unfolded the newspaper. I started in on the food while flicking through the pages. When I hit the entertainment section, the eggs turned to ash on my tongue. There it was—an article about the movie coming out, and the whole scandal surrounding me and Amber and Holden. There was a photo of the three of us in happier times, accompanied by an inset of Amber and Holden, an obscenely large engagement ring flashing on her finger.

The chair across from me scraped on the hardwood floor, and I quickly folded up the paper. Fuck. All I needed was for Paige to put two and two together and give me the pity face. I didn't want a pity fuck from her either.

"Don't bother hiding the article," a man's voice said. "I already know it's you, Riley. Saw you yesterday at the afternoon tea. Not that you noticed me."

Oh shit. Kenji Tamashiro. I'd gone to college with the guy. We'd even fucked a few times. And then I'd blown him off when he'd asked me for help with finding a literary agent after I'd become famous. Ken could wreck things with Paige for me, and I'd fucking deserve it. "Ken, I didn't know you were at the retreat too."

Kenji smirked. "Yeah, you only had eyes for pretty Miss Paige. Didn't give two shits about the rest of us, did you? Typical."

"It's not like that. I—"

"Give me one reason, 'Carter,' why I shouldn't tell everyone, starting with Paige, who you really are."

My partially eaten meal turned to stone in my stomach. "Look, man, I know I was an asshole to you. And I'm sorry I got caught up in all the attention I was getting. It was all fake. And so was I. I realize that now."

Kenji crossed his arms. "Do you?"

"I *am* sorry."

Ken shook his head and let out a breath, his arms relaxing to his sides. "I want to fucking hate you, but"—he gestured to the newspaper—"I guess you got it in the slats, man."

"I did."

"So, you and Amber and Holden? That was really a thing?"

I nodded, my gut knotting up again. Emphasis on "was." Eight months had passed since our relationship had ended, and part of me still hadn't accepted that fact.

"So what's the deal? Are you in denial and using the 'I'm bi' excuse?"

I barely held back an eye-roll. "Don't give me that bi-erasure bullshit. I'm not *pretending* to be bi. I am. Are you *pretending* to be gay?"

Ken raised an eyebrow. "Methinks thou dost protest too much, Lady MacBeth."

"Yeah, yeah. And denial ain't just a river in Egypt. I've heard it all."

"You wouldn't be the first guy who liked fucking guys but didn't want a relationship with one because it was too 'gay' for him."

"That's not it. I just haven't found a guy I want to settle down with." *So what is Carter, then? A fuckbuddy?*

"I think you're afraid."

"I'm attracted to *both* men and women. I always have been." I forced a smile. "Don't knock it until you've tried it."

"Sounds complicated."

"It doesn't have to be."

Kenji laughed. "Oh it is. But that's Riley Kendrick for you. One big complication."

I nodded. Ken was right about that. I was one big, complicated mess. "So, you'll keep my secret?"

"For now. We'll see how long that lasts." Ken made a show of looking at his watch. "I'm guessing it'll be a whole ten minutes until you do something shitty."

I wanted to roll my eyes again, but Ken had a point. I had been a total jerk to the man, too busy getting high and having "fun" to be a decent human being. "I'm not that asshole anymore."

Kenji held my eyes, his own dark ones reflecting the hurt buried under his attitude. "I hope not. You used to be a great guy, back in the day. When you brushed me off…" He paused, frowning. "I couldn't believe it."

Heat flashed up my neck and over my cheeks. "Christ, Ken. I hate thinking about it. You still need help?"

Ken laughed. "You need to pick up *Publishers Weekly* every now and then. You're not the only one out there who's done well. My Victorian gay romance series just got optioned for cable."

"Wow! That's fantastic."

"It is, but no thanks to you."

I winced. "I deserve that." I took a sip of my coffee. "It's probably better that way anyhow."

"Probably."

Paige came back to the table. "Sorry I abandoned you," she said to me, then looked at Kenji. "But it looks like you made a new friend."

"An old one, actually," Ken said, standing up and exchanging places with her. "Carter and I did our master's degrees at the same university."

"How nice you have this chance to get reacquainted," Paige said. She sounded like she really meant it. God, I should just leave her alone. She was so… sweet.

I looked at her delicate hand splayed over the cover of *Amber's Conquest*.

So sweet and yet, Paige Sutherland had a secret dirty side.

And damn it all, I was going to enjoy every bit of it before our time together was up.

Chapter 3

RILEY

I had to get more time with Paige. I lagged behind as she handed out our tickets to the British Museum as well as virtual tour equipment. There was something about her—maybe it was her take-charge attitude or her apparently genuine interest in ensuring we had a great time—that really attracted me. Of course, she did look pretty spectacular in the fitted sleeveless blouse and narrow flowered skirt she wore with low sandals. It was summery, yet classy. Amber would have gone naked rather than wear something similar. If it didn't show at least an inch of ass and plunge dangerously low between her oversized tits, she wouldn't go near it.

A tug on the sleeve of my blazer drew me out of the dark tunnel of my recollections and back into the bright lobby of the British Museum.

"Everything okay?" Paige asked.

I forced a half-smile, one that always worked on my conquests. "Nothing the pleasure of your company wouldn't cure."

Her eyes widened and color highlighted her high cheekbones. "Uh… sure." She cleared her throat and raised her hand, drawing the group's attention. "Everyone, you're free to tour the museum on your own. Of course, I'm happy to have you join me. Let's meet back here at four o'clock. Oh, and please call my cell phone if you need me."

I stuck to Paige's side as everyone broke off into smaller groups and went inside, leaving me alone with her.

"Looks like it's just the two of us." She frowned and adjusted her purse strap over her shoulder. "I guess no one else wanted to hang out with me."

Or, it might have been the death glare I'd sent to anyone who looked her way. From behind her back, of course. Today, all I wanted was to have pretty Paige to myself.

"Their loss," I said, taking her arm. "Where do you want to start?"

She unfolded the map of the museum. "What time period are you writing in?"

"Good question." I rubbed my jaw. I'd only ever written contemporary fiction.

"Why don't we wander through the second floor first? There might be less people, and it will take us through ancient Egypt, Greece, and Rome, as well as Europe up to present times."

As we walked up the stairs to the second floor, I rested my palm at the base of her spine, thoroughly enjoying the little catch of breath in her throat when I touched her. She'd made the same noise yesterday, when I'd done it in the lounge.

So responsive. She had no idea how much I loved that.

We entered the first exhibit. "What do you write, Carter? I'm afraid I'm not familiar with your work."

Christ. She'd gone for the jugular without even realizing it. "A little of this and a little of that." Hopefully she'd drop the subject.

"Come on," she said, a teasing note in her voice. "It can't be 'a little' of anything if you're on this tour. I'd never be able to afford this trip if I wasn't working it."

"Total Indulgence doesn't pay its tour guides well? I might have to complain to the boss."

"I'm not really a tour guide. I'm actually the marketing director. But…" She glanced at me, then quickly looked away. "This is miles beyond my means."

I chuckled. "It's miles beyond mine too. My publisher's footing the bill." It wasn't exactly a lie. Until more money from my books and the movie rolled in, I was as poor as a church mouse.

"They must think you're very promising then."

I smirked. "Something like that."

"You still haven't told me what you write." She turned away from the Egyptian mummies on display. Her head tilted to the side and several long strands of sandy-blonde hair fell forward.

Before she could push them back, I caught the strands and let them slide between my fingers as I curled them behind her ear. Pure silk. Shit. Now I wanted to grab a handful and tug her head back so I could lick the pulse in the notch at the base of her throat. I could almost hear her heart pounding in the near-empty room.

I brought my lips to the curve of her ear, inhaling the fruity, floral scent of her perfume. "I write erotic romance," I whispered, ending with a quick flick of my tongue before pulling back.

Paige pressed a hand to her chest. "You must be very good at it." The huskiness of her voice and the haze in her eyes went straight to my cock.

Wow. This woman was lethal. Good thing I'd worn tight-fitting briefs, or the tenting in my dress pants would be all too visible. I took off the blazer and folded it over my arm, using it to shield my rebellious dick from her view. I needed to get a handle on my libido before things got out of control and I ended up scaring the crap out of Paige. I had a feeling she was just what I needed to get my writing mojo back.

"Ready to check out the next exhibit?" I asked.

She blinked as though I'd woken her from a dream—or fantasy. Yeah, I'd been having a few of those myself. Me… her… no clothes… a big bed… and… *Carter.*

Fuck.

What the hell was wrong with me? This woman was ripe for the picking, so why was Carter intruding into my mind? We were taking a break. Nothing that happened on this trip had anything to do with Carter. It was all about me and my muse.

Entering the next exhibit, I spotted some primitive manuscripts that reminded me of what Paige had been reading that morning. "What's your favorite scene in *Amber's Conquest*?" I asked.

"Well, I haven't finished it yet, but in *Amber's Fall*, I really liked that Riley took Amber to the museum on one of their dates. It's so much more original than going to see a movie."

I had to laugh at that. Jesus. What Amber and I had done had been so much worse than necking in a movie theater.

"What's so funny?" Paige frowned.

"Didn't you figure out what they did at the museum?" The publisher hadn't let me be too explicit for fear it would get me or Amber arrested.

Stopping, she put her hands on the curves of her shapely hips and stared me down like an errant schoolboy. "They toured the exhibits, like we're doing now."

Shit. She was going to have me creaming my pants.

"Ah… no. They had sex." I looked around the room, suddenly realizing where we were. "In a Greek gallery, much like this one."

Her eyes rounded. "No!"

"Yes. They got so turned on looking at the erotic etchings, they couldn't help themselves."

Her brows furrowed. "How would you know?"

I gulped as my mind raced. Had I included those details in the book, or at least enough to lead the reader to that conclusion? Fuck, I hoped so.

"It's all there in chapter ten."

"You seem very familiar with Mr. Kendrick's work." Her eyes lingered over a rather detailed drawing of a naked man and woman engaged in an intriguing sexual act. Sweat began to gather at the back of my neck.

"He's one of my favorite authors." Jesus. Talking about the book had been a really bad idea. Unfortunately, all I knew about Paige was that she liked my writing.

"You must really be looking forward to the release of the movie next month then."

"More than I can say."

She smiled at me over her shoulder. "Maybe it will inspire you."

And keep a roof over my head. Unless I wasn't able to write again. Then I'd have to use my earnings to repay my advance from Exotica.

As though sensing my change in mood, Paige lightly touched my shoulder. "Are you having writer's block? Is that why you don't want to talk about your work?"

I let out a huge sigh, surprising myself at the depth of my feelings about this. I'd told Carter I was fucked up, but could it be more than that? Was I depressed?

I clenched my fists and blew out again. There was no way I'd let Amber and Holden affect me that much. I was Riley fucking Kendrick, and I didn't fucking do depression.

Writer's block? Yes.

Depression? Not happening.

"I'm having a little trouble figuring out my next book. My editor suggested this trip to see if a change in direction might work."

"So you're hoping to find your muse?"

I winked at Paige. "I think I may have found her."

Her cheeks reddened again. Could she be any more perfect? I couldn't remember a single conversation with Amber where she'd taken even the slightest interest in my writing beyond how much money I'd make from it.

When Paige excused herself to use the restroom, I pulled out my phone to check my messages. There was an email from Nora. Nothing from Carter.

Why was I even expecting one? The break had been my idea. I was the one putting the moves on a woman. I was the one getting hard at the thought of taking Paige to my bed. So why did Carter keep entering my thoughts? Was I actually feeling guilty about leaving him behind? That was ridiculous. He understood that I needed this trip. And the need was both personal and professional.

Right now, what I needed most was to know that Carter was all right.

Navigating to the messaging app, I sent him a selfie of me with my arm around a bronze sculpture of a rather poorly endowed Greek male.

A few seconds later my phone pinged.

Carter: Where are you?

Me: At the British Museum. What are you doing? Have you started the books?

Carter: I have.

Me: What part are you at?

Carter: Where Amber is giving you a blow job in your office at the college and there's another student waiting right outside.

Me: What do you think so far?

Carter: I'd have been hot for teacher too if you'd been my sociology prof (devil emoji)

My cock went from a semi to a hard-on at the image Carter's words formed in my mind.

Me: Would you have gotten down on your knees for me?

Carter: In a heartbeat.

Jesus. My cock was rock hard now. My balls pulsed with the need to come, and I was stuck in the fucking British Museum for the rest of the afternoon. I was going to die of blue balls. How embarrassing. A couple years ago, nothing would've stopped me from rubbing one out in some dark alcove. What had happened to me? Where had that carefree bastard gone?

An idea popped into my head. Looked like the bastard was still around after all. After a quick glance around the room to confirm no one would see me, I went behind the statue and undid the button on my slacks, and pulled my briefs out to snap a photo of my crotch. With a flick of my thumb, I sent it to Carter. That would teach the fucker to turn me on like that.

"They've got some really great manuscripts in here."

Paige. Startled, I jumped and fumbled my phone. It went flying out of my hand and landed face up at Paige's feet.

"Shit. Fuck."

Trying to cover my open fly with my jacket at the same time that I lunged for the phone, I failed at both, tripping and sprawling on the floor.

Smirking, Paige gracefully retrieved the phone and stared down at it in her hand, the dick pic clearly visible.

She arched a brow, turning the phone to the left, then the right. Her gaze met mine. "Is this you?"

"No." Heat blazed up my neck, and I thought for sure my entire head would go up in flames. Angling my back to her, I did up my pants as I got to my feet. With all the things I'd done in my life, the good, the bad, and the oh-so-very ugly, this slip of a woman was making me feel more ashamed than I'd ever felt before.

Her gaze roamed down my body, a smile playing with her lips. "Really? The pants are the same color. And the shape of the… member… looks the same."

So she wanted to play, did she? I took Paige's hand and pressed it against my cock. "What do you think now?"

She squeezed it gently, then licked her lips. "Definitely the item pictured."

Was it my imagination, or was her voice as desire roughened as mine?

I moved in closer so my chest pressed against her breasts, her hand trapped between our bodies. Cradling her jaw in my palm, I whispered for her ears only, "Now you know what I feel like. Maybe later I can find out what you feel like?"

"Naughty boy," Paige said, her warm breath brushing my skin. I shivered at the thought of it on my cock.

"Boy? Does my age bother you?" Paige looked to be around her mid-thirties, not that I cared. But she might. I kissed her neck, the line of her jaw, the corner of her mouth.

Paige cleared her throat as she stepped away. "Let's… uh… go check out those manuscripts."

PAIGE

All I could think about was the feel of Carter's hard cock under my palm, his lips caressing my throat, my jaw, the edge of my mouth, his velvety voice whispering in my ear.

I'd been wet and aching for hours, all through the museum, the ride back to the hotel, the walk up to my room. As soon as I was able to shut the door behind me, I dropped onto the nearest chair and plunged my fingers into my panties, frantic to assuage my throbbing clit. I came in less than a minute, imagining it was Carter touching me, Carter's fingers on my clit, in my pussy, his tongue parting my folds…

I panted, boneless, sprawled on the delicate chair in the sitting room of my hotel room. I almost laughed at myself. When was the last time I'd been so turned on? And he'd barely even touched me. Jesus. I could hardly imagine what it would be like if he did.

When he did.

There was no way I was ending this trip without sleeping with him. It was inevitable.

I scrambled for a quick shower and changed my clothes before heading down to the Grosvenor's Grand Imperial Restaurant, its beautiful gold walls giving the room a sensual glow. I took a seat at a table for four, my heart pounding in anticipation of seeing Carter again. Maybe I should've chosen a larger table, so there'd be less chance of getting too caught up in him?

Oh, who was I kidding? I wasn't going to stop thinking about him, even if there were fifty people at our table.

Our table. Sheesh!

I had to get a hold of myself. I was the guide on this tour; I was representing Total Indulgence. I needed to act like a professional, not some lovestruck teenager.

I glanced at my watch as a clump of folks from the tour traipsed in. They waved at me, but took their own table, since they'd have to split up if they sat at mine.

I wished I'd brought my book, so I'd have something to distract myself with. Each time someone stepped into the restaurant, my pulse jumped, then fell back to normal when it wasn't Carter.

Gah! Maybe it was those Riley Kendrick books that had worked me into this state in the first place. They were so deliciously wicked, so… inspiring. And then there was Ari, encouraging me to get laid on this trip.

It was no wonder that a few words, a few touches, and I was ready to explode.

More people filed in, but not the one I wanted. I looked at my watch again. 8:15. Where was Carter?

I fiddled with my water glass, then took a sip of tea from the steaming cup the waiter had poured for me. A delicate jasmine tea. Emma would like it.

Emma! I'd forgotten to call her earlier. I pawed through my purse and pulled out my cell phone. It was 3:15 PM in Miami. I hit the entry for Emma, then listened to the phone ring. And ring. And ring. And then go to voicemail. I left a brief message and said I'd call back in a few hours. After I hung up, I stared at the phone. Was Emma okay? She'd seemed fine when we'd spoken yesterday. And Ari had promised to check in with her every day.

Still… This was the longest I'd ever been away from Emma. And I had the better part of three weeks to go yet.

My phone buzzed with a text. Emma.

Emma: at spa with ant ari cant talk must be quiet!

I smiled at her endearing typos, then answered.

Me: Have fun. I love you. I'll leave you alone.

Emma: ant ari says stop worrying!

Me: I bet she does.

Emma: she realy means it!

I giggled. I could picture Arianna's face.

Me: I'm not worrying.

Emma: please dont, mom im fiiiiine :-)

Me: You're right. Have fun!

I punched in several goofy smiling emojis, not quite sure what some of them meant.

My phone buzzed again, this time with a text from Arianna.

Ari: Chica, I swear, she's fine! Stop fretting. We're about to get our massages. Maybe you need one too.

Me: Point taken. Enjoy!

Ari: Oh I will. Mario has very talented fingers.

Me: I'm not going to ask.

Ari: I'm not going to tell either. (smirking emoji)

"What's with that big grin on your face?" Carter asked as he took the seat to my right.

"A funny text from my friend." I wasn't about to mention Emma. Carter had already hinted that he thought I was bothered by our age difference. No need to pour gas on the fire and talk about my daughter. My adult-but-not-exactly daughter.

"Did you tell her about me?" he asked.

I smiled. "You must think quite highly of yourself."

He mock winced. "Oh, the burn!" He clutched his chest. "Way to wound a guy."

"Just teasing."

He leaned toward me, lowering his voice. "And I deserve it." His fingers brushed against my bare knee, shooting sparks straight between my legs. "You make that dress look damn good," he murmured, his gaze dropping to the low-cut front of the little black dress I'd packed on a whim.

"Thank you. You look quite nice yourself." Carter was wearing a burgundy suit with a charcoal tie, the color of the linen bringing out the deep brown of his eyes.

"Figured I'd dress up for this place."

A couple of older women on the tour headed our way. "Mind if we join you?" one of them asked.

I started to answer, but Carter beat me to it. "Sorry. We have someone joining us already."

He must mean Kenji. I was surprised to register some disappointment at the idea. They'd probably start reminiscing about their college years while I nodded and smiled at all the right places. Still, I might learn a thing or two about Carter.

Not that it mattered. *This is just a fling. Right?*

Right. I had to keep reminding myself of that. There was no way Carter was going to want something long-term with a thirty-six-year-old single mom with a disabled daughter.

"Hey, what's wrong?" he asked. His fingers caressed my knee again, and I brushed them away.

"Nothing." I plastered a smile on my face, then picked up my teacup.

"It wasn't nothing. Tell me."

When his hand returned to what seemed to be its favorite spot on my leg, I returned it to his own. "I'm too old for you."

"I'm twenty-eight. You're what? Thirty-three? Thirty-four? Big deal."

"Thirty-six."

"So?"

"Eight years is a long time. Especially when you're still in your twenties."

He leaned forward again, his voice low in my ear. "For fuck's sake, Paige, I don't care about numbers." He took my hand and placed it on the bulge at his crotch. "If the fact that just smelling your sexy-as-fuck perfume, just being next to you, does *this* to me doesn't convince you that I don't care how many birthdays you've celebrated, I don't know what will."

I pulled my hand back, my heart hammering, my stomach fluttering. I opened my mouth to speak, but he held up a finger.

"I'm not finished," he said. "All I thought about all day is getting you under me. And if that doesn't happen soon, I'm going to die from an epic case of blue balls. Or I'll wish I had."

I let out the breath I'd been holding. "Well, then. Consider me convinced." *And flattered.*

Kenji Tamashiro was approaching our table. Tall and lanky, with a tennis player's build, Kenji was certainly the kind of guy who turned heads. Just like Carter.

A thought occurred to me. Had the two of them ever…?

"May I join you?" Kenji asked.

Before I could say yes, Carter rose. He put an arm around Kenji's shoulders and dropped his voice, but I could still make it out. "Normally I'd say yes, but I don't need you, or anybody else, cock-blocking me tonight."

Kenji laughed. "You *were* serious this morning."

"One-hundred percent."

"Good luck to you then."

Ken headed for another table, and Carter took his seat beside me. Hmm…. "Did you somehow scare everyone off at the museum today?" I asked.

He settled back in his chair. "I might have."

"Want me all to yourself, do you?"

He leaned in, his hand cupping my knee. "I'm a greedy little shit sometimes."

"Only sometimes?"

He burst into laughter. "Busted."

Oh this man was going to be the ruin of me. But I couldn't seem to resist him. If I was going down in flames, I'd hang on and enjoy the heat.

We ordered a meal for two, the conversation flowing smoothly. At least when the subject was me. When it came to Carter, he'd often clam up or switch the subject back to my job.

As if he had something to hide.

I looked at his hands. No telltale traces of a wedding ring. But that didn't necessarily mean anything. Lots of men didn't wear their rings.

A fling was one thing; a fling with a married man?

Not going to happen.

I swallowed hard and patted my lips with a napkin. "Carter, tell me the truth."

"About what?" His gaze narrowed as he looked at me.

"Are you married?"

The crease between his brows melted away. "No. Never have been either. You?"

"Once. It ended shortly after it began."

"He was an idiot then." His hand slid up my thigh, pausing to make circles right below the hemline.

"Yes, he was. But then again, we were young."

"How young?"

Damn it. I shouldn't have said anything. "Eighteen."

He whistled. "You weren't pregnant, were you?"

Now which one of us was busted? I shook my head. *Forgive me, Emma.* "Just high-school sweethearts. It was… a mistake."

Carter grimaced. "I've been there. Not that same mistake, but I fell hard for someone who turned out to be… well, too young to reciprocate."

Interesting. "How old was she? Or he?"

"We met when she was nineteen. And I was twenty-six."

"Like Riley Kendrick and Amber McCallan."

Carter's eyes dropped to the table and a muscle ticked in his jaw. "That's probably why I was so attracted to those books. It was kind of my story, you know?"

And Riley Kendrick was bi too. No wonder the story resonated with him.

"Is she the reason you can't write? She broke your heart, and now you can't write about romance?"

Carter's jaw worked a bit more, and he played with a pot sticker on his plate. Then he looked up at me. "She ripped my heart out of my chest."

His voice was low, raw, the words thick with emotion. I placed my hand over his on my thigh and squeezed it. "I'm sorry."

"Yeah, well, it's better I found out she didn't love me before I married her."

My mouth dropped open. "You were engaged?"

"Not yet. But I'd planned to ask her. I'd started shopping for a ring right before she handed me my ass on a platter."

"Oh Carter." I squeezed his hand again.

He shook his head and forced a smile. "If it wasn't for her, I wouldn't be sitting here, with you. So it was a good thing, in the end." His gaze dropped to my lips and he relaxed, his grin turning wolfish, his hand under mine inching higher, grazing the hem of my skirt. A spark of electricity zapped me between the legs, and I shifted restlessly.

Down, Paige! He didn't mean anything by that.

His fingers slid under the fabric and he leaned closer. "Let's forget the past and focus on the here and now. On you and me." His smile was full of wicked promise, and his hand was on the inside of my thigh, the tips of his fingers so very close to where I wanted them to be.

Damn, he did *mean something by that.*

The waiter brought the check. Thank God the tablecloth was long. Carter surreptitiously withdrew his hand from between my legs and signed his room number on the check before I had a chance to react. All I could think about was almost getting caught.

I reached for the bill. "Wait a minute. I have an expense account."

He waved the waiter away. "Let me treat you."

"But..."

"But what?"

"I'm working. I'm supposed to pay for my meals. This isn't—" I almost said "a date," but stopped myself.

"I'm going to pretend that the only thing you said was thank you."

I shook my head in amusement. "We'll have to add 'pushy' to your list of flaws."

"Right next to 'greedy.'" His lips brushed the hair beside my ear and his hand went back to where it shouldn't have been but seemed to belong. "When I want something, I get it. So let's add 'spoiled' to that list too."

His warm breath washed over my skin and made me shiver. "How about 'wicked'?" I asked.

"Oh yes. That certainly belongs on the list."

"Incorrigible?"

He smirked. "Of course."

"Arrogant?"

"In spades." His fingertips brushed against the crotch of my panties, and I barely stifled a moan.

"Presumptuous?" My voice was ridiculously breathy.

"Mm-hmm." He took a sip from his water glass. "Now let's get out of here before we add 'arrested for public indecency' to that list."

He withdrew his hand from between my legs and placed it on the small of my back. I really shouldn't be letting him touch me like that in front of the other guests. Or walk me to my room.

I rose. "Good night. Thank you for the lovely company and the meal."

He rose as well. "I'll say goodnight to Ken. That'll give you a head start. But don't think the night is through."

I waved to the other tables, not trusting myself to say anything intelligent over the pounding of my heart.

Was I really going to do this? After knowing him for what? A day and a half?

I fought to keep my strides purposeful, without seeming hurried. I felt like a rabbit that had been spotted by a hawk. I needed to take a breath, gather my wits. Slow things down.

He caught up to me at the elevator, and again he placed his hand on the curve of my back. How I wanted to melt into that touch, say "Screw it," and do what I wanted.

But that just wasn't wise.

The elevator opened and we stepped inside. We were both on the same floor, and I pressed the number, my mouth suddenly so dry I craved a glass of water.

"What's wrong?" Carter asked.

"It's so early. Too early."

He glanced at his watch. "It's after ten."

"No, I mean—"

He chuckled. "I know what you mean. And maybe it is." He brushed the hair from my shoulder, then kissed the skin he'd bared. "And maybe it's not." He licked the spot he'd kissed, and my knees turned to jelly.

The elevator dinged, and I bolted forward.

Carter grabbed my wrist. "Whoa there. You've gone all skittish all of a sudden."

I tugged at my wrist. He didn't release it, but he did follow me when I started toward my room. "I don't do this kind of thing."

"Until now."

I stopped at my door and fumbled around in my bag for the key card. "There you go again, being presumptuous."

I found the card and slid it into the slot, my haste making me pull on the knob before the mechanism unlatched. The light turned red. "Fuck," I mumbled.

"Yes. Let's do." He placed his hand over mine. "Here. Allow me."

My fingers tightened on the key card, but I let him take it and open the door. He herded me inside. "Carter, I can't do this."

"Not now, or not ever?" He touched my cheek, made me look up at him. His eyes held mine, intense and serious.

"Not now. Not yet."

"You're killing me, Paige. But I want you to be ready." He leaned down, his lips hovering over mine. "A kiss isn't too much to ask?"

I shivered, looking into those eyes, so dark with promise. Then I rose up on tiptoe and pressed my lips to his, a muffled whimper escaping me as I did so.

"Christ," he mumbled against my lips. "You *will* be the death of me." Then he took control of the kiss, his tongue running along my lower lip, coaxing my mouth open, allowing him to invade. He slid an arm around my waist, his left hand on the side of my throat, his thumb caressing my jaw, and I melted against him.

Had I ever been kissed before? It didn't seem like it now. Carter's mouth moved on mine like I was a feast he couldn't get enough of. Dear God, I needed to stop this…

He pulled back and grinned. "Stop thinking so damn hard."

"I'm sorr—"

He pressed a finger to my lips. "Don't apologize. We'll do this at your pace, not mine." Then he released me. "I'd better say goodnight before we add 'liar' to that list."

I smiled. "Thanks for understanding."

He shook his head. "I don't understand it, actually. But I respect it."

"See you tomorrow."

"Hopefully all of me." He stepped into the hall.

I winked at him. "Hopefully."

"I will happily make that wish come true."

"Goodnight, Carter."

"'Night, Paige."

I shut the door, then pressed my forehead against it and took a deep breath. I was going to have to start making a list of Carter's good qualities too.

"Sweet" was going right at the top of the list.

RILEY

God, when was the last time a woman—or a man—had refused to jump into my bed? We'd spent the last two days traveling from London to Scotland, stopping at various castles and manor homes along the way. Again and again, I had tried to get more time with Paige, but she carefully kept me at arm's length.

I'd forgotten how fun the chase could be, the heady thrill of pursuit, the anticipation of the conquest. Paige was making me work, and I didn't mind one bit. Well, my dick might beg to differ. But it wasn't in charge. For once.

I was sprawled across the immense bed in my hotel room in Edinburgh, staring out the window at the city lights below. Energy pulsed inside me. I was itching to do something, to show up at Paige's door and knock, and keep knocking until she let me in.

But I'd promised to do this on her terms. I picked up my cell phone and flipped through the pictures I'd taken that day. At least half of them featured Paige, though she was usually unaware that the picture was being taken. She really had no idea how lovely she was. I stopped on one I'd captured in York. She was standing by a tree on some estate we'd stopped at, and the wind had blown her hair out of its ponytail. She was re-securing it, and the delicate lines of her neck, her jaw, her collarbone, called to me. I traced them in the photo, remembering the kiss she'd allowed me two days ago, that too-brief moment of bliss and torment.

Had she received the roses yet? Probably. But she hadn't called.

Well, fuck waiting. I could call her. That wasn't breaking the rules or pressing too hard.

She picked up on the second ring. "Carter, I was about to call you. They're lovely."

"I wasn't sure what color to get. Pink seems to suit you."

She laughed, that musical sound I couldn't get enough of. "I love them. And pink is one of my favorite colors." She paused, then said, "But you shouldn't have. You know I can't take them with me."

"I know. I just wanted you to have something nice in your room."

"The whole room is nice, Carter. It's not like we're staying at Motel 6."

"My room is huge. And lonely."

She sighed. "Mine too."

"I have the cure for that." I palmed myself in my slacks, my balls already aching from hearing her voice.

"I bet you do."

"What are you wearing?" I asked.

She giggled. "I am *not* having phone sex with you."

"Why not?"

"Because!"

"No one has to know."

"It's not happening, Carter."

"Even if I beg?"

She snorted. "Incorrigible."

"And that's how you like me." I unzipped my slacks and eased my cock out. "Okay, you talk, and I'll listen."

She was silent for a moment. "What do you want me to talk about?

And what are you going to be doing while I do?"

"What do you think I'll be doing?"

"If I know anything about you, my guess is you've got your hand in your pants."

"You do know me, Paige."

"Good Lord." She laughed again. "You have no limits, do you?"

"Hey, it was this or go knocking on your door. So don't lecture me on limits, missy."

"I'm adding 'impossible' to that list."

"Do you think about it?" I asked, my voice deepening. "About when you kissed me?" She said nothing, so I continued. "I think about it. All the time. How soft and delicate you are. That little noise you made."

Her breathing hitched. "I do think about it. A lot."

"Do you touch yourself when you do?" I stroked myself, from the root to the tip, circling my palm over the head, spreading the slickness of my pre-cum. "I do."

"You aren't playing fair, Carter Templeton."

"Never said I would." I paused, then asked, "So, do you?"

"That's a very personal question."

"That's a yes, then."

She gasped. "I didn't say that!"

"But you didn't deny it. And that's the same as admitting it."

"Is not."

"Come on, Paige. You can tell me."

She laughed. "I'm hanging up now."

I sighed. "Not going to indulge me?"

"You've got an imagination. Use it."

"Oh, I will, Paige. I will."

"Goodnight, Carter. And thanks for the roses."

"Enjoy." I ended the call and pictured her leaning forward, her eyes closed, inhaling the scent of the blooms. Then she was on her knees, taking me into her mouth, those petal-pink lips stretched around the tip of my cock, her hazel eyes locked on mine, her right hand disappearing between her legs…

Christ! I came with a low grunt all over my hand, my breath whooshing out in a rush. I'd barely touched myself. Then again, she made me feel like a horny eighteen-year-old, and apparently I'd regressed physically as well as mentally. And we were only on day four of this trip.

Fuck. I'd probably trashed my pants, and I wasn't about to call down to the concierge for someone who could remove the cum stains.

I shimmied out of my clothes, then went to the bathroom and washed off. I came back with a damp washcloth and inspected the damage. Only a few drops near the zipper. I dabbed at them, grinning like a fool. The day I finally got Paige Sutherland in my bed was going to be one of the highlights of my life. I hadn't felt like this since… Well, since the day I'd locked eyes with Amber McCallan while teaching Sociology 101.

I looked at the laptop sitting on the desk. An idea was forming… a younger man/older woman story. I'd camouflage the details this time. I'd learned my lesson about putting too much truth on the page. But the essential truth, the truth that mattered?

That could go on the page. It should. It had to.

I took a seat at the desk and pressed the power button on the laptop, my heart drumming in my chest.

For the first time in a long time, I felt the need to write.

CARTER

My lungs pumping as though I'd just run a marathon, I slammed *Amber's Fall* shut and set the book on the end table. I arched my back and pushed the heel of my palm down on my straining cock. Reading about Riley in scene after scene of him having sex with Amber, sometimes alone, sometimes with another man or woman, was making me crazy. I'd alternated between being half hard and completely hard since starting the damn book. It was definitely a one-handed read. And there were still two more books to go. Jesus. As though I weren't missing Riley enough as it was. The five days since he'd left on his trip to Great Britain felt like five hundred.

Of course, I missed the sex, but more importantly, I missed the man. Even though we weren't living together, the booty calls arrived, without fail, every two or three days. And those times I got to wake up with Riley in my arms were my favorite. I loved curling myself around that long, hard body, the scent of sex and Riley's cologne teasing my senses.

Christ. How was I going to survive another seventeen days of this? Assuming, of course, that Riley didn't meet someone who fed his muse better than I did. My chest ached at the thought.

Three months or three years, it didn't matter. I couldn't lose Riley without getting my heart broken. Somewhere along the line, I'd fallen and fallen hard. I was already far too invested to give Riley up without a fight.

If you really mean that, call him.

I checked the time. It was five o'clock in Burlington. It would be about ten in the evening in Inverness. Early enough to reach him. Pulling up the video call application on my tablet, I tapped Riley's name in my contact list and held my breath. I really wanted to see his gorgeous face.

When said face filled up the screen of my tablet, I blew out a huge sigh of relief and smiled. "Hey, sexy."

Riley smiled back, a crooked grin that made him look even cockier than usual. "Hey, Carter. Aren't you a sight for sore eyes. What's going on? You look like you just rolled out of bed, even though it's what? Five o'clock for you?"

I snorted. "It's your own damn fault."

"My fault? How so?"

I swiped a hand over my jaw. "You and that book of yours."

Riley's laughter, deep, throaty, and sexy as hell, burrowed into my heart. How the fuck had the man gotten so far under my skin in such a short time?

"What chapter are you on?"

"Near the end of the first book. You and Amber just went to the sex club. Gotta tell you, Rye. That was hot as fuck. We should go together someday."

"Oh yeah? It intrigued you that much, Mr. Upstanding Educator?"

I lifted my hips and pushed my sweats down to my thighs, exposing my straining cock. "I'm getting carpal tunnel and my dick is chapped. See?" After wrapping my fist around the base, I angled the tablet's camera down so Riley could see me stroke myself.

It felt so good to jerk myself and watch Riley's face on my screen at the same time. To hear the sharp intake of breath and the low moan he let out.

"Jesus, Carter. You weren't kidding." Riley licked his lips, his eyes glued to my cock, where beads of pre-cum slipped from the slit.

"Come on, Rye. Join me."

For a moment, all I could see was the ceiling of what had to be Riley's hotel room. Then the screen was filled with the man's glorious cock.

"Oh God," I groaned. "Stroke yourself. Pretend it's me."

"You too," Riley said breathlessly.

"Yeah." I moved my hand up to the head of my cock. Using the pre-cum as lube, I jerked myself slowly, from head to base, back up, adding the twist, right under the head, that I knew drove Riley crazy. The moan that rang out proved me right. But hearing it wasn't enough. "Move the screen back a little so I can see your face at the same time."

Riley's harsh breaths as he shifted the screen of his laptop increased my desire, ratcheting it up to near-unbearable levels. "I need to come so fucking bad."

Riley nodded. "Show me your face, too. Show me how much you want me."

"Yeah, yeah," I panted, setting my tablet on the coffee table between my spread legs so my hole was clearly visible, along with my cock, chest, and face. "I'll show you everything."

I'd give him everything I had too, everything I was, if only Riley wanted it.

I sucked a finger and began to circle my hole with it.

"Oh shit. Yeah, just like that, Carter." Riley opened his thighs wide and fingered himself, plunging in up to the second knuckle.

My eyes rolled back in my head at the decadent sight. I'd never get tired of Riley's body, of feeling it tighten around my fingers or cock. Yet, seeing Riley finger-fucking his own asshole did something else to me. Seeing him spread out and vulnerable, ignited a desire, a need to protect, a possessiveness I'd never experienced before, not even with my ex-wife. "Oh God, Riley. Give it to me. Fuck me."

Riley's fingers pistoned in and out of his ass as his other hand gripped his fat cock, stroking almost frantically. Either this was really working for him or he'd already been horny. The thought gave me pause. Riley was at a romance writers' conference where, undoubtedly, most of the participants would be women. Had he—?

No. I shoved the thought aside. By miracle of the Internet, Riley was with me now. That had to mean he hadn't given up on me, didn't it?

"Unh… Oh God. I'm going to come," Riley said on a moan.

"Do it," I ordered. "I'm right there with you."

Seconds later, Riley's back arched, his breath caught, and he called out, "Carter! Oh God. Carter!"

Cum spurted onto his flat stomach, rope after creamy rope. It was sexier, more perfect, than anything I had ever seen before, in person or in porn. And it pushed me over the edge into my own release.

My cock pulsed, and hot cum coated my hand and abs. The entire time, I kept my gaze fixed on the screen, watching Riley watch me with avid interest.

"Wish I were there to lick it all off you." His voice was thick, his pupils blown.

My abdomen contracted and another spurt of cum shot out. I shivered. "Jesus, Rye. You're killing me."

He chuckled. "Serves you right for booty calling me."

I pulled off my T-shirt to mop up the rapidly cooling mess I'd made. On the screen, he did the same with a hotel towel. When I was done, I picked up the tablet and set it on my stomach. "Wasn't the only reason I called you."

Riley shot me that half-grin again. "But it was part of it."

"A man can hope." I loved seeing the light in his eyes, and I realized it had been a while since I'd last seen it. Not since we'd first started dating, in fact. Had he met someone?

"How's the muse search going?" I asked. When Riley looked away, my stomach lurched. It was one thing to think he might have moved on and that this sexual interlude had just been a convenient diversion; it was another thing entirely to know it. "Forget I asked. It's none of my business anyway."

"It kind of is. I mean, if you were serious about what you said before I left."

When I'd told Riley I was falling for him. "Of course I was." Suddenly I felt naked and wished I hadn't used my T-shirt to clean myself up. "Tell me about her. Or is it… him?" I didn't know why, but in some way, a him might be worse. Maybe it was because we'd shared women before. Only women. Never men.

"Her."

I swallowed hard. "She another writer?"

"She's part of the tour," he said vaguely. His face disappeared from the screen to be replaced by a document containing some sort of outline.

"You're writing again?"

Riley's face came back. A big happy grin touched his eyes. He was like a little boy, spying a mountain of presents under the Christmas tree.

"I'm happy for you, Rye." Why was this so hard? Why did I feel like something had taken a bite out of my side? Tears burned the backs of my eyes. I willed them away before he caught on.

Riley tilted his head, holding his chin in his palm. "Really?"

"Yeah." I nodded insistently. "It was the purpose of the trip, wasn't it? To find your muse, to get the words flowing again."

"I should be able to get the outline to Nora soon. I've also written a couple scenes." He averted his gaze, uncertainty dimming the joy that had lit his face. "It's not much, but it's a start. I just hope it's good."

I hated the lack of self-confidence in his expression. Amber and Holden had certainly done a number on him. I smiled, despite the pain in my chest. "It's going to be great. You never write shit."

"Let's hope you're right."

"I am."

There was a long pause, because what could you say when the sound of your own heart shattering was all you could hear?

"Carter?"

I looked up at Riley's soft voice. "Yeah?"

"We aren't over."

"You sure about that?"

"I still want you." He met my gaze, head on. "That's not about to change."

I shifted uncomfortably on the couch. "What about her?"

"What about her?" Riley shrugged. "I've only known her for five days.

Nothing's happened."

"Yet. Losing your touch, lover boy?" I teased. He'd had me in bed the first night we'd met. The thought sobered me. Why hadn't Riley fucked her yet?

"She's a little skittish."

"I'm sure you'll get her, if that's what you want. You always do."

"Have faith in me," he said softly. "In us."

Time for a change of subject before I embarrassed myself and started bawling. I cleared my throat. "So, where are you headed to next?"

"Loch Ness. Maybe I'll get to see if good ol' Nessie measures up to our Champ."

"My dad used to swear he'd seen Champ once." He'd loved telling that story to us when we were kids. Man, I missed him.

"Well, I've lived on Lake Champlain my whole life, and I never once saw the fucker."

"That's 'cause you scared it away with Little Riley."

"It's *not* Little Riley. Need another look?" He palmed his spent cock.

I laughed. "After Loch Ness, then what?"

"Some Highland games in a village about an hour and a half from Inverness. Should be fun."

"Scots in kilts. You're sure to get an eyeful."

Riley winked. "Don't I wish. You ever going to wear a kilt for me?"

"If you stick around, I'll wear whatever you want." Fuck. Why had I said that? I wished I could pluck the words out of the air and lock them back up in my brain where they belonged. I'd meant it to be light and flirty, not desperate.

"Talk to you soon?"

I plastered a bright smile on my face, one I didn't feel at all. "You bet."

After the end of the call, I remained staring at the blank screen of my tablet for several long minutes. What had Riley been getting at? He seemed to be going after this woman. Did that mean he wanted us both, or that this thing with her was just to get his muse going, and they'd part ways at the end of the trip?

My gut rolled. Damn. I hated feeling so out of the loop, so helpless. Like others were controlling my life.

No. If I wanted Riley, I had to fight for him.

Getting up, I went to the kitchen counter and picked up the red brochure that contained the itinerary to Riley's trip. On day nine, they'd be in Liverpool. What if I joined him there? Would he be happy to see me or pissed that I'd crashed the tour?

If I was making the wrong decision, it could mean the end of a relationship that meant everything to me. Question was: What did it mean to Riley?

Chapter 4

RILEY

A breeze blew over my legs and under my kilt, tickling my balls. I felt half-naked, but given the fact that many of the men around me were in kilts, I didn't feel alone. And I had to admit, I was enjoying the novelty of letting it all hang out. I'd certainly gone commando before—it drove Carter wild—but always in pants or shorts. Letting my tackle swing free under a heavy kilt? That was something else altogether. I *was* supposed to be wearing something under it, but fuck that. When in Scotland… pretend you're Jamie Fraser.

I really had to hand it to Paige—Total Indulgence definitely knew what they were doing when they put a tour together. Today we were in a small town north of Inverness to see the Highland games. Total Indulgence had even arranged for a local costumer to provide us all with appropriate attire—thus my kilt and the traditional dancing costumes the women were wearing. Paige looked like a sweet country maid crossed with a Catholic schoolgirl. The combination was enough to keep me at half-mast every time I saw her.

It seemed that every person in the area was at the games, which were a combination of country fair and sporting event, where the men and boys got to show off their skills. Not to be left in the dust, plenty of women and girls were participating too, especially in the lively dancing competitions.

Although it was July, the day was cool, and clouds scudded across the sky. Everyone joked that it would probably rain (it was Scotland after all), but I didn't care. The grass was green, the beer was flowing, and fuck it, I was wearing a kilt, and not much else.

I'd watched a few competitions, marveling at the brawny souls who dared to toss the caber, essentially a tree-sized log. I'd been offered a chance at it, but didn't dare try. I'd make an ass of myself and/or break something, and I didn't want to risk the latter. I had a mission to accomplish. I was getting Paige in bed before the day was through.

True to form, she'd stayed out of my orbit for the first part of the day, but we were all meeting at 6 PM for a special dancing class that Total Indulgence had arranged just for us. And I was determined to have Paige as my partner.

I showed up at the open-sided tent where we were to meet. A wooden dance floor had been set up for our use. I spotted Kenji and we traded nods. He was deep in conversation with a couple of the women, so I let him be. I scanned the group, looking for Paige, my heart giving a funny little flutter every time I caught a glimpse of sandy-blonde hair, followed by a pang of disappointment at each false alarm.

And then I saw her, and this time my stomach flipped as well. I felt like a teenage boy at my first dance, afraid to approach the girl of my dreams.

But I was no teenager. And this wasn't my first dance.

I cut through the crowd and reached her side just as Kenji approached her on the left. "Fancy meeting you here," I whispered in her ear.

She reddened then touched her neck, shyly meeting my eyes. "Having fun?" she asked.

"Very much so," Kenji said before I could open my mouth.

A smirk played around his lips. That fucker! He knew exactly what he was doing.

"Me too, Paige," I said, then inwardly groaned at how lame I sounded.

"Of course Carter's enjoying himself," Ken said. "All these men… in kilts."

I was going to punch him. That's how this was going to end. I stepped forward, and Kenji burst out laughing and put up his hands to ward me off. "Just kidding. Couldn't resist." He winked at me, then gave Paige a peck on the cheek. "It's really amazing what you've done."

"You organized all of this, personally?" I asked.

She blushed again and nodded. "This tour is my baby."

"Well, it's freaking fantastic."

"Thank you." She met my eyes for a moment, then looked away when Ken touched her arm. "Do you have a partner?" he asked.

Fuck being Mr. Nice Guy. "She does," I cut in, putting a hand on Paige's waist. "Me."

"Ah," Ken said and raised a brow, nostrils flaring with barely repressed laughter. "I guess that's my cue to leave." He winked at me again and leaned in. "I've got some kilts to peek under. Enjoy."

I watched him wander off until I was certain he wasn't coming back. When I turned to Paige, she said, "Now what was *that* about?"

"Ken's trying to keep me from what I want."

"Why?"

"It's payback. And trust me, I earned it."

"That sounds like an interesting story."

"I've got a story that's even more interesting."

"Oh?"

"My blue balls have blue balls."

She chuckled. "Sounds painful."

God, she was cute. I resisted the impulse to grab the thick French braid hanging down her back and twist it around my fist. I wanted to pull on it, to make her arch on all fours beneath me while she moaned my name. *Riley.* Not Carter. *Riley.*

My cock sprang to attention and I thanked God that the sporran and heavy kilt kept it weighted down. Still, if anyone paid close attention… I stepped behind Paige and pulled her to my chest, pressing my cock against her ass. "Feel what you've done to me."

She subtly rubbed against my kilt, and I had to stifle a moan. Good Christ, this woman didn't appreciate her power.

Our dance instructor, a trim redhead around thirty, clapped her hands. "Claim your partners."

Total Indulgence had arranged for a number of male dancers to act as partners for the women and assist in their instruction. The women and men paired off; I kept a tight hold of Paige's hips all the while.

"How do you know I didn't want to dance with someone else?" Paige asked.

"You're dancing with me. End of story," I growled in her ear.

She grinned, turning toward me a bit. "You are far too demanding, Mr. Templeton."

"I'm at the end of my rope," I said and touched her cheek. "And you know why, you little minx." I whispered the next words. "Kissing me, and turning me down. Kissing me, then avoiding me for days." A tremor coursed through her, a tremor I could see and feel. "That running ends tonight, Paige."

"We'll see," she said, a challenge in her eyes.

Challenge fucking accepted.

The instructor called us to order. "We're going to learn a traditional ceilidh dance. I'll call out the steps, and you follow your partners."

My possessiveness was for naught. The ceilidh (kay-lee) resembled a square dance in many ways, right down to the called out dance moves, such as "swing your partner" and "do-si-do." Although I had plenty of opportunities to touch Paige, I often traded her off to other men. And yet, every time we touched, electricity flowed between us. I could sense it in the way she'd drag in a breath, her cheeks flushing, her eyes widening, a smile lighting up her face to match my own.

By the end of the hour, we were both breathless and laughing, and when I asked her to accompany me to get a beer and cool down, she didn't argue.

We got our pints and found a bench under a tree. I pulled her onto my lap, and she shrieked in protest, but I muffled the sound with my lips. She let out that breathy little whimper again and shifted in my lap, her thigh rubbing against my aching cock.

"Let's go back to the hotel," I whispered.

"I can't. I should stay in case anyone needs anything."

I kissed her neck, then licked the spot I'd kissed, and this time her whimper turned into a moan.

"You have to stop that," she said, her voice husky.

"I think I need to keep going." And I did, kissing down to the notch at the base of her throat, my hand creeping under the hem of her plaid skirt.

She took hold of my hand, forcing it back to her knee. "I need to get off your lap. And we need to stop kissing."

As if to make Paige more embarrassed, Ken walked up to us. "Get a room already!" he said with a laugh, then walked away.

"See?" she said and shifted onto the bench. She was breathing hard, her face red, and I knew she was thinking of running off.

I took her hand. "We both want this. Why fight it?"

She met my eyes, some old hurt flashing through hers. I wanted to strangle the guy who'd wronged her. "I don't know how else to be," she whispered.

"I won't hurt you, Paige. I swear it." I kissed her palm and she shivered.

"You won't?"

"I won't." I crossed my heart. "Shall we get that room?" My pulse pounded wildly in my ears, and I fought to keep my grip on her hand light instead of tight and desperate. When was the last time I'd wanted anyone this much?

She squeezed my hand, her trembling voice betraying her. "Oh God, yes. Let's get that room."

PAIGE

My fingers wouldn't stop shaking as I let Carter into my room at the hotel. Dear God, did I even remember how to do this?

Recalling my conversation with Ari before I'd left Miami, a giggle rose in my throat. It was like riding a bike, right?

I just hoped I didn't fall off. Carter stepped up behind me and swept my braid to one side. Then he kissed my nape, and I swore every inch of my flesh broke out in goose bumps. He kneaded my shoulders lightly, and I moaned softly. When was the last time anyone had touched me like that?

"Relax, Paige," he murmured. "I don't bite." He chuckled, the sound dark and wicked. "Well, not hard."

I laughed and turned in his arms. "That's better, and"—he touched my lower lip with his thumb—"you have the prettiest smile."

"Thanks."

I threaded my fingers together, trying to keep them from shaking.

"Look at me," he said. I took in his dark hair, his beautiful brown eyes, the neatly trimmed beard and mustache. How was it a man that gorgeous was interested in me?

"Stop worrying, Paige. Relax and enjoy yourself."

"I'll try. It's just… been a long time."

He smiled, one corner of his mouth quirking up. "I promise not to break out the Olympic scorecards."

I laughed again. "Okay."

He leaned in and kissed me, his hands cupping my cheeks, and I opened to him with a sigh. He licked along the inside of my top lip, and I shivered. Then his tongue stroked mine, sending sparks between my legs.

Why had I resisted this for so long? It felt damn good to be kissed like this. Carter smelled so incredible, a mix of spices, the outdoors, and something that was his alone.

I wrapped my arms around his neck and pulled him closer. Something hard pressed against my belly. "Is that your sporran, or are you just happy to see me?"

It was his turn to laugh. He removed the sporran, and his cock tented the front of his kilt.

"Swinging free?" I asked.

"It's not every day I'm in Scotland. If it works for Jamie Fraser…"

I reached out and caressed him through the wool. He groaned in my ear. "I swear I've had a hard-on from the first time you kissed me."

"You flatter me."

"It's true." He started unbuttoning the red vest I wore over the short-sleeved white blouse underneath. "Let's see what's got me so inspired." One of his hands crept inside, cupping my left breast, his thumb finding my stiff nipple and stroking it. When I opened my mouth to gasp, he latched onto my lips again, and I threaded my fingers through his thick hair, pouring all my excitement into the kiss. Carter's hands made quick work of the blouse and my red and white tartan skirt, until I stood there in only my bra, panties, and the argyle knee socks I'd been wearing. "Did I tell you how unbearably cute you are in this getup?"

I tugged at the black vest he wore over a long-sleeved white shirt. "And you, Mr. Templeton, are incredibly hot in this kilt. But now I'd like to see you out of it."

"You don't have to ask me twice." He yanked at the blue tie that matched the blue and green plaid of his kilt, then untucked the shirt and unbuttoned it as quickly as his fingers would allow, bearing an impressively lean and toned torso.

I touched my own belly, lightly silvered with stretch marks from my pregnancy. Would he notice? Would he ask about it? What would I say if he did?

Clad only in the kilt and black socks with matching swatches of plaid, he toed off the black dress shoes he was wearing, then flexed for me. "Not quite Jamie Fraser, I know."

"I'm not complaining." I stepped closer. "Besides, Carter Templeton looks damn fine to me."

He reached behind me and unhooked my bra. I caught it before it fell, holding it in place like a shield, then laughed and let it drop with a nervous thrill running through me. "You're a lovely lass, Paige," he said, putting on a thick Scottish brogue. Then he bent down and took one of my nipples in his mouth, drawing on it gently, before biting down. I cried out, the mix of pleasure with a hint of pain making my knees weak. He switched to the other nipple, using his fingers to tweak and pinch the one he'd abandoned.

"Oh Carter," I gasped.

Each time he sucked hard on my nipple, a wave of heat tore through me. His hand left my breast and slid down to cup my sex, his thumb stroking over the fabric, grazing my clit when he pressed between my lips. "Oh God," I whispered, not sure I could stay upright much longer. My thighs quivered, and my legs seemed made of Jell-O.

Carter yanked the fabric covering my crotch to one side, then plunged his fingers in his mouth, slicking them up before finding my clit again, and this time I tilted my hips forward, giving him better access. He supported me with one hand across my back, his mouth still on my nipple, his fingers stroking between my legs.

I moaned and twisted in his arms, widening my stance, and he worked a finger inside me, the invasion making me pant unashamedly.

Carter's hard cock pressed into the flesh above my waist, and I reached for it, fumbling around with the kilt until I found the opening at his hip. Snaking my hand underneath, I took hold of him, delighted to find that he was well-equipped. I stroked him lightly, and he groaned against my nipple, then released it. His hands went to the belt at his waist and unbuckled it, the kilt falling to his feet. He stripped off his socks and made swift work of the rest of my clothing.

He knelt before me and kissed my belly. "Let down your hair," he said, his voice husky with desire.

I reached up and unfastened the tie at the end of my braid, then loosened the twisted strands and let my hair tumble around my shoulders.

He smiled up at me. "You are a fucking goddess. When I first saw that braid, I wanted to wrap it around my fist while I was fucking you from behind."

The words were low, his voice filled with grit, and I shuddered, the image he'd conjured in my mind flooding my sex with moisture. The idea of being taken, roughly, seared through me.

"Get on the bed, Paige, unless you want me to fuck you on the carpet."

I went to the bed and threw the coverlet back while Carter rummaged around in his sporran. He held up two foil-wrapped condoms and came to join me. I leaned forward to get onto the bed, and he placed a hand on the small of my back. "Stay there."

I wondered how much he could see of me, bent over the bed, my legs spread. I arched my back like a cat in heat, pushing my bottom out, letting him see me, offering myself shamelessly.

"Fuck," he murmured. "You have no idea how much that turns me on."

I looked at him over my shoulder, watching as he licked two fingers, then slid them inside me.

"Oh," I moaned, pushing out to meet him, chasing his fingers when he withdrew them before plunging them back in.

"Jesus, Paige, you're so fucking tight. I can't wait to get my cock in you."

"Then don't wait." I couldn't believe I'd said it. Then again, I couldn't believe I was doing any of this. Me, staid Paige Sutherland, single mom, hard worker, woman who hadn't had sex in five years. Having a casual fling with a man eight years my junior. A man I barely knew.

But somehow I trusted Carter. And this was just a fling after all.

"Get on your back," he said, plunging his fingers in again, making me moan. I was so close already, and we'd barely started.

I climbed onto the bed and rolled over. Instead of entering me as I'd expected, Carter hauled my hips to the edge of the mattress and knelt beside the bed. "What are you doing?" I asked, propping myself on my elbows to look at him.

He grinned up at me. "Something you're going to like."

Was he really going to…? I'd barely formed the thought before he nipped at my inner thigh, his beard caressing the soft skin and making me shiver. I tried to close my legs, but he pushed them apart. "Don't move," he said, his voice low and commanding.

Heat bloomed in my belly, and I tried not to squirm when he ran his tongue along the seam of my sex, parting me to reveal my swollen clit. He blew on it, and I twisted away, then reminded myself to lie still.

"That's better," he murmured. "You taste so good, Paige." He dipped his tongue inside me, penetrating me gently with it, and I arched to meet his mouth. Damn, he was good at this.

His tongue replaced his fingers and he concentrated his attention on my little nub. My breathing came hard and fast, and I knew I was getting close.

He withdrew the two fingers inside me, then his hand came back, and something felt different. He'd split his fingers apart, two inserted inside me and the other two caressing my other hole. I stiffened in surprise. Did he want *that*?

Pulling back, he looked up at me. "Don't worry. Nothing's going to happen that you don't want. Just indulge me here. It's called the Venus Butterfly, and if you don't like it, tell me to stop."

"Okay," I rasped and let out the breath I'd been holding. Lying back, I closed my eyes. *Relax, Paige, and go with it.*

He resumed sucking on my clit, his fingers at work inside me, the other two he'd added circling my pucker, gently pressing and sometimes tapping on it, then finally penetrating it. The sensation was strange, but exciting too. I'd never tried anything anal, but clearly I'd been missing something, because this felt… great. And kind of overwhelming.

Sensation was coming at me from three different places, tension coiling in my belly so fiercely I thought I might cramp up. "I need… I need…" I couldn't quite say the words, but Carter seemed to understand.

He sped up his movements, his fingers plunging into me quickly, his caresses more insistent, his tongue moving on me furiously. I arched to meet him, trying to impale myself on his fingers, chasing the unusual sensations he was stirring in me. What would it be like to let him take me *there*?

Heat flooded my face and chest and I came, moaning so loudly I shocked myself. I lay there trembling as Carter rose until he was standing between my legs, his rigid cock pressing into my thigh.

He picked up the condom packet and tore it open with his teeth. "Ready for more?" he asked with a wicked grin.

I nodded, a hand pressed to my chest. "Let me catch my breath." He started to roll the condom on, but I sat up and took his arm. "Wait."

He raised a brow in question.

"Don't you think I should return the favor?" I asked.

A broad smile spread across his face. "I'm not one to refuse a lass," he said, slipping into the Scottish brogue again. "Especially one so bonny."

I smiled up at him, and patted the bed beside me. He sat down and I slid to the floor, acutely aware of how wet I was, how I ached to have him inside me. Soon.

It was my turn to impress him. I took his cock in hand, happy to see a drop of pre-cum at the tip. He'd definitely been enjoying himself so far, and I was going to make sure this night would be one he wouldn't forget.

I circled him with my fingers, loosely stroking, then gliding my thumb over the tip to collect up that bit of slickness so I could spread it over him. He groaned at my touch, particularly when I tightened my fingers around him.

"Fuck yeah," he murmured, thrusting into my hand.

Time to take it up a notch. I leaned forward and took the tip of him in my mouth, swirling my tongue around the head, then descending on the shaft until my lips met my fingers curled around his base. He shivered when I withdrew, flicking my tongue around him as I went. I descended on him again, sucking hard.

"That feels fucking incredible."

I hummed my appreciation, keeping up what I was doing, squeezing him a bit harder and adding more suction until he was groaning.

"Fuck, fuck, fuck," he murmured, his hips bucking, then he pulled back and swore again. "Got to stop, sweetheart, or it's going to be all over."

I sat back on my haunches. "You sure?"

He sucked in a breath and nodded, his fingers finding the condom he'd set aside. "I want to come inside you." He rolled the condom on as his breathing started to slow. He patted the bed. "Get back up here."

I sat beside him. He rolled to his feet, pushed me back, and yanked my hips to the edge of the mattress. "Ready?" he asked.

"Am I ever," I said, the ache between my legs intensifying.

A mischievous look in his eye, he grinned. "This bed is the perfect height," he said, bumping the blunt head of his cock against my clit. I sighed in pleasure, and he did it again, rubbing himself up and down between my labia, getting slick with my juices. Thumbing my clit, he positioned himself, then thrust inside me, the sensation making us both moan.

I closed my eyes and wrapped my legs around Carter's waist as he skillfully strummed my clit. He was big enough to stretch me deliciously. Jesus, had sex ever felt this good before?

We quickly built a rhythm, our bodies slapping together, our breathing harsh. Pleasure coiled within me, and when Carter gave my clit a little tug, I spilled over into bliss, crying out and shuddering beneath him.

"Fuck, Paige. You're squeezing me," Carter panted. "I'm not going to last if you keep that up."

I opened my eyes, taking in the sheer animal beauty of this man who had already brought me so much pleasure. I deliberately tightened my inner muscles, making him close his eyes, his dark lashes fanning over his cheeks. He was biting his lower lip, his face tight with concentration as he drove into me. He took both of my hips in his hands, his thrusts deepening, growing frenzied, before he stiffened and shuddered through his release.

"Damn," he muttered, bending forward over me, taking my head in his hands and kissing me deeply. "You feel so fucking perfect, Paige." He kissed my neck, chuckling in my ear. "The Olympic judges would have given you straight tens for that bit where you squeezed me."

I couldn't help laughing. "I guess it is like riding a bike."

"Except a lot more fun."

He kissed my nose, my cheeks, then just looked at me, grinning like someone who'd won the lottery.

It was the same grin I had on my own face, I was sure.

Ari was right; I did need to get laid. And often.

And even if I never saw Carter again after the trip was over, I wasn't going another five years without this. It was time I started living again.

RILEY

Feeling a little like a thief, or worse, an adulterer, I closed the door to my hotel room. I understood why Paige insisted on keeping our sexual relationship a secret from the rest of the tour group, but I hated it.

Even when I'd been in the thick of things with Amber and Holden, I'd never denied my relationships with either of them nor that our relationship had included all three of us. It had been unconventional and people had been curious, envious, disgusted. You name it, I'd heard it. None of that had mattered to me. I'd been more than willing to deal with the flak if it had meant having both of my lovers by my side, in bed or out of it. Clearly, Paige didn't feel the same way about me. At least not yet.

That's not why you feel like an adulterer.

I shrugged off my shirt and pants, then dropped onto the big, lonely bed in only my underwear as pangs of guilt ate at my gut. I *wasn't* an adulterer. First off, I wasn't married. Second, Carter knew the score. We were taking a break, and both were free to—

Bile rose in my throat at the thought of Carter pounding his fat cock into someone else's ass, or pussy for that matter. That's what Amber and Holden had done, snuck off to fuck, leaving me out of the equation entirely.

How is that any different from what you're doing now?

Fuck. I banged my fist on my forehead two times, three times. It *was* different, despite how it might seem from the outside. I wasn't cheating on Carter. I was searching for my muse. And it was looking like I'd found her. Okay, the couple of scenes I'd written were a bit flat, but I was writing again. That had to count for something, didn't it?

So, you're just using Paige?

"No, and get the hell out of my head!" I shouted into the darkness. Jesus, I was losing my damn mind. I enjoyed Paige, enjoyed spending time with her, talking about books, about England and Scotland, about history and politics. Anything, really.

And the sex had been phenomenal. Not better than what I shared Carter, but certainly very different. It had been fun to woo her, to draw her out of her shell, to coax her into letting loose, and finally, to have her get a little wild with me. I'd pushed her limits a bit, and I would push them even more before this trip was over.

Being the pursuer had given me a thrill, and when I'd finally caught my prey, she'd been delightful. A revelation. Like the librarian who wore a red silk thong and matching lace bra under her conservative pinstriped skirt and ruffled-neck blouse. I smiled at the memory of Paige sucking my cock, the way she'd squeezed me with her pussy while we were fucking. Sex with her had been really fucking hot.

So why wasn't I still lust-drunk? Why was I lying in bed arguing with myself instead of sleeping the deep slumber of the well-sated?

Because something had been missing.

Someone.

Goddamn. Why did I have to go and develop a conscience all of a sudden, and one so determined to work overtime? I wasn't doing anything wrong. For fuck's sake, I'd even told Carter about Paige. I wasn't sneaking around, I wasn't doing to Carter what Amber and Holden had done to me. If anything, my feelings for Carter were even stronger now than they'd been before I'd left Vermont. My chest tightened.

Shoving myself into a sitting position, I cradled my head in my palms. I *missed* Carter. Missed him to the point that the missing was a physical ache in my heart. One I didn't recall ever having for Amber.

Was I in love with Carter?

If so, why hadn't being with Carter been enough to spur my writing when thoughts of him were clearly enough to spur my imagination, as my growing erection could attest to?

A vision of Carter fucking me from behind while I knelt over Paige, eating her out, danced on the backs of my lids.

Oh God. I'd just had sex with Paige, but my traitorous cock was ready for round two, while I was alone in this damn hotel room. Alone with my hand, which after hooking my boxers under my balls, I put to good use. Moaning, I lay back on the bed and imagined Carter pounding into me while Paige sucked me off. Imagined plunging my fingers deep into her hot pussy and lapping up her sweet juices with my tongue.

A full circle. Infinity.

"Oh fuck," I cried out as the orgasm hit me like a ball hitting a bat, fast and hard. Covering my eyes, I worked on catching my breath, while I continued to stroke my softening cock. When was the last time I'd come like that? If I hadn't already been virtually naked, I'd definitely have come in my pants at the mere thought of a threesome with Paige and Carter.

Hmm… An idea percolated in my brain. I waited patiently as it bubbled to the surface, afraid to push, in case I lost it completely. Then it was there, clear as day.

I had to write. Had to get this down. Every emotion. Every action, every moan, gasp, and cry.

After quickly cleaning up, I threw on some sweats and a T-shirt, and powered up my laptop. I sat in the desk chair, cracked my knuckles, and started typing. Ideas flowed, tumbling over each other. My fingers hit the wrong keys, creating a mess of typos in my haste to get my thoughts on the page. But I didn't care.

Nothing mattered except the words.

Words that formed into sentences.

Sentences that formed into scenes.

Scenes that would form into a book.

Hallelujah! I was finally back on track.

Chapter 5

PAIGE

Carter leaned over to me and wagged his eyebrows. "Dinna fash yerself, lassie," he said in the most outrageous brogue.

Glancing at Hamish, the tall, tawny-haired Scot who'd been hired as our guide around Kilmartin and the surrounding sites, I put a finger to my lips. "Shh! He'll hear you."

"Don't you mean, 'Hold yer wheesht!'"

I laughed. "Do you even know what you're saying?"

"I'm a writer. I make shit up all day long."

My hand brushed Carter's as he strode beside me, and I had the insane impulse to thread my fingers through his. But we weren't alone. And I had no idea if he wanted a repeat of what we'd shared the night before.

We'd both enjoyed ourselves, sure, and from what I knew about Carter, he was no stranger to casual affairs.

The question was: How casual was this? And would it last for the rest of the trip?

"Penny for your thoughts," Carter said.

My cheeks heated. Should I be honest? "I was thinking about last night."

He smiled at me. "You're adorable when you blush."

"I feel like a child compared to you," I said, glancing around to make sure no one was within earshot. Most of the group was on the bus headed to our next stop, the Nether Largie standing stones. But some of us had elected to walk there with Hamish, who pointed out various cairns and other items of interest along the way.

"A child how?"

"You're so… experienced with—with everything, and I've been content with just my little corner of the world."

"You mean sex."

My face burned. "Yes."

"That doesn't make you a child. It makes you normal."

"So you're abnormal?"

He shrugged in his slate-gray jacket. "I'm certainly not Mr. Vanilla."

I grinned, remembering what we'd done. And that had probably been nothing to him. "No, you're not."

"I think it's why I got into the study of sexology. I wanted to understand how I fit into the world. If I did at all."

"And that led you into writing romance?"

"Not exactly. I used to teach sociology. But as it turns out, it wasn't a good fit for me."

"Why?"

"Well, when you realize that half your students only want to get in your pants, it's a bit disconcerting."

"If I'd been your student, I don't think I'd have been an exception."

One corner of his mouth turned up. "You say that *now*. You lead me on a merry chase this past week."

My pulse quickened. Should I ask what I wanted to know? I took a steadying breath. "And now that you've had your fill?"

"Had my fill?" He stopped walking. "I'm far from having had my fill of you, Paige."

Oh. "So we aren't done?"

He shook his head. "Unless that's what you want?"

"No." I tried to suppress my grin of relief, but he caught my eye, the twinkle in his telling me it was okay to want more.

"Good. Because I don't think I can survive another two weeks of blue balls."

I giggled, and Kenji caught up to us. "What's so funny?" he asked.

"Long story," I said.

He looked from me to Carter's crotch and grinned. "I know."

Ah. "So you two"—I looked from one to the other—"were involved?"

Kenji shrugged. "Briefly."

"Does that bother you?" Carter asked me, his voice filled with tension.

I supposed it should, but… "No. It doesn't."

"You're an unusual woman," Kenji said. "Most people would be running in the other direction."

"As long as everyone's been responsible and upfront, I don't see the problem."

Kenji looked at Carter. "You are two peas in a pod."

Not quite. But maybe someday… Oh don't go there, Paige. Messing around for the duration of the trip was one thing. Beyond that?

Probably not going to happen.

Hamish stopped to collect the group that had ridden the bus. I took a quick headcount to make sure no one was missing, and then we set off for Nether Largie.

A light breeze snatched at my hair, which I'd braided again, thinking of Carter's little fantasy about taking me from behind. Maybe we'd make that a reality soon. Maybe even tonight.

Hamish asked if anyone had any questions so far.

"Where's Craigh Na Dun?" Carter asked.

Hamish chuckled. "I dinna ken. There's nae such place. But there are plenty o' standing stones like what's described in *Outlander*. Nether Largie could be the model for Craigh Na Dun."

"Hoping to get in some time travel?" Kenji asked Carter.

"Only to go back to a time before I met you."

Ken slapped a hand over his heart. "Third-degree burn!"

He and Carter laughed, then Kenji wandered off to another group.

"Seriously, if you could travel through time, where and when would you go?" I asked.

Carter stuck his hands in his pockets, a furrow creasing his brow. "To a future when no one gives a fuck about your sexual orientation, gender, or religion."

"That would be utopia."

He shrugged. "It's something to hope for. To strive for. It's something I try to promote with my writing."

"How so?"

"Well, like Riley Kendrick, I write about threesomes of all sorts."

"How is your writing going?"

The smile he gave me was tentative. "It's actually *going* again. Thanks to you."

Warmth spread through my chest. "I'm so glad to hear it."

"So," Carter asked, "if you could time travel, where and when would you go?"

"I'd like to visit your utopia. I'd also like to meet Jane Austen."

"Aren't we going to her house later in the tour?"

"We'll be visiting a couple places she lived. That's as close as I'll ever get."

We followed Hamish toward a cluster of stones he identified as Nether Largie.

"It's a good thing we can't really do either one," Carter said. "Otherwise, we'd get too hung up on trying to fix the past or influence the future. But all we really have is now."

"So true," I murmured.

And it was. There was little point in obsessing about where this was going, or how I'd messed up in the past. Enjoying the here and now—that was what I should be doing.

Enjoying Carter, for however long he was a presence in my world.

RILEY

I kept my gaze on Hamish, our tour guide, as he finished up the escorted portion of the day's adventures in Nether Largie. "For those of ye interested in a more in-depth explanation of how these standing stones were used as a lunar observatory, gather 'round. As for the rest of ye, 'tis been bonny."

I glanced at Paige and cocked a brow. I'd love to get her in bed again, but we wouldn't be anywhere near a hotel until we hit Glasgow. So for the next few hours until we set out, I was happy to do whatever she wanted.

"If anyone stays, I should stay too," she said.

"Of course." I smirked. "We wouldn't want old Mrs. Clark getting lost on her way back to the village," I said dryly as the older woman headed toward the bus Paige had hired to taxi us around the area.

Paige laughed. "Fine. But I still want to stay."

"As my lady wishes." I bowed dramatically, ushering her toward the small group now circling Hamish. Rising, I winked at her and nodded toward the gorgeous Scot. "At least the view is nice."

Her cheeks colored sweetly, even as her eyes strayed toward the man, a tall, broad-shouldered, kilted specimen of masculine perfection. Okay, he wasn't quite as sexy as Carter, but he was damn close.

"Come on, now," I teased. "I'm sure you noticed those thighs when we were trekking up here." While some members of the group had ridden up on the bus, many of the younger ones had hiked over from the castle we'd visited prior.

"Yes, I noticed. I'm not dead." She turned back to me, her fingertips tapping her plump lips. I could almost see the cogs turning in her head. "Mmm… I'm not sure how to ask this, but you did bring it up. If it's too personal"—she pushed a loose strand of hair behind her ear—"just say so."

I stepped close, so my breath feathered her neck, and inhaled her delicious scent, flavored from a half-day of walking around in the crisp Highland air. "What could you ask me that would be more personal than what we did last night?" Given the hitch in her breathing, she had to be remembering what we'd done, how good it'd felt.

"You've got a point, Mr. Templeton."

I closed my eyes. God, I loved her lust-thickened voice. It shot from my ears to my cock, and I began to harden.

While Hamish explained the significance of the alignment of the stones in indicating the extreme positions of the moon during its nineteen-year cycle, I drew Paige away from the others. The outcropping of rocks I'd spotted a dozen yards away would give us some much-needed privacy.

"You didn't ask me your question," I said, taking her into my arms from behind as she kept her gaze on her charges.

"Oh." Her body stiffened, and she waved her hand dismissively. "It was nothing."

I nibbled the spot behind her earlobe, a spot, I'd discovered, that turned her into jelly. "Ask me. I'll tell you anything."

"You said you were bisexual, and we've talked about threesomes…" She swallowed.

"Yes…" I prodded gently, pleased, really pleased, with the direction of her thoughts.

"Is Hamish the kind of guy you'd go for, or do you prefer threesomes with two women?"

I observed the Scot from my perch over Paige's shoulder. He was absolutely the type I went for. Tall, blond, built, patient…

Like Carter.

A surge of longing welled in my chest. Yes, like Carter. But Carter wasn't here. Paige was, and Hamish was. Not that I had time to seduce the guy. Hell, as far as I knew, Hamish was as straight as an arrow.

None of that mattered though when one was blessed with a writer's imagination, and when it came to sex, mine was more vivid than most.

Slipping my hands under Paige's blouse, I began to massage her midriff, working my way up to her chest. "He's very much my type. Is he yours?"

She caught her lip between her teeth, and her brow wrinkled adorably. "I'm not really sure what my type is. I'm obviously attracted to you, but you don't look anything like my ex." Smiling, she brought her lips to mine. "You're much more handsome than he was."

"Am I more handsome than our *braw* guide?"

Laughing at my attempt at a Scottish accent, she glanced over her shoulder at Hamish then back at me. "Honestly, I can't say. You're both so different. But…"

I spun her around so her back was to my chest again. "It's okay to be attracted to both of us." Teasing her nipples, I pressed my hard cock against her ass.

She moaned and leaned into me, her stance widening.

Slowly, I trailed one hand down her side until I could snake it under the hem of the long, thick skirt she'd worn with the sexiest knee-high leather boots. "Keep your eyes on Hamish. Imagine my hand is his. Imagine that he's kneeling in front of you. Imagine that it's him removing your panties." Lowering myself behind her, I pushed them down her legs and pocketed the small scrap of material.

With my hands on her hips, I nudged her over to a rock that she could lean on. From this angle, she would be able to see the group and, more importantly, see Hamish.

I knelt between her legs and ran my fingers over her smooth skin, pushing the skirt up as I went. She gripped my shoulders. "We should stop."

"*Should* we? You really want to stop?"

She looked at me for a moment, then slowly shook her head.

"Have you ever had sex outdoors, Ms. Sutherland?"

Wide-eyed, she shook her head again.

"You are today." I grinned. "When in Scotland, do like the Scots: flip that kilt."

And with that I dove between her thighs, letting her skirt fall over my head. In the heat and darkness of my hiding spot, I gripped her ass and pulled her pussy against my mouth. My tongue darted out to flick lightly against her clit. She moaned and clasped my head on either side. Her hips pushed forward, encouragingly.

"Imagine it's me behind you," I said. "I'm stroking your ass and rubbing my cock between your beautiful cheeks." I mimicked the words with my index finger, spreading her juices along her crack. "And between your legs, pleasuring you, is Hamish." I parted her pussy lips and circled her clit with my tongue.

"Oh God, Carter." She gripped my head tightly between her hands as though afraid I'd leave. Silly woman.

I slid my pointed tongue into her, probing, teasing, readying her for me. Easing back, I worked a finger, then two, deep inside, hooking them up to caress her G-spot. She cried out, her back arching, impaling herself on my fingers.

"You're so good at that." She whimpered and twisted her hips as she chased my mouth. "Oh, I'm…" One hand left my head, to cover her mouth no doubt, and her body convulsed. And like a contented cat, I lapped at her while I continued to pump my fingers into her pussy.

Several long minutes later, she quieted, and all I could hear were her soft pants. I poked my head out from under her skirt. "How was that?" I asked, licking the taste of her off my lips.

She gave an embarrassed chuckle before returning my grin. "Better than I ever imagined."

I pushed to my feet. "But wait, it gets even better," I said in the voice of an infomercial host.

The shadows lifted from her eyes, and this time her laughter was full and joyous. Yes. This was how I wanted to see her: free and loving life. Too often she gave the impression of having the weight of the world on her shoulders. I was happy to relieve her of it, if only for a short while.

"What do you have in mind?" She palmed my cock and rubbed her thumb over the mushroom head clearly outlined in my jeans, a pair of Levi's I felt would go well with my professor persona. No labels, no artful holes.

"Turn around." I couldn't wait to fuck her. "Face the group and watch Hamish."

Her eyes rounded. "Have I shocked you?" I asked.

"Maybe a little."

"But you're also excited." I tweaked a peaked nipple that prodded the thin material of her blouse.

She gasped. "Yes."

"Bend over, sweetheart."

"Yes."

She laid herself over the rock she'd been leaning on. Once again, I flipped her skirt up. I cupped one firm cheek in my hand, caressing it lightly as I undid the buttons on my jeans. My eager cock pushed against the waistband of my trunks, and I sighed in relief when I was finally able to free it from the confines of the tight denim. Those Scots were definitely on to something with the kilts…

Reaching into my back pocket, I got out the condom I'd stashed there earlier that morning and quickly suited up, careful to return the wrapper to my pocket before sidling up to her. I eased my cock between her thighs, bumping the head of it against her clit. "Ready?"

Her body jerked and she groaned. "Yes. I want you inside me."

I rocked against her a few more times, slicking my cock with her moisture. "And Hamish? Where do you want him?"

"In my mouth."

Oh, she was a naughty one all right. She might not know what it was to be spit roasted, but she wanted it. "You don't want him to pleasure you?" In my experience, given the chance to direct activities, most women generally preferred to have both their partners focused on their pleasure.

"He would be. I've recently discovered I love"—she paused and threw me a shy glance over her shoulder—"having a cock in my mouth."

Holy shit. My dick throbbed with the need to be inside her. Inside this woman who was so ripe for a threesome. I pushed into her, sinking in up to my balls in one sharp thrust that had us both gasping. When I pulled out and did it again, she moaned and pressed backward, as eager for this as I was. Leaning over her, I placed my hand around her throat and slid my thumb between her parted lips. "Suck. Imagine Hamish's big cock thrusting into your mouth. You're taking it. All of it." My voice deepened. "And you're loving it."

"Yes, yes." She closed her lips and twisted her tongue around my thumb. As the suction increased, my legs wobbled.

Fuck! My cock was inside her pussy, pumping in and out, yet I imagined I could also feel her tongue wrapping around the head, teasing that spot under the rim. "Jesus, woman. You're dangerous."

Dangerous to my sanity. Dangerous to my plans. Dangerous to my h—

No. I shook my head. This was a fling. Part of my quest to regain my writing mojo. I had Carter waiting for me in Vermont.

Carter.

Shit. I was going to come. My gaze on the Scot, who looked more than a little like Carter, I drilled into Paige. Moving my free hand from her hip to her pussy, I pinched her clit between my thumb and forefinger, slowly increasing the pressure.

"Oh." She wailed around my thumb, her muscles squeezing my cock.

Stars blurred my vision. My balls drew tight and when she came, her walls pulsed around me. I let the climax take me over. My eyes closed, and all I could see was Carter, and all I could feel was Paige.

I fell forward to cradle her against my chest. It felt so good, so right, to hold her like this with my cock slowly softening inside her. Her light laughter piqued my curiosity. "What is it?"

Arching her neck, she looked back at me. Her beautiful face was lit up by a well-satisfied smile, her eyes sparkling with humor and a touch of self-deprecation. "That was amazing. We absolutely have to do it again."

It was and we would.

"Have I turned you over to the dark side, young padawan?" I asked, landing a peck on her lips that quickly turned into a deep kiss. One that caused my cock to twitch inside her.

When I released her mouth, her eyes were dewy. "I'm afraid I'll never be pure again."

"Pure?"

A corner of her lips quirked up. "Every time you're near, and heck, even when you're not, my mind fills up with you, with us, with…" She looked away, a bashful expression on her face.

I stepped back, letting myself fall out of her, and smoothed her skirt back into place. After stuffing the condom, wrapped in a hanky, into my jacket pocket, I tucked myself back into my jeans, and caught her chin between my fingers. I stared deep into her eyes. "Never be ashamed of your wants and desires. Sex is beautiful, fun, intense, whatever we need it to be. Our sexuality is meant to be enjoyed, however it presents itself. If your fantasy is to have sex with two men, there's nothing wrong with that."

"As long as it remains only a fantasy."

"Why not live it out? As far as fantasies go, this one is pretty harmless."

"Oh, I couldn't. I'm a m—" She stopped speaking and tried to turn away, but I held her in place.

"You're a what?"

"A m-marketing director. I have an image to uphold... for the company."

"No one need ever know," I said gently.

"Do you really think we could keep it a secret?"

"People are funny about things like that. Even when presented with the truth of a situation they don't understand, they deny what's right before their eyes."

She ran her hand along my shoulder, gently massaging it. "Are you speaking from personal experience?"

I nodded mutely. The press had salivated over photos of me with Amber and me with Holden, but all they'd said regarding photos of all three of us was that we were caught up in a love triangle of sorts. Reporters had skirted the truth, but never admitted it, despite what I'd written in the books. The movie would change all of that.

"I am. But the day is far too beautiful to talk about dreary stuff like this." I hooked my arm through hers. "How would you like to head back to the village and find a nice pub where we can get a bite to eat?"

She pressed her lips to my jaw in a tender kiss. "I'd love that, Mr. Templeton."

My heart tightened at the gentleness of her tone, while my stomach roiled at her lighthearted use of my false name. Carter's name.

What the fuck have I done?

Chapter 6

PAIGE

I hadn't been on a date in ages, and certainly not with a man so much younger. *Relax, Paige. You're not dating. You're just hooking up, as the kids call it.*

I really had to learn to go with the flow. I'd followed Ari's advice so far, and it had been working out great. All I needed was a fruity drink, some good music, and to get in the right frame of mind. Having the attention of someone like Carter was a fantasy come true, and I needed to run with it and stop thinking about the future.

Even though I was a bit tired, I was really looking forward to a fun evening with him. We'd just arrived in Liverpool, after a long day of traveling from Glasgow, including a pit stop in the delightful town of Gretna Green, a place that had featured heavily in many of my favorite historical romances.

I walked down Mathew Street, a narrow cobblestone lane, looking for the red sign that indicated the entrance to the world-famous Cavern Club. Thankfully, I'd opted to wear my sandals with the block heels instead of the stilettos, or I'd have face-planted for sure.

The entrance and stairs to the legendary cellar were well-lit, but with the black-painted brick walls, I could never forget I was descending below ground. And then I was there, inside the historic venue that had seen six decades of musical greats like the Beatles and Queen. These days, the

Cavern Club hosted any number of new and established groups and singers with live music every day. I hoped whoever was playing tonight would be good. After all, this was a special treat for the tour participants.

As I glanced around, I hoped my black cropped pants, sleeveless burgundy blouse, and lightweight blazer would fit in with this younger crowd. The last thing I wanted to do tonight was draw attention to my age. Unlike Carter, who always looked stylish regardless of what he was wearing, I had to put some thought into it. I was far more comfortable in a skirt suit than I was in jeans and a T-shirt.

The club was dark, with multicolored spotlights illuminating music-industry memorabilia throughout. The stage at the far end of the space was empty at the moment, and only soft music played in the background. Since the live music was supposed to be nonstop until midnight, I guessed this was a short intermission while the next band prepared to take the stage.

Fortunately, it was early in the week, so the club wasn't too crowded. As my eyes adjusted to the dimness, I was delighted to see quite a few tour members already having a drink or examining the photos on the walls. The outing to the Cavern Club was an optional activity, so I'd had no idea who, if anyone, would show up. I stopped by a table where Kenji was sitting with Lori Graham, a reserved woman in her mid-thirties who wrote fairly sweet romances.

"I'm happy you decided to come out for drinks tonight," I said to them.

Kenji craned his neck and made a show of looking behind me. "Where's your boy toy?"

I frowned. "If you're referring to Carter, he stayed behind at the hotel to finish up a scene. He said he'd join us later."

"Good, good." Kenji raised his arms and undulated his body. "I hope he'll show us some moves. Carter was quite the… dancer back in college."

Why did I think he'd been planning on saying something else entirely?

Lori stirred the ice in her glass and made a moue. "I can't dance."

Kenji patted her arm. "Nonsense, sweetie. You've just never had a good teacher." He opened his eyes and thumped his hand on his chest dramatically. "I know. Maybe Carter can show you tonight. What do you say, Paige? Think he'll do it?"

I rolled my eyes, pretending to be exasperated with Kenji, but secretly, I had to admit I enjoyed their low-key rivalry. Having had no brothers, I wasn't used to the teasing and ribbing common between young men. "I have no idea," I said, then changed the subject. "Are you both enjoying the tour so far?"

Kenji's face glowed. "I adored the Scottish kilts… ah… kirks and castles, I mean"—he winked at me—"but I really *needed* this. Music, a crowded bar, maybe some dancing. You know?" He tapped me on the arm. "You didn't tell me King's Cross is playing tonight. I loooove them!"

"That's because I don't even know who they are." Laughing, I leaned close as though preparing to impart a royal secret. "I can't tell you how much I'm looking forward to a mixed drink. I've had about all I can take of ale and whiskey."

"Preach, girl." Ken held up his beverage, a frothy green thing. Beside him, Lori tittered and brought her own glass, what appeared to be vodka and orange juice, to her lips. By the looks of her, it was clearly not her first.

I leaned over and whispered in Ken's ear. "Can you look after Lori? She seems to have had a few too many."

"Don't worry, Mama Paige," Ken teased. "I'll make sure she gets back to the hotel safely."

"I appreciate that." I touched Lori's arm. "Have fun."

"Oh, I will," Ken and Lori both said at the same time.

Leaving them to their laughter, I leaned on the bar and waited patiently for the bartender to take my order. When he nodded at me, I said, "May I have a strawberry margarita, please?" After the coolness of Scotland, I was in the mood for something summery and flirty.

"Straight away, ma'am."

A minute later, I was taking my first sip of the sweet liquid wonder. When was the last time I'd enjoyed a drink on a warm summer night without a single worry to cloud my mind? Ari did her best to drag me out every now and then, but she usually spent the evening prodding me to put myself out there and get back into the dating world. If Ari could see me now, she'd certainly be proud.

I spotted an empty table across the club. I checked in with some other tour members along the way, asking how things were going and if they needed anything. To my immense relief, everyone appeared to be having a great time and were looking forward to the England portion of our trip.

I settled onto a stool at a tall table to listen to the band that was starting up and await Carter's arrival. The lead singer and the guitarist were both quite cute, and I could see why Ken liked their music. As I finished off the last drop of my margarita, a fresh one was placed in front of me. My eyes shot to the waiter. "Not that I don't appreciate it, but I didn't order this. It must be for someone else."

"No mistake, ma'am." The waiter pointed to a tall, blond man standing at the bar. "That gentleman sent it over."

"Is that so?" I smiled at the blond. What could it hurt? I was hardly alone, and Carter would be joining me soon. Raising the drink in his direction, I mouthed "Thank you."

Drink in hand, the blond approached, stopping just short of my table. He indicated the empty stool across from me. "May I?"

His accent was American, from New England, if I were to guess. I held my hand out toward the stool. "Please."

My heart skipped a beat when he took my hand and kissed the back of it. Laughing nervously, I pulled it out of his grip and tucked it into my lap.

Relax, Paige. The man was flirting with me, that was all. As he took a seat, I introduced myself. "I'm Paige. From Miami."

"Hello, Paige from Miami. I'm Carter from Vermont."

His deep voice washed over me like a warm ocean wave, and it took a few seconds for what he'd said to register. "Carter? What a coincidence. I'm… traveling with a Carter."

The man grinned. "Don't tell me he's from Vermont too."

Was he? Had Carter ever said where he was from? For some reason, Vermont sounded right.

"How strange," I murmured, before saying a little more loudly, "Either way, I imagine there are quite a few Carters in Vermont."

"And they're probably all better-looking than me," Carter said, his mouth drawing down into a sad expression.

Obviously, he was joking. The man had to know how attractive he was. "Oh, I don't know about that." Playing along, I batted my lashes in an exaggerated fashion. "You seem pretty good-looking to me." Would Carter like him too? He did remind me of Hamish, who Carter had definitely been attracted to. Maybe the threesome we'd fantasized about could come true.

"Why thank you, Paige. I must say I wasn't expecting to meet someone like you here tonight."

"Oh?" Did he mean someone old like me? Granted, I wasn't the youngest patron, but I wasn't the oldest either. Besides, this Carter looked to be only a few years younger than me, if the fine lines at the corners of his eyes were to be believed.

"Are you kidding? I was expecting to have to wade through a bunch of twenty-year-olds with shaved heads and bad teeth. You, my dear, are a definite breath of fresh air."

"My, my. You are quite the flirt. Are you a politician, Carter, or maybe a diplomat?"

He scoffed and took a drink of his beer. "Hardly anything quite so lofty. I'm just your average over-worked, under-paid public school teacher."

From where I sat, there was nothing average about the man. He was gorgeous, with his broad shoulders and trim waist. "A teacher. Really?" I cocked my head to the side, observing Carter, imagining him in a classroom full of children all clamoring for his attention. It fit. "I've always admired teachers. I don't know how they deal with so many kids at once. I'd go crazy."

He chuckled. “The kids are nothing. The parents?” His eyes widened and he shuddered. “Sca-aaary.”

“I can imagine.” I smiled, remembering my own clashes with the parents of some of Emma’s classmates. “What do you teach?”

“Special education. I’ve specialized in children with developmental disabilities, such as autism and intellectual disability.”

“Intellectual disability. Does that include Down syndrome?”

“Yes, among other conditions.”

“What made you specialize in that direction?”

“My younger brother has severe autism, and I realized that there are fewer programs available for kids like him, who have little chance of mainstreaming. I feel like they often get forgotten in the shuffle, which certainly doesn’t help them as they get older.”

Hearing Carter put into words everything I’d felt about Emma’s education, my heart contracted and heat spread throughout my chest. There’d been so many struggles, so many ups and downs. And in the end, I’d felt almost blessed that Emma had mosaic Down syndrome rather than one of the other types. Her intellectual disability was minimal compared with that of many other people with Down syndrome.

I swallowed to clear the emotions clogging my throat. “No child left behind has left more than a few behind,” I said.

“Are you a teacher too?”

“Oh no. But, I have a… niece who has Down syndrome, and I’ve heard a lot about her difficulties with the school and various government programs.”

Carter’s bright blue eyes connected with mine, seeming to see everything I wanted to keep hidden. He placed his hand on top of mine where it rested next to my glass. “I’ve had some delightful and very memorable students with Downs over the years. There’s something so joyful and honest about them. They make you see life through their eyes.”

“And it’s all one big party, isn’t it?” Emma had been a bundle of excitement during our earlier video call as she’d explained to me her entire visit to the zoo with Ari. I sipped my margarita and thought about Carter’s words. He seemed to really understand what it was like to have a child with special needs like Emma.

If we didn’t live hundreds of miles apart, I could really see myself becoming friends with him. His quiet confidence made me feel safe, like I’d met a kindred soul.

“So.” Carter cleared his throat. “You’re on a trip? Work or pleasure?”

How to answer that? This trip had turned out to be both work and pleasure. More pleasure than work, if I were being honest. Carter had seen to that. I couldn’t help the small smile that curved my lips. “I’d say this has been one heck of a vacation so far.”

His eyes glimmered with mischief as he leaned in close and whispered, "I have a question for you, Paige from Miami: How do you feel about vacation flings?"

"As it turns out, Carter from Vermont," I said with a wink, "I rather enjoy them."

RILEY

Man, I can't wait to see her again. I walked into the Cavern Club, scanning the crowd for Paige. When I spotted her, my stomach did that funny little flip I'd been getting ever since I'd first met her. What did it mean?

You know what it means, Kendrick.

Maybe. *Maybe* that's what it meant.

She was talking to someone, a man whose back was to me. It definitely wasn't Kenji, Mr. Clark, or David Laughton. The broad shoulders and thick, flaxen hair made that clear. I stepped sideways so I could see the guy's profile, and my heart leapt to my throat. It was Carter. Holy shit!

My pulse pounded with excitement. What was Carter doing in Liverpool?

And why was he talking to Paige, of all people?

I started toward them, then stopped. Maybe I ought to observe them for a second before I barged over there.

Carter already knew about Paige, but what was I going to tell her?

I went over to the bar and ordered a vodka Collins, then sipped it while I studied them.

Carter was smiling at Paige, casually touching her arm. And she was definitely smiling back. He was listening to her attentively, his eyes focused on hers. God, he was a good listener. He sucked you in with those blue eyes, the depth of his attention…

Shit. Carter was hitting on her. I was almost sure of it. When he leaned in and whispered something in her ear, his arm brushed the side of her breast. Classic Carter move. I'd seen it often enough to know.

A strange thrill ran through me. Shouldn't I be jealous? But that wasn't what I was feeling. Not at all. They looked good together. They'd look even better naked together in my bed. I took another sip of my drink. I'd fantasized about the three of us before. I'd written scenes of us together in the story I was working on right now.

And the idea turned me the fuck on.

Maybe it could really happen. I'd have to figure out how to approach them, how to broach the subject with her. She'd already sort of agreed to it…

Carter turned and our gazes clashed. His face lit up, and I was off the barstool and over to them before I could give it too much thought.

He rose from his seat and opened his arms to me. "Man, did I miss you, Riley," he said, tugging me into his embrace and planting a big kiss on my mouth.

I kissed him back, my eyes flicking to Paige, whose jaw was hanging open. Fuck.

I pulled back from him and looked at her, trying to think how to explain.

"Riley?" she said, her eyes widening. "Oh my God. You're Riley Kendrick. And all this time, you've been calling yourself Carter Templeton." Her gaze swung to Carter. "Let me guess. That's *your* name."

Carter stepped away from me, his gaze darting between us. "What the hell, Riley?"

Paige rose from her chair, her eyes blazing. She grabbed her purse. "You can add 'liar' to the list." She stomped off, and I started toward her when Carter's hand clamped around my bicep.

"It's her, isn't it?" he asked, his tone clipped.

Fuck, fuck, fuck. I turned to him. "Yeah it's her. What are you doing here?"

"Thought I'd surprise you."

I half smiled. "I'm surprised, all right."

"I'll bet." He crossed his arms.

I needed to talk it out with him, but right now I needed to talk to Paige more. She was at a severe disadvantage. She'd had no idea about Carter.

And I should've told her before now.

I touched his cheek, and he jerked back. Damn it. "Listen, I have to go make sure she's okay. But stay here. I'm coming right back. I'll explain everything."

"There's nothing to explain."

I took a deep breath. This might earn me a punch in the face, but it was worth the risk. I stepped close to Carter, placed my hands on his cheeks, and kissed him. "Please wait for me. We'll talk when I get back."

He reached up and took hold of my hands, gently pushing them away, his eyes pools of hurt. "Fine. Not like I have anything else to do." He picked up what looked like a shot of whiskey and downed it, before shouldering past me and heading for the bar.

Goddammit. I watched his retreating back. I'd fucked this all up, hadn't I?

Maybe I could fix it. I had to try.

I hurried over to the hotel and up to Paige's room. I pounded on the door. "Paige, open up. It's me, Riley."

I waited, listening to her approach the door. She yanked it open. "Go back to your boyfriend. I'm going to bed. *Alone*." She slammed the door in my face.

"Paige!"

The door flew open again, and she stepped out, jabbing a finger into my chest. "I *asked* if you were involved with someone, and you said no."

"You asked if I was married. I'm not."

"You have a boyfriend!"

"We were on a break." I hesitated, then added, "But, yeah, Carter is my boyfriend."

That was the first time I'd said it. *Boyfriend*. It felt… right. Hopefully Carter would think so too—if he ever gave me the time to explain.

"On a break? Boyfriend? Not married?" She threw her hands up in the air. "Semantics!"

"I'm sorry, Paige. I should have realized—"

"That you weren't being honest? Yeah, you should have realized that, and you should have had the decency to try it out for a change." She shook her head. "But what should I expect from the infamous Riley Kendrick?"

My shoulders slumped. I was so tired of people believing all the lies. I'd hoped she'd be different, now that she'd spent some time with me. "What you see in the press, that's not me."

"But the books? That is all you, right?"

I nodded. Had she read the third book yet? Did she understand what had happened? "Did you finish the trilogy?" I asked, my voice rasping in my throat.

"Not yet. And I'm not going to now."

She went to slam the door shut, and I put out a hand to block it, wedging my foot against the wood at the same time. I could barely look her in the eye. I'd never meant to hurt her, and I had. I was every inch the asshole Ken had accused me of being. "*Please* finish them, Paige. And then we should talk."

Something softened in her gaze. "Okay." She pushed against the door, tears starting to well in her eyes.

Please don't cry. I reached out, touching her cheek. "I fucked up. I'm sorry. Please… Let me explain."

She sighed, and put her hand over mine, holding my palm against her cheek, closing her eyes for a second. Then she nodded. "We'll talk tomorrow. When I can think straight." She stepped back and I released the door. It swung shut, and I stared at the white painted wood for a moment, my gut one big knot.

Could I fix things with her? With Carter?

I hoped to God I could. I headed down the hall, back to the Cavern Club.

Carter, please wait for me to figure this out.

CARTER

Standing at the bar, I deliberately avoided looking toward the exit. I didn't want to see Riley chasing after Paige. For fuck's sake, I had come all this way, over three thousand miles, to see him, because after the calls and text messages, I'd felt certain our relationship had reached the next level. What had happened? Less than five minutes after our "epic" reunion, I was alone.

Again.

Should I have gone after Riley? Insisted that we talk then and there?

Isn't that what you always do? Chase after Riley?

That was what made this so awful. Seeing him run after Paige like that… I pressed a hand to my chest in an attempt to massage away the ache in my heart. This proved it then, didn't it? Our so-called relationship didn't mean to him what it meant to me. I'd come after him, only to have him dump me and go after Paige.

It was her Riley wanted.

And could I blame him? Hadn't I been flirting with her myself? Hadn't I secretly, in some twisted part of my brain, been feeling her out as a potential third for me and Riley?

Guess the joke was on me.

It was finally my turn at the bar. I glanced at the menu. "I'll have a pint of Green Beret IPA and a shot of whiskey, please," I said to the bartender. I was definitely in need of the hard stuff tonight. "Make it a double."

Would Riley even return to get me? I hoped so, or I'd be sleeping on some park bench tonight. Good thing it was warm and not raining.

A thought hit me, sudden and hard, like lightning. What if Riley and Paige were sharing a room? I shook my head. I really hadn't put enough thought into this trip. What a fucking stupid idea it had been to fly to Liverpool.

Someone bumped into my side. A good-looking Asian man, tall and lean, with a swimmer's build. He looked to be about Riley's age. He flashed me a broad smile, showing his gleaming pearly whites, as he laid a twenty pound note on the counter. "Drinks are on me."

I frowned and reached for my wallet. "Thanks, but I'm good."

"Please. No one should ever be as sad as you look in the birthplace of the Beatles."

"Man's got a point, mate," the bartender said, palming the cash.

Knowing when it was best to go with the flow, I acquiesced. "As long as the next round's on me."

"I do love a man who knows when to submit." The Asian guy ran his hand lightly along my arm. "By the way, I'm Kenji."

"*Kon'nichiwa*, Kenji-san," I said, totally showing off the bit of Japanese I'd learned from watching anime.

"Please, no need to be so formal. I've lived in the States too long for that. Ken or Kenji will do." Ken smiled and rested his head on his hand as though waiting for something.

"Oh, right. Sorry." I held my hand out. "I'm Carter."

"Oh, so you're—" Ken's smile broadened, and he pressed down on his bottom lip with his teeth. "Not Chris Hemsworth's younger brother Liam."

I blushed and put on a bad Australian accent. "Unfortunately not, mate."

Kenji picked up his drink. "I've got a table over here. Join me?"

What the hell. I was alone anyway. I followed him to a table for four near the stage. Two women sat there, giggling as they checked out the men gathered in front of a band performing some sort of indie rock. I had never been into music much, but when I did listen to it, I preferred '70s classic rock or '80s pop. Yeah, yeah. I was old school, and I knew it. No wonder Riley and I had been doomed. The guy embodied everything young and cool.

As we took our seats, I expected Kenji to introduce me to the women, but instead, he leaned over to one and whispered something in her ear. She nodded and helped her friend gather her things, and together they exited the club.

"What was that about?" I asked with only mild curiosity. I was far more interested in my double shot of whiskey.

"Lori's had too much to drink, and I promised a friend I'd make sure she got back to the hotel safely. Vicki agreed to see her to her room."

"That was nice of you."

"Was it?" Ken grinned. "Maybe I just wanted you all to myself."

I raised my glass, and clinked it against Kenji's sweet-looking green drink. "Looks like you got your wish."

"Lucky *moi*." Kenji winked. "So tell me, what brings you to Liverpool?"

"Chased after a dream, and got nothing but egg on my face for my troubles."

"Oh dear." Kenji touched his hand to his lips and frowned. "I can't imagine anyone being stupid enough to abandon a handsome hunk like you."

"That's the trouble with people." I leaned closer to Kenji. The whiskey was already relaxing me. Unfortunately, it was also loosening my tongue. Whatever. I was entitled to let off a little steam after that show Riley had put on. Kissing me like that, slow and deep, like he'd really meant it. Like he'd actually been happy to see me. Right before crushing my heart. "If you let them in, they hurt you. Doesn't matter if you're falling for them or not. They see someone better, and off they go. Without even so much as a backward glance."

Ken's hand pressed lightly along my spine, up from my waist to my neck, before rubbing in big soothing circles. "Hey, sweetie. It's okay. Whoever made you feel like this doesn't deserve you. Especially after you came all the way to see h—" Kenji stopped and raised a brow.

"Him," I answered. It was fairly obvious that Kenji was gay, so there was no risk in being honest.

Kenji clucked his tongue. He returned his hand to my lower back, then raised his gaze to look over my shoulder. "Any man who'd leave you for someone else is clearly an idiot who doesn't know he's got someone worth keeping."

A hand swooped between us, and suddenly Kenji was being shoved against the wall. "What the *fuck* is going on here?"

That voice. Riley.

I jumped to my feet, a little unsteadily, and tried to intervene. I couldn't believe what I was seeing. Riley had Ken by the collar of his shirt, against the wall. His face was red, his eyes narrowed. Enraged. I had seen Riley lose his patience with some particularly persistent paparazzi, but I'd never seen him get violent.

Riley shook Kenji. "Why were you hitting on my boyfriend? Or were you filling his head with lies about me?"

"How the fuck was I supposed to know he was your boyfriend?" Kenji pushed against Riley's chest with both hands. When Riley didn't budge, Kenji flailed about half-heartedly with his fists. Even I could tell he wasn't trying very hard. "You've never even mentioned having one, asshole. Or should I say *Carter*?" He scoffed, looking disgusted with Riley and the whole situation. "You say you've changed, but you haven't. Not one fucking bit."

Wait. Did they know each other? My gaze swung between them before settling on Riley. "Who is he?" I pointed to Ken.

"Someone I knew in college."

"In the biblical sense, of course." Ken smirked, and Riley winced.

"Of course." I rolled my eyes. What did I expect? Given Riley's past, there were probably ex-lovers scattered around the four corners of the globe. I grabbed hold of Riley's wrist. "Let him go. We were only talking."

"Yeah. Let me go," Ken said. When Riley stepped back, Ken

straightened his button-down shirt, then the fitted vest he wore over it. When he was apparently satisfied that all was in order again, he stepped in front of Riley. His eyebrows lowered, and even though I had just met the guy, I prepared for a load of some pretty hefty snark. "Isn't it interesting that both your names are… Carter?" He popped his eyebrows. "That must get so very confusing in bed."

"Jesus, Ken." Riley ran a hand through his hair. "Knock it off with the fucking drama. He already knows."

"I know what?" I asked. I was so fucking frustrated with the whole damn night, I couldn't keep the conversation straight.

Ken sidled up to me and trailed his fingers along my arm. "That he's been using your name, sugar. Hiding in plain sight as it were. The great Riley Kendrick."

Riley smacked Kenji's hand off my arm.

"Ow." Ken drew his hand to his chest, rubbing at the redness that was already showing. "What's your fucking problem?"

"Keep your paws off my boyfriend."

My gaze snapped up. His boyfriend. Warmth flooded my chest. That was the second time Riley had called me that tonight. The second time ever.

Kenji's brows furrowed in an exaggerated fashion. He pressed a long finger to his mouth. "Hmm… Does your *boyfriend* know you've been—"

Riley cut him off. "I swear to God, Kenji, stay out of this, or I'll—"

"You'll what?" Kenji got up in Riley's face. "What are you going to do? Beat me? Kick my teeth in?"

Riley snorted. "Of course not."

I put my hand on Kenji's shoulder, trying to draw him back. "I wouldn't let him anyway."

"Carter." Riley's voice sounded broken, and it revived in me a desire to protect him. To take care of the one I loved. "Come on. Let's get out of here and talk," he pleaded.

Kenji stood and kissed my cheek. "I do hope I'll see you around, handsome."

I shrugged. "That depends on Riley."

"I see." Kenji leaned into Riley and stage whispered, "I guess I'll go see how Paige is doing. I'm thinking she could use a friendly shoulder to… cry on."

"No!" Riley shouted.

At the same time I found myself on my feet, my hand on Kenji's arm. "No."

Riley stared at me, his expression blank except for his eyes. Those brimmed with questions.

Kenji's gaze bounced between Riley's and mine. "Now this is a surprise." He shrugged his arm out of my grip and placed his hands on his hips. "Want my advice?"

"No," Riley said.

I had to agree. "No."

"Well, you're going to get it anyway. Riley, my friend, take this gorgeous man back to your room and do what comes naturally. A good fuck has a way of resolving any number of misunderstandings." He rubbed his hand down my chest. "And he certainly looks like he'd be up for a really great fuck."

"There's no misunderstanding." I ignored Riley and stared at Kenji. Why? I had no idea, except it seemed like the man had been on the receiving end of Riley's shifting attentions himself. "Riley has a girlfriend now. He doesn't want me anymore."

Riley growled loud enough to surprise me into looking at him.

"Do you hear that?" Ken cupped his ear and swiveled his head around. "Sounds like my cue to leave. Goodbye, darlings. I'm outtie."

And with that, he sashayed away to be swallowed up by the crowd. I dropped heavily onto my stool and finished off the rest of my whiskey, then washed it down with half my beer.

"Easy." Riley put a restraining hand on mine.

I pinched the bridge of my nose and used the time to get a handle on my emotions. They were all over the fucking place. I couldn't decide if I wanted to strangle Riley or kiss him. It had actually been hot as fuck seeing Riley push his way so possessively between me and Kenji. On the other hand, seeing him leave in Paige's wake had nearly killed me. "Why shouldn't I drown my sorrows? I came all this way for you—for *us*—and what did you do? You ran off in the opposite direction almost as soon as you laid eyes on me."

Riley let out a long breath. "I'm sorry about that. Really. I just had to be sure she was all right."

"You never did that for me."

He swung his arm around my shoulders and brought his lips close enough to my ear that I felt his hot breath when he whispered, "That's because I know you'll be okay. You always are."

I shook my head. "Not this time." My voice cracked as tears welled in my eyes. "Not this time, Rye. You broke my fucking heart." I swiped a palm across my wet cheeks. "I should have stayed home."

"Fuck, man. No. I'm thrilled that you're here."

My jaw hardened as I remembered Paige's expression. "Your girlfriend sure isn't."

Riley ground his teeth so hard I could hear it. "She's not my girlfriend."

"But you are sleeping with her." I met his gaze. "Don't bother lying. I know your tells."

"I know yours too." He shot me a penetrating gaze.

I swallowed. Yes, I'd been coming on to her. Paige was attractive, funny, and intelligent. No wonder Riley was so into her. "I didn't hear any denials."

"Okay, yeah. All right. I've slept with her, but it—"

"Don't try to tell me it didn't mean anything. In the three months we've been together, you've never cared about anyone else's feelings. Hell, you barely care about mine."

"That's not true, Carter." He kissed me gently on the mouth, adding a swipe of his tongue against my hungry lips. I bit back a moan even as my cock twitched in my jeans. Christ, I was a needy bastard, letting him kiss me when I was still mad enough to eat iron.

"You're special, Carter," Riley continued. "I really care about you. More than anyone since…" He trailed off.

I cleared my throat. "Since Amber and Holden."

"Yeah."

This was killing me. Fucking killing me. Riley was saying everything I had been dying to hear. So why did it feel so hollow? Why wasn't I ecstatic, my heart bursting with love and joy?

Because there's more to it.

"I'm not the only one who's special, am I?" I inhaled deeply before continuing. "She's special to you too, this Paige."

"Yes. No." Riley's hand balled into a fist on the tabletop.

I snorted. "Which is it, Rye? You can't have it both ways."

"Maybe?" He grabbed my beer and drained it. "Look, I don't know what I need long-term. Hell, I don't even know what I want. All I do know is that right now?" He gripped the back of my neck and his eyes held mine. "The one person I know, one-hundred percent, that I need in my life is you." He pressed our foreheads together. "You, Carter. I need you and I want you. I've missed you so damn much."

Riley put two fingers under my chin and tilted my head up until our gazes met again. "Will you have me, Carter? Will you give me the chance to show you how much I want you in my life?"

Fuck. My pulse pounding in my ears, I sank into those dark blazing pools. For once, all of Riley's thoughts and emotions were clearly written on his face. Could I trust them? Could I trust that this connection between us was real? Lasting? I didn't know if I could believe, but I really wanted to.

Threading my fingers through his thick hair, I brought our heads together. My mouth hovered within kissing distance of his, and as his soft pants tickled my lips, I made up my mind.

"Take me to your room, Riley. Show me what I need to know."

Chapter 7

RILEY

Had Carter really forgiven me? I was about to find out.

Fumbling the key card and almost dropping it, I opened the door to my hotel room, Carter at my back. Christ. I was so aware of him, his every breath, his every movement.

How badly I'd hurt him.

I turned to Carter, who stood just inside the door, his duffel bag in hand. We'd collected it from the front desk. He wasn't putting it down, wasn't making himself comfortable. His eyes were darting from surface to surface, lingering on the laptop I'd left on the desk.

"You're really writing again," he said.

"Yeah. I am."

Carter still made no move toward me, no move to settle into the room. He looked like he wanted to bolt.

"Come here," I said. "Put your bag down."

"You know, I think I should get my own room. I don't want to disturb your writing. Whatever you have going with Paige, it's obviously working."

Fuck. "It is, and it isn't. If you read what I wrote, you'll see how much I've missed you. Yes, she got me started, but it hasn't felt… complete to me."

He shook his head. "You said I was your boyfriend, and you don't know how happy that made me to hear it. But fuck, when you talk about her, there's something in your tone, in your expression…" His voice cracked.

Goddammit. Maybe Kenji was right. Maybe we needed to stop talking and start fucking. I needed Carter to stop doubting. I needed to show him what he meant to me.

In two long strides, I was right in his face. I stripped the bag from his arms and tossed it on the floor with a thud. Then I pressed forward, taking his cheeks in my hands, his light stubble prickling my palms.

Tears welled in his eyes, and I felt my own start. *I'd* done this to him. I'd hurt him. "I'm so fucking sorry, Carter. I am. I'm a fucked up mess, I know it. But I'm trying not to be. I'm trying to get my shit together. I need you to bear with me while I sort all this out."

"I should walk away," he said in a ragged whisper. "I should, and I know it."

My pulse pounded, my heart stuttering. *No, no, no.* "You can't. You just… can't."

I brought our mouths together, and he groaned, whether out of passion or frustration or both, I couldn't tell. I ran my tongue along the seam of his lips, but he wouldn't let me in. He ripped his mouth away, his chest heaving.

"I can't do this, Riley. I can't. I can't be some toy you play with and toss away when you're done."

He bent to pick up his bag, and my heart thrashed in my chest. If I let Carter go, that would be the end of it. And I didn't want that, I didn't want that at all.

I grabbed his arm, the one holding his bag, and I pulled the duffel out of his grasp and dropped it on the floor again. This time I kicked it away and pushed him back into the door.

His eyes widened. "What the fuck, Riley?"

"You're not leaving. You're not running away."

"Me, run away? You should know—you ran off to fucking England!"

"I'm not running anymore." I leaned in to kiss him, but he shoved me back.

"You think you can fuck me and make it all better?" His face was flushed, his cheeks bright red.

"I'm not letting you walk out the door. I'm not letting you walk out on us." I stepped forward again, pressing my chest against his, pinning his wrists to the door. He could break away; we both knew it. He was stronger than I was, and I often let him manhandle me a bit. But tonight, that's not what he needed. He needed me to take charge, to take control. To show him how I felt.

He eyed me, questions in his gaze. "I'm so fucking angry, Riley." His voice had a tremor in it, his body shaking in my grasp.

"You have every right to be," I whispered, bringing my lips right to his, but not kissing him, just hovering on the brink. "Now let me make it up to you." I waited a second for him to pull away, but he stood there, trembling, his eyes glistening.

I closed the gap, and this time when our lips touched, he groaned in surrender and opened to me. I twined my tongue with his, and he tried to break my grip on his wrists. I held firm, pinning him more securely to the door. The wood creaked, and he sighed into my mouth, the fight flowing out of him.

I ground our hips together, my hard cock rubbing against his, making us both moan. I pivoted us away from the door, shifting my grip to his waist and walking him toward the bed. When his knees hit the mattress, he pushed back against me, and I finally broke our kiss and started pulling off his shirt.

I tossed my glasses on the nightstand, and Carter's lips curved up. "You know, your sexy professor look really does it for me."

I smiled, my hands cupping his pecs, the light hairs tickling my palms. "You want me to leave them on?"

He nodded, and I yanked off my own shirt, then put the glasses back on. I could see him better that way.

God, Carter was gorgeous. All lean muscle, his torso ripped to perfection. I ran my hands down his arms, the muscles like granite under my touch, his chest heaving like he'd been running. He was radiating heat, and I craved that warmth. I pressed our chests together, our cocks sliding against each other and reminding me we were both still too clothed for my liking. I tugged at his belt and kissed him again, plunging my tongue into his mouth. He grabbed me by the shoulders, pulling me closer, then spun me around and started to push me onto the bed. I resisted and pulled back, shaking my head. "This isn't business as usual."

He raised an eyebrow. "Okay."

"Now strip." I unbuckled my belt, and the two of us made quick work of the rest of our clothes. Once we were both naked, he looked at me, his eyes roving down my body, lingering on my cock. "On your knees," I said, my voice coming out raw and demanding.

He lowered himself to the floor and took my cock in hand and looked up at me. "Go ahead. Suck it," I said.

He shuddered out a breath, then he leaned forward and twirled his tongue around the head of my cock, and fuck, it was so perfect. I shivered all over and pressed forward, my hand going to his neck, and his mouth opened to let me in, swallowing me in one thrust, and I felt myself on the verge of coming already. "Slow down," I murmured. "Don't want this over before we get started."

He eased back, his hands gripping my thighs, his tongue swirling along my shaft as he let me out of his mouth. He gazed up and I nodded, and then he engulfed me again, his lips touching my balls. I sighed with how good it felt to be this deep in his throat. He swallowed and I shivered, the sensation making my balls tighten. I was close, so close. But this wasn't all I wanted from him.

I stepped back and looked down at Carter, who waited patiently, staring up at me. "What do you want me to do?" he asked, his voice a bit hoarse.

"Get on the bed. On your back." I went to the nightstand and pulled out the condoms and lube I'd put there with Paige in mind. I rolled on a condom, my eyes on Carter, who was lying on the mattress, his big cock curving up toward his belly.

We were both breathing hard as I approached the bed, lube in hand. I dribbled some on my palms, then leaned over him, taking his cock in one hand, while the other slid down to his hole. He groaned when I stroked his cock, and he spread his legs to give me better access as I worked a thumb into his tight pucker. He shifted under my touch, pressing himself onto my thumb and helping me work it in and out. I swiveled my palm over the head of his cock, making him groan. "Fuck," Carter moaned. He opened his eyes and looked up at me. "Fuck me," he said, the vulnerability in his eyes making my throat tighten.

I loved Carter; I really did. No more doubts. I brought our mouths together, the kiss heated, Carter writhing under the invasion of my thumb. "I love you, babe," I whispered.

"God, Rye, you know I love you too," he said, his voice thick.

I kissed his neck, my heart slamming in my chest. I *felt* how deeply he loved me, and I let it wash over me, then poured it back out through another deep kiss. I pulled back and looked into his eyes. "Ready?"

He nodded, and I replaced my thumb with my cock, pushing against the tight entrance, both hands gripping his hips until I breached the ring of muscle and slipped inside. I groaned, enjoying how he moved beneath me, his hips shifting to give me better access.

I took his cock in my right hand and started stroking it in time with my thrusts, both of us breathing hard, his eyes locked on mine. "Fuck me, Rye. Fuck me *hard*."

The demand roared through me and my pelvis snapped forward. I released his cock and grabbed him by both hips, driving into him harder, making sure my cock dragged across his prostate with each thrust, his moans taking on a guttural quality. He was close, on the verge of coming, and so was I.

We moved together frantically, our chests heaving, the slap of our bodies, our harsh breathing, the only sounds in the room.

I drove into him, almost doubling him over, my balls slapping against his ass, and suddenly he stiffened, his cock spasming, ropes of cum shooting onto his chest. The sight tipped me over the edge, and I came with a great shudder, collapsing on of top him. I rested on his chest for a moment, then withdrew, letting his legs fall over the edge of the mattress.

"Jesus," he said as I pushed my glasses back up my nose. "I should fight with you more often."

I laughed and shook my head. "I'd rather not. But we can do this anytime you want."

"Sexy, Demanding Professor?" he asked.

I smiled. "Whatever you like." I went into the bathroom to dispose of the condom, then brought a wet washcloth back and wiped Carter off.

"Thanks," he said.

I pressed a kiss to his neck. "Anytime," I murmured against his skin. I pulled back and looked into his eyes. "I do love you. Very much. I think I just realized how much."

"Me too," he said, stroking my cheek. "But we still need to talk about the pretty elephant in the room."

My stomach clenched. "Paige."

Carter nodded. "What is she to you?"

CARTER

I held my breath, waiting for Riley's response to my question about Paige, not sure what answer I wanted to hear. Whether what he felt for Paige was nothing, or something.

He sighed and ran a hand through his hair. "There's something about her. Something that calls to me. She's so sweet, and smart, and damn, I have fun with her. I like her, Carter, a lot more than I thought I would."

I could see the struggle on his face, could hear it in his words. Riley was falling for her. Maybe he didn't want to admit that yet, but he was.

My chest tightened. "So what does this mean for us?"

He shook his head slowly. "I honestly don't know. I mean"—he kissed me—"not that you and I aren't solid, but that I think there could be something with Paige too."

"You mean like you and Amber and Holden?" I almost whispered the words.

"Yeah." He was silent a moment, and I turned over the idea in my head. Would it be so terrible? Sharing Riley with someone else? How would that even work?

"What are you thinking?" he asked me.

"Are you saying you want to see her for the rest of this trip, or past it?"

"I don't know yet. Can you just… have fun with me—us? See where this goes?"

I took a deep breath. I did like Paige, and I definitely was attracted to her. I'd had the idea of sharing her with Riley at the back of my mind when I'd first spotted her. But that was supposed to have been a one-night thing. Nothing more lasting.

I glanced over at the open laptop, at the papers scattered around it, at the signs of Riley finally back at work again. Paige obviously was good for him somehow.

I met his gaze. "Let's give it a try."

His face lit up, and I felt a little pang in my chest. What if this thing with Paige was stronger than what Riley and I had? What if—

He touched my cheek. "I can see the doubts on your face. Please, trust me. I wouldn't ask if I didn't think our relationship was strong enough."

"Is it though? I had to chase you halfway across the planet."

He shook his head. "I wasn't running, Carter. I wasn't sure how I felt when I left Burlington, but this trip has made it clear. I missed you. No matter what happened with Paige, I knew I was going back to you. Back to my *home*."

I exhaled, the tension leaving me in a rush. Home. The way Riley had said it, the little catch in his throat, that convinced me more than anything. "Okay. I'll relax and see where this goes."

He pulled me into a kiss, our tongues tangling briefly before he lay back. "This is going to be good, Carter. I feel it in my bones."

Maybe. I wished I felt as certain. I closed my eyes, remembering the tingle of attraction that had run through me when I'd first spotted Paige at the bar. In that sea of people, she'd called to me.

The same way she'd called to Riley.

That had to mean something. Right?

RILEY

Armed with Carter's permission to pursue Paige, I'd started out the day with high hopes, but she had returned to her pre-Highland games tactic of ignoring and avoiding me whenever possible.

I still couldn't believe Carter was actually here, that I'd spent the night in his arms. We sat together, our legs touching, on the bus as it made its way down from Liverpool to Stratford-upon-Avon, the hometown of William Shakespeare. Despite the tension with Paige, I'd enjoyed visiting The Beatles Story exhibition at Albert Dock that morning. Carter and I had rocked out to *A Hard Day's Night* in the Discovery Zone. So what if the area was designed for children? I'd always been young at heart.

And wasn't that the issue right there?

My gaze landed on Paige at the front of the bus as she told interesting anecdotal stories about the sites we passed. Her dark-blonde hair gleamed in the sun streaming through the windshield, where it hung in a thick tail out the back of the pink bedazzled Beatles cap she wore. It was so odd to see her wearing something so out-of-character. Not that she didn't look great in her white blouse and light gray slacks. But it was almost as though she wore the hat to draw attention away from her face.

I found myself leaning forward to get a closer view.

"She looks tired," Carter said, as though reading my mind.

I frowned. Yeah, and it was all my fault.

"It's what you were trying to see, wasn't it?" Carter tugged on the new Beatles "Abbey Road" T-shirt I had bought him at the Fab4 Store. The sky in the image of the boys crossing the street perfectly matched the blue of Carter's eyes. Not to mention that the dark material hugged his muscles just right. I had also picked out a few vinyl albums missing from my collection and a surprise gift for Paige. Not that she'd accept anything from me right now.

Sitting back in the seat, I scratched my beard. Having facial hair had some advantages, like the way Carter had squirmed and moaned this morning as I ate his ass, making sure to press his thighs against my rough cheeks. I placed my hand, palm up, on his leg, and was relieved when he twined our fingers together. I swallowed, then took the bull by the horns. "I feel terrible about how things went down with Paige last night."

Carter looked toward the front of the bus. "She can't be happy that I showed up like that. I imagine the two of you had… plans for the night?"

His statement ended on an insecure note that hurt my heart. How could I answer that without making myself feel more like an asshole and making him feel even more uncertain?

When Carter had said he loved me last night, I had experienced so many emotions: elation, joy, excitement. But fear was in there too. What if I couldn't love Carter enough? What if he turned on me like Amber and Holden had? What if this thing with Paige ruined what Carter and I had going? It was the most caring and honest relationship I'd ever had with anyone. I really didn't want to fuck it up. And that meant being transparent with him… and Paige, even when it made me uncomfortable, maybe especially then.

"Yeah, we did." I brought our joined hands to my lips and lightly kissed his knuckles. "Does that upset you?"

Carter stiffened and his fingers tightened around mine. "Of course it does," he snapped before leaning his head back against the seat and sighing. He closed his eyes, depriving me of those deep pools of blue.

"I-I'm sorry," I stammered. "I shouldn't have—" I cut myself off and turned to stare out the window at the countryside flying past. I shouldn't have what? Taken a break from my relationship with Carter? Slept with Paige? Run after her last night? Had sex with Carter?

Fuck! I probably shouldn't have done any of those things. Not when my head was such a damn mess and my heart was giving me confusing messages. I probably should have spent the trip alone, focused on my writing. It certainly would have been easier.

Truth was I didn't regret any of the things I'd done, only *how* I'd done them. I'd hurt two people I cared about. And I had to find a way to make it up to them.

"Car—," I started, then leaned toward him and whispered, "What should I call you?"

Carter rolled his eyes. "You can use my middle name."

"Uh, sure. Umm… what is it?"

He gave me a look that said *Really?* "It's Eric. We've talked about this. Yours is Christopher."

I blushed. "Forgive me?"

Carter nodded and coughed. "I'm sorry I snapped at you." He paused and tugged on his jeans. "After you fell asleep last night, I thought about things. About what we discussed, about what you wrote in *Amber's Triumph.*" He turned his head toward me and I did the same. "On an intellectual level, I understand that you can be attracted to two people at the same time. That you can care for, or even love, two people."

"Whoa. I'm certainly not there yet," I interrupted. "Not with her."

"No." He offered me a sad smile. "But you'd like to be. Right? Tell me that in your heart of hearts, you don't want both of us, me and Paige, and maybe not just for the duration of this trip either."

"I don't know about after the trip." I cupped Carter's smooth cheek and searched his face for any sign of his thoughts. "But you're right. I do want both of you. At least for now. If she's willing." I glanced at Paige at the front of the bus. "And given the fact she refused to speak with me yesterday, this whole discussion might be academic at best."

"Ooh." Carter grinned. "I do love when Professor"—he dropped his voice to a low rumble that went straight to my cock—"Kendrick comes out to play."

I chuckled. "I would so have done you on my desk."

"Would you have used my body for a chalkboard?"

"Chalk is bad for you. I'm a whiteboard guy."

He flicked his tongue against my lips. "Dry erase markers are more fun anyway."

My stomach flipped and my pulse raced. I was so fucking hard. "Oh God." I moved my mouth next to his ear and whispered, "I want you so bad, Carter. I want to straddle you, sink down on your big cock, and ride you until we both scream."

Moaning softly, he pressed his face into the crook of my neck and shifted his hips so his back was to the aisle. "You fucking sadist. How am I supposed to finish the day with that thought in my head?"

I closed my eyes and breathed in the scent of his shampoo. "I love you. I really fucking love you."

Carter's lips pressed against my neck and his hot breath bathed my sensitive skin. "I love you too, Rye." There was a pause, then he continued. "And I'll help you work things out with Paige."

I pulled back, my eyes popping wide. "You will?" I captured his face between my palms and gave him a big, smacking kiss that drew a few amused glances from our trip mates in the seats around us. I ignored every one. "Thank you, thank you."

Carter shrugged. "Don't thank me yet." He motioned toward the front of the bus where Paige stood glaring at me.

I groaned. "I need to speak with her, sooner rather than later. I hate seeing her so upset."

"Slow your roll there, Casanova. I think you've done enough damage already."

I huffed. He was right, but what the hell else was I supposed to do? "Flowers then?" She'd liked the ones I'd sent her in Scotland.

"Nah. I'm pretty sure they'd end up in the trash." He smirked. Then his lips thinned out and he sat up straight. "I'll talk to her."

"You?" I said, skeptical.

"We really did have a good rapport last night."

"You'd do that for me?" I was touched. My stomach fluttered again, and there was an odd burning sensation behind my eyes.

Carter's gaze softened and he captured my hand in his, bringing it to press against his heart. "No. But I would do it for us."

"Us?" My voice wavered.

He smiled. "I'll do it for the *three* of us."

Chapter 8

PAIGE

I'd been feeling the weight of Riley's stare all day, but I was damned if I was going to forgive him so easily. Or at all. He'd lied to me.

My lover had a boyfriend.

"Bravo! Bravo!"

Shaking off my thoughts, I joined the crowd's enthusiastic applause as the curtains closed on the cast of *All's Well That Ends Well*. It had always been one of my favorite Shakespeare plays, and the Royal Shakespeare Company had done it justice.

After the final encore, the lights turned on, and I left my row of seats. I stopped at the exit to the theater to talk with the members of the tour. "Ms. Sutherland," Marietta Clark said, her face flushed with excitement. "Thank you so much for organizing all this. The play was marvelous."

I patted the elderly woman's hand and smiled at her husband Tom. "We have much more in store for you in Bath."

"Oh!" She tittered. "The house party?"

"In just two days." I smiled at Marietta's obvious excitement.

"I can't tell you how much I'm looking forward to it. I've written about house parties in many of my novels, but I've never actually attended one."

"I hope it meets your expectations," I said, a tendril of nerves fluttering in my belly.

"Nonsense, dear. I've had more fun on this trip than I've ever had before."

"I'm truly glad. See you at dinner?" I asked.

"Of course."

The Clarks left to catch the bus that would take those who wanted to rest back to the hotel, and I joined a group of younger tour members who were joking about all the bed hopping in the play.

"Paige," Kenji called, as he squeezed in between me and Lori. "Did you hire some young studs to dance with us at the ball?"

"Certainly. After all, what's a ball with no dance partners?" I joked.

"Funny," he grinned. "I was thinking what's a house party with no *bed* partners."

The temperature around me rose ten degrees. "Uh… well." I giggled. "Matchmaking is a little beyond my duties."

"Are we going to have dance cards?" Lori asked, pushing her way in front of Kenji, who huffed, looking more than a little put out.

I did my best not to laugh. "I hadn't thought of that, but it's a brilliant idea."

Kenji frowned. "If you do, Paige, make sure my name's on your card. I want to dance a waltz with you."

Something lightly bumped my hand. A throat cleared, and when I turned, I was surprised to see it was Carter. My belly did a little flip and my pulse raced. Even though he was Riley's boyfriend, I couldn't deny my attraction to him. His piercing blue eyes held mine in thrall. "Sorry Kenji, her dance card is already full." He winked at me, then grinned at Ken.

With a snort, Ken folded his arms over the shiny red shirt he wore with calf-length skinny white slacks. "I bet it is. She certainly isn't lacking for suitors."

"Jealous?" Carter asked, raising a brow.

What the heck was going on here? It was bad enough when Riley and Kenji butted heads. I attributed that to them having been lovers. But Carter and Kenji? I didn't think they even knew each other.

Lori stepped over to Carter and stuck out her hand. "I don't think we've met. I'm Lori."

"I'm C-Eric. Nice to meet you."

"Carrick? What an interesting name." Kenji's dark eyes gleamed as he asked the question that had been on the tip of my tongue. That's when it clicked. Of course. He couldn't use his real name without blowing Riley's cover.

Carter coughed. "Sorry. Frog in my throat," he said in a strangled voice. His ears going red, he pounded on his chest. "Eric. My name is Eric."

"What do you write, Eric?" Kenji asked.

"Oh, I'm not a writer. I'm…" He turned to me, his eyes pleading with me for help.

I wanted to roll my eyes. Riley had gotten Carter into this mess. He should be the one to clean it up, not me. But as I looked at Carter and remembered our conversation before Riley's arrival at the Cavern Club, the way we'd laughed, the way we'd talked like we'd known each other forever, I took pity on him. The poor man was in love with Riley, and Riley had used his name and cheated on him.

With me.

Damn. I took Carter's arm. "C-uh-Eric is a friend of Carter's. He couldn't make the first part of the trip, but he'll be finishing up the tour with us."

"Oh good," Lori and Kenji said at the same time, although their tones were quite different.

God, Arianna was going to kill me for this. I'd just added an unpaid guest to our roster. At the thought, I bit back a smile. Who was I kidding? "Carter" was Riley Kendrick, world-famous erotic romance author. He had to have more money than he knew what to do with. He could certainly afford to pay for his boyfriend's trip. That brought on another thought: if word got out that Riley was on the tour, the paparazzi would descend in droves on my group of famous and semi-famous authors and ruin all my carefully laid plans.

I rubbed at my temple as a headache began to brew.

Carter leaned in close and whispered, "Want to get out of here? I'd like to talk with you for a bit, if you don't mind."

"Okay." If he was to spend the next twelve days with us, we needed to clear the air. Good thing Riley and I had been fairly discreet. I caught Kenji watching us, a serious expression on his face. A warning?

"There's a little park across the street," Carter said, pointing it out. "Let's talk there."

I waved to the group. "Dinner's at the hotel restaurant tonight. See you all at seven?"

Side by side, Carter and I crossed the street and took a path that meandered around a small lake where a raft of ducks bobbed on the water.

"It's beautiful here." Carter knelt and took a short video with his phone of some ducks diving for food, their round butts sticking up in the air. "The kids will get a kick out of this."

A sigh bubbled up in my chest. How had a special-ed teacher, someone as good and down to earth as Carter, gotten mixed up with someone like Riley? Guilt stabbed at my gut. I'd gotten involved with Riley too. To my credit I hadn't known he'd been posing as Carter Templeton, college professor-cum-romance writer.

"I imagine you want to tell me to keep my hands off Ri—" I cut myself off and glanced around to make sure no one was in earshot before continuing. "—Riley. But don't worry. It's over. I had no idea he had a boyfriend."

Carter rose and walked back to me. "I wasn't going to say that."

I frowned. "He did tell you…" Lamely, I batted my hand around.

"Yes. I knew he was interested in someone on the tour."

"And that didn't bother you?" My voice rose. I'd have been livid in his place.

Carter shrugged. "We were on a break."

"His idea or yours?" I asked, already knowing the answer.

"His." He shoved his hands into the front pockets of his jeans, which made his shoulders roll forward. I watched the muscles ripple and desire dried my mouth.

Then I remembered the previous evening, and my anger returned. This time it was directed at the man standing in front of me. I glared at Carter. "You certainly took advantage of it."

A corner of his lips curled up. "How could I resist when I saw the most gorgeous woman in all of England, sitting by her lonesome in a bar?"

I didn't know whether to laugh at his flirting or to be even more put off by it. "I don't get you two. Are you in a relationship or not?"

"We are." Carter hooked his thumbs in the pockets and let his long fingers dangle over his hips. It had the effect of showcasing the nice bulge in his jeans. Did he even know the effect he had on people? On me?

I threw my hands up in frustration. "Then why the heck did both of you…"—I skipped over the embarrassing words by rounding my eyes—"with me? Am I a pawn in some sick game you two are playing?"

"No." He stepped closer and cupped my shoulders in his big hands.

I shrugged out of his hold. "What then?"

His jaw ticked as his gaze scanned the park. He nodded to the left. "There's a bench over there. Let's sit down."

Silently, I followed him the short distance to the wooden bench that overlooked the lake. The blue sky, the clear water, the quacking of the ducks, the entire serenity of the scene was in direct contrast to the overwhelming chaos now ruling my mind. I needed answers and I needed them now.

"So explain it to me," I said as soon as my rear made contact with the wood.

Carter sat beside me and stretched out his muscular legs. He had to be at least two or three inches taller than Riley. "Riley and I have been seeing each other for about three and a half months now. It's been casual. At Riley's insistence." He swallowed and leaned forward, resting his elbows on his knees. "We're both bisexual, and every now and then, we like to add a third, a woman, to our… into the mix."

"You have threesomes." It made sense now. Riley's constant talk about threesomes, his game of pretending Hamish was a part of our escapade at Nether Largie. "I'm so stupid."

Carter's piercing gaze landed on me, his brow knotted. "Why?"

"He brought it up almost every time we talked. And it's all there in his books, isn't it? He and Amber often invited a third to their bed."

"But you didn't know he was Riley Kendrick."

"No," I conceded through gritted teeth. But the idea had turned me on each time we'd discussed the possibility.

And that's why you flirted with Carter at the club. Admit it.

Fine. I'd admit it. I'd been scoping Carter out, thinking Riley might like him. I steeled my spine. I needed to know where I stood. After all, this was just a vacation fling. If either Riley or Carter had other ideas… "Have any of these women become part of your relationship?"

Carter stared at the gravel under his shoes and bent to pick up a stone. "No, never. They were all one-night stands, and they knew that from the get-go."

"So." My tone was snippy, and I didn't want it to be. I took a deep breath. "Is that what I'm to be? A one-night stand." I laughed bitterly. The ending of my affair with Riley had been so abrupt. Too abrupt. I'd really hoped it would last until the end of the trip, but everything had changed with Carter's arrival. "I guess it doesn't matter. One night, two if I was lucky, was all I'd really expected from Carter… uh, I mean Riley." I rubbed my aching head at the temple. "God, this name thing is confusing."

Carter tossed the stone from one hand to the other. "What do you mean you expected only one night? You don't seem the type."

I closed my eyes. "Do I really need to spell it out? I'm almost a decade older than him. He's young, fit, sexy as heck. He can have anyone he wants. And that was before I knew who he really was." I let out a sigh and fixed my gaze on the calming water. "He was lonely, and I was interested. We had some fun together. That's all it was."

He sat up and raised a knee onto the bench so he was facing me. "I don't buy it."

"I was never more to him than one of those other women. And that's how I wanted it to be."

Placing his elbow on the top of the bench, he leaned closer to me. "From what Riley's told me, you two have been sleeping together since the Highland games. That makes you more than a one-night stand."

I barked out a laugh. "So I'm somehow special?"

He touched my arm and brought his mouth next to my ear. I shivered as his hot breath hit my skin. He whispered, "I think you might be. You're already special to me."

This time my laughter was genuine. I tossed my head back and let loose. Let all the tension drain from me as my belly shook. "You are so full of sh—crap."

He grinned. "Maybe. But I'm actually serious. You make Riley happy, and that makes me happy."

Once again, he leaned into me and brushed his lips against my neck. When his tongue flicked out to toy with my lobe, I shivered. He drew back and smiled. "You think maybe we can make you happy?"

"Until the end of the tour?" I asked. Because no matter what did or didn't happen, in twelve days, I was flying back to Miami, back to Emma, back to reality.

Carter took my hand and squeezed my fingers gently. "Our very own high-end vacation fling."

"In that case..." I shot him a sassy grin. "I dare you to try."

"You play hard, woman," he growled.

I dropped my gaze down to the sizable bulge in his jeans and slowly licked my bottom lip, channeling Arianna. "I hope you do too."

He brought my hand to his crotch and pressed it against his impressive erection. "You can bet on it."

RILEY

What was keeping Carter? I glanced toward the bathroom door. Was he having second thoughts?

I checked my watch again, then rolled up my sleeves and loosened my tie. Paige was supposed to be here soon.

Crossing the hotel room, I peeked in and spotted Carter looking at himself in the mirror over the sink. He was fidgeting with his hair, raking his wet hands through it, something I had often seen him do when he was nervous.

My chest ached for him. At the group dinner in the hotel restaurant, Carter and I had invited Paige up to our hotel room for a nightcap. At least that's what we'd said in public, but we'd really asked her up to talk and see where things might go from there.

Carter wanted this, didn't he?

I eased up behind him and smoothed my hands over his broad shoulders before meeting his gaze in the mirror. I massaged his tight muscles and grinned when he moaned. "Relax," I murmured. "Everything is going to be all right."

Carter dropped his head back on my shoulder. "What the fuck am I doing?"

"Only what you want to," I answered. The last thing I wanted was to force Carter into something he wasn't comfortable with.

"It would've been so easy, you know." Carter opened his eyes and met my gaze in the mirror." I could've turned her away at the park, made it clear that you're mine."

I kissed his neck. "I *am* yours. This isn't about that. It's about us."

He snorted. "I eased the path for you. Like a dumb schmuck. Like some fucking matchmaker."

"Hey, what's going on?" I tightened my hold on Carter's shoulders and spun him around. "Talk to me."

"God, where should I start?" He shook his head. "What if this vacation fling with Paige doesn't work out?"

"Then it doesn't work out." My tone was matter-of-fact, though inside I felt anything but. I didn't know how I'd react if things fell apart with Paige, and that terrified me. But not more than not trying. "What about you, Carter? How would you feel?"

"I don't know. As soon as I saw her, I knew she was someone I could be friends with. She's easy to talk to, seems dependable enough, and most importantly, she's down to earth. She has a nice job as a tour guide, but it's a job. Not a career. She's not power-hungry like Livia." He glanced at me. "She even seemed impressed that I'm a teacher."

I took a moment to unravel everything Carter had just said. Should I tell him that Paige wasn't a tour guide, that she was the marketing director at Total Indulgence? He wouldn't be too happy with that. But he'd be jumping to the wrong conclusions about her; Paige was nothing like his career-driven ex-wife. I didn't know Paige very well yet, but I knew that. Of course, none of that mattered. If this was just a fling…

As he inhaled deeply, Carter's chest expanded, touching mine. "Okay," he said, shaking his shoulders as though shaking off his serious thoughts. "We'll play this by ear. If nothing else, she's great to talk to."

I grinned. "And to look at."

"That she is."

"You know who else is great to look at?" I kept my tone playful and from the glint in his eye, I knew I had his cock plumping.

Carter smirked. "You?"

"Well." I winked and eased my arms around his neck. "That goes without saying. But, I was talking about you. Those jeans do some sinfully interesting things to your…" I glided my hands down his back to grab his butt. "Ass." At the same time, I jerked him against me, and we both moaned when our cocks bumped together. God, I loved it when Carter got like this. When he let me do whatever I wanted.

I slid one hand around his waist, and slowly trailed it down his abdomen until my palm rubbed against the ridge his erection made in his jeans.

He pushed his hips more firmly against my hand. "Jesus, Rye. She's going to be here any minute."

I loved the rasp in his voice. It made me want, no, it made me *need* more. "I know." Dropping to my knees, I pressed my face to his crotch, inhaling deeply. He gripped the counter behind him, his back arching, pushing his cock against my cheek.

Just as I gave in and reached for Carter's zipper, there was a knock at the door. He lowered his chin to his chest and blew out a frustrated breath. "You're evil, man. The devil. Satan incarnate." He reached out and pulled my face against him as he thrust forward. I couldn't help it. I laughed and nuzzled his erection. We both wanted this. And we were both going to go out into the living area with glazed eyes and hard cocks.

When there was another knock, he gently shoved me away and did his best to adjust himself in his tight jeans. "Go answer the door, you dirty bastard," he said gruffly.

Climbing to my feet, I chucked Carter's chin and when he looked up, I smiled and kissed him. Love for this man made me giddy. "I'll make it up to you later."

"Fucking A," he grumbled.

I hooked my arm around his shoulders. "I love it when you're horny and flustered."

"Let's hope Paige does too."

I winked. "I'm counting on it."

"Fucker."

God, I loved that we could joke like this, tease each other. I'd never had that before, not even with Holden. Together we walked into the living area. Carter stopped by the couch, while I went to open the door. When I saw her, my breath caught in my throat and my heart beat a mad rhythm. I prayed she didn't turn tail and run the other way. "Thanks for coming, Paige."

Her gaze took me in, a slow up and down, then drifted over to Carter. She smirked. "Am I interrupting something?"

I took her hand and tugged her inside. "No, you're just in time."

I closed the door, taking care to lock it, then went to stand beside Carter. I slid my arm around his waist and leaned heavily into his side.

"Hi, Paige," he said, using my body to hide his hard-on. I wanted to laugh. Even a blind man would be able to see how turned on he was. And by the barely suppressed humor in Paige's expression, she wasn't blind. Not at all.

"You two look cozy." She set her purse on the coffee table and looked up at me. "I take it Carter told you what we talked about."

I dropped a kiss on Carter's cheek, then went to stand in front of Paige. "It means a lot to me that you came here tonight."

She crossed her arms, pushing her breasts against the thin fabric of her blouse. Christ, her tits were perfect. My mouth salivated with the desire to taste her again. She frowned and bent her head to catch my gaze. "I'm still angry with you."

"Just a sec." I reached under the coffee table and pulled out the bag with the gift I still hadn't given her. I handed it to her. "Does this help?"

She opened it and took out the stuffed teddy bear that I'd bought for her at the Fab4 Store. She smiled slightly. "Thank you. This is very sweet, but it doesn't change anything."

My stomach bottomed out. Was I going to lose her? I grasped her arms lightly. "I'm really sorry, Paige. I should have told you about Carter. We were on a break, but"—I smiled at Carter—"he's important to me, and you had every right to know I was in a relationship."

"Carter told me you'd told him about me, or at least that you'd met a woman, so I can't be angry about that." Her eyes went to the carpet and she pressed a hand to her chest. "It hurt though. I can't say it didn't."

I rubbed my hands up and down her arms. "Can you forgive me?"

She glanced at Carter behind me, and nodded. "But no more lying."

"Agreed."

"Thank you." And with that I pulled her against me and pressed my lips to hers. Her body stiffened, but moments later she let out a little moan and melted against me. My hands roamed up and down her back as I licked her lips with my tongue, savoring the taste of her.

Remembering what tonight was about, I released her mouth, and taking her hand, led her to the couch. I sat beside her and patted the spot on my other side while looking at Carter.

Carter got the message. He always did.

Once he was seated, I placed my hands on Carter's and Paige's thighs. A sense of elation warmed my chest even as a tendril of fear gripped my gut. Tonight was make it or break it.

If I fucked up, it would all be over. But if I did things right, it could be like those magical months with Amber and Holden before it had all gone to shit. It could be the start of something really fucking beautiful.

"So…" I smiled at Paige, then leaned in to resume our kiss. With my tongue twirling around hers, I tightened my hold on Carter's thigh, moving it up a few inches. When Paige and Carter moaned at the same time, I felt like a god. This was the heady feeling I'd been searching for and never quite found with the other women I'd shared with Carter.

I eased off the kiss with Paige and turned to Carter. The heated look on his face said it all. "You really are an asshole," he said, his voice a hoarse, breathless whisper.

I groaned and locked our lips together, swallowing his moans. I knew how aroused he got watching me kiss a woman. I knew because seeing him kiss a woman did the same to me.

And that's what tonight was really about.

With a comical pop, I released Carter's mouth and patted both their sides. "Now that we're all warmed up…" I rose to my feet, turning to look at both of them. "It's your turn."

Paige's brow crinkled in a way that was cute as hell. "Our turn to do what?"

"To kiss." I took a moment to look at her. I hadn't miscalculated, had I? If seeing Carter and me kiss had turned her off, this whole adventure was a non-starter.

Her cheeks were flushed, her nipples pressed firmly against her blouse, and her beautiful hazel eyes were slightly dilated. I smiled. "You like him, don't you? You're attracted to him. I can tell by the…" I let the words hang and ran a hand along my own cheek, teasingly.

She blushed and shot a timid glance in Carter's direction. Had any woman ever looked more gorgeous and sexy, especially when she was a little embarrassed? This was going to be so much fun, if she allowed it.

Carter's eyes were fixed on Paige. If her pupils were a little dilated, Carter's were blown. Our earlier play had something to do with it, but I could tell how much he desired her. I'd seen that look before. Never quite as powerfully because, in all honesty, we'd barely known the women who'd shared our bed.

Paige was different.

As though our minds were running on the same wavelength, Carter took Paige's hand and peered into her eyes. "I really would like to kiss you, Paige, but only if you want it too."

Squirming, she looked up at me imploringly and gave a nervous laugh. "It seems so… I don't know. Sixth grade spin the bottle?"

I raised a brow in challenge. "Does it matter?"

Stepping between Carter's outstretched legs, I leaned down and kissed him, a slow and exaggerated French kiss, just the way he loved them, wet with lots of tongue. He retaliated, twining our tongues together with our mouths open wide.

Jesus. I groaned, my cock throbbing against the zipper of my slacks. I was getting too caught up in this. Reluctantly, I pressed our mouths together before slowly backing away. Carter looked wrecked, crazy turned on. Like he wanted to ram his cock into my ass over and over. He didn't care that we had an audience—or maybe he was so turned on because of it.

My hands still on his shoulders, I sucked in a deep breath and barely managed to string some words together. "You want to kiss him too," I said to Paige in a rough voice.

Given her heightened color, the rapid rising and falling of her chest, the pressing together of her thighs, I already knew her answer. Still, I needed her to say it.

She bit her lip. "I-I do."

Taking a few backward steps, I swung a hand between the two of them. "Then have at it." Doing nothing to hide my actions, I adjusted myself and gave them a pained grin. "I'm going to go to the hotel bar for a bit. Give you both some privacy."

"No, stay." Carter jumped up and grabbed my wrist. He whispered next to my ear so only I would hear, "It's always been the two of us when a woman is involved. I'd… uh…" He looked into my eyes. "I'd feel like I was cheating."

Damn, this was not what I wanted, but how could I make them understand? "I think you two need to get to know each other better," I hedged.

"Sure, but first let's get to know each other together," Carter said.

"Please," Paige added, her eyes rounded and worried.

I took in their mutual discomfort with the idea of being left alone. Their connection to me left them feeling like they were doing something wrong by being together. Maybe my presence was exactly what was needed to break the ice. I had to show them that it was okay. That I wanted them to touch, to kiss. And most importantly, that I wouldn't feel left out when Carter and Paige were together. "Okay," I said. We'd take this one step at a time.

"So," she said, folding her hands in her lap. The whiteness of her knuckles betrayed her nervousness. "Where do we go from here?"

Giving him a sidelong glance, I caught Carter's attention.

He blinked.

I nodded.

Carter grinned and put his arm around Paige's shoulders, pulling her against his chest. "I think we were right about here… weren't we?"

Smiling, she touched his cheek, her fingers sliding down to rest on his lips. "Yes," she breathed.

It was sexy and beautiful. God, I'd missed this. I watched avidly as Carter pressed his mouth to Paige's, as he gently swiped his tongue along her lips until she gasped with pleasure and opened for him. I knew exactly how that felt: like heaven.

When he released her mouth to nibble at her neck, Paige looked at me and smiled. Arousal tightened like a knot in my belly. She was so gorgeous. They both were, and at least for the time being, they were mine.

I sat next to Paige, sandwiching her between Carter and me. While Carter alternated between kissing her mouth and torturing her neck, I untucked Paige's blouse and snuck my hands under the silky material, gliding upward until I found my prize: her glorious breasts. She moaned and arched against me, laying her head on my shoulder. Carter raised his eyes to look at me and there was so much love and desire in those deep blue pools. Lust burned brightly in them, surely a perfect echo of my own. I smiled and mouthed, "I love you."

Carter grinned, then ducked his head to lick the nipple I had exposed. I loved when we worked together as a team to bring pleasure to a woman. It was especially sweet this time… because it was Paige. A woman we both liked and admired. A woman we both wanted more from.

My fingers on the buttons of her blouse, I whispered in Paige's ear, "Is this okay?"

"Yes," she said on a moan. "Oh yes."

Chuckling, I finished unbuttoning it and slowly slid the blouse off her shoulder and went to work on her bra, a delicate pink thing. A quick twist of my fingers and off it went too. Carter grunted his disapproval at having to release his treat, then dove back in as soon as the offending lace was removed. Paige laughed softly.

"That's our Carter," I said. "A boob man all the way."

"And you, Riley?" Paige asked, twisting her head to see me better. "What kind of a man are you?"

In response, I slid my hand down her thigh until I reached the hem of her skirt. Keeping my eyes on hers, I inched it up to her waist. Not appreciating the interfering material, Carter quickly undid the button and zipper at the small of her back and drew it down her legs, then tossed it to the coffee table. "That's better."

I had to agree. I moved my hand to her inner thigh, lightly swirling my fingertips over the soft pale skin, zeroing in on the object of my attention. Once again, I caught Carter's eye. He winked and worked his way down her body, nibbling, sucking, kissing, while his hands continued to toy with her ruched nipples.

Paige's eyes were closed, her fists clenched by her sides.

With my free hand, I brushed Paige's hair off her face. I pressed my cheek to hers. "Open your eyes, sweetheart."

When she complied, I drew her attention to Carter. "I love how he looks there, kneeling on the floor between your legs."

Her pink tongue snuck out and licked her bottom lip. I was sure she didn't even realize she'd done it, and that made it all the more sexy.

"Tell him what you want," I ordered.

She closed her eyes and shook her head, rolling it from side to side. "I-I can't."

My heart stuttered, stopped. My gut knotted. Similarly, Carter froze and searched her face. "You can't what? Open your eyes, Paige. Look at me. Look at Carter. We're here for you. Whatever you want."

She swallowed, her slim neck working as she struggled with her words.

"I can't say it."

"Do you want us to stop?"

"No!" Her shout reverberated off the walls.

Oh, thank you, God.

Carter's chest emptied of air, and he rested his head on her thighs. "Jeezum Crow, woman."

A tiny smile graced her face. "Sorry?"

I chuckled. "It's Vermont-ese for Jesus Christ. You flatlanders don't understand."

"Flatlander? Is that like outlander?"

Carter broke in with a growl. "Something like that. Now let's get back to the program." He tore Paige's panties off and threw them onto the table to land on her blouse and skirt. "You still haven't told me what you want me to do. But don't worry, I know exactly what you want."

"Oh, you do, do you?"

My heart swelled hearing their playful taunting. I had a sense of what Paige really wanted, but that wasn't going to happen tonight. No, as I'd told her, tonight was about her. About her pleasure.

Carter nodded and parted her thighs. He dipped his head and took one long lick from her opening to her clit. She gasped, moaned, and arched. "Oh Carter." Her hands went to his head, kneading and tugging on his hair even as she pushed him more firmly against her.

Unfortunately, for me, I couldn't see anything anymore. But I still could touch. Trailing my hand down her hair, I brushed lightly along her skin, making her shiver. "How does it feel, Paige? Do you like having his mouth on you?"

"It feels…" She gasped and her hips bucked. "So, so good."

I cupped her breasts and pinched the nipples. "Do you like this?"

"Yes, harder."

Licking the side of her neck, I complied. "You're so beautiful like this. Laid out for our pleasure." I bit her softly. Her moans and the sounds of Carter licking at her pussy were driving me crazy. I skimmed the fingers of my right hand down the center of her body until I reached my goal. Understanding immediately, Carter cleared the way by moving his mouth lower, spearing into her with his pointed tongue.

I slicked my finger in her juices, rubbing over her clit and along the sides of her interior lips. The sensitive skin was smooth and wet. Her thighs trembled and bumped on either side of Carter's head. I suspected she was doing that on purpose to feel his soft hair on her heated flesh. After all, that was what I always did.

I increased the pressure of my finger and the speed of the circles I was rubbing on and around her clit. Catching on, Carter did the same, thrusting his tongue into her like he would his cock. Oh, I couldn't wait for Paige to be ready for that. I loved watching Carter fuck almost as much as I loved having him fuck me. My cock leaked pre-cum as I pressed myself, fully clothed, against Paige's back. I loved the feel of her in my arms, her warmth, her softness. The only thing that would make this moment more perfect was if I could sink into her, balls deep. But that would be for another day.

Today, tonight, was for her and her alone. I needed her to know how important she was. That this wasn't just a kink I shared with Carter. That she wasn't just another warm body in our bed, or in this case, on our couch. She was a part of us. Integral to our pleasure. At least for the duration of this trip. After that, would we have to give her up? My belly flipped at the thought.

Glancing at her face, I saw she was there, balancing on the precipice. I'd get her over. I waited for the perfect moment, and when Carter swirled his tongue at her entrance then penetrated her deeply, I used a finger to pull back the hood of her clit and rubbed it, exactly the way I knew she loved.

She screamed, pushed her head against me and gripped Carter's hair, squeezing his head between her thighs. Her body shook. She squirmed and arched, then trembled through the aftershocks.

After a few moments, she chuckled softly and grinned. "Holy moly."

I removed my finger to let Carter give it a swipe of his tongue. She shivered and laughed, pushing his head away. "Stop, oh God. Stop."

Wearing a big grin, Carter sat up on the couch. His gaze traveled up her sated body to her face. "I take it you enjoyed yourself."

Her cheeks pinkened. "I can't imagine how it gets any better."

I wrapped my arms around her waist. "Did that answer your question about the kind of man I am?"

Turning her head to look up at me, she frowned. "But Carter did it while you played with my breasts… well, until you were both…." She turned her head as though too shy to look at me as she spoke, only to end up looking at Carter.

He grinned at her. "Riley and I know what we each like and it pleases us to do that for each other." When she frowned, he rubbed his jaw. "Yeah, I'm not explaining this well. Riley?"

"Hmm… let me see if I can do a better job." Taking her by the hips, I shifted her so her back was no longer to me. I missed the heat of her body, but loved the light in her eyes. "Carter loves me, and he loves breasts. Which means he loves watching me—"

"Play with breasts," Paige finished, understanding dawning on her pretty face.

Carter laughed. "It's like a two for one."

I settled against the back of the couch, my chest full with all that had happened that evening and with all that could happen in the coming days. It felt like Christmas in July.

CARTER

"Wow," I said, shaking my head. "That happened." Our first time with Paige had gone even better than I'd expected. She was both innocence and seduction, all wrapped up in one enticing package. I could see why Riley was so intrigued by her; I was too. I plopped down onto the couch as the door closed behind her.

Riley sauntered into full view. Seeing him rubbing his crotch, my eyes bulged. The thin material of his trousers perfectly outlined his erection. I swallowed hard. "Looks like you've got a problem there."

"Yep. A big one."

He continued walking toward me, tugging the tails of his shirt out of his pants. His fingers worked to undo the long line of buttons on his shirt. My mouth watered more with every additional inch of flesh that was revealed. "You're so fucking sexy."

The shirt hit the floor and Riley went to work on the button and zipper of his pants. My breath caught at Riley's teasing dance. His hips swayed, and he turned around coquettishly while flashing me the dimples at the base of his spine. My hands tightened into fists when he lowered his trunks to expose one fleshy cheek.

He winked at me over his shoulder. "You gonna get undressed, handsome?"

"Shouldn't we talk about what just happened with Paige?"

"Later. Right now, I'm horny as fuck, and I know you are too."

"No argument there." Jumping to my feet, I reached a hand down the middle of my back, grabbed the T-shirt and whipped it off. Then I quickly unsnapped and unzipped my jeans, wiggling and shimmying my hips, as I shoved them down my legs where they bunched around my ankles. "Shit." I'd forgotten to remove my sneakers. Quickly, I toed them off, then hopped around on one foot then the other as I tugged my jeans and boxers off.

When I was finally undressed, I returned my attention to Riley, who stood looking at me, in all his naked glory. Humor lit his eyes as his lips broke into a wide smile.

"Not too graceful, was it?" I asked.

"But oh-so-enthusiastic!" He pointed at the couch. "Now sit."

"Woof," I barked as I obeyed.

Riley stroked his thick cock. "Ready?"

"I've been fucking ready all evening." I was on the verge of a medically-critical case of blue balls. Riley and Paige had seen to that. I reached down to jerk my own aching cock. "What are you going to do about it?

"Hmm… let's see," he said, right before he launched himself onto the couch and onto me. I barely had time to spread my arms wide before his gorgeous ass landed on my lap. Riley's strong thighs encased mine as he straddled me and perched right above the head of my cock. He flicked his hand up. Between two fingers, he held a condom packet.

I took it from him and in two seconds was covering my dick. Even the light touch of my own hands was making me tremble. I licked my lips in anticipation. "I need you, Rye."

"I know." He placed his hands on my shoulders and kissed me tenderly. Deeply.

Unable to wait any longer, I moved one hand to his ass. "I have to prepare you."

He shook his head. "All taken care off." And with no further ceremony, he sank down onto my cock.

"Oh Jesus. Fuck," I cried out as my dick was encased in Riley's heat.

His long answering groan of pleasure twisted my heart. I wrapped my arms around my boyfriend, tugging his head down until our lips met.

Moaning, he whispered against my mouth. "I can taste her on you."

He delved in again. Our tongues danced around each other in an openmouthed kiss, similar to the one we'd shared in front of Paige. One I hoped to someday share with her.

Is that what Riley wanted too? Would he have preferred for Paige to be with us right now? Was he just slaking a need?

"Hey," he whispered. "Where'd you go?"

Embarrassed by my own traitorous thoughts, I averted my gaze.

But Riley was having none of it. He gripped the sides of my head and forced me back. "Look at me, babe. What's going on?"

"Do you really want me, or are you horny because of what we did with Paige?"

He rocked his hips, which lowered him even farther onto my cock. We both gasped at the incredibly deep penetration. "Paige can't do this to me, can she?"

The continued rolling of his hips, the sensuous and sinuous motions, were clouding my brain. "So, you're saying you just want to be fucked?"

"No." Riley swiped his tongue over my lips, then nipped along my jawline. I squirmed under the torturous onslaught. "I want to make love to you." He raised his head and looked deep into my eyes. "You, Carter. The man I love."

"You wouldn't rather be with her right now?"

He shook his head. "It's not a question of rather or not. Of course, I can't wait to have sex with her again. Both with you and without you. Just like I want us to all have sex together. But right now, I'm very happy"—he rocked his hips as though punctuating his words—"to be with you." His voice lowered and grew raspy. "Remember what I said on the bus? I'm going to ride you until we both scream."

I wanted that. That and so much more. Was this really happening? Was Riley really as committed to our relationship as I was? I'd certainly had reason to doubt his profession of love, especially given that Paige was on the scene, but with every passing minute, I believed him more and more. He seemed transformed. Like a happier, more self-assured version of the Riley I'd known and fallen in love with. Was this Paige's doing?

I ran my hands over his back, pressing into the muscles and smoothing over the knobs of his spine. Riley watched me with a heated gaze, filled with lust and love, and my heart soared. No, this wasn't only about Paige. But she was definitely a part of it.

With my hands on his hips, I arched my back, keeping the man suspended, impaled on my cock. "You're so beautiful." Swinging back, I thrust up again. He matched me move for move, and in mere minutes, Riley got his wish. We were both screaming as our mutual climaxes hit.

Sliding down onto the couch, I brought him with me, clutching him tightly against my chest. He snorted. "I'm not going anywhere."

"Sorry." I loosened my hold a smidgen, not really sorry at all. We lay like that, in each other's arms, only the sound of our rapid breaths breaking the complete silence of the hotel room.

Riley played with my sparse chest hair, an action that was surprisingly soothing. He cleared his throat. "I hope you understand now, Carter. Whatever we may or may not have with Paige in no way takes away from what we have together."

I cocked my head to the side to better see his face. "What I don't get is why you're thinking so much about this. I mean, that little speech you gave… don't get me wrong. It was enlightening. I feel like I understand you better now. But if this is just a vacation fling, why does it matter so much to you?"

Shifting in my arms, he pressed a kiss to my nipple, right above my heart. He raised his head, his face open and vulnerable for perhaps the first time in our whole relationship. Elation and worry consumed me as I waited for him to speak. Because Riley was about to say something, something monumental. I felt it in every cell in my body.

"What if this wasn't just a vacation fling?"

I frowned, gripping his waist. "What are you saying, Rye?"

"What if…" He inhaled deeply before continuing. "What if this could be something more?"

Holy shit. My gut churned painfully. This was what I'd been afraid of. I wasn't enough for him. "Is that what you want? Something more?"

Riley sighed as if the sound were torn from his soul. "Stop. I can see the wheels turning in your brain, and I know you're imagining all kinds of things that have nothing to do with reality. I've been honest with you from the beginning."

"Have you? I mean, an occasional third isn't the same thing as a full-blown three-way relationship."

"You're right. I think I was too scared to hope. But my dream is to have a poly relationship. A triad, where each edge of the triangle is as strong as the others. And I want you to be a part of that. Maybe with Paige, maybe with someone else." Riley kissed my chest again.

"Jesus." I scrubbed at the top of my head and laughed uncomfortably. "I couldn't even make it work with one woman. What makes you think I can make it work with a woman *and* you?"

His face brightened. "Because we love each other. More importantly, because we *like* each other."

"And you have feelings for her," I added, slowly coming to terms with the inevitable.

"She's the first woman since Amber I feel anything for."

I closed my eyes. "You know she lives in Miami, right?"

"Yeah."

"So you want a long-distance relationship?"

Riley pushed himself up on his elbow and rubbed his palm along my stubble. "I don't know. Anyway, we're getting ahead of ourselves." He shot me a hesitant look. "Can we approach this the way we would any woman we wanted to date?"

Sliding my fingers through Riley's hair, I clarified, "Get to know her. See if a relationship with us is even something she wants?"

"Yeah. Is that something you'd be willing to do?" Riley smiled and the sight of it, so soft and hopeful, melted me. Undid me completely.

"You do know what you're asking me? Since Livia, I haven't even thought about having a relationship with a woman again."

"But this is Paige, and she's different. Just think about it."

"Okay," I whispered, reaching up to press my lips to his. "No promises. But I'll consider it."

Who was I kidding? If a triad was something Riley wanted, I'd go along with it, even if it killed me.

No one had ever owned me the way Riley Kendrick did.

Chapter 9

PAIGE

What was I doing? *Two* men? Two men who were *involved* with each other?

I was losing my mind. "'Go on a tour,' Ari says. 'Get laid,' she says," I muttered to myself as I unlocked the door to my room. I had a minibar in there, and I intended to take full advantage of it.

I pulled a can of Coke and a mini Jack Daniels out of the fridge. I mixed the combination in a glass, then took a sip and lay back on my bed, memories of Carter touching me, kissing me, my excitement when Riley stayed in the room, watching at first, then joining in. I touched my left breast, the nipple instantly beading under my fingers. Jesus. I was becoming a sex addict.

And it was all Arianna's fault, wasn't it? She'd suggested I have a fling. Of course, she hadn't suggested I have it with two men…

I groaned. What was I doing? I rolled onto my side and took another sip of the drink I'd placed on the nightstand. My purse and phone, along with the cute little teddy bear from Riley, lay beside it. I checked the time. Ari would be leaving the office soon.

If anyone in my life had run into this particular situation before, it would be Ari. And even if she hadn't? She'd still listen and not judge.

And maybe she could tell me what the heck to do.

The phone rang twice before Arianna answered. "*Hola, chica*. How's the trip? I hope you're calling because you got laid and you want to thank me."

I laughed despite myself. "Something like that. You're never going to believe it. Are you somewhere private?"

"Just a second." I heard some rustling, then the sound of a door closing. "Okay, you can spill."

"Well, I met someone."

"Details! Age, height, etc. Is he hot?"

"He's hot, Ari. Dear God, is he hot." I described Riley and what we'd done together before Carter showed up.

Ari whistled. "I feel like a proud mama right now."

"I'm not so sure how you're going to feel about this next part." My stomach fluttered. I knew Ari was fine with gay people—Javier Cordero, our CFO, was gay, and he and Ari had always been tight—but what would Ari think of the mess I'd gotten myself into?

"Paige? You still there?"

"Yeah." I exhaled into the phone. "Riley has a boyfriend. Carter. And he showed up here a couple days ago."

"Oh, *chica*, I'm so sorry!"

"That's not all of it. Earlier this evening, I went to their room to talk. They're both bi, Ari."

"And…?"

"And we… we… um…" God, could I say it out loud?

"You *didn't*!" Ari said.

"Yeah, I did."

Arianna's chuckle was low and knowing. "You've always been an overachiever. I should've known!" she crowed. "So, was it fab-u-lous?"

I closed my eyes. "It was heaven. Overwhelming. I can't stop thinking about it."

"Are you going to do it again?"

"I'm not sure I should've done it at all. I have a *daughter*. I'm a *mom*. I'm not supposed to be doing this kind of thing." I paused. "And they're both younger than me."

"So fucking what? You're having a good time, right?"

"Yes, but…"

"Calm down. You're not a grandmother yet. You're gorgeous, sweetie. I don't tell you that to blow hot air up your skirt. It's true."

"I guess."

Arianna snorted. "You just had two gorgeous guys all over you, and you're worried that you're not hot?"

"There's something I left out. Something you have to swear to keep to yourself."

"I know how to keep a secret, *chica*. Spill."

I took a deep breath and picked up the teddy bear, clutching it to my chest. "You know that book series you loaned me for inspiration?"

"Yeah, the Amber books…" I could picture Arianna's eyes widening, could hear the sharp intake of her breath. "Wait. Are you telling me Riley is Riley *Kendrick*? *The* Riley Kendrick?"

"Yep. The one and only."

"Holy shit! Girl, you went for the gold!!!"

"So now you see the problem."

"Problem?"

"Ari, he's Riley Kendrick. He's rich. He's famous. He's eight years younger than me. And he's already involved with someone."

"Did you read the books?"

"The first two. He wants me to read the third one, but now that I know they're about him, I'm not sure that I can."

When Arianna spoke, all the levity had left her voice. "You need to read it. Trust me."

"Why?"

"You need to know what you're getting into."

"Can you give me the Cliff's Notes?"

"I could, but I don't think that's what you need."

"Ari—"

"I don't want to scare you, but there's a reason he asked you to read it."

"What reason?"

"I think your little vacation fling is more serious than you think."

"Serious how?" God, was Riley hiding something *else* from me?

"You need to understand what happened to him."

"He lost his girlfriend to some other guy, right?"

"It's more complicated than that. Read the book, then Google the rest. He wants you to know him, Paige. *Really* know him."

My pulse quickened. "So you're saying he's not just fooling around with me."

"*Sí*, *chica*. I think he's not fooling around at all."

"I can't do this, Ari."

"One baby step at a time. I could be getting ahead of myself. Read the book. And then talk to him about it." After a pause, she added, "And be sure to enjoy yourself plenty during the rest of the trip."

"And after?"

"Don't worry about after. If it's meant to be, it's meant to be."

"But with two guys? They don't even know about Emma!"

"So? They don't need to know. At least not yet, and if you get to that point, they'll handle it."

"My ex-husband, Emma's *father*, couldn't handle it. Every guy I've dated since couldn't handle it."

"All two? Three? You've hardly dated, Paige. And Emma is eighteen. She's out of the house."

"It's a trial."

"And she loves it. If you could see how happy she is, you'd know it's the best thing for her."

I took a deep breath. "She does seem happy when I talk to her."

"She is. She really is. I'm not bullshitting you."

"Okay." My gaze fell to the copy of *Amber's Triumph* on the nightstand, peeking out from beneath my purse. "I should read the book?"

"Yes. And call me when you're done and after you talk to him. I want all the dish!"

"You always do." I chuckled. "This time I'm the one who has something to report. First time ever!"

Ari laughed. "Like I said, overachiever is your middle name."

We ended the call, and I picked up *Amber's Triumph*. Why wouldn't Ari—or Riley—tell me what had happened?

And what if I didn't like what I read?

I stared at the book's cover. Was Ari right? Did Riley have some deeper purpose for wanting me to read it?

Was my vacation fling not really a fling at all?

A strange excitement stirred in my belly. There was a reason he wanted me to know him. A reason I wasn't sure I wanted to examine too closely just yet.

I set down the teddy bear and opened the book. Time to meet Riley Kendrick, warts and all.

PAIGE

I tugged at the corset I'd been laced into and huffed. How had women put up with these for so long? And how was I going to survive an entire evening in this getup?

"You want it a bit looser?" Gail, the costumer assisting me, asked.

I gazed at myself in the mirror. My breasts were threatening to spill over the top, and my waist looked incredibly small. What would Riley and Carter think when they saw me?

My hips flared out from my waist now. I turned around, scrutinizing myself. The chance to play dress-up, to attend a "real" 19th-century masked ball, had seemed like fun when I'd dreamed it up back in Miami.

Now it seemed like something more. A chance to seduce someone… someones.

I met Gail's eye and shook my head. "I'll get used to it."

She smiled. "You will, dear. Just don't try to take any deep breaths."

I laughed. "I won't be jogging in this, I promise."

Gail motioned to the selection of vintage reproduction dresses laid out on the bed. "The green silk, I think, would look smashing on you."

"Let's try it."

"First the petticoat." Gail strapped the petticoat on, then helped me put on the dress.

It was a near perfect fit. The bodice was a bit tight, and I tried to pull it upward. No luck. I was showing more cleavage than I thought was appropriate to the time period. Or appropriate, period.

"Help!"

Gail smiled. "It looks lovely, dear."

"I'm not showing too much?"

She shook her head. "It looks like more to you because you're looking down. From my view, it's perfect."

I bent forward, eyeing myself in the mirror. A lot of breast seemed visible. "I don't know…"

"Trust me. It's fine." Gail motioned for me to take a seat before the mirror. "Now let's put your hair up." She drew my hair into a bun at the back of my head, leaving some tendrils loose at the front and sides, which she quickly curled into ringlets.

I had applied my makeup earlier, keeping it simple, as I imagined a fresh-faced Jane Austen heroine might look like. I almost laughed out loud. What would Jane think of me, and what I'd done the night before with Riley and Carter?

A virginal girl making her debut I certainly was not. No, I was a courtesan, or someone's paramour, a mistress to a powerful man. Or perhaps a widow seeking a lover? Or two?

Gail held out a selection of fans. "This lovely Japanese one with the cherry blossoms picks up the pink in your cheeks."

I took the silk fan and experimentally held it up to my face, fanning myself coquettishly. "I love it."

"And the last pieces." Gail handed me a set of elbow-length white gloves and a mask, a black, beaded piece that covered only the area around my eyes and gave me a somewhat feline look.

I pulled on the gloves and donned the mask. I looked like myself, but not. "You've done an amazing job," I said.

"My pleasure." Gail beamed and clapped her hands together. "I've almost forgotten—your reticule and dance card."

I had added dance cards after Lori mentioned them in Liverpool. As at the Highland games, I'd hired a local acting company to provide dancing partners for the women. Everyone would be in period dress, and there was liveried staff and a string quartet to provide live music. The event cost a fortune, but it was meant to be thc highlight of the tour. A chance to go back in time, to pretend for one evening that the modern world didn't exist.

I flicked the fan closed and looped its cord over my wrist, then put the dance card and a pencil in the small beaded reticule. I took a last look, swallowed down a flutter of nerves in my belly, and headed for the bedroom door. Everyone was due downstairs in fifteen minutes. I'd have just enough time to check in with the staff and make sure everything was running smoothly.

Total Indulgence had rented out a lovely manor house and its surrounding grounds for the party. The grounds featured a beautiful garden, complete with a boxwood hedge maze at the center. We'd gotten lucky with the weather; it was a balmy night, perfect for leaving the windows open. Not too hot, not too cool.

I descended the curving staircase to the foyer below, unable to stop myself from smiling. I really did feel like a heroine in a Jane Austen novel, especially when I saw the liveried footman in the parlor, ready to assist me however I required.

But it wasn't the footman I required. No, I wanted Riley. And Carter. Heat crept up my neck; if only the staff knew what I was thinking as I checked in on the caterers and musicians.

Riley and Carter had given me a taste of what things could be like between us, a taste that had whetted my appetite for more.

I was rounding the corner to enter the great ballroom when Kenji appeared in a top hat and tails. "Ta-da!" he said, doing a twirl to show off his close-cut breeches, knee-high leather boots, embroidered gold waistcoat and navy-blue jacket. His mask was like mine, black, and it gave him a mysterious air.

"How Beau Brummel of you," I said.

He straightened his coat with white-gloved hands and picked at a speck of imaginary lint on his sleeve. "You like?"

"I do, very much."

He put out his hand. "Your dance card, please, my lady."

"I think my first two dances are already taken," I said, handing him the card and pencil.

He laughed. "Losers weepers. I'm here and they're not." He added his name to the card in the first slot and the second.

I couldn't help grinning when I saw what he'd written. "Duke Tamashiro?"

Kenji buffed his nails on his waistcoat. "Prince seemed a bit much."

"I'm sure you could carry it off."

He sighed. "Heavy is the head that wears the crown. Besides, dukes have all the fun, don't they?"

I pulled out my fan and snapped it open, eyeing him over the top edge. "I daresay they do, Your Grace."

He tapped a finger against his bottom lip. "Your Grace. I do like the sound of that."

The others started filing in, joined by the actors who'd been hired to provide dance partners.

The costumes and masks seemed to be having the desired effect; there were smiles and laughter everywhere, as well as plenty of good-natured flirting.

Where were Riley and Carter? I scanned the crowd as the waitstaff circulated through, offering champagne and hors d'oeuvres to the attendees. The quartet started playing, and Kenji held out a gloved hand to me. "My lady?"

Losers weepers, indeed. I took his hand and let him sweep me into a graceful waltz. As I'd suspected, Kenji was an excellent dance partner, surefooted and graceful. He easily navigated around the other couples, offering nonstop commentary about everyone's clothing.

"So how many of these guys are gay, do you think?" he asked.

I shook my head. "No idea. They're all actors, so some, I'm sure."

"I've got my eye on that tall chap in the brown coat," Ken said, nodding to a couple nearby.

The man was looking our way, his eyes raking us up and down, and I smiled. "Could be he likes us both."

Ken grinned and shook his head. "Oh honey, I don't think so. Check out where his eyes are now."

I turned to look, following the man's gaze to a pair of tall men entering the ballroom. Riley and Carter looked resplendent in top hats and clothing that fit as though it had been tailored for them. The black masks covering their eyes made me think of highwaymen, and a shiver of anticipation flowed over me. Oh, to be stopped at night in a carriage and to have the two of them come aboard with nothing but money and lust on their minds…

"The nerve of you, Lady Sutherland, drooling over other men when you've got me in your arms," Kenji teased.

I gave his shoulder a light squeeze. "Trust me, if I thought you were interested, they'd be in trouble."

His gaze flicked away from mine, and flags of crimson appeared on his cheekbones. But… wasn't Ken solidly in the gay camp?

"You aren't, are you?" I asked tentatively. Could Ken be bisexual? He always wore his homosexuality like a badge of honor.

"Of course not. I'm as gay as nineteen pink balloons." His dark eyes were stormy, his grin a tad forced.

Deciding that it was none of my business, I inclined my head. "I'm afraid Riley and Carter make me think everyone is bi."

He gave me a peck on the cheek. "His Grace forgives your unseemly behavior."

"How gracious of you." I smiled at my own pun and glanced over Kenji's shoulder, my gaze colliding with Riley's as he headed my way, Carter close behind.

Kenji spun me around. "Here they come. Riley looks pissed. Pistols at dawn, do you think?"

"Let's hope it doesn't come to that." I whirled around again, and a gloved hand that wasn't Kenji's slid over the junction between my neck and shoulder.

"May I cut in?" Riley asked as we came to a stop. Ken drew himself up to his full height. "I laid claim to the lady's first two dances. You may wait until she is free."

I giggled. Kenji really was great at being imperious. I smiled up at Riley as we spun away. "How good are you at swordplay?" I asked Kenji.

He burst into laughter at my double entendre. "My Lady Sutherland, you're damned good fun." He nodded at Riley, who stood at the edge of the dance floor with his arms crossed. "The only way I want to cross swords with Riley again is if we're both naked."

"Even though he pissed you off?"

Ken shrugged. "Have you looked at the man? I can forgive a lot of things in his case."

"Yeah. And I bet he knows it."

Ken winked at me. "Of course he does, honey. Part of his charm."

Yes it was. Maybe it did make Riley a bit spoiled. But he didn't seem irredeemable.

The quartet started a new piece, and Kenji switched direction, steering us across the floor. I caught sight of Riley several times in between the other twirling couples. He hadn't budged an inch, his lips set in a firm line.

Carter was dancing with Lori, and he gave me a wide smile and nod as they passed by.

So Riley wanted to pout. Well, the wait would be good for him then.

The dance ended, and Kenji started to escort me off the floor, but I stayed him. "One more, Your Grace?"

He bowed to me and steered me back into the crowd. I caught Riley's gaze as we whirled by. His mouth was open, a slight crease between his brows.

I'm not that easy, Mr. Kendrick. I smiled at Riley and winked. *You want me? You have to work for it.*

"Can you make sure we're near Carter and Lori when we're through?"

"You mean Eric. And yes."

"Thank you, Your Grace."

Kenji was true to his word, wrapping up our third dance right next to Carter and Lori. "Off to see about some… refreshments," Ken murmured, his eyes locked on the actor in the brown coat.

"Good luck," I said and turned to Carter. "I seem to have an opening on my dance card."

Carter's gaze slid to Riley, but I didn't look, hoping Carter would pick up the hint. He did, and extended a hand to me. "At your service, Lady Sutherland."

Like Kenji, Carter was a confident dancer. Unlike the rest of the men though, he was decked out in a kilt. "Is the kilt yours, Lord…?" I waited for him to supply a last name.

"Thornton. Eric Thornton. Duke. And yes it's mine. Riley mentioned liking them when you were in Scotland."

I laughed. "Everyone wants to be a duke tonight, I see."

Carter grinned. "Thought Ken would go for royalty."

"I thought so too, but he chose mere dukedom."

"Riley is going to be peeved with you," Carter said.

I shrugged. "He should have been on time then."

Carter chuckled. "My fault. Well my kilt's fault, I suppose."

I looked up at him through my lashes. "He couldn't resist peeking under it?"

"You know Riley."

"I'm beginning to. I think."

Carter squeezed my waist. "I approve of your strategy, by the way. I think sometimes Riley has no idea what we mere mortals go through. It's good to remind him that he can't always have what he wants when he wants it. I think I've forgotten that too many times."

"Then let's give him a good reminder, shall we?"

We spun around the floor for two dances. God, Carter smelled wonderful. And he felt wonderful too, his shoulder like iron beneath my glove, his large hand dwarfing my fingers, the other steady at my waist, gently communicating which way he wanted me to turn.

And all the while Riley's gaze bored into me like a laser beam. I felt the heat of it every time we passed by him, but I barely acknowledged his presence.

When the second dance ended, he stalked our way and wordlessly extended a hand to me. His eyes held mine, daring me to turn him down again.

This time I didn't. I took his hand and murmured my thanks to Carter as he stepped away.

Riley spun me back out onto the floor, his back ramrod straight, his feet nimble and quick.

"You enjoyed making me wait," he finally said, his dark eyes holding mine.

"Couldn't help myself. I've never been the belle of the ball before."

A smile played with a corner of his mouth. "You are far too modest, Lady Sutherland."

"Not modest. Honest."

He gently squeezed my hand. "Then you spent your life among men who are blind," he murmured, the huskiness of his tone making heat gather between my legs.

Damn him; he always knew what to say to make me melt.

"Is there somewhere more private we could go?" he asked.

"We have the run of the house." I couldn't look at him as I said it; instead I studied the faces of the other dancers, the onlookers. Did they know what Riley had asked me?

No one seemed to be paying us any mind. Ken had disappeared—hopefully having fun with Mr. Brown. And Carter was whirling Vicki Lozier around the floor, looking like he was having a great time.

Riley gradually directed us to the edge of the dance floor, then tugged my hand and led me down a candle-lit hallway. From my earlier explorations, I was pretty sure the study and the library were close by.

Riley steered us into the nearest room, both of us freezing when we saw Kenji on his knees in front of the man in the brown coat. With the actor's hard cock in his hand, Ken half turned at our entrance. "Should've locked the door, I see," he said.

"Sorry!" I called and tugged Riley out of the room. I tried the handle of the next door, and it led us into the library. Riley closed it behind us and latched it, the sound making me slick between the legs.

There was a desk along one wall and a chair behind it. The windows were open to the garden beyond, where dusk was falling. A few couples were strolling the grounds.

"We need to close the curtains," I said.

He took my wrist and pulled me close, shaking his head. "No need." He walked me over to the desk. "Take off your panties," he said as he sank to his knees.

Sweet Jesus. His eyes were smoldering as he looked up at me, his cock pulsing against the fine fabric of his trousers.

I hiked up my dress, trying to get to my panties, but the petticoat got in the way. "Help me?" I asked almost desperately.

He fished around under my skirts. "No wonder everyone was a virgin until marriage," Riley grumbled. He yanked at the petticoat. "How does this thing come off?"

"There are some straps." I felt around for them and untied them, and Riley tore the fabric away, then got down on his knees again and lowered my panties. I stepped out of them.

"Now get on the desk and spread your legs," Riley commanded me.

I was careful not to sit on the dress, instead bunching it to my hips. Riley pushed my legs apart as though too impatient to wait for me to get there on my own.

My back was to the window, but the way I was posed, my knees wide apart, my skirt hitched up to my waist, wouldn't fool anyone. "Can't we close the curtains?" I asked.

Riley slid a hand up my inner thigh. "I'm not waiting a minute longer, Paige."

His fingers found the folds of my sex, and I instinctively arched my back and widened my legs even farther, scooting to the edge of the desk, the dark wood cool beneath my buttocks, the comforting scent of old books surrounding me.

Riley nuzzled my thigh, his thick facial hair rasping against my soft skin, and I whimpered with pleasure. He inhaled deeply, then exhaled against my slick flesh. "You smell so fucking good, Paige. They ought to bottle it like perfume. It would be better than Viagra."

His tongue darted out, licking the seam of my lips, and I stifled a moan. "You are such a dirty boy," I whispered.

"That's what you like about me." He parted my folds with his fingers, then sucked my clit into his mouth, his tongue playing around it. I jerked and bit my lower lip, fighting not to cry out and draw attention.

He pressed one finger, then two, inside me, and I couldn't help pushing my hips forward, not caring what I looked like to anyone who might be outside. "Riley," I panted.

"Yes?" he asked, sitting back and looking up at me while his fingers continued to explore.

I met his gaze, saw the lust there, the encouragement to say what I wanted. "Make me come," I whispered, still too shy to say it with more confidence.

He gave me a wicked grin. "I'm not one to refuse a lady." He pushed my legs farther apart, then went back to sucking my clit, his fingers curling up inside me and stroking my G-spot.

I was panting hard and shaking, clutching at his shoulders, my thighs trembling as I struggled to stay silent when all I wanted to do was scream his name. He started flicking his tongue rapidly back and forth over my clit and something detonated inside me. I stifled a scream, sucking in air, my eyes closed as my hips bucked against Riley's face.

He kept going until I had to push him away, my limbs weak, my flesh so sensitive I wasn't sure I could close my legs without setting off another orgasm.

Riley rose and started unbuttoning the flap of material at the crotch of his pants. "I'm going to fuck you over this desk."

I nodded and rolled onto my stomach, bracing myself on my elbows, my ass jutting into the air.

The doorknob to the library rattled and someone knocked on the wood. "Ms. Sutherland?" a female voice asked.

Yikes! I straightened up and shoved down my skirt. "Just a minute," I called. "Petticoat!" I said to Riley, motioning to the ruffled fabric at our feet.

He snatched it off the floor along with my panties, which he shoved into one of his coat pockets while I hastily strapped the petticoat back into place.

My face burning, I strode to the door, thankful Riley hadn't been kissing me and I hadn't messed up my hair. Maybe I could pull this off.

I opened the door to the woman in charge of catering. "Yes? Is something wrong?"

The woman smiled. "We've run through all the champagne on the order. Should we open a new case or switch to wine?"

What the hell. "Yes, more champagne, please."

The woman's gaze flicked to Riley, then back to me. I did my best to keep my expression bland. "Anything else?"

"We'll be offering cakes, tea, and coffee soon, along with cordials. And more champagne, of course."

"Thank you." I closed the door behind her and said a silent prayer that the woman could be discreet.

"Well, that wasn't awkward at all," Riley said, coming up behind me. He kissed the back of my neck. "You look gorgeous in this gown."

I shivered at his touch, my insides heating up again. "We should get back to the party before we're missed."

He pressed his hard cock into my buttocks. "Forgetting something?"

I looked at him over my shoulder. "Waiting is good for you."

He raised a brow. "Is it now?"

I turned to face him and played with the silk cravat at his neck. "Humbles you, a bit."

He grinned. "You think I need humbling?"

"I know you do."

He leaned down, his lips hovering over mine. "I'm keeping your panties."

"You expect me to go out there and talk to people without them?"

He nodded. "Only you and I will know." He kissed a corner of my mouth, then along my jaw to my ear. "And Carter."

I trembled as Riley's hot breath washed over the sensitive skin of my neck. *And Carter.*

A fresh flood of moisture gathered between my legs, making me ache. Riley and Carter. I wanted them both.

And I was going to have them before the night was through.

CARTER

Riley and Paige had been gone quite a while, and all I could think about was what they were doing. Without me. Would the three of us still end up together before the night concluded? I certainly hoped so.

I was dancing with Lori again when they reappeared. Paige had that loose-limbed grace to her of someone who'd been well satisfied, though Riley seemed anything but as he headed for me.

I handed Lori off to Kenji as the dance ended, then made my way over to Riley and Paige. I caught his eye. "Everything all right?"

He looked at Paige and grinned. "I think you should ask Paige that."

She smacked his arm. "You're incorrigible."

"And that's how you like me." He reached into a pocket in his jacket and pulled out something that he then pressed into my hand.

It was soft fabric, lacy… *Oh.* I didn't look at the item in my hand. I didn't need to.

Paige's panties. I met her gaze, and the way she bit her lip made me chuckle. I stuffed the scrap of fabric into my pocket, then brought my fingers to my nose. The faint aroma of her arousal lingered on my fingers, and I couldn't look away from her. I wanted her, now.

Riley spoke, low enough for both of us to hear. "It's her punishment. She got hers, but I didn't get mine."

"We were interrupted," she insisted.

"And Lady Sutherland apparently felt the game was over."

"Your Grace…" Paige said, her tone caught between pleading and exasperation.

"So, I think, Thornton, that it is your duty to take the situation in hand, as it were." Riley's grin was pure wickedness.

I chuckled at Paige's open mouth and wide eyes. "Come, Lady Sutherland," I said, extending my arm to her. "We have matters of great import to discuss."

She took my arm, her footsteps slow and stiff as we headed toward the terrace just off the ballroom. "We're going outside?" she asked.

"I do believe we could use some fresh air." I leaned down, whispering the last in her ear. "And I bet there are plenty of secluded alcoves in the garden maze."

Full dark had fallen, and the garden paths were lit here and there, but shadows spread out before us as we walked toward the maze, pea gravel crunching underfoot.

"Are you both trying to get me fired?" Paige asked when we reached the entrance to the maze.

I stopped her. "Of course not. Look, if you don't want to…"

She stared up at me, one side of her gorgeous face lit up by a nearby lamp on a post. "The problem is that I do want to. You two keep tempting me."

Whew. I didn't want to push her too far. Sometimes Riley didn't seem to know—or care—where the line was, but I wasn't a boundary breaker.

"We'll never do anything you don't want to."

She started into the maze, giving my arm a tug. "I feel like I've lost all restraint. Like something in me has been unleashed, and I can't stuff it back into the box I was keeping it in."

"Do you want to? That's the question I think you need to ask yourself."

She was silent for a moment, her hand tightening on my arm. "I *should* say yes. I want to say yes. But if I'm honest…" She trailed off. When she spoke again, there was a catch in her voice. "The truth is, my life kind of sucked before this."

"How so?"

"All I did was work." She let out a little laugh. "The last time I had sex before this trip was five years ago."

"*Five* years?" I shook my head. "I find that hard to imagine."

"It wasn't by choice."

It was my turn to laugh. "Come on, Paige. That can't possibly be true."

She started to protest, then abruptly shook her head. "Okay, maybe I turned down some opportunities."

We reached a dead end in the maze, one that had a stone bench and a small fountain in it. The perfect spot for what I had in mind. I drew Paige to a stop. "I'm sure you did." I motioned her to the bench and remained standing. I could faintly see her in the light cast by the moon. She was looking up at me expectantly, and my cock swelled, the scent of her panties once again flooding my mind.

I took her hand in mine, then pressed it against the hardness at my crotch. "Will you turn me down too, I wonder?" I murmured.

She caressed me through the cloth, saying nothing, but her fingers spoke for her as they teased me. She unbuttoned the fall of my trousers, her hands slipping inside and pulling me free.

"Paige," I whispered, my voice deepened with desire.

She bent forward and took the tip of my cock in her mouth, and I groaned when her lips closed around me, her tongue swirling around the head.

"Fuck," I gasped, fully hard in an instant. I rocked my hips forward slightly, reminding myself that she wasn't Riley, but she met me more than halfway, increasing the suction as she took me in.

"Jesus, Paige." I cupped her bare neck and let myself thrust shallowly, testing her limits.

She clutched my ass cheek with one hand, the other clasping me at the root, holding me back a bit. She twirled her tongue around the shaft, swishing it along the underside as she pulled back up to the tip. Then she plunged down again, taking me deeper than I'd expected, and I couldn't stifle the groan that came from somewhere deep in my gut.

I looked down. She worked back and forth, her pretty mouth stretched around me, her eyes gazing up to meet mine. "You're out of this world," I said.

She hummed her appreciation and took me in a bit deeper, speeding up the pace, and I had to close my eyes. The sight of my cock sliding in and out of her mouth was going to make me come. I'd expected her to turn me down, but she'd surprised me with her eagerness. There was something prim and proper about her, but underneath?

She was a fucking tigress.

Her fingers tightened around me and she increased the suction.

"Fuck, I'm going to come," I said, starting to withdraw, but she held me in place, surprising me yet again. My ex, Livia, had never swallowed. But Paige, fuck, Paige was going to—

I came hard, convulsing with a groan as I shot down her throat, her silky skin under my hand, her hot tongue swirling around the head of my cock and making me shiver. "Stop, beautiful, stop," I murmured, pulling back, my breath coming hard.

She wiped at her mouth, grinning up at me. "Have I been properly punished?" she asked, a lilt in her voice.

I laughed. "Wait until I tell Riley about this."

She chuckled. "He's going to be sad he missed out."

I tucked my spent cock away and buttoned my trousers. "Who says we're done with you?" I pulled her up from the bench and took her in my arms. "We're only getting started," I whispered in her hair. "How soon can we leave?"

She looked up at me, and I couldn't resist kissing her. She tasted of me, and the memory of what she'd just done made me groan. God, she was amazing.

When we parted, she answered my question. "We can leave soon. Probably should have some cake and a drink. Then we can go."

I offered her my arm again. "Well, then, Lady Sutherland, let's take our leave of the other guests. I'm not done punishing you yet."

She squeezed my arm. "I should hope not, Your Grace."

PAIGE

My God, I really am doing this. Having a threesome with two gorgeous men.

I made sure everything was progressing smoothly at the ball, then Riley, Carter, and I slipped upstairs. I still felt slightly guilty, but judging by the outrageous flirting going on at the party, the guys and I weren't the only ones who'd be extra happy by the end of the night.

We ended up in my room, the three of us giggling like idiots. Too much champagne coupled with a bit of giddy anticipation—at least on my part. To think, when I'd come on this trip, I'd hoped to maybe hook up with someone once, maybe twice. And now I was sleeping with two guys? Together?

Riley and Carter were looking at me expectantly, as if waiting for me to make the first move. Where did I start? Maybe with my clothes, which weren't the easiest to get out of. I turned my back to them and cast a shy smile over my shoulder. "I'm going to need some assistance with all this." I motioned to my gown.

Riley grinned and looked at Carter. "It appears we have a damsel in distress on our hands."

"Don't let her fool you," Carter said.

"I'm right here, guys."

"We're well aware of that," Riley whispered in my ear, one of his hands wrapping around my throat, his thumb lightly stroking my skin and making it tingle.

I started to turn to kiss him, but he held me fast. "Don't move. We can't get you naked if you're all over the place."

Oh. Carter joined Riley behind me and kissed me on the shoulder. "What about her punishment?"

"We'll get to that." Riley started working on the buttons along my spine, and I pressed my thighs together. Exactly what "punishment" did Riley have in mind?

He nibbled my earlobe, making me shiver as he quickly finished undoing the buttons at the back of the gown. The green silk rustled as it slid into a heap on the floor. I stepped out of it, and Carter picked up the dress and laid it over a chair.

I stood before them in my petticoat and corset, while they were both still fully clothed. "Aren't you going to undress?" I asked, my voice suddenly seeming so small.

Carter looked at Riley, then back at me. "In time." He motioned to the petticoat. "How is it attached?"

I pointed out the straps, untying them myself and letting the garment fall to the floor. Now only the corset and thin chemise stood between me and complete nudity.

The cooled air of the room made my nipples form peaks, and the rub of them on the corset when I shifted made me take in a quick breath. Every inch of my skin felt hyperaware, as if the gazes upon me were feathers lightly stroking my body. Everything seemed magnified, and perhaps it was. After all, I was the object of desire for two men. Two men who stared at me in open admiration.

I half turned away again, gesturing to the ties at the back of the corset. "Can one of you please free me?"

Carter started to step forward, but Riley shook his head. "Maybe we should keep her in it."

A glint came into Carter's eyes. "More punishment?"

"If you leave me in this while we're..." I let my voice trail off. "I'm liable to pass out."

Riley chuckled. "That wouldn't be much fun." He came up behind me and started on the corset.

I groaned in relief as the constriction of my rib cage eased. "Thank you."

"How grateful are you feeling?" Riley asked.

"Very," I said as he removed the corset altogether. I took a deep breath and turned to face them. Looking down, I saw the peaks of my nipples poking almost through the tissue-thin chemise.

Carter's and Riley's eyes seemed glued to this obvious sign of my arousal. Reaching up, I gently tweaked both nipples at once, the sensation sending sparks between my legs.

Riley grabbed his crotch and groaned. "Fuck, Paige."

"I aim to," Carter said, and I giggled. This would be my first time with Carter. What would he feel like inside me? His cock was comparable to Riley's. But it would be different. *He* would be different.

"Take off the chemise," Riley said, his voice low and rasping.

I took hold of the delicate fabric and started to draw it upward, butterflies swooping and diving in my belly. This was it. I was really, truly, doing this.

The fabric caressed my thighs, my belly, my breasts, as I pulled it overhead and dropped it. The only thing I still wore were the white silk stockings and ballerina-like slippers I'd donned earlier to complete the costume.

"On the bed," Riley said. "Sit on the edge, and spread your legs."

I went to the bed and sat, opening my legs as little as I thought was reasonable. "Wider," Riley said. "Show us how much you want us."

Heat flooded my face and chest. I was slick already, and they hadn't even touched me. I parted my thighs, looking away from them, pretending to be fascinated by the drapes.

"What a pretty pussy," Carter murmured.

"It's so tight. Wait until you're in her."

It was strangely exciting to be discussed this way, as if I were a painting they were admiring. I wanted to touch myself, but I couldn't. That was just too intimate. Too revealing. Too needy.

That's what I was. Needy.

I shifted restlessly, wanting to press my thighs together, anything to ease the ache between my legs.

"Touch yourself," Riley said. My eyes snapped to his, but I made no move to comply. "I know you want to," he said. "So do it."

Could I? I closed my eyes and let my right hand drift down to cup my mound, the well-manicured curls springy against my palm.

One of the men took an audible breath. Which one? Riley? Carter? I'd have to open my eyes to know. But I couldn't.

I parted the lips of my sex, my fingertips encountering the flood of moisture that lingered there. I lightly circled my clit. Were they touching themselves as they watched me?

The thought made me shiver, and I pressed a finger more firmly against my clit, my breathing growing faster, heavier.

There was a rustle of cloth, then footsteps as someone approached.

Did I want to know who?

But I didn't need my eyes to know it was Carter who tipped me back onto the mattress. I could smell him, feel him. "Look at me," he said.

I opened my eyes. God he was perfect, his blue eyes holding mine as he picked me up, easily spinning me so my head was at the edge of the mattress where I'd been sitting. Carter climbed up beside me, still fully clothed aside from his jacket, his bare cock poking out from the fall of his trousers. I looked over my shoulder at Riley, who likewise had shed only his coat. He too had freed his cock, which he lazily stroked as he watched us.

I turned my attention back to Carter when he leaned over me, his mouth seeking mine. His tongue plunged between my open lips and I sucked on it, making him groan. He palmed my breasts, squeezing them lightly, their aching tips not at all appeased by his touch.

He took one of my nipples into his mouth, his tongue swirling over it before he lightly bit down and tugged, making me arch and cry out.

"I think she's ready," Riley said.

"She tastes so sweet," Carter muttered. He caught my eye and grinned. "Someday I want to drizzle maple syrup all over you."

Someday? What did that mean? Was there some kind of future for us beyond the trip?

Stop it, Paige. Don't go there.

Because that wasn't going to happen. This was just… for now.

Carter rubbed his stiff cock against my clit, and I cried out again. "You want it?" he asked. "You want my cock in you?"

"God yes." I almost didn't recognize my voice. Who was this breathy hussy in my body?

He released me for a second while he retrieved a condom from his trouser pocket and put it on. Then he was between my legs, rubbing himself against my lips, making me groan. "Please, Carter."

The smile he gave me was pure masculine satisfaction as he thrust inside me.

"Oh," I moaned and wound my legs around his waist, meeting his thrusts. He pounded into me hard a few times, then backed off and rolled me onto my side so he was straddling my left leg. He extended my right one into the air and then entered me again.

Jesus, he was so deep this time, the curve of his cock rubbing against my G-spot and making me moan. "Oh yes, oh yes. Right there."

Riley tapped on my shoulder, and I realized he was standing at the edge of the bed, his cock millimeters from my lips.

Ah. Now I understood why Carter had repositioned me. They'd obviously done this before.

Riley bumped the head of his cock against my lips. "Time for your punishment."

I grinned as I took him in my mouth.

It was so odd to have them both inside me at the same time, Carter's cock thrusting in and out of my sex while Riley's slid over my tongue.

What must I look like to them? I'd never thought I'd do such a thing in my life—well, I'd thought about it sure, especially after the Amber books, but to actually do it, to actually have two men inside me at once? I shuddered suddenly, my orgasm taking me by surprise.

I clenched around Carter and he cried out, thrusting into me harder, and Riley said, "I told you, didn't I?"

"Yes, you did," he muttered. "Fuck, Paige, you have to stop."

I didn't want to. I wanted Carter to come, wanted him to lose control the way I had. I sucked harder on Riley and clenched around Carter again, and both of them swore.

Riley tunneled his fingers into my hair, holding me in place, and thrust harder, and I let him in deeper, swirling my tongue over the head again the way he liked, and he came with a shout.

I swallowed his cum as Carter's thrusts grew frantic. He climaxed, breathing hard. "Jesus Christ, Paige, I thought you were going to kill me."

I laughed and looked up at them, all of us panting. "Maybe *I* was punishing you two."

Riley grinned and knelt, taking my face in his hands. "You can punish us any time." His kiss was light and sweet, so tender my heart fluttered.

What was I doing? As much as I'd tried to tell myself it was just sex, it wasn't.

Carter crawled up beside me and slung an arm across my waist, then he kissed me too after Riley released me. My heart gave another little flutter.

I caressed Riley's hair and Carter's at the same time, my throat tightening. I'd walked right into danger, and I hadn't realized it.

These two were stealing my heart, despite everything I'd told myself.

Despite every *lie* I'd told myself.

And despite the big truth I'd kept from them.

Emma.

Chapter 10

RILEY

Praying no one recognized me, yet eager to experience Bath's highly touted thermal spas with Carter and Paige, I herded them through the modern lobby of the city's premier establishment. I'd had to opt for contact lenses since glasses would have been awkward to wear in the water and steam rooms, so I'd covered up with a ball cap and sunglasses. Hey, it worked for Superman.

I stayed back while Paige and Carter went up to the reception desk to book our afternoon treatments. They returned to my side a few minutes later. Paige had a huge smile on her sweet face. "I'm so looking forward to this. It's been ages since I've pampered myself like this."

Watching her with an indulgent expression, Carter handed us each a basket containing a robe, flip-flops, a towel, and a bottle of water. "We'll meet you right outside the changing rooms, okay?" I said to Paige.

She practically danced. "Yes, but hurry. Carter convinced them to let us all do the couples massage at four, and I can't wait. But first, the spas!" She skipped away to the door marked "Ladies."

Seeing her so excited did something to me. My throat tightened. She should always be this happy.

Carter bumped my shoulder. "Ready? We should get changed too."

Startled out of my reverie, I looked up. "Yes, we should."

"She seems happy."

I laughed. That was putting it mildly. "She's been working so hard. I'm glad to do this for her."

Carter grinned. "For her. Sure."

"What?" I asked, forcing my features into what I hoped was a look of pure innocence.

"You wanted to have her all to yourself."

"Myself? I think I've more than proved I'm the sharing type." I arched a brow and poked a finger into the hard muscles of Carter's chest, before opening my hand to smooth my palm over his abdomen. God, I loved his body. Each muscle so well-defined and strong. I took a step closer as I let my hand fall to his waist. "Are you a figment of my imagination? You feel solid enough to be real."

Carter grunted and trapped my wrist before my hand could drift lower.

I pouted. "Party pooper."

"Come on, Mr. One-Track-Mind. Paige will be wondering what's happened to us."

We entered the changing rooms and quickly put on our bathing trunks. Armed with towels, robes, flip-flops, and water, we rejoined Paige. She held a map in her hands. "This is the route for the self-guided baths."

I bowed low. "Lead the way, milady."

Beside me, Carter smirked. "That was awful, man. And you call yourself a writer?"

Laughing, Paige hooked her arms through ours and tugged us toward the first stop, the open-air rooftop pool. Still arm in arm, we paused for a moment to enjoy the breathtaking view of Bath and the surrounding hills. "It's so beautiful here," she said.

I looked at her, or rather the top of her head. My gaze collided with Carter's. There was a warmth in his eyes, a tenderness that hadn't been there before. I smiled. "It sure is," I said. I doubted Carter would catch on, but I'd meant both Paige and him. Standing in the sun, its rays reflecting off the water and bathing them in shimmering light, both my lovers were resplendent. And, for now at least, they were mine.

Lifting my hand from Paige's waist, I touched Carter's arm, needing to connect with him as well.

He cleared his throat. "So, Paige, tell me about this spa."

"Well, this particular bath is kept at 33.5 degrees Celsius and is very mineral rich."

We walked to the edge and down the steps. When the heated water reached the tight muscles in my lower back, I arched and groaned.

Carter's amused look arrested my thoughts. "What?" I asked.

"We wearing you out, kid?"

Paige started to laugh. "You guys never stop. Are you going to break out the measuring tape next?"

"Oh, we've already done that," I said.

"You two are incorrigible."

"Just the way you like us."

Her cheeks colored and she fanned her face. "Wow. This water really is hot."

"Right," Carter said, sinking in up to his neck. When he sat on the ledge lining the wall, a jet piston at his back, he practically purred.

The sound, low and throaty, went straight to my cock. "Fuck," I muttered under my breath, taking a seat to Carter's left, while Paige settled on my right.

Closing my eyes, I did my best not to think about the previous night, or that morning, or the quickie we'd had after lunch. After all that sex, I'd thought I'd be able to go one hour without getting a hard-on. I was wrong.

Ten minutes later, Paige urged us out of the water. It was time for the Roman steam room. We spread out our towels on the stone ledges in the eucalyptus-scented room. Luckily, given the boner I was sporting, we were alone.

Carter teased me by covering my crotch with his heavy foot and gently squeezing with his toes. The weight put the right amount of pressure on my balls. I moaned in delight.

"Oh the joy of being young," Carter said, winking at Paige.

I held my breath, awaiting Paige's reaction to the reminder of our age difference. Why she was sensitive about it, I had no clue. The woman was gorgeous, regardless of her age.

Her eyes seemed to glaze over with memories. "All that stamina can be quite… entertaining."

Moving up to the ledge behind us, she began to massage Carter's shoulders. Why was he getting the royal treatment? When I frowned at them and shoved Carter's foot off my dick, both of them burst out laughing.

Before I could cobble together a bitchy response, Carter caught me by the arm and dragged me onto his lap. I gasped as his very hard cock pressed against my ass. "Yeah," he said, dropping a kiss onto my gaping mouth. "I'm not that old."

Paige took my hand and pushed it down the front of her bikini bottoms until my fingertips touched her soaked pussy. She moaned and trapped my hand between her thighs. "Seems I'm not too old either."

I retrieved my hand and sucked on my index finger. "No," I said, arousal thickening my voice. "You definitely aren't."

Carter grabbed my hand and licked my middle finger down to the last joint. Paige and I both moaned.

"Jesus."

The door pushed open. My heart beating like mad, I jumped up from

Carter's lap and reached for my towel, bunching it up in front of my groin. Ignoring the newcomer, I popped open my bottle of water and drank deeply.

A woman in her early twenties sat beside me. "Hi." She waved at us. "Where's everyone from?"

Paige smiled from her perch behind Carter, who crossed one leg over the other knee and folded his hands in his lap. "We're American."

"Oh? Are you here on a tour or something?"

"Yes. We're touring England and Scotland."

"And enjoying Bath's baths," Carter added.

The woman's face went blank and Carter's reddened. I smothered a laugh. Obviously, the man's brain was as debilitated by lust as my own.

"Where are you off to next?" the woman asked.

Carter and I both turned to Paige. "We're heading to Chawton tomorrow, then Cambridge after that, and finally on to London for the last few days."

The woman clapped her hands together. "How exciting."

"What about you?" Carter asked. His eyes were a little narrowed, and I couldn't decide why. Unless he wanted her to leave us alone. But then, why ask her any questions at all? The less we engaged, the sooner she'd be on her way.

Her eyes widened. "Oh, I'm sorry." She opened her robe enough to show us her uniform. "I work here."

Here it comes.

She was going to toss us out on our asses for indecent behavior, only we hadn't done even one-tenth of the indecent things I was dying to do.

Paige scanned the room. "What time is it? We have a massage scheduled for four."

"All together?" the woman asked.

"Yes." Paige raised her chin, a little defiantly if I was reading her right.

"Splendid. You have plenty of time. It's only three. Listen, if you're interested, we do have private suites. I can move your massages to there, so afterwards you can take your time in the private spa… hot tub, I think you call it in America. The room also has showers. I can have the staff bring in your belongings. It will be more private, and the lady won't have to be alone."

"That would be great," I said. "Thank you."

Carter held up a hand. "How much extra will this cost?"

"No charge. We like to pamper our special guests."

"Special?" Paige asked.

What was up with the question? It almost seemed like they were suspicious of the spa employee's kindness. This kind of thing happened all the time at spas, restaurants, and hotels, at least to me it did.

"Tour people. We love becoming a regular stop on tours. It's good for business."

"We appreciate it. I'll be sure to tell our tour company how well we've been treated here," I said, barely holding in a grin when Paige frowned at me.

I spent the next hour freezing my balls off in the ice room, sweating my balls off in the steam room, and then revving up my libido again in the rainforest shower. If I didn't know better, I'd think Paige was some sort of dominatrix with the way she was edging me, stoking my arousal, then backing off, keeping me on the precipice. And judging by the tent in Carter's swimsuit, he was having the same experience.

"I don't know if I'm going to make it through a massage," he grumbled, confirming my assessment.

"Come on, boys," Paige teased. "Big men like you, men with *stamina*, can surely get through a sixty-minute massage."

Carter and I looked at each other. I blinked first.

"Sixty minutes?" I said, on a strangled groan.

Paige's laughter ushered us down the hall to our private room while Carter and I limped after her.

PAIGE

"Oh. My. God. This feels amazing," I moaned as my masseuse, Wendy, dug her fingers into the muscles of my upper back. My men lay on their own tables on either side of me, attended to by their own masseuses. From the smiles on the women's faces, it was clear they felt they'd lucked out as far as clients went. And they were right. Riley and Carter looked like sinfully tasty treats, all long limbs and firm muscles. I salivated with an overwhelming desire to lick them from the top of their heads to the tips of their toes.

Despite the differences between them, I was drawn to them equally. Riley was youth and exuberance, despite his tendency to wall-off his emotions, except where Carter was concerned, although I sensed that was a recent development. Carter was maturity and infinite patience. I could well imagine him in a classroom full of students or in his home surrounded by his own children.

Both men made me feel special. Riley, in the way he treated me, like I was the most beautiful woman in the world. And Carter, in that way he had of giving me one-hundred percent of his attention, as though he hung on my every word.

Wendy's fingers dug into my glutes, and I was unable to hold back the moan that roared up my throat.

"Fuck." Riley swore and squirmed, his eyes trained on me. Sweat beaded his brow, and his face seemed unnaturally red. Weren't massages supposed to be relaxing?

"You okay?" I asked him.

He gritted his teeth. "Peachy."

I turned my head to see how Carter was doing. "Oh my." His teeth were bared. His gaze on my… exposed butt. "Carter," I said, a warning in my tone. His eyes snapped to my face, well, to my lips at least.

His masseuse prodded his hip. "Sir, please turn onto your back."

Carter's eyes widened as panic seeped into the deep blue of his irises. He searched out Riley. "Dude," he said. His voice, deeper than I'd ever heard it, vibrated throughout my body and centered on my sex.

"Sir," the masseuse said again.

Carter angled himself toward me and away from his masseuse. His face beet red, he shook his head in silent refusal.

I eyed him with concern. What on earth was going on? I observed the tic in his jaw, his wild and frantic eyes, the flush on his face, neck and chest, his clenched abs, his… Oh!

Riley must have reached the same conclusion at the same time, because he grabbed his own masseuse's arm, drawing everyone's attention to him. His eyes, which I'd rarely seen without his glasses, blazed. "How much would it cost for you to leave us alone for an hour?" When the woman frowned, he rushed to add, "Forty minutes tops."

The woman rolled her eyes and signaled the other two. "You've already paid for your massages." She wagged her fingers at us like we were errant schoolchildren. "Do *not* make a mess. This job is taxing enough as it is."

Resting on my elbow on my side, sheet clutched to my chest, I held my breath until the door shut behind the women. Then I let loose the giddy laughter that bubbled in my chest. "The looks on their faces. They're going to think I'm the most depraved woman alive."

"No," Carter said. "They're going to think you're the luckiest woman alive." He rose from his table, his erection jutting out from its nest of short blond hair, only slightly darker than the hair on his head.

My pulse beat a rapid tattoo at the sight of his naked body, all those muscles, his hard… Wow. I hadn't seen many aroused males in my life, but I knew beyond a shadow of a doubt that Carter was magnificent.

Strong arms wrapped around my waist and a warm chest blanketed my back, drawing me into a seated position. Riley kissed my neck. His teeth scraped along the tendon I exposed by tilting my head to the side.

Yes, I was the luckiest woman on the planet. To have not one, but two exquisite men eager to please me was truly heaven on earth.

Carter moved between my thighs, parting them wide. His erection rubbed along my slit. I shuddered as pleasure swamped me. Bending down, he brought his lips to mine. I reached up and wound my arms around his neck, flattening my breasts against his hard chest.

"Oh," I cried, startled to feel Riley's hands cup my mound. His fingers pressed into my opening and I arched my back, eager to feel him more deeply. When Carter moaned into my mouth, I noticed the rhythmic motion of Riley's other hand stroking Carter's shaft.

It hit me then, how truly selfless and giving my lovers were. While the men had certainly experienced their share of orgasms in the last few days, I also had to acknowledge that, during each encounter, I'd been the focus of all their attention. Heck, that first night in their hotel room, I'd been the only one to climax. No doubt they'd pleasured each other after I'd left, so why hadn't they done it while I'd been there? In fact, I hadn't ever seen them do more than kiss, and not much at that.

Did I want to see it? Did I want to see them kiss each other, touch each other, make love to each other?

My answer was a resounding "Yes!"

Carter drew back from me a little and arched a brow. "Yes?"

"She's just telling us she likes what we're doing. Right, sweetheart?" Riley asked while his hand continued its relentless assault on my sanity.

"I-I do. So much." I paused and laid my cheek against Carter's broad shoulder. So much temptation. The scent of his skin, imbued with massage oil, toyed with my senses. I nibbled along his clavicle and swiped at the notch at the base of his throat, where a few droplets of moisture had accumulated. The salty taste of his skin erupted in my mouth, and my mind went blank. What had I wanted to say? Oh, yes. "But this time, I—oh!" I cried out as someone's finger brushed my anus.

When Carter laughed, I looked down and saw it was his hand. My mind exploded. How was this happening to me? And why was I enjoying it so darn much?

I was going to—"Oh God. Stop. You'll make me come."

Riley chuckled next to my ear. "It's kind of the point, sweetheart."

"But I-I want to see you," I blathered.

His hands stilled. "Me? You mean you want me to come around to the other side of the table? Sure. I can do that."

"Yes, well, no." I pressed my face against Carter's chest and blocked the sides of my head with my hands.

At least I tried to.

Carter took my hands in his and kissed them. "What is it, Paige? What do you want?"

Riley's hand left my mound and his warmth left my back. What had I wanted again?

I raised my chin and looked at both men. Standing side by side, they were so perfect. So beautiful. So incredibly out of my league. But for now, at least, they were mine. And I intended to enjoy them to the fullest.

I placed a hand on my belly to calm my fluttering nerves. "I want to see the two of you together."

A confused look on his face, Riley glanced at Carter, then back to me. "Together? We're right here, next to each other."

"No, I..." I stopped and looked down at my clasped fingers, too embarrassed to put into words what I so clearly wanted in my heart.

Strong hands cupped my cheeks. I looked up into Carter's dancing eyes. "You want to see me and Riley together? Making love together?"

Mutely, I nodded.

"Sweetheart," Riley said, capturing my attention with his gruff voice and his dark piercing gaze. "Are you sure you're ready for that?"

"Why wouldn't I be?"

"Sex between two men can be... ah..." Carter exchanged a chagrined look with Riley. "A bit animalistic."

"What are you talking about? You're both beautiful. How could the expression of your love for each other be anything but beautiful as well?"

A corner of Riley's mouth kicked up. "Love can take many forms."

I crossed my arms over my naked chest. "Or are you too chicken to do it in front of an audience?"

"Ha-ha." Riley winked at Carter. "Been there, done that."

"Many times," Carter added.

"Then what's the problem?"

Carter shrugged. "No problem. You game, Rye?"

Riley plastered himself along the full length of Carter's body and hooked his arms behind Carter's head. "I'm always game."

When Carter cupped Riley's bottom and lifted him so Riley could wrap his legs around Carter's waist, a thrill raced through me, lighting me up from the inside. Seeing them like this, well, it was incredibly hot.

Carter turned and set Riley on his massage table, then knelt between his spread thighs. His long fingers closed around Riley's thick shaft and he began to stroke him, adding a circular motion each time he reached the head.

Riley's moans were music to my ears. When he tossed his head back and gripped the sheet covering the thin mattress beneath him, my fists closed also. I remembered Carter's mouth on me, Riley's fingers as he'd worked my clitoris. They were both well-versed in how to make me tick.

And clearly, Carter was familiar with all of Riley's buttons as well.

Rising up, Carter kissed the head of Riley's erection, then he opened his mouth and took him deep, deeper than I'd ever been able. Riley cried out, his hips bucking. Droplets of pre-cum would be leaking from him now, hitting Carter's tongue. The bittersweet taste. So addictive. I licked my lips.

"Touch your breasts, sweetheart," Riley ordered.

Surprised, I stared at him.

"Please."

Slowly, I brought a hand to my right breast, cupping it, massaging, circling the areola until, finally, I pinched the peak between my thumb and forefinger.

"That's it, sweetheart. Harder."

When I returned my attention to Riley and Carter, Riley had his eyes fixed on me and his hands fisting Carter's hair as Carter's head bobbed up and down between his legs. Riley groaned loudly, then tugged Carter off. "Stop, man. It's too intense."

A grin on his face, Carter rose and closed his mouth over Riley's. Their kiss was deep and tender. Every now and then, I caught a glimpse of pink tongue, a flash of white teeth, and my belly ached, wound tight with need.

I switched hands, using my left to squeeze my breast, while my right drifted down my torso, over my waist. I paused at the loose skin on my abdomen. Neither man had remarked on the stretch marks, although surely they'd seen them? My fingers smoothed over one silver line, before toying with the soft curls at my apex.

Across from me, Riley's breath hitched, and he gripped Carter's shoulders. "Fuck me, Carter. Right now."

Carter frowned, then whispered something in Riley's ear. Riley smiled, his eyes going soft. "I trust you. Do you trust me?"

"Fuck yeah." Carter's fingers dug into Riley's sides as he yanked him closer. "With my fucking life." Their mouths crashed together, and now I understood what Carter had been trying to explain earlier.

They resembled sleek lions battling for dominance. Passionate, aggressive. Rough even. Yet, at the same time, the act was more sensual than I could have imagined, perhaps because every touch, every look, and every word reflected the love Riley and Carter shared.

Coming up for air, the men exchanged a glance, a silent communication I hadn't yet learned to interpret. Would I ever get the chance?

Riley turned and knelt on the table on all fours. Carter stepped on a pedal to lower the table, gripping Riley's waist to steady him until the table stopped. Standing at the foot of the table, directly behind Riley, Carter picked up a small bottle of massage oil and poured some into his hand, then caressed the line between Riley's round butt cheeks.

Groaning, Riley closed his eyes and pushed back. "Hurry," he ordered.

I'd never seen Riley like this before, and I marveled at his courage. Not in giving himself to Carter, but rather in how he was exposing himself to me.

In our interactions together, he'd always been the one in control, the one directing our time together. For some reason, despite Carter's size but maybe because of his easygoing personality, I'd imagined that the dynamic would be the same between the men.

Riley's eyes were still closed. Another thing I'd rarely seen him do. I'd assumed he was a very visual person who needed to always see what was happening.

Are his eyes closed because he's embarrassed?

The thought pained me. "Riley," I whispered.

When he looked at me, I realized my error. Hunger, need, and desire poured out of him with such intensity, I felt it like a physical caress. Heat pooled low in my belly, and my sex grew slick with my arousal.

Riley's nostrils flared. "Open your legs, Paige," he growled.

I did.

"Wider," Carter said, his hand pumping Riley's shaft, coating it with oil.

Gulping, I parted my thighs as wide as I could. Cool air brushed over my heated flesh, and I shivered. Goose bumps erupted over my body. "Oh," I moaned.

"Jesus." Carter poured more oil on his hand and palmed his own erection. It was long and hard, the head a purplish red. When he took himself in hand, a tingle of pleasure shot through me.

Oh God. I needed to touch myself. Sliding my hand down, I cupped my labia, relishing in the heat, all the while keeping my attention fixed on the men before me.

Carter's hand latched onto Riley's hips and the head of his penis was poised at Riley's entrance. His face red and tense, Riley seemed to be holding his breath.

"Ready?" Carter asked.

Riley nodded but didn't make any sound. Slowly, Carter's hips flexed and the air whooshed out of Riley. He dropped his head and fisted the sheets in his hands.

From my angle, I witnessed Carter's generous shaft disappear into Riley's bottom. When Carter's abdomen was finally firmly pressed against Riley, I gasped, only then realizing I'd been mimicking Riley's breathing.

Both men held themselves as motionless as statues. Maybe to give Riley time to adjust to the invasion. I'd never had more than a finger in my bottom, and Riley had been the first to do that. Seeing them connected like this, I wondered how it felt. Surely it would be different than having a man in my vagina?

What if I had a man in both holes?

What would it be like to be joined to both my lovers at once? My thighs clenched, and with a desperate cry, I found my clitoris with my index finger. Circling it gently, I allowed the sensations to fill me.

At the same time, Carter pulled back and I caught a glimpse of his shaft, shiny with massage oil, before it quickly disappeared again. Both men groaned, pleasure contorting their expressions.

"Harder," Riley shouted.

"I'm too close."

"Do it."

Carter nodded even though Riley couldn't see him and pistoned his hips. It was amazing to see the flex of his cheeks, the curve of his back, the taut muscles rippling, not to mention the way Riley pushed with his palms to brace against each violent impact. The tendons in his neck stood out in sharp relief as he raised his head and cried out.

My fingers pressed against my clitoris, rubbing back and forth in time with each rock of Carter's hips. And when he reached around Riley's side to grasp his erection, my groans rivaled his.

"Get over here," Riley said, his eyes drilling into me, tracking every movement of my fingers.

My gaze shot to Carter. When he nodded, I hopped off my table and stood beside theirs. Riley patted the space in front of him. "Sit."

I climbed onto the table and straddled it, facing Riley, and awaited his next request.

"Lie down. Legs on my shoulders."

My brows popped. The position would be… delicious. Again, I checked with Carter. If he didn't want me to—

He licked his lips. "Now." His voice had gone incredibly deep, raw even. With a bite. Like that first sip of tequila.

Okay, then. Shifting my hips, I lay back on my elbows. The position opened me up to the men. Exposed all of me to their hungry gazes.

Before I had a chance to reconsider, Riley swiped his broad tongue along my center. "Oh God." When I caught my breath again, I swung my trembling legs over Riley's shoulders.

Carter took hold of my ankles, circling them with his fingers. A loud moan escaped me. When had my ankles become erogenous zones? Heat rolled up my thighs, and another bolt of pleasure shot through my entire body.

While Riley licked and sucked every inch of my sex, Carter began to roll his hips. Riley held his hand up so Carter could pour some oil into it. Should I be concerned that they worked so incredibly well in tandem? Of course, this was hardly their first threesome. The men had openly admitted it.

Seconds later, Riley plunged two slick fingers into me and I forgot all my worries. My hips shot up and took on a rhythm to match Carter's and Riley's thrusts.

My arms quivered and ached with the effort of holding myself up. I lay down and found myself staring into Carter's heat-filled eyes. The pupils were so dilated, the blue was gone except for a single dark ring. He let go of one of my ankles and used his free hand to smooth up and down Riley's spine. Riley arched into his touch like a cat seeking to be petted.

Carter pulled my leg to the side, revealing what Riley was doing to me. It was decadent, sinful, and more exciting than anything I'd ever done.

I brought my hands to my breasts and pinched my nipples the way Riley had done to me. I imagined it was Carter's strong fingers tweaking the tips, squeezing to just this side of pain. My gaze flicked between the two men, my two men.

The tingling sensation spread from my clitoris, linking to Riley's fingers deep inside me, and then filled my entire body with an electric hum. "Oh, God. I'm coming!"

Riley lightened the touch of his tongue to keep me writhing on the edge of the precipice, several seconds that felt like an eternity. Until finally, he raked me gently with his teeth.

I exploded. Soaring on a wave of pleasure. Colors collided behind my eyes, reminding me of what I really wanted to see. Even as my body shook, I trained my gaze on the men in front of me.

Riley raised his head and inhaled my scent as he reached between his own legs and pumped his erection. Carter wrapped his arms around Riley's chest and pulled him up so he was kneeling, then grabbed my calves to tug me closer.

Swatting away Riley's hand, Carter took hold of Riley's erection and moved his tight fist up and down, swirling his oiled palm over the head. I could see the pre-cum leaking from the small slit.

Riley moaned. "Oh, yeah. Fuck. Yeah."

"That's it. I've got you, Rye," Carter whispered. The sweet words and tender expression on his masculine features had tears burning at the backs of my eyes.

Riley must have felt similarly, because his arm snaked up and hooked behind Carter's head, drawing him down for a kiss. The men held onto each other, each with a hand on one of my legs, as they reached completion.

Riley looked down at me. His eyes were soft with lust and something else. He smiled, then cried out. Carter angled Riley's shaft toward me and he emptied onto my belly. Shot after shot of warmth hit me, branded me. Drew my tears.

Carter grunted, his fingers tightening on Riley's flesh and around my calf. His eyes rolled back and his entire body shook. When he finally opened his lids, his gaze landed on me. On Riley's cum on my abdomen. Something flashed in his stare moments before he nudged Riley forward.

Riley braced himself over me. Carter blanketed him and ran a finger between my thighs, slicking it up with my juices. I gasped, then gasped again when he scooped up some cum from my belly before popping the well-coated finger between his lips.

"Mmm... so good," he said on a groan. "Your tastes are the perfect mix."

Riley elbowed him in the ribs. "Selfish bastard."

Carter glared. "Get your own."

Laughing at their antics, I forgot to be self-conscious of my position. Okay, "forgot" might have been too strong a word. Either way, I didn't care. Joining in the fun, I eased a finger along my folds, taking care to dip it into myself. A small moan escaped my lips and both men's jaws tightened.

This was a new experience for me, this sense of power, of being able to hold the undivided attention of not one, but two very strong and able men. Devoid of any remaining sense of decency, I scooped up some cum on my finger and brought it to my own mouth. I could taste myself and Riley. But something was missing.

Carter.

As though he'd read my thoughts, Carter eased off Riley's back and came to stand beside me. His large hand cupped my cheek. "Share?"

Smiling, I nodded. He bent to kiss me, swirling his tongue around mine, coating it, combining all our tastes in his mouth.

"Mmm... yes," I said.

Carter smiled and kissed Riley, and Riley kissed me.

"Perfect," Riley said.

"Perfect," Carter and I echoed.

The three of us were perfect together. And for the next nine days, I wanted to enjoy this perfection to the utmost, because the memories of these few days with these amazing men would have to last me a lifetime.

CARTER

Riley had been right about everything. The two of us with Paige, the three of us together. Maybe this could actually work.

Feeling on top of the world, I strode through the streets of Chawton with my two lovers. The quaint village had been the home of Jane Austen during the last eight years of her life. I'd loved seeing Paige fan girl as we toured Chawton House, Jane Austen's house and garden. Even Riley had been a little moved seeing the Elizabethan manor, especially the library, where Jane was thought to have penned her final three novels.

After visiting the house and museum, the tour group had split up, and I found myself enjoying the beautiful afternoon in the presence of two of my favorite people. We strolled along the old-fashioned streets admiring the shops and boutiques as well as some old thatched-roof cottages.

We were just about to enter a tea shop for some refreshments when Paige's phone rang. She squinted down at the number and frowned. "You guys go ahead. I have to take this."

"No problem," Riley said.

"We'll wait for you here," I insisted. Even though we'd probably be able to see Paige through the shop's windows, I wasn't comfortable leaving her alone outside in a foreign town.

"Thanks," she said, then answered. "Hello, Vanessa. What's going on?"

Paige listened as the caller talked, her expression hardening. After a minute or so, she interrupted, "Vanessa. Vanessa"—her voice rose—"Vanessa. Are you listening? Yes, okay. Now, before I left, I gave you very clear instructions about everything you needed to do each day to get the advertising campaign rolling for the Extreme Sports-aholic tour. Did you or did you not send the graphics to the printer two weeks ago?"

Hearing Paige's tone, the hair on my nape rose, and I arched a brow at Riley. Riley shrugged and looked away. Paige seemed very angry at this Vanessa person, whoever she was. Probably another guide who worked with Paige. But why then would she be taking instructions from Paige? Unless Vanessa was a junior tour guide or a new hire, in which case, perhaps Paige was being a bit hard on her.

"Vanessa, that's not what I asked. Yes or no?"

There was a moment of silence, during which Paige pressed two fingers to her brow. "And why not?"

Vanessa's panicked squawking reached a level I could hear although I couldn't make out the words.

"And you didn't think to call me? Or ask Arianna?"

Paige's jaw clenched and her fingers whitened around the phone. "You told me I could count on you, but clearly I can't. Now, make sure you do exactly as I say. Save the graphics on a USB key and go down to Miami Pro Print. Talk to Joe, the owner. Tell him we will pay him double his rates if he can print the portfolios by tomorrow at four—then do what you have to do to get him to agree. Second, you'll wait at the printer's tomorrow, and as soon as the copies are ready, get in your car—then hire a darn cab—and go hand-deliver them to Brenda at Dream Sports."

Paige inhaled deeply and curled a strand of hair behind her ear. "It'll be okay, Vanessa, but you shouldn't have let it get to this point before calling me. We'll talk about that when I return." Fortunately, Paige had calmed down. Vanessa must have fucked up badly for Paige to get so upset.

Riley nudged my shoulder and when I turned to him, he waggled his brows up and down. "Rawr. I love when the claws come out."

I glanced down, and sure enough, Riley was raring to go. "Strong women can be sexy as hell, but in this case, I feel sorry for Vanessa. Paige reminded me a bit too much of my ex-wife."

"Livia? How so?"

We'd never discussed my marriage in much detail, but it was time Riley knew. If Paige was anything like Livia, I wanted no part of her. "Livia was all about her career: driven, cool under pressure, organized, and intelligent. I really admired her when we met while she was in law school. But after she ended up at a high-powered firm, she changed. I used to find her need for control challenging and kind of endearing. Until it turned into her way or the highway. The final straw was when she admitted she'd lied about wanting to have kids. She moved on to a senior partner at her firm. He could get her a junior partnership, and I sure as shit didn't look as good on her arm."

"Fuck. I had no idea it was that bad." He rubbed my back. "That bitch didn't deserve you."

Paige approached us. "Sorry you had to hear that."

I crossed my arms. "Problem at work?" I needed to know why she'd gotten so worked up.

When she slid her phone into her purse, Paige's hair fell over her face. Riley brushed it back and she smiled at him, as warm and sweet as ever. The dichotomy was unsettling.

"Vanessa, one of my employees, dropped the ball on a big ad campaign we're working on," Paige said, rubbing her temple. "I told Ari—she's my boss—that it was a bad idea for me to act as tour guide on this trip."

The bottom fell out of my stomach. "Act as?"

"Didn't Riley tell you? I'm the marketing director at Total Indulgence Tours. The tour guide assigned to this trip broke her leg, and Ari asked me to fill in at the last minute."

I glared at Riley as I clarified things. "So you're *not* a tour guide?"

"No." Paige laughed. "All that traveling would wear me out, besides I have to stay—" Her cheeks reddening, she cut herself off and looked away.

"Have to stay…?" I prodded.

"In Miami. Anyway, I love planning the trips far more than I enjoy taking them. Well…" She blushed. "Usually. I'm pretty much a homebody."

"Hey," Riley said, stepping between us. "What do you say we go in? I'm starving."

Paige's stomach growled. She patted it and her eyes sparkled. "Me too. I guess I'm not used to so much… exercise."

Chuckling, Riley circled his arm around her waist and led her inside the tea shop to a round table toward the back. Even in a small place like this, Riley always had to be mindful of being spotted. Fans weren't really a problem, except that they tended to post snapshots online of their celebrity sightings, and within minutes, the paparazzi would swarm. It had happened too many times for me to be fazed by it anymore. Luckily, I'd always managed to keep my face out of the photos, and remain Riley Kendrick's "mystery man." Which was way I still had a job. I wondered how Paige would feel about dealing with the press.

After ordering, Paige excused herself to go to the restroom. I stared out the front window and considered the similarities between Paige and Livia. They both held positions of authority at work, but was Paige as single-mindedly focused on her career as Livia had been? I hadn't gotten that sense, but I'd been wrong before, and it had cost me years of my life.

Riley's foot connected with my shin. "Ow!" I glared at him.

He glowered back. "What crawled up your ass?"

"You kicked me!" I countered incredulously.

"For good reason. Why are you so gloom and doom all of a sudden?"

"You should have told me."

"Told you what?"

"Don't play stupid, Professor Kendrick."

"Shh!" Riley hissed, glancing surreptitiously around the small space.

"You know why I'm pissed."

"Yes, and this is exactly why I didn't tell you. Paige is the same woman, whether she's a tour guide or a marketing director."

"I don't know, man," I said, unconvinced. "You heard her out there. I'm going to have recurring nightmares now."

Under the table, Riley rested his hand on my thigh. The weight and warmth steadied me. He shook his head. "That ballbreaker ex-wife of yours gave you PTSD."

"I don't have PTSD," I shot back.

"You sure?"

I crossed my arms and stared down at the scarred tabletop. I wasn't sure at all. "So, I'm a little gun-shy. Can you blame me?"

"Don't you think I am too? I wasn't married to Amber and Holden, but that didn't mean I wasn't invested in the relationship."

Goddamn, it was embarrassing talking about my feelings like this. But Riley wasn't going to stop until we'd had it out. "At least you didn't give them seven years of your life. At least you didn't uproot yourself, leave your family, and trudge off to New York City to work in an inner-city school while she mingled with the who's who of Manhattan." I shook my head. "Man, the things I saw there. It was a far cry from Essex, Vermont."

Riley barked out a laugh. "And Starr Farm Beach is a village compared to LA."

"Uh-uh, professor boy. Starr Farm Beach is the Manhattan of Vermont," I teased. "Maybe if I'd had a house on Lake Champlain like you, I could have tempted Livia to stay in state for law school."

"Nah." Riley tapped on the table. "It didn't work for Amber, and it certainly wouldn't have worked for Livia. If anything, they're the ones who were alike. They both wanted more than they had. Desperately. Neither cared who they had to use to get it."

I cocked my head. Now we were getting somewhere. "You think Amber used you?"

"Not at first. I mean, I was a lowly college professor when we met." Riley's expression turned from one of sweet remembrance to one of a bitter aftertaste. I knew how much the breakup with Amber and Holden had hurt Riley. Not to mention that she'd taken him to the cleaners in court afterward. "But when the books started, then the movies… she had our LA condo picked out before the ink was even dry on the contract."

I dropped my head onto the table. "Makes me wonder if we can ever trust any woman again."

"Oh hey now. Stop generalizing. Livia was as driven as you can get. Amber too, in her own way."

"And Paige isn't?" I sat up. "The way she sounded out there… You have to admit the similarities are rather striking."

Riley shrugged. "Personally, I think she sounded more like an angry mom. Tough love and all that." He gave my thigh a last squeeze before resting his elbows on the table and cupping my fists. "Paige is a warm, caring, and generous woman. In bed and out. Can you say that, could you *ever* say that, about Livia?"

I thought back to the early years of my relationship with my ex-wife. Even then, she'd been a selfish lover, wanting to be lavished with attention while returning only a fraction of it. At the time it hadn't bothered me… much. She'd been sexy as hell, and I'd just wanted to sink my cock into her. But as I grew up, I'd matured, become more empathetic, and she hadn't. In the end, our relationship had devolved into a toxic dynamic where I gave everything, and she took everything.

On the other hand, given her age, Paige was already the woman she was destined to be. And that was one who was independent and determined while still remaining down to earth and fun.

Her career wasn't the problem, my perception of it was.

Returning to our table, Paige smiled at both of us. "I'm so happy to be here with the two of you. I want you to know that."

"I am too." I took Paige's hand, and Riley placed his over mine.

Riley beamed at us. "It's a dream come true."

Although a ménage relationship had never been my dream like it had been Riley's, I was beginning to see the appeal. These last few days had been some of the best of my life. But could such a complicated relationship stand the test of time, of society, and its judgments?

I was getting ahead of myself. First we had to see if what we had could endure through the end of the trip.

Chapter 11

RILEY

How had I gotten so lucky, finding my two perfect muses? I flipped through the photos I'd taken with my phone earlier that afternoon when I, Paige, Carter, and a few others from the group had opted to go on a river tour of historic Canterbury. A guide had rowed us up the river to The Grey Friars, a small Franciscan island. We were treated to gorgeous views of the King's Bridge, as well as several medieval structures, like the Old Weavers House, the King's Mill, and a Cromwellian iron forge.

Each successive location had made my fingers itch with the need to write. So while Paige and Carter had gone to afternoon tea at the hotel's rooftop restaurant with the group, I had hightailed it back to the hotel.

Setting the phone aside, I returned to my manuscript and layered setting details into the scene I'd just written: a sexy romp where my characters—Riley, Paige, and Carter—yes, I would change their names later—engaged in a sinfully delightful escapade under the stars as their gondola drifted over the calm waters in a canal city oddly reminiscent of Canterbury. Literary license, what a wonderful tool to have in the writer's toolkit.

I read over the scene one more time, correcting a few typos, making the dialogue a little snappier, and deepening the emotional connection between my characters. My entire body buzzed with the knowledge that what I'd written worked. Really worked. The writing had flowed from my fingertips like blood from a vein. It wasn't yet as good as the Amber books. I'd need Nora's input to reach that level. Still, it was a great first draft. And most importantly, I was writing again. Writing and enjoying it.

Coming on this trip had been a stellar idea. I'd have to buy Nora an appropriate thank-you gift. Not only had I found my muse, but I'd found it in the guise of Paige and Carter. The combination of my two lovers had been the magic missing ingredient. Paige had gotten my ideas percolating again, but it wasn't until that first threesome at the hotel in Stratford-upon-Avon that I'd felt the surge of energy, the focus that made everything else fade away.

The zone, some called it. I loved being in the zone. Hours would fly by as my fingers pounded the letters off my keyboard. Afterward, I'd feel drained, yet immensely satisfied. My mind finally relieved of the task of giving birth to my characters through the telling of their journeys.

God, it was great to be a writer again.

Pushing back my chair, I stood and pressed my fists on either side of my spine at the base, then leaned back to stretch it out. These hotel chairs left something to be desired. Nothing a hot shower wouldn't cure though.

I glanced at my watch. Paige and Carter would be back soon. I'd have to make it a quick one. Tossing off my clothes on my way to the bathroom, I couldn't resist imagining what shenanigans we'd get up to that evening. I could hardly wait to get my hands on Paige's creamy breasts and Carter's rock hard glutes. My life was damn near perfect right now.

After turning on the water and adjusting the temperature, I hopped in and quickly took care of the business of washing my hair and body while I let the hot water soothe away the lingering tightness in my lower back. I thought I heard the room door close, but when I called out, there was no answer.

Once I was done, I stepped out of the narrow shower stall and dried myself off. Naked, I walked over to the wardrobe and searched for my distressed Balmain skinny jeans and favorite Fendi monster eyes T-shirt. Since we had no plans to go out this evening, I could leave Professor Templeton in the closet for a few more hours.

I tossed the clothes onto the bed, then scooped up the remote to switch on the TV so I could catch the news. That's when I spotted Carter sitting at the desk, scrolling through something on my laptop.

A sick feeling of dread cramped my stomach. No one read my work before Nora. No one. "What the hell are you doing?"

Carter swung the chair around. His brow was furrowed so deeply a V shot up from the point between his eyes. "What am *I* doing? What the hell are *you* doing?" He jabbed a finger at the screen.

I stalked across the room and tried to slam the laptop shut. Hopefully, he hadn't read more than a page or two. "Don't read that. It's just a draft."

Carter stood and blocked my arm. "Too late."

When he released my arm, I tried again to close the laptop, but once more he stopped me. "Tell me, Riley. Are you going to write about this too?" He picked me up and dropped me on the bed. "About how your incensed lover manhandled you?"

Carter jammed his fists on his hips and snarled, "What comes next? Does 'Riley' seduce his boyfriend? Does he make 'Carter' forget how 'Riley' is using him and 'Paige' for sex and for story ideas?"

I stared at Carter, my mouth hanging open. In awe. In astonishment. Certainly, in concern. But never in fear. "I-I found my muse," I tried to explain.

"So you've said."

I pushed myself up into a sitting position and rested my elbows on my knees as I thought about what to say. How to explain it better.

Carter gripped his hair so tightly I was sure he'd rip it out of his skull. "Jesus Christ, Rye." He picked up my clothes and threw them into my lap. "At least have the decency to get dressed."

"The decency? You've never minded my nakedness before."

"A fuck won't make this go away."

"No?" I pouted, then shrugged into my T-shirt. I scooched over to the edge of the bed and slipped my legs into my jeans.

"Riley," Carter growled.

"What? You said get dressed. I'm fucking getting dressed."

Carter arched a brow. "Commando? Really? You know what that does to me."

Yes, I did know. In fact it played into the plans Paige and I had made for tonight. Plans that now seemed rather moot. Damn. And I'd really been looking forward to our night together. It would have been the ideal reward for a productive writing session. Instead, I was getting irritated, my high ruined. "You're a big boy. Deal with it."

"Fine." Carter walked over to the sliding glass door and leaned his forehead against it, his powerful arms braced on the frame. "Explain to me what's going on. This thing between us, between you, me, and Paige, is it real, or is it something you instigated just so you could write another damn book?"

"Fuck, no. Of course not." I sent Carter what I hoped was a sweet smile. "Truth is, you inspire me. Both of you."

Carter turned around and leaned against the glass. His face was tight, angry, his eyes disappointed. He shook his head. "What are your characters' names, huh? Riley, Carter, and Paige. Sound familiar?"

Oh God. How could I explain my writing process to Carter? "The names will be changed in the final version."

"Uh-huh. Like they were changed in the Amber books."

"That's different. Amber wanted her name in the books."

"Riley, for fuck's sake."

"All right. All right." I opened my arms wide. "So I get a little inspiration from my real life. Why is that such a big deal to you?"

"Because"—Carter pushed off the door—"you can't keep manipulating the people around you into situations that make for a good story."

"Manipulating?" My face heated like I'd walked into a wall of fire. "I've never manipulated anyone in my life. *I'm* the one who was manipulated. *I'm* the one who was betrayed. *I'm* the one who's fucking broke while Amber and Holden are living it up on my goddamn dime."

Chest heaving, fists clenching and unclenching, I glared at Carter, whose eyes had widened with each successive word. "Well?" I prodded when the silence went on for too long. If we were going to fight it out, we'd damn well do it right. "Say something."

"I don't know what to say." Carter rubbed his jaw as he approached, stopping right in front of me. "Are you a fiction writer or an autobiographer? Things didn't go so well for you on a personal level last time. You sure you want to repeat history?"

"It's the only way I know how to write."

"Bullshit. Thing is, if you honestly care about me and Paige, if we're all equals in this relationship as you claim to want, then you need to get your head out of your ass. There are *three* of us involved. This isn't just about *you*." Carter ended on a thunderous note.

My heart stuttered, seemed to stop, then started racing. Was Carter going to leave me over this?

"Carter." I reached for his hand, but he pulled it away.

"I can't—" Carter cut himself off. Teeth clenched, he crossed the room to the door.

Completely bewildered, I chased after him. "Where are you going?"

"To think. About me. About us. About what *I* want." His face darkened. "You should do the same."

"But you'll be back, right?"

Carter blinked, then left the room.

He blinked? Oh fuck. Did that mean yes or no?

This can't be happening.

I lurched over to a chair. Fuck. Fuck. I stamped my foot on the floor. I wouldn't lose Carter, or Paige for that matter, over a book. Whatever I had to do to get them back, I would.

But what? What are you going to do, Kendrick?

All I knew was that I needed these two people in my life. Not just for the duration of the trip, and especially not for a book.

I had to make them understand, even though neither of them was ready to hear the truth.

CARTER

I marched down to the hotel bar. God, Riley could be infuriating. He didn't seem to understand that not everyone wanted to live their lives on the front page. Did he even remember that I taught kids? That schools and parents were incredibly concerned about the character of the people interacting with their children for eight hours a day? I couldn't be frolicking on the pages of an erotic novel, for Christ's sake!

I entered the dark wood-paneled pub and took a seat at the bar. "What can I get you, mate?" the bartender asked.

"Whiskey, neat."

The barman nodded and took down a bottle and poured out two fingers of rich brown liquid. He slid the glass over to me. I took a sip, the whiskey igniting a mild fire as it slid down my throat. How could I make Riley understand? While I was overjoyed that he was writing again, I couldn't be a star in whatever story he was spinning for the public.

Someone nudged my elbow. "Hey there," Paige said. "You look like you could use some company."

"You're probably right."

Her brow crinkled adorably. "What's wrong?"

"Not sure I should tell you." I stared into my drink, but no answer was forthcoming.

"Well, I'm willing to listen. No matter what it is." She placed a hand on my forearm, squeezing gently.

I sighed. I should tell her. She deserved to know. "Riley is writing again."

She nodded. "I'm glad he's worked through the writer's block."

"He spoke to you about it?"

"A few days after we met, I realized how keyed up he was. He seemed really unhappy. So I asked him about it."

Wow. No wonder Riley liked her so much. I had been with him for three months, and I'd never thought to ask. Even worse, I hadn't realized the stress Riley was under until right before he'd left.

He was right. Paige was nothing like Livia. Paige actually cared about people.

And that meant she'd probably be as upset as I was about what Riley had done. I took a deep breath. "Have you read any of what he's written?"

She shook her head. "No. Why?"

"He's writing about us, Paige. The three of us."

She frowned a bit, then shrugged. "It's fiction, right?"

"That's just it. He used our names. He described things we've done, where we've done them. It reads more like a diary than a novel."

Paige's eyes went round. "He used our *names*?"

"In all fairness, he said he plans to change them."

"I should hope so!"

I reached out and took her hand. "Am I out in left field here? I feel like this is Amber and Holden all over again."

"That was real?"

"More or less. My understanding is he took most of it from what actually happened."

"He's really writing about *us*?"

I nodded. "Seems like it."

Paige clapped a hand over her open mouth, then let it drop to her lap. "My God, he did say I was his muse…" She shook her head frantically. "I can't have him writing about me. What will everyone say?"

"Riley seems to believe I'm blowing it out of proportion."

"Doesn't he realize he'll wreck our lives? Especially yours. You could be fired."

"Exactly. I wouldn't care so much if it was only me who'd be affected, but I help support my mom and my little brother." I waited a moment for her to mull things over, then I said, "What are we going to do?"

"I don't know," Paige said, slowly shaking her head. "I need to think about this. This is turning out to be way more involved than I had planned." She hugged her arms around herself, and I took off my jacket and placed it around her shoulders. She looked at me and touched my cheek. "I haven't even had sex in the past five years, and now I find out I'm going to be in a book? Having sex with two men?"

I placed my hand over hers on my cheek. "Don't worry. I won't let him do this to you. To us." I leaned forward and pressed my lips to hers.

And I wouldn't. I didn't want to kill Riley's desire to write, but he couldn't be allowed to ruin our lives either.

PAIGE

Riley might be more trouble than he was worth sometimes, but Carter was the kind of man you could lean on. I could really see myself falling for him. He'd known exactly how to calm me down, keep me from charging up to their room and giving Riley a piece of my mind about using us in his writing.

"Thanks for hanging out with me this evening." Switching off the television, I smiled up at Carter and sank deeper into his hold.

"Mmm..." He kissed my neck. "It was dinner and a movie with you or more fighting with Riley. The choice wasn't a difficult one."

"Wow," I joked. "That certainly puts me in my place."

"Oh shit." Carter's lips left my neck and when he sat up, his face was red. "Paige, I'm so sorry. That's not what I meant at all."

I patted his thigh. "Relax, I'm teasing."

He laced our fingers and kissed my knuckles. "I'm not sure what I would've done if I hadn't run into you." He shot me a sidelong glance. "Probably gotten drunk and regretted it in the morning."

"I'm glad too." I rested my head on his chest. The steady beat of his heart, so strong and bold, wrapped around me. "It gave us a chance to get to know each other better."

"And I've loved every second of it."

"But?"

He kissed the top of my head. "I should be going."

"You could stay, you know."

Releasing my fingers, he took my chin in his hand and pressed his lips to mine in a soft, sweet kiss that made my insides quake. I opened my mouth wider, deepening the kiss.

Much to my disappointment, after a few minutes Carter lessened the intensity of our embrace until he ended it with a last tug of his teeth on my bottom lip. "As soon as I walk out the door, I know I'm going to regret leaving."

"Then stay."

"You sure you're ready for that?" he asked, searching my face. "Because if I stay, there's no way I'll be able to resist all this"—his hand moved up and down my side before settling over my breast. "I will have you."

Could I have sex with Carter without feeling like a cheater if Riley wasn't present? Sure Carter and I had kissed and, well, *more* at the masquerade ball on our own, but that hadn't been behind Riley's back while we were in the middle of a serious disagreement. I was upset with Riley, and quite frankly, I wasn't certain I could forgive him if he tried to publish what he'd written about the three of us. Perhaps my intense desire for Carter tonight was really just a need for comfort.

My eyes met the banked fire in his gaze and took in the tender, loving way he held me. No, my feelings for Carter went beyond the need for comfort, beyond mere attraction. I genuinely enjoyed spending time with him, with or without Riley.

But sex?

"Good question," I said, finally.

He stroked a finger through the hair that clung to the side of my cheek. "That's answer enough for me."

"What about you? Would you be ready?"

"Physically?" He pushed his hips up, drawing my eye to the front of his jeans, which were definitely no longer flat. "Emotionally? Not so much."

"You miss him."

"I love him, and I'm worried. In retrospect, I realize now that before this trip, he'd really been struggling to write, and both psychologically and financially, it had been weighing on him. Not that he'd mentioned any of this to me until right before he left. But that's no excuse; I should have seen it." He pursed his lips, then shook his head. After a moment, he looked into my eyes and smiled. "But the last few days, he's been so excited about his work. He can't wait to sit at his laptop and write. Last night, I woke up to the clickety-clack of his keyboard. I watched him work for a while. He was so into it, laser-focused. Honestly, I've never seen him like that before, and I really don't want to take that away from him."

I looked down and flicked my nail against a rivet in the pocket of Carter's jeans. "I don't either, but, like I said earlier, I really can't have him writing about me."

"I know." He cupped my cheek in his large, warm palm. "We'll talk about it tomorrow. All three of us together."

Releasing me, he rose. "Thank you for everything. Despite the circumstances, I had a great time."

I followed him to the door. "Me too. Are you going back to your room?"

He grinned. "Yeah. I think I've given Riley enough time to stew."

"You're good for him, you know that?"

"You are too. For both of us." Stepping closer to me, Carter kissed me once more. "Good night, Paige."

"Good night."

After watching his retreating back all the way to the elevator, I quietly closed the door. I leaned against it and pressed my hands to my flaming face. What was I doing? At first it had been Riley, a consummate star, passionate and commanding in any disguise, who'd enchanted me. Then Carter had shown up, and I'd been drawn in by his compassion and the warmth of his personality. A natural-born caretaker like me, he was easy to talk to and a pleasure to be around.

There was no question I was attracted to both men. Thank goodness this could never be more than a vacation fling. Here, it was easy to hide the fact that I was involved with the two of them, especially since everyone had caught on to Riley and Carter being a couple. But in the real world, this kind of thing just wasn't possible.

Riley did it with Amber and Holden.

Yes, and look how that had turned out. Riley had been a rising star in the book world, a celebrity hunted by the paparazzi, with his photos published in entertainment magazines. And even then, the three-way relationship that had seemed so loving and solid in *Amber's Triumph*, had crumbled under the pressure of public scrutiny. My investigations on the Internet had provided me ample evidence of that. Some of the photos of Riley after the breakup, looking so dejected and heartbroken, had literally brought me to tears.

I didn't want him to be hurt like that again.

You mean you don't want to be hurt like you were when Dylan left you and Emma.

Damn it all. Why did life have to be so complicated? Shoving off the door, I went to get ready for bed. When I slid under the covers, my phone rang. It was Ari.

"Hello, Arianna."

Ari snickered, putting me immediately on alert. "I heard you had some fun at the house party."

"W-what? What did you hear?"

"Oh, you know something about the tour guide getting a lot of attention from two rather hunky men."

"Oh God." I buried my face in my pillow.

"What was that?" Ari asked.

"Nothing."

Arianna burst into laughter. "You're my hero. Seriously, Paige, I didn't think you had it in you."

Hearing the double entendre, my entire body went up in flames. I kept my lips cemented shut, hoping Ari wouldn't catch on.

No such luck.

"Oh! Oh my God. And Daniel always said I didn't have a funny bone. Wait until I tell him about this."

"No!" Realizing I'd just yelled at my boss, I took a deep breath and tried again. "Please, don't tell anyone about this. Especially not Daniel or Javier."

"Okay, okay. Calm down. I was only having some fun with you." There was some rustling over the phone line followed by the crack and pop of a soft drink can being opened. "But seriously, I heard from the staff that the actors you hired had a hell of a good time."

I groaned. "No kidding. Doors were opening and closing all night long."

Ari laughed. "Yep, sounds about right. I swear people go on these tours for the sex rather than the sights."

"I had no idea."

"I did," Ari said, and her meaning was instantly clear to me.

My boss, my friend, had sent me on this trip, knowing my chances of getting laid were extremely high. "Ari!" I scolded her.

"Don't take that tone with me," she teased. "*I* only gave you the opportunity. *You're* the one who hopped on and rode it."

"Oh God." I buried my face in the pillow again.

"Come on, girl. Own it. Tell me, how are things going with Misters Hot-as-Fuck and Fucking-Hot?"

"Exactly as the caterer tattled," I said, deadpan.

"Lucky bitch."

I cracked up at that. I could always count on Ari to lighten the mood. "Seriously though, they're both amazing. But"—my smile fell—"today, Carter discovered that Riley's been writing about us."

"What do you mean? About you and him?"

"No. About the *three* of us. According to Carter, Riley's writing a story that involves three characters named Paige, Riley, and Carter. Oh yes. He used our names. And although the settings are different, the actions and dialogue are a little more than 'inspired' by actual events." Simply saying it had my blood boiling.

"You can't be serious."

"Oh, but I am."

"Well, first off, don't jump to any conclusions. Talk to him. Maybe this is just part of his process. Or maybe it's not his actual book. Maybe it's like therapy. Either way, talk to him and find out what's really going on."

"It's pretty clear. His Amber books were true to life. He told Carter that this is the only way he knows how to write."

"Did he seem like he was using you? In the Amber books, Riley really did seem to fall for Amber and Holden."

I sat up and used the pillows to cushion my back, then banged my head against the wall. Repeatedly. "I feel like I'm going crazy. I must have been lust-drunk. That's what this is, right?"

"I don't think you have to be crazy or lust-drunk to enjoy the attention of two gorgeous men. Women the world over would kill to be you right now."

"Until this happened, I'd been having a fabulous time with them." I thought back to my pleasant evening with Carter. Maybe I was a one-man kind of woman after all. An image of Riley popped into my mind, making my belly clench. Oh, who was I kidding? I didn't want one without the other.

"I don't know what to think about how I feel," I said softly.

"Oh, honey. It's simple. I can hear it in your voice all the way from Miami. You're in love with both of them."

I shook my head even though Ari couldn't see me. "That's impossible."

"Is it?"

Ari was wrong. I wasn't like that. I didn't fall in love at first sight. "I've known Riley for two weeks. Carter for less than one."

"Sometimes," Ari began, "it's that fast. Look at me and Daniel. We got married two weeks after we met."

Brilliant example, I thought uncharitably. "And look how that turned out."

"We were in love."

"I think you still are." Despite their divorce a year ago, I often caught Ari and Daniel sneaking glances at each other. The longing between them was palpable.

Ari huffed. "We're not talking about me right now. We're discussing you and your two hotties."

I groaned. "I don't know what to do."

"Talk to Riley and see if you can get past what he's done."

"But a threesome? Or is it a triad?" I sighed in frustration. "Is that really me?"

"Look, you don't have to put a label on it. See what develops. Just have fun."

We said our goodbyes, her words echoing in my head. *See what develops.*

Sure, I could do that. Except something developing was exactly what I was afraid of. If I did fall for them, then when the trip ended in a week, and everyone went home, Riley and Carter would go together. I'd be left alone. And heartbroken.

You can't be heartbroken if you aren't already in love.

I silently screamed at the voice in my head and threw a pillow against the far wall. I was *not* in love with two men.

Definitely not.

Chapter 12

RILEY

How was I going to fix this? Carter and Paige had barely spoken to me all day, and even though Carter had come back to our room last night, he'd slept on the couch instead of sharing the bed with me, and when I had tried to talk to him about it, he'd said he wouldn't discuss it without Paige being there.

We'd toured the cathedral at Canterbury in the morning, and with my gut in one big knot, I was barely able to follow a word of what the guide said. All I could think about was how I'd tried to give Carter a blow job after we'd woken up, but he'd brushed me off. "No more games," he'd said.

Is that what Carter thought, what Paige thought? That this was all a *game* to me?

It wasn't a game. It was my life. If I couldn't write about it, what was I going to do? I'd tried to write something else. But that hadn't worked. So now what?

I lay back on the bed in our room. We'd reached London around midafternoon and were back at the Grosvenor Hotel. We'd spent the afternoon at Covent Garden, and now Carter was having dinner with Paige at The Lamb and Flag pub, one of Charles Dickens's favorite watering holes, and I hadn't been invited.

Was I going to lose Paige and Carter to each other? Was this going to be Amber and Holden all over again?

Fuck that. That was *not* happening. I needed to fix this. And I needed to fix it now.

By the time I reached The Lamb and Flag, my heart was pounding. And when I looked in the front window and saw Paige and Carter laughing over their pints, I had to take a deep breath before I stormed in there and said something I shouldn't.

But I *had* to say something. *Do* something. That much was clear. I opened the door and headed to their table. Paige saw me first, and she paused mid-sip and put her pint glass down, her face shifting from laughter to something far more somber.

I pulled out the chair beside her, sat without asking permission, and crossed my arms. "Enough with the bullshit. We need to talk. All three of us."

Carter set his pint down with a thunk. "I don't think you're in a position to make demands."

"I'm not? What about asking for you both to hear me out? Instead of pushing me away and turning your backs like we're kids on the playground."

"We're not being childish—" Carter started, but Paige cut him off.

"We kind of are," she said. "It's okay for us to be upset, but the silent treatment is pretty passive-aggressive."

Carter was silent for a second, then he smiled. "You're right." He dipped his head in acknowledgment. The smile faded when he looked at me though. "We're listening."

Thank God. My gut was still a mess, but I could breathe a little easier now. "I'm sorry. I didn't think about the consequences of what I was doing. I was so excited to be writing again. Really writing. I haven't been this happy in a long time." I shifted in my chair and uncrossed my arms, reaching for and taking their hands in mine. "I haven't been this happy since Amber and Holden. And yesterday and today, all this tension, the two of you going off together, stirred up a lot of shit for me. A lot of fear." My insides quivered as I looked from Carter to Paige.

She squeezed my hand. "Were you more upset about losing Amber or losing Holden?"

"Both. I wanted them both."

Carter leaned forward, his face so stern I wasn't sure what to think. "Is that what you want now?"

My heart started beating fast, my breathing going shallow. I swallowed hard. "Yes." The words slipped out, my voice barely audible above the clamor of the lively pub.

"You can't write about us, though," Paige said, her voice soft but firm.

"I'm not. I'm really not. I know it seems like it, and I'm sorry. And if it's making you so unhappy, I'll write a different story. I just don't know how to do that."

Paige smiled, the first one she'd directed my way in what seemed like ages. "You're at a writers' retreat. There are lots of people you can ask for advice."

"Who? Lori? She can barely put a kiss on the page without turning red."

"What about Kenji?" Carter asked.

"God no." I could imagine the look on Kenji's face. His utter glee at my coming to him for help. No doubt he'd enjoy telling me "Hell no." And I would deserve it.

"Kenji is a good choice. He knows your situation," Carter said. "And I've read his work. He's really, really good."

"He is?" I asked.

"You haven't read him? He won a Lambda last year."

"He did?" How did I not know this?

Carter shook his head. "Now I understand why he's so mad at you."

I reddened. "Well, it's not only that. He asked me for help finding an agent a few years ago. And I was too wound up in my own shit to help."

Paige spoke up. "He really seems like a nice guy. I think he would help you if you asked."

"He's going to make me grovel."

Carter chuckled. "That would be good for you."

I took a deep breath. Fuck. I let the breath out. "You're probably right. On both counts." I looked at Carter, then at Paige. "So, can we continue as we are, at least for the rest of this trip?"

He nodded, and Paige leaned forward and kissed my cheek. "Thank you for listening to us."

Carter still seemed a little unsettled though; I could see it in the stiff set of his shoulders. "What's wrong?"

Carter's jaw worked and he took a gulp from his pint, withdrawing his hand from my grasp. His eyes flicked to Paige, and she nodded.

Fuck. So there *was* something they were keeping from me. "Tell me."

"Do you even remember what I do for a living?"

"You teach. Like I used to."

"Yeah. And remember what happened when people found out about you and Amber?"

"I got fired. But she was my student. That's not the situation we're in."

"But I teach young, especially vulnerable, kids. Not to mention I have a morality clause in my contract. And having my sex life—my unusual sex life—splashed all over the pages of a novel or the front page of the National Enquirer isn't 'proper and fitting' behavior for a special-ed teacher."

Oh. My cheeks flamed. "I'm sorry. That didn't even cross my mind.

We're all adults here. We should be able to do what we want."

"We should," he said. "But I can't."

"I get it," I said. "Message received."

Staring at the table, Carter nodded, then he looked up at me. "I took a risk just being with you, Rye. Once I knew who you were, I thought about staying away. I really did."

I stared at him openmouthed. "You did?"

"But I couldn't." His eyes misted. "I can't."

"Carter," Paige said, and she reached over to take his hands.

I felt frozen. Carter had thought about leaving me? Because of who I was? He'd never said a thing.

Probably because he shouldn't have had to. If I'd thought about it, for even a minute. "Christ," I said, my voice sounding rusty. "I'm such a pig. It's one thing for me not to keep up with Kenji's life, but to not even think about what being with me would mean to your life, your job?" I shook my head. "You *shouldn't* forgive me."

Carter laughed but there wasn't much joy in it. "I don't think you've been listening to me. I don't have any choice. I love you."

"And I love you." I glanced at Paige. She was smiling, her own eyes welling up. God, I wanted to say it to her too. But it felt too soon, like I'd be pressing her for a commitment.

I still had six days before we were due to part. And that meant I had six days to show her that what I felt for her was real. So that when I told her, she'd believe it. Carter too.

Because all three of us had to be together. Anything less was unacceptable. I leaned over and kissed Paige's cheek. "What do you say we go back to the hotel?" I asked the two of them.

Paige and Carter looked at each other, then at me, before nodding. What was that look about? There was heat there, and something else. Another secret?

Well, I was getting to the bottom of that before the night was through.

This time we went back to my and Carter's room instead of Paige's. We'd barely shut the door before Carter was in my arms, kissing me roughly, then he turned to Paige and drew her close, kissing her deeply just inches from my own lips. When Carter released Paige's mouth, he urged me to kiss her, and God, she tasted so sweet. My cock ground against her belly, and she whimpered into my mouth, that sound that got me rock hard in a second.

We parted, the three of us loosely draped around each other, all of us breathing hard. My pulse was throbbing in my cock, urging me on, but I had to know first what was going on between Paige and Carter.

"The two of you looked at each other before we left the pub. Like you're keeping something from me."

And there it was again, that look passing between them. Finally Carter spoke. "We almost slept together last night."

"Why didn't you?"

"Because it felt like cheating," Paige said. "We were fighting. It didn't seem right."

"I would've been okay with it," I said. But was that the truth?

Carter shook his head. "I wouldn't have in your shoes."

"If this is going to work, if we aren't going to end up like me and Amber and Holden, then we need to be okay—and open—about our relationships with each other," I said.

"But obviously, we're not there yet," Carter said.

"Yet." I smiled. "So there's hope."

Carter looked at Paige, and she nodded, then she kissed my cheek. Tears glistened in her eyes and I held her close. "I mean it, Paige."

"I know you do," she whispered.

Carter kissed the back of her neck and cupped her breasts in his hands, his fingers playing with her stiff nipples through her bra. She moaned, and I took her mouth, my tongue twining with hers. She was sandwiched between us, and I ran a hand down her hip and gathered up the fabric of her skirt, before slipping my hand up along her inner thigh, seeking the slick heat between her legs.

She gasped when I touched her pussy, and Carter growled, grinding against her ass and pushing her against my aching cock.

God, I wanted them both, so very much. How had I gotten lucky enough to meet two such incredible people? Especially when they were willing to forgive me, even when they shouldn't.

I stripped off Paige's blouse and kissed the tops of her breasts, then slid her skirt off. Carter was busy undressing himself, then he stepped up behind me, kissing the nape of my neck, biting down on it gently in that way that made me shiver all over. Fuck. He knew what that did to me.

My fingers working at the clasp of Paige's bra, I turned to look at Carter over my shoulder. "I want you in me before we're done tonight."

Carter grinned. "Thought you would."

I laughed. "Cocky bastard."

Palming his erection, Carter smiled and Paige giggled.

"You two," she said.

I turned back to her, cupping the beautiful breasts I'd bared, then sucked one hard pink nipple into my mouth. She groaned, and the sound went straight to my cock. I had to be in her soon. I wanted everything, now.

And I still hadn't removed a stitch of clothing. I started unbuttoning my shirt while Paige stepped out of her panties and Carter worked on my belt.

In a matter of minutes, all three of us were naked, and for a second, we just looked at each other. Then I realized exactly what I wanted, how good it had felt to be sandwiched between them.

I scooped Paige off her feet, and she shrieked in protest, making me and Carter laugh. I dropped her on the bed, then climbed over her on all fours. I looked over my shoulder at Carter, whose eyes dipped to my ass then came back up, questions in them. I nodded, and he opened the nightstand drawer, pulling out the condoms and lube.

Paige looked at us. "You two have a plan in mind?"

"Always," I assured her. I bent down and kissed her neck. "I want you both at the same time," I whispered.

"Oh," she said. "A Riley sandwich?"

Carter chuckled. "Best sandwich there is… except maybe for a Paige sandwich."

Her eyes rounded, then flared with heat. "I wonder what that would be like."

"Play your cards right, and you'll find out," I said with a waggle of my brows. I kissed down to her breasts, then took a nipple in my mouth while my right hand slipped between her legs and between her folds. She was wet for me, already, the top of her thighs slippery with her arousal.

I circled a finger around her clit just as I felt Carter part my ass cheeks and tongue my hole. God it felt good. So damn good. I pressed back against him while Paige quivered beneath me, her hips rocking as she rubbed against my hand.

I plunged two fingers inside her and used my thumb to work her clit, her breathing speeding up, those little pants, her breathless "Riley," egging me on. I bit down gently on her nipple, and she cried out, her hands clamping onto my head, her fingers twining in my hair.

Carter dribbled some lube over my hole, then used his fingers to work it inside. I groaned against Paige's skin at the invasion and pressed back onto those fingers, the two working in and out and stretching me.

My stiff cock ground against Paige's hip. I wanted inside her, her breathy little moans driving me crazy. I released her nipple. "Paige, grab a condom and put it on me." I looked over my shoulder at Carter. "You ready?"

He worked his fingers in deeper, and I shuddered. "Are you?" he asked.

"Always."

"If you're sure."

"I am," I said. I was *so* ready for this.

Paige nimbly rolled the condom on me, and I didn't hesitate. I positioned myself at her entrance, slicking up my tip with her juices, then I drove inside her, making us both cry out.

"Fuck," I groaned. I looked back at Carter, who was smoothing a condom over his own rigid length. "Fuck me, Carter."

"God, you are greedy," he said with a chuckle.

"I think you mean he's a bossy bottom," Paige said, and we both swiveled to look at her. She shrugged and moaned when I thrust deeper. "I do read, you know," she said.

I raised an eyebrow. "Apparently."

I felt Carter pressing against my hole, and I stilled for a second, waiting for the pressure, the bite of pain that always followed. And then the sheer bliss of Carter sinking into me.

I sighed in pleasure, and he wrapped an arm around me right below the collarbone, his chest pressed to my back.

"You fill me just right," I said, then I pressed forward into Paige, Carter following, the two of us seeming to fuck her with my dick.

Fuck. I pulled out of Paige slightly, pressing back against Carter, driving his cock deeper into my ass. Then Carter pressed forward, and I sank back into Paige, her tight walls clenching around me.

I opened my eyes and looked down at her. "We're both fucking you. Can you feel it?"

We pulled back, then pressed forward again, and her mouth opened, only a throaty groan coming out. "Oh, I feel it," she finally managed. "And I'm probably going to feel it tomorrow too."

I pressed her knees flat against the bed, giving myself a little more depth inside her. I increased the pace, Carter easily following me, and soon I was slamming into Paige whenever Carter thrust into me. I imagined it was Carter's cock passing through me and into her, one long shaft that was bringing us both pleasure.

She clutched my shoulders, a high keening cry coming out of her as she shuddered and bucked beneath me.

Carter pistoned into me, his breath coming in heavy gusts. "I'm so close, Rye."

"Me too," I murmured as Paige's internal muscles fluttered around me. She clenched me hard, and I tipped over the edge with a guttural cry as Carter slammed into me again and bit down on my shoulder.

The combination of Paige's release, my own, and the sound of Carter groaning his own bliss against my back was something I'd never really experienced before.

Oh, Carter and I had certainly done this combination with other women. So had Holden, Amber, and I. But I'd never felt this bone-deep connection before to the two people with me.

I'd never had this much trust before. Not even with Amber and Holden.

I wanted to blurt out my heart to Paige and Carter. Wanted to tell them how happy I was. How much I loved them both.

I collapsed to the bed beside Paige, Carter withdrawing and going off to clean up. When he came back, he lay down beside me, and the three of us intertwined our fingers on my belly.

I wanted to tell them. I really did. Was it too soon?

I looked at Paige. Her eyes again welled with tears. "What's wrong?" I whispered.

"Nothing," she said and smiled, dabbing her eyes with her free hand. "Sometimes sex just makes me emotional."

"Good sex always does," Carter said and pressed a kiss to my temple.

I reached up and cupped the nape of his neck. I looked at Paige again, and this time she was smiling. But there was still something there, some lingering sorrow.

If I said something now, in the heat of the moment, she wouldn't believe me. But soon—yeah, I was going to say it soon, in some quiet moment. I didn't want her to doubt me, didn't want her to brush off my feelings as sex-induced euphoria.

I wanted her to believe in my love with every fiber of her being.

PAIGE

"Oh wow. This place is amazing!" Riley gushed as we entered the Carwash main room at LOOP Nightclub, London's premier disco and '80s/'90s dance bar.

I was pleased with everyone's reactions so far. The seventies and eighties didn't quite count as historical in the romance world, so one could argue that this event didn't fit in with the rest of the tour, but after researching the club and viewing the effort they'd put into recreating that era, I'd been unable to resist.

"Great choice, Paige." Carter stepped in close behind me to be heard over the thumping beats of Abba's "Dancing Queen." Already, my feet were itching to move.

"And great outfit," Kenji said, bumping my hip.

I preened and fluffed out my hair, laughing when my bangles jingled. I'd dressed as Madonna in *Desperately Seeking Susan*, and on the way over from the hotel, it had been all I could do to keep Riley away. Somehow he'd managed to sneak his hand under my decidedly short skirt, and Carter kept glancing at my cleavage. Maybe Ari was right. Just knowing how much Riley and Carter wanted me made me feel free. Freer and happier than I'd ever been.

I hip-bumped Kenji back. "You look pretty amazing yourself." And almost unrecognizable as "Karma Chameleon"-era Boy George. The makeup, the hair beads, and the hat were exact replicas.

Everyone looked fabulous, dressed as various music icons from Tina Turner to Cyndi Lauper. But in my mind, Riley and Carter stood out from the crowd. And I wasn't the only one to think so, if I went by the looks they were garnering from all the women and quite a few men.

Riley, of course, had chosen bad boy George Michael from his "Faith" days. He was sexy as heck with his combed-back hair, aviator shades, white T-shirt, black leather jacket with multicolored pins, and blue jeans, faded and threadbare in all the right places. He'd even trimmed his beard to make it look more like the one George had sported back then. Needless to say, it was a far cry from Riley's Professor Templeton disguise.

And Carter, well, he was also completely transformed into a perfect, albeit much more muscular, incarnation of Billy Idol. He was dressed in jeans so tight they had to be Riley's, a silver-studded sleeveless leather jacket over a bare chest, leather boots, rings, and chains. The curved lip, raised fist, and outrageous British accent rounded out the entire outfit. Everything about him screamed sex and danger.

I shivered with barely contained desire for my two men.

Kenji and I trailed after the hostess in hot shorts on rollerblades, who'd already commandeered Carter and Riley to show them to the VIP booths I had reserved for the group.

Enough tour members were there to fill two booths of ten or so. We settled in to chat about the place and enjoy our glasses of champagne served with dry ice. The result was bubbles, bubbles, and more bubbles.

Before long, the party mood had taken us all over, as we grabbed our party favors off the tables, showering each other with glitter and blowing into our horns. When "Carwash" by Rose Royce came on, I grabbed Carter and Riley by the hands and urged them out of their seats. "Let's dance. I love this song!"

Before I knew it, the entire group had crowded onto the packed psychedelic dance floor. Beneath our feet, large, differently colored rectangles pulsed in time with the music. The disco ball above us shot shards of color across our faces and the strobe lights made everything flicker.

Hands in the air, I swayed to the music, letting it wash over me. Dancing was a great release, a chance to let my body move, to work out the kinks from all the activity I'd been doing lately, both in and out of bed. When I opened my eyes, Riley was watching me, and his worn jeans did very little to hide his enjoyment.

The music changed to "Do You Love Me" by The Contours, a sexy song from *Dirty Dancing*. How I'd loved that movie when my mom had convinced me to watch the '80s classic. Letting loose, I started doing the twist and the mashed potato.

Riley shook his head, his lips curved into a smirk. "Oh no, you don't." He grabbed me by the waist and slammed me against his chest. Once I was firmly in place, he thrust his hips, adding a half circle in either direction. "I might not do ballroom, but I can sure as shit dirty dance."

Heat bloomed in my belly… and below. I'd never danced like this. Imagined it, dreamed about it, but never done it. And here I was, in the middle of a crowded London nightclub, grinding against one of the two most handsome men in the place. Was I trapped in a dream? If so, I hoped to never escape.

Fantasy or not, I was having a ball. Hooking my arm around Riley's neck, I let myself be carried away by him and the music.

Beside us, Carter danced a more sedate version with Lori. The woman was flushed, starry-eyed, and I knew exactly how she felt. Carter as Billy Idol was incredibly potent.

Riley gripped my leg and brought my knee to rest on his hip, then he bowed me back. I whooped with delight at the erotic position, and quickly revised my earlier thought: both men were extremely potent.

When Riley finally righted me, I clung to his shoulders and gasped through my laughter. "Baby was a lot younger than me, I'll have you know."

"But not nearly as sexy," he teased.

We smiled at each other, the air thickening between us. An ache started in my belly, a throb between my legs.

"I want you so fucking bad right now," he said, his voice husky, the lust in his expression raw and powerful.

He crushed me to his chest and buried his face in my hair. Riding his thigh as I was, my panties were getting soaked, and his erection rubbed against my own leg with each movement he made.

Over Riley's shoulder, my gaze collided with Carter's. He'd escorted Lori back to the table and was headed toward us. Without a word, he positioned himself behind me and gripped my hips, placing his hands over Riley's.

And we danced.

The three of us, pressed together, moving against each other. There was only one way to describe it: sex standing up.

Carter ran his nose up my neck and blew on my skin. The coolness of his breath on my damp skin made me shiver. Deliciously. Winking at me, Riley lowered his head to my other shoulder and nibbled my earlobe.

"Oh God," I cried as desire coursed through my body, igniting every nerve ending, rendering me even more sensitive to the touch of these two very wicked men. "You need to stop. We can't do this here."

Behind me, Carter rolled his hips and pressed his erection against my bottom. The groan that tore out of his chest had Riley's head popping up.

I couldn't see his eyes because of the sunglasses he wore, but the tight line of his lips and the sharpness of his jaw told me he was as affected by Carter's need as I was.

"Fuck, Carter," Riley said, confirming it. He scanned the area. "There's got to be somewhere we can go."

Carter's fingers dug into my hips, pushing Riley's into them as well. I was literally the filling in their Oreo, the jam in their PBJ sandwich. The thought pushed a nervous giggle past my lips.

"You think this is funny?" Riley's eyes narrowed in on me.

I giggled some more. "I think we need to sit down. Have a drink. Cool off a bit."

Blowing out a miserable sounding sigh, Carter backed off, and I immediately felt cold. "You're right," he said. "Let's go."

"Everything okay?" Kenji asked as we passed by him. From the glint in his eye and the way he did a slow up and down of the men's bodies, zeroing in on their crotches, he knew exactly what had been happening.

"Just getting a drink," Riley said a little curtly.

"Avoid the bar."

When Kenji gave a slight nod, Riley's jaw clenched and he hissed out a breath. "Thanks, man. I owe you one."

"Oh, hon. You owe me much more than that." Kenji waved us off after shooting Carter a playful grin.

Once we were out of earshot, I turned to Riley. "What was that about?"

"What was what about?" he asked, helping me into a seat at the booth.

I smacked his arm. "Don't give me that. You know exactly what I'm talking about."

He sat beside me and squeezed my knee. "Of course you do. Ken was reminding me that he backed off Carter when I asked him to stand down."

Carter laughed. "Asked. Right."

"What are you two talking about?"

"At the Cavern Club," Riley explained. "After you and I left, Kenji tried to put the moves on Carter."

I grinned. "I'm sure he knew exactly who Carter was when he did it too."

Carter snarled à la Billy Idol. "Hey now. Hot men don't need an excuse to hit on me."

"I know, babe." Riley reached up and gripped Carter's neck. "You're the hottest man in this club."

The huskiness in Riley's voice when he called Carter "babe" and the intimate way he held Carter by the neck was more of a turn-on than anything... okay, it wasn't more of a turn-on than watching Carter take Riley like he'd done at the spa, but it was a very close second.

And clearly Carter agreed. Red raced up his exposed chest, neck, and face. His voice was like gravel when he tugged on his jeans, looked around, and said, "Christ, where's that waitress? I need a drink."

As if by magic, a gorgeous woman with long black hair done up in a ponytail roller-skated right up to him and laid her hand on his shoulder. "What can I get you, love?"

"Righto," Carter popped off in his overdone British accent. "A whiskey for me." He turned to me and Riley, full Billy Idol sneer in place. "George, Madonna? What's your fancy?"

It took several minutes before we stopped laughing enough to place our orders.

"I don't know about you guys, but I'm having 'The Time of My Life,'" I said, barely holding back a snort.

Carter raised his lip. "The only question is 'Should I Stay or Should I Go?'"

"Please stay," Riley countered. "'We've Only Just Begun.'"

Kenji dropped down into a seat across the table from us and shot me a look of pure disdain. "Pun wars. That's beneath you, my 'Caribbean Queen.'"

"Oh, I'm not used to being 'Under Pressure,'" I challenged.

Carter rubbed his jaw. "It's a 'Shock to the System' for sure."

Riley opened his mouth. There was a slight look of panic in his gaze until the waitress returned with our drinks. "Ah," he said, taking his vodka Collins. "*Saved by the Bell.*"

"Cheater!" Kenji shouted. "That's a television show."

"Ah, well. What can I say, Ken." Riley grinned like the cat that ate the canary, and I knew something good was coming. "'You Spin Me Round.'"

"From what I can see, you should be saying that to Paige." Kenji tapped a brightly painted nail to his bottom lip. "Or should I say C-er-Eric?"

Riley wrapped his arms around both our necks and tugged us in close so our faces were all scrunched together. "Both," he said. "You both spin me right the fuck around."

Maybe it was the alcohol. Maybe it was the music, the surreal atmosphere, or the scent of desire in the air. Or maybe it was knowing that, at least for now, I was a part of something unique, something special. Whatever it was, I didn't feel even a shred of self-consciousness when our playful huddle turned into a not-fit-for-public-consumption three-way kiss. Or maybe it was that kissing both these men at the same time in front of God-knew-who was possibly the sexiest, most exciting thing I'd ever dared do in my thirty-six years of existence.

Maybe heaven really was a place on earth.

RILEY

What if Kenji laughed in my face?

Man up, Kendrick.

I looked up from my breakfast at the Grosvenor Arms to see him headed my way. I swallowed hard. Ken had agreed to eat with me, though he didn't know why I had asked.

"So, Professor Templeton," Kenji said, plopping himself onto the chair across from mine, "to what do I owe the pleasure?"

"I need to ask a favor."

Ken's eyes twinkled. "A favor, you say?"

"Yes. I want to talk to you about writing."

"*Moi?*" Ken put a hand on his chest. "The great Riley Kendrick seeking advice from little old me?"

I looked around. No one seemed to be paying us any attention. But still… "Could you *please* not say my name so loudly?"

Ken grinned. "Honey, I haven't even started to get loud."

"Kenji, please."

Ken stared at me for second, then he signaled the waiter, Gerry, who'd once again been good-naturedly flirting with me. He was cute, but I was off the market. "Okay," Ken said. "But no more demands until I've had some caffeine." He ordered a cup of coffee and a light breakfast. "And you're paying."

"Of course." I waited until Ken's food was served, the two of us rehashing the prior night at the club, Ken regaling me with the tale of "flexible Brian," who apparently had made Ken's night.

After Gerry left the table, Ken took his time doctoring his coffee with cream and sugar. Finally he took a sip, then fixed me with a not entirely friendly stare. "So, you want a favor. Something about the old typey-typey?"

Here goes. My cheeks grew warm, and I cast about for a way to ask. "I need some advice. So far, everything I've written, I've taken from my real life. Some details got changed along the way. But most of it was more or less what actually happened."

"So when you fucked Holden in the hot tub, that happened?"

I nodded.

Ken clapped his hands together. "I always knew that one would love it in the ass."

We were getting off-track. "So, what I was wondering was how do you write something that's entirely fictional? I don't seem to get it. How to make the story up, the characters. I've tried, but they don't seem real. Or that exciting to me. Not like when I write about what's actually happening in my life."

Ken clasped his hands on his crossed knees and leaned forward. "You've never actually studied writing, have you?"

"Well, academic, technical writing. But not fiction."

"That's the whole issue. You need some grounding in plotting, character development, and GMCs."

"GMCs?"

"Goals, motivations, conflicts. They're the things you structure the plot around. There's an entire book on the subject."

"And once I understand this stuff, I'll get how to do it?"

Ken nodded and took another sip of his coffee. "More or less. You really should be discussing all this with your editor."

I reddened for real this time. "I… kind of didn't want to tell her."

Kenji laughed. "Honey, she already knows."

"How?"

"I'm sure she's figured it out, especially after everything came out in the papers."

"She hasn't said anything."

"Why would she? You're Riley Kendrick. You could take a dump on a page, and people would pay for it."

"That's not true."

"As long as it had sex in it? Yeah, it's true."

"But…" How to make him understand? "I don't want to write crap. I want to write books people can't put down."

"Look at you, all Mr. Quality."

"Ken, I'm serious."

"You are?"

"I am. I can't write about Paige and Carter. They've made that abundantly clear."

"So you got a scolding and then came running to me."

"Something like that."

Ken nibbled on a croissant and took another drink of coffee. "Okay, I'll send you a list of the best books about writing commercial fiction. And I do recommend talking this over with your editor. She can help you refine your plot and make the story and characters stronger." He grinned. "You could've avoided this whole convo with me."

I took a deep breath. "I know I lucked out. I get that, Ken, I do. I know I didn't bust my ass in the trenches for years and years trying to break into publishing."

"You're a fucking unicorn. No one hits it that goddamn big on the first go. No one. Until you."

"I got lucky."

"Yes, you did. But now you have to do all the work you skipped over the first time." He regarded me over the rim of his raised coffee cup. "I shouldn't do this, I should let you wallow in your crap, but I occasionally like to think I'm the bigger person."

"I owe you majorly, man."

"I'll take payment in sexual favors."

"Um..." What the fuck did I say to that?

Ken roared with laughter. "OMG. Your face!"

I laughed weakly. "I'll give you whatever you want. Just not that."

"I know. And if you could blurb my next book, I'd really appreciate it."

"Can do. Gladly."

"Even if there is a jackass character named Riley in it?"

"Even if."

Gerry came back to the table, his eyes fixed on me. He pulled a copy of the *Daily Mail* out from under his arm. "Almost forgot your paper," he said as he handed it over. There was a strange look on his face, and I stopped him. "Is something wrong?"

"You'd best look at page six, is all I'm saying."

Uh-oh. A sick feeling started in my stomach. Had someone seen us at the club and put two and two together? I opened the paper and Ken leaned forward. I angled it so we could both read it.

I turned to page six and my stomach plummeted. There, splashed across a two-page stretch, was a full-color photo of me with my arms around Paige and Carter, the three of us engaging in a kiss.

The caption sealed my fate. "Infamous Riley Kendrick Finds New Love—and It's Another Trio!" More pictures were featured on the subsequent page.

Kenji patted my hand, then sat back. "Oh, honey. You done screwed the pooch."

"You think?" I stared at the picture, my breakfast threatening to spew all over it.

I had to tell Paige and Carter before they heard about it from someone else. They were both going to freak.

And Carter would lose his job as soon as the news hit stateside, if it hadn't already.

Fuck, fuck, fuck.

It had all been too good to be true, hadn't it?

Chapter 13

PAIGE

My heart in my throat, I walked down the hall to Riley and Carter's room. Riley had called me a few minutes ago, and his tone had instantly put me on alert. Something was wrong, something we needed to discuss in person.

I knocked on the door, taking a deep breath. Maybe it wasn't that bad? When the door opened, the grim looks on Riley's and Carter's faces confirmed my worst fears. Something was definitely, seriously wrong. I stepped inside and followed Riley over to the sofa in the room's sitting area. I sat across from them, looking from one to the other. "So, what's wrong?"

Riley looked at Carter, then turned to me. "I have bad news. Someone recognized me at the club last night." He pulled a folded copy of the *Daily Mail* out from under his arm and opened it, laying it down on the coffee table facing me.

A two-page spread showed a large picture of the three of us kissing and embracing, with more photos on subsequent pages. And it was quite obvious that all three of us were involved. Intimately involved.

And in case the message hadn't been obvious, the headline made it abundantly clear that the London press had no trouble recognizing our ménage for what it was. The three of us, together.

My stomach a hard knot, I scanned the article, looking to see if Carter and I had been identified. So far, it seemed not, but it was only a matter of time before someone recognized us and said something.

"I'm so sorry, Paige," Riley said. He reached over and took Carter's hand. "And Carter, shit… I'm so damn sorry. I hope your work doesn't find out."

Carter squeezed his hand. "I knew there was a risk. And I took it. So don't blame yourself."

"How did this happen?" I asked.

"Ken warned me about some reporters being in the bar. I should've listened to him. I just didn't want to end our fun," Riley said. He looked so miserable. "It's my fault. I should have been more careful."

"You haven't been recognized anywhere else," Carter said.

"I think the employee at the spa who sat with us in the sauna recognized me."

"Do you think she had something to do with the paparazzi finding you here?" I asked.

Riley raised his hands palms out. "We'll never know." He turned to Carter. "I hope this doesn't cost you your job."

Carter shrugged, trying to seem nonchalant, but the gesture was stiff. "What happens, happens. I made my choice."

"You didn't ask for this," Riley whispered.

"It was my choice to kiss you—both of you—in public. It was my choice not to be more careful."

"I still feel like it's my fault." Riley ran a hand through his dark hair, leaving it rumpled. "If they fire you, I'll do what I can to help your family."

My eyes widened. My parents! What were they going to think? My mom had been almost as bad as Ari, urging me to get back out there, but this… this was not what she'd meant.

"Paige, you look like you've seen a ghost," Carter said.

"My parents," I whispered.

Carter crossed his arms. "My mom has barely accepted my interest in men. She's going to freak when she finds out about us."

"Mine too. And my dad…" I could imagine what he'd say. My parents had been supportive when I got pregnant with Emma and when Dylan left me. But I'd been a lot younger then. I was certainly old enough to know better now.

Riley came over and crouched down beside me. "Paige, it might not be as bad as you think."

I shook my head and snorted. "You don't know my dad. He'll be mortified to see this in the press."

Riley started to rise, looking like I'd slapped him, and I took his wrist. "It's not your fault. Really. I wanted everything that happened. I knew what I was doing. I just didn't think I'd get caught."

He bent over and pressed a kiss to my lips. "I swear I'll make this up to you somehow. I'll make it up to you both." He touched Carter's cheek.

My cell phone started ringing, and I glanced at the display. It was Ari. "It's my boss. I better take it." Had Ari already heard the news? Was she planning to chew me out?

I walked onto the balcony for some privacy and pressed the answer button, mentally bracing myself for Ari's disappointment. "Ari?"

"Paige, first off, I wanted to let you know Emma is okay. But she needs an x-ray. I'm going to hand you over to a nurse so you can authorize it."

"X-ray? What happened?"

"She slipped and fell on a drink someone spilled at the coffee shop. They think her wrist might be broken. Not sure."

"Is she scared?" I ought to be there, taking care of Emma, instead of making a public spectacle of myself with Riley and Carter.

"She's okay. A few tears, but they gave her something for the pain, and she's even flirting with the doctor." Ari said something to someone, then came back on the line. "Let me put the nurse on."

I listened as the nurse explained that the x-ray was a precaution, then I authorized the procedure and gave my insurance information.

Ari came back on the phone. "They're taking her down to radiology."

"Can I talk to her first?"

"Not yet. But she's fine."

"Maybe she shouldn't be working there. The pace is so fast—"

"Paige, Emma loves it there. You know she does. She could've been a patron and slipped and fallen. You can't cover her in bubble wrap."

Ari was right. But still… "I feel terrible that I'm not there with her."

"Am I chopped liver?" Arianna asked, the indignation in her voice making me smile. "Your parents are on the way. Emma is fine."

That was probably true, but I needed to be with my daughter.

And I needed to tell Riley and Carter about Emma. Which meant there'd be no point hanging around afterward for the awkwardness. No need to force them to make excuses and dance around the truth.

It was over; I'd known it was coming. And if I left now, I'd just spare us all a lot of grief.

"Ari, could you take over the trip for me? I'd really like to go home and be with Emma."

"Paige, that's not necessary."

"I *need* to be there."

Something in my voice must have gotten through. "You're upset about something else. What's going on?"

I sighed. I might as well tell her and face the consequences. Ari, Daniel, and Javier would know soon enough. And if they wanted to fire me, I'd deserve it. "Riley got recognized. And Carter and I were with him. And we were all kissing. It's all over the papers here."

"Shit," Ari said.

"If you're going to fire me, tell me now. Please."

"*Fire* you? Why?"

"It's going to look bad for TI. It's only a matter of time before the press figures out who I am."

Ari laughed. "*Chica*, you're not going to get fired. Teased, for sure. But not fired."

"Why not?"

"In this business, there's no such thing as bad publicity. This will only make Total Indulgence more popular."

"I don't think—"

"Paige, this is what we do. We sell luxury adventure, fun, excitement. And if you get laid along the way, so much the better, right?"

"But—"

"Everyone is going to be jealous of you."

"Everyone is going to think I'm a slut."

"Fuck them. Fuck anyone with that shitty attitude." Ari lowered her voice. "The people who matter won't care."

"My parents are going to care. A lot."

"They'll get over it. As long as you're happy."

My eyes welled. "That's just it. I am. But—" I let out a sob. "It's over."

"What happened?"

"I haven't told them about Emma. But I'm going to. And that's going to be the end of it. No more lies, no more fantasies."

"Calm down, *chica*. Give them the benefit of the doubt."

I laughed, but it was humorless. "I know how this is going to go, Ari. I need you to get on a plane and take over for me tomorrow."

"How about you talk to them first, then call me back."

I shook my head. "Please, Ari."

"Okay. But I'll wait an hour to book a flight. You call me if I don't need to fly out."

I agreed and hung up. I wiped my eyes and took a deep breath. I could do this. I *had* to do this. It was time to tell them the truth.

I stepped inside, and they both turned to look at me, concern all over their faces. "What's wrong?" Riley asked.

My insides quivered and my knees felt weak. I sat down before I fell down, then clasped my hands together. "I have a daughter. She's eighteen, and she has Downs. She was injured today at work. That's why my boss called me."

"Is she okay?" Riley asked.

I nodded. "Her wrist might be broken, but she'll be all right."

"That's good," Carter said.

I looked from one to the other, but saw no anger there. "Well?" I asked.

"Well, what?" Riley said.

"I *lied* to you."

"It's not like I asked if you had kids."

"But I didn't mention it. Though I kept hoping you wouldn't notice the stretch marks. And I told Carter I had a niece with Downs. Not a daughter." I turned to him. "I'm sorry."

"I understand why you did," Carter said. "I'm not mad."

"You never have to hide anything from us. Don't you know that?" Riley said.

I rolled my eyes. "Really, Riley? You're telling me you would have been excited about my having a child?"

He shrugged. "You have a kid. So what?"

"A *disabled* kid."

"Again, so?"

I looked at Carter. "You know what a responsibility it is."

He nodded. "Yes. But all kids are."

"It's not the same."

"No, it's not. But everybody has something to deal with."

I crossed my arms. "And yet, it's not like guys have been lining up to be Emma's father. Not even her own father wants that burden."

Riley rose. "Then he's an asshole. That doesn't mean that's how I feel. Or Carter."

Carter nodded. "The idea doesn't scare me. I've always known I'd probably be the one to take on the responsibility for my brother when it gets to be too much for my mom."

"Then you hardly need any more headaches." I shook my head. "But none of this matters anyway. I just needed to be honest with you."

Riley drew me out of the chair and pulled me close. "I wish you'd trusted us all along. But thank you for telling us now." He kissed me on the mouth, then smoothed my hair back behind my ears. "I love you, Paige. I've been dying to say it, and I think you need to hear it now. I was going to wait a few more days, but that seems silly."

Stupid, runaway heart—mine was pounding, a thrill of hope running through me. Then I closed my eyes, took a deep breath, and pressed it down. Riley was sweet, he was young, he was naive. And he might say this now, but he didn't know what it meant to be a father. To take on such a responsibility.

Carter knew. And though he'd said he wasn't scared, he wasn't holding me either. He wasn't doing anything. And that told me everything I needed to know.

Riley might love us both, but Carter's heart had room only for Riley.

And I wasn't going to be the third wheel in their relationship any longer.

I stepped back from Riley. "I really... like the two of you." My voice cracked and I swallowed hard. "But I'm a mom, and I need to be a mom, and the two of you need to go back to your lives. The fantasy is over. You both gave me something I'll never forget, but a memory is all this can ever be."

"It doesn't have to end here," Riley said.

"Of course it does. You two are a couple. There's no room for me, as anything more than a fling. I see the love in your eyes when you look at each other." My voice cracked again, and I couldn't hold back the tears threatening to spill any longer. I let out a sob and grabbed my purse, turning for the door.

"Paige, wait." Riley took hold of my arm.

I shrugged him off, reaching for the handle, and he held the door shut. "Listen to me."

I couldn't look at him. I wiped my eyes and tried to calm my breathing. "Let me go, Riley."

"No—"

I smacked him in the arm. "Let me go!"

"Paige—"

"Let her go," Carter said, rising.

I turned to look at him. "Thank you," I hiccupped, my voice thick with tears. At least Carter wasn't going to prolong my misery.

Riley hissed in frustration, then stepped away from the door. "I love you, Paige."

The sadness in his voice twisted in my gut. "I know you think that's true." I opened the door. "But it's best to leave things be. You'll see that soon enough."

I slipped outside, my vision nothing but a blur. The door clicked shut behind me, and it sounded like a gunshot.

I'd ended this farce; I'd just saved us all a lot of misery. So why did it feel like my heart was shattered beyond repair?

RILEY

Sticks and stones can break my bones, but words will never hurt me.

Whoever had said that was a fucking liar. I watched in stunned silence as the door slammed shut behind Paige. The harsh metallic sound reverberated throughout my body. My heart banged against my ribs. Blood roared in my ears. And behind all the noise was the pain of my heart rending.

None of the past fifteen minutes made any damn sense. Had I suddenly been transported to a parallel universe where initially everything appeared to be the same, but upon closer inspection turned out to be as alien as the visitors to Area 51?

The effect was disorienting, and I had to swallow to push down the bile burning my throat and stealing my breath. I wiped my stinging eyes, then turning to Carter, I raised my arms in an awkward acknowledgment of the alternate reality we'd just experienced. "What the fuck happened?"

Slumped against the wall, Carter briefly closed his eyes and rubbed the side of his face, the scratch of his beard adding to the clatter in my brain. When he looked at me, his normally bright eyes were sunken and wrecked. He looked as miserable as I felt. Carter shook his head. "I don't know, Rye. I think we got dumped."

"Fuck. It can't be over." I'd already reached that conclusion, but hearing him say the words was another attack on my battered heart. The burning sensation in my eyes intensified and heat ran down my cheeks. I hurt so bad, I needed to let the pain out. "Fuck me!" I yelled as I slammed my fist into the wall.

Carter's eyes opened wide. "No. God. Don't, please don't," he said, pushing off the wall. With long steps, he crossed the room and took me in his arms. "I'm so, so sorry." His hands slid to my back and held me tightly.

I cradled my throbbing hand against my chest and sank into Carter's embrace, let him be the power that supported us both. "She's gone," I whispered.

"I know, and it's all my fault."

The mournful tone in his admission twisted my gut into a knot. This wasn't Carter's fault, not by a long shot. Before I could speak though, he went on. "I shouldn't have come here. If I'd stayed home, none of this would have happened. Paige would still be here, and you'd be together."

I squeezed his waist, trying to comfort him as best I could. He lowered his head and rested his cheek on my shoulder. "I just wanted to be with you," he said softly.

"I know, babe. And I wanted to be with you." I rubbed his back with my good hand. "This isn't your fault. Before you arrived, what Paige and I had were a few good times and some hot sex. But we didn't have a relationship really. You made that happen."

He sniffed. "Look where that got us."

"It's my fault," I said, unable to let Carter continue to blame himself. "I pushed her to have both of us. Hell, I'd been bringing up the idea of a threesome practically since the minute I met her." A groan burst out of my compressed chest. "But I really wanted to have both of you. And for the shortest, most miraculous time, I did." I struggled to get any air into my aching lungs.

Was it possible to die of a broken heart? Because it really felt like I was about to take my last breath.

Carter gripped both sides of my head. "Listen to me, Rye. You didn't force anyone into anything. Paige wanted everything that happened."

Through my tears, I held his gaze. "Did you want it? Or did you do it for me?"

He exhaled, then hung his head. "I was attracted to her from the beginning. But in my mind, it was a one-night stand, maybe two. After I started getting to know her and seeing how happy you were, especially when the three of us were together, I let myself consider something more." He raised his chin and pinned me with his stare. "So yes, I did want it. I do want it."

"But? I can hear a 'but' there."

Carter lowered his hands to my shoulders. "Let's sit down."

I followed him to the couch. We sat next to each other, our thighs and shoulders touching. He took my hand. "Do you understand what happened earlier? Why Paige was so upset?"

"Her daughter was hurt."

"A daughter neither of us knew about," Carter added, arching his brow.

Flexing my sore fingers, I mulled that over. "I don't get why she didn't tell us about Emma earlier."

"Don't you?"

No, I didn't care that Paige had a kid. Hell, many women her age did. It was hardly unique. Did I care that she was eighteen? Okay, I was man enough to admit that it took me aback a bit, but really, what did it matter?

"I guess she thought her daughter's age would be a hard limit for me." I shifted on the couch, lifting my knee onto the cushion so I could look at Carter. That's when I saw the tears on his cheeks. I wiped them off with my thumb. He immediately flushed. I gave him a weak smile. "Our age difference was an issue for her, not me."

"So it doesn't matter to you at all that when you were ten, Paige was already a mom? Or that Emma is just a few years younger than Amber?"

I shook my head. "Not in the slightest."

His expression brightened. "I didn't think it would." He gripped my arm. "But besides Emma's age, I think Paige expected us to walk away as soon as we heard about the Down syndrome."

Anger rose in my chest, but before I could give voice to it, Carter put a finger on my lips. "Hear me out." He waited for my grudging nod before continuing. "I see this a lot with the parents of my students and my own mother. Many of them have lost family and friends because people are uncomfortable around children with disabilities. And it only gets worse as the kids get older." He squeezed my thigh. "We don't know a lot about Paige or her background, but I can bet that similar things have happened to her. She's lost people, probably boyfriends over this."

A lightbulb went off in my head. "She never talked about having been pregnant, but she did say she married too young and that her marriage only lasted a few years. I'm betting her husband, Emma's father, walked out on her and Emma."

Carter sighed. "Children with Down syndrome can be very challenging."

"But to walk out on your own kid?"

"Financially and emotionally, it's a lot to carry." The hand Carter had left on my thigh clenched. "Fuck, people can be such assholes."

"Yeah, and she expected the same from us. I could see it in her eyes. When she told us about Emma and that she had Downs, she expected us to turn tail and head for the hills." But why? Carter was a special-education teacher. His younger brother had autism. He was used to dealing with children with disabilities. I had never met a more patient and understanding man. So it had to be me. She didn't trust me to handle the situation well. She didn't trust me to want to even try. "Correction: she expected *me* to run for the hills. God, do I really come across as that shallow?"

"Hell, no."

"Then why?"

Carter gripped my nape and brought our foreheads together. "She's scared, Rye."

"We should go to her room." I reached up to take hold of his arm. I needed to touch him, draw strength from this man I loved so much. Linking our fingers together, I stood. "We'll explain to her that we're okay with everything. That there's nothing for her to be scared of."

He rose and ran his fingers over the edge of my jaw. "I really love this about you. How accepting you are. I don't think it's something most people see, but I do. You're a good man, Riley Kendrick."

Warmth spreading throughout my chest, I pressed against Carter's fingers. He cupped my cheek. The heat of his palm seeped into my face. It felt so damn good. Our connection had grown from nothing to everything. I wasn't going to lose Carter too. "You're a better one, Carter Templeton." I grinned. "Or should I say Eric Thornton?"

"God." Carter grunted. "I fucking hate that name."

I smiled. "So, what do you say? We march over to Paige's room and make our case?"

"I don't think she's ready for that. Remember that night in Liverpool? She wouldn't talk to you. I say we give her time to calm down first."

"Shit, you're right. But what are we supposed to do? Hell, she could be on her way to the airport right now."

"Riley, you saw her. She's too upset to hear reason at the moment. If we press her, it's only going to make things worse, not better. Give her some time, and have a little faith."

I took a deep breath and nodded. Paige needed time. And I needed to get myself in check. I cradled my throbbing fist to my chest. I'd punched a wall, for Christ's sake. And I'd had a damn hard time letting her walk out of the room. If Carter hadn't been there, who knew what I'd have done? Probably something that would have made things a hell of a lot worse.

I looked up at him. "I hope you're right. Because I can't lose her."

He touched my cheek, his expression so solemn, I wanted to cry. "I know. We'll fix it."

I hoped to God we could. Losing Paige wasn't something I could live with.

CARTER

I woke up in the suite I was sharing with Riley, not surprised to find myself still alone in bed, the other side undisturbed, the sheets cool to the touch. The faint clicking of Riley's keyboard came from the next room. I'd fallen asleep to that sound. It was good that Riley was working, trying to get his feelings on paper instead of pounding the walls again.

I looked at my phone. Three AM. Paige had left the room almost twelve hours ago. Was that enough time?

Probably. Of course, if she was sleeping—something I wished Riley could do—I didn't want to disturb her. But I didn't want to miss her in case she'd decided to fly out to Miami. Maybe we should go camp out in the lobby, just to be sure.

I rose and dressed, then checked on Riley. God, he looked like hell, his hair sticking up in clumps, his right hand purple and swollen around the knuckles.

"Did you ice it?" I asked, motioning to Riley's hand.

"Yes, Dad." The sarcasm in his tone made me smile. He removed his glasses and rubbed his eyes. I touched his cheek, tracing the dark circles that hadn't been there before. "You should get some rest."

He shrugged, then shook his head. "I'm too keyed up."

"And apparently well-caffeinated." I gestured to the half-full mug beside the keyboard and the large coffee urn sitting on the other side of it.

"Ordered some room service, I see."

"I'm not sleeping until I talk to her. You don't know how hard it's been not to jump out of this chair and march over to her room and demand that she talk to me." He rubbed a hand over his bleary eyes again. "But I know that would be a disaster, especially without you there." He flexed his bruised hand and winced. "It's not like me to do something like this."

"I know." I'd seen Riley come a bit unglued once when the paparazzi had followed us somewhere, but he hadn't been violent. Just very unhappy.

"I mean, I wasn't like this when I lost Amber and Holden. I was angry and upset, and I damn sure yelled a lot, but I didn't go around punching things."

I felt a little pang. Would Riley have done the same over me? Or was it only Paige who affected him so deeply?

"Why don't you take a quick shower? I was thinking we should go stake out the lobby, in case she tries to slip away."

"Good idea. I'll be right back." Riley shut his laptop and wagged a finger me. "No peeking. I'm not sure about what I've written. Let me digest it first, and then you can look when I'm ready. Okay?"

"Okay." I poured myself a cup of coffee while Riley headed to the bathroom. Might as well try to perk myself up. We had a long night ahead.

CARTER

Someone shook my shoulder. The hand on my arm was small, feminine, the fingernails lightly pressing into my skin. Paige? I opened my eyes to take in a gorgeous Latina standing in front of me. Riley was still snoozing, his head pillowed on my other shoulder.

The woman motioned to him. "That must be Riley. And you must be Carter." She was wearing a dark green figure-hugging dress that made me want to whistle in appreciation.

"And you are?" I asked, my voice raspy with sleep.

"Arianna Rodriguez. Paige's boss."

I looked around the hotel lobby, my gut tightening in alarm. "Has she left already?"

Arianna flipped a mass of shiny black hair over her shoulder and took a seat in the chair next to the couch we were sitting on. "You'd better wake him up for this."

I shook Riley awake, glad that he'd gotten some sleep instead of spending the whole night fretting. I glanced at my watch. Seven AM.

"What's going on?" Riley asked, yawning and stretching, his eyes finally latching on to Arianna and widening. He looked at me. "Who's this lovely creature?" he asked.

I smirked. Riley never missed a beat. Except when it came to Paige. "Arianna Rodriguez. Paige's boss."

He straightened and ran a hand over his hair. "Fuck. I mean—"

Arianna smiled and waved his words away. "I've been cursing since I was twelve. Don't worry about my tender ears."

"Is Paige here?" he asked, the hope in his voice giving me another pang.

Arianna shook her head slowly. "I'm afraid not. She checked out yesterday afternoon and spent the night at Heathrow waiting for a flight out. We crossed paths a few hours ago."

"Fuck!" he said, and slammed his bruised hand onto the cushion beside him. "I knew we should have gone after her."

I put a hand on his shoulder. "I'm sorry I made the wrong call."

Arianna shook her head again. "I don't think you could've stopped her, no matter what you did. She was still a mess when I saw her right before she got on the plane."

Riley swore again and ran a trembling hand over his mouth. Then he stilled and looked at Arianna. "How much has she told you?"

"Everything, I think."

"About the three of us?"

She nodded. "And her fears that you couldn't accept Emma."

"Which is stupid," he spat. "I don't give a fuck if she has a kid. Or a kid with issues. So what? It doesn't change how I feel."

Arianna leaned forward, her dark brown eyes flashing. "Emma has been the sticking point for several men before. Including her own father. So if Paige doesn't believe you, it's not because she doesn't have ample reason."

Riley slumped back against the cushions. "I can't believe she left like that. Without even hearing us out."

Arianna looked from him to me. "And you? How do you feel about this?"

She was a sharp one, this Arianna Rodriguez. "I want what Riley wants." I gave his knee a squeeze, and he placed his hand over mine.

Arianna shook her head and made a buzzing noise, as if I were a game-show contestant who'd given the wrong answer. "Not fucking good enough. He"—she indicated Riley—"loves her. But you? You love him, not her. And I think she sees that."

He turned to look at me. "Is that true, babe?"

My gut clenched. Was it? Was what I'd been feeling, this weird anxiety when Riley had punched the wall, when he'd talked about how devastated he was by Paige leaving, was that a sign? A sign I didn't love her, wasn't ready, would never be ready?

Or was I just fucking jealous and needed to get over my damn self?

"Babe?" Riley prompted me.

I closed my eyes. He started to say something, and I held up a hand to shush him.

Paige wasn't Livia. She was kind, caring, supportive. When Riley drove me crazy, she was there to reel me back in, to reel both of us back in. I liked her so damn much, loved being with her in bed, loved sharing Riley with her, loved the way she gave of herself with no expectations. Loved the way she'd listen, really listen, and hear more than what was being said.

I loved… her. And I wanted her in my life, regardless of what Riley wanted. He and I could move on without her, sure.

But Paige made us better. Paige made us complete.

I opened my eyes. "I love her," I said, my voice creaking like a rusty hinge. I looked at Riley. "But I admit, I've been a bit jealous." I touched his bruised knuckles. "I don't think I'd have ever inspired this."

He shook his head, his eyes grave, then he kissed my cheek. "Don't sell yourself short, Carter Templeton. I'd have done the same for you." He swallowed hard, muscles jumping in his jaw. "I can't see my life being complete without both of you."

I smiled. "I was just thinking the same thing." I leaned forward and kissed him, really kissed him. We didn't stop until Arianna cleared her throat.

"While I am enjoying the show, boys, I have to get my act together before everyone starts coming down for breakfast."

"So what should we do?" Riley asked her.

Arianna pulled a card out of her purse and wrote something on the back of it. "This is her cell number. I suggest giving her a few days to calm down and reassure herself that Emma is okay. And talk to her parents. They saw the news, and while Paige's name wasn't mentioned yet, they recognized her." She handed the card to me.

"I need to talk to her," Riley said.

"Text her." Arianna shot him a sad smile. "Let her know you're thinking of her and that you love her. Don't be surprised if she doesn't answer, and don't be surprised if she tells you—in her polite Paige way—to fuck off. She's spent the last fifteen years or so believing she'd never be loved again. Words won't be enough to convince her. You're going to have to fly your cute little behinds down to Miami and woo the hell out of her." She looked at me. "Especially you."

I nodded. "Message received."

Arianna raised a beautifully manicured finger in the air, her nail polish gleaming blood red. "And I swear if you break her heart, I'll make you regret it."

"I have no doubt," I said.

She held out her hand for me to shake. "Call me Ari." She smiled with genuine warmth. "I have the feeling we're going to be good friends."

I took her hand. "I sure hope so."

Riley shook her hand as well. "Me too."

She collected her purse, then headed for the concierge's desk. Riley turned to me. "We could leave now."

I resisted rolling my eyes. "Did you even hear what she said? We need to give Paige a bit of space, let her calm down."

His knee jiggled against mine. "I feel like I need to do something." He motioned for the card Arianna had handed me. "At least let me text her."

I handed over the card. "Don't press. Just tell her we love her."

Riley's fingers flew over the screen, then he set the phone down. "Okay, let's plan to fly to Miami directly from London. That would give her three days."

"You do remember what's happening in five days?"

He looked puzzled.

"The press junket in LA. For the movie."

"Fuck the junket."

"Really, Rye? Fuck the junket? And what about the book? Nora gave you a deadline. You won't make it if you don't knuckle down."

"I don't care."

"Riley, come on."

"What?"

Thank God I'd finally read the Amber books, because I'd never have understood him otherwise. "Don't do this. Don't make the same mistake you made with Amber and Holden."

"What mistake would that be?"

"You put them up on a pedestal and made them more important than yourself."

His jaw worked and he looked away. "I'm not doing that."

"I don't want you to lose yourself."

"You think that's what I'm doing?"

"Answer this: What's the most important thing in your life?"

"You and Paige."

"Besides that."

"My writing."

"Yet you're willing to drop everything and tank your career. You're willing to set aside your writing, this book you've been working on every spare moment. Shit, Riley. I've seen the blood, sweat, and tears you've poured into these new chapters. How happy you've been while doing it too. Why would you so easily give up something that makes you feel alive? That's such a central part of who you are?"

"I'm not giving it up. Only putting it on hold for a bit."

"Paige wouldn't want you to trash your career."

"So, what? We lose her while I take care of business?"

"No. You go to LA, you write. You knock 'em dead on the junket. You take care of business, and when you're done, we win her back."

Riley shook his head. "I don't know. I'm worried, Carter, about waiting too long."

I squeezed his hand. "Listen to me, and listen good. You are worth just as much in this relationship as Paige. As me. You are the one who brought us all together. And if you don't learn that you fucking matter, then this relationship is doomed."

His lashes glistened with unshed tears. "I want this to work." He wiped at his eyes. "But I'm scared I'm going to fuck it up. Like I always fuck everything up."

Oh damn. I cleared the lump from my throat. "You have the sweetest heart of anyone I know. Well, besides Paige. And yeah, you're not perfect, but no one is. Not me, not Paige. No one. You think we'd both love you if you weren't worth it?"

"She didn't say it back." Tears slipped down his cheeks, and I kissed them away.

"She will. She's just scared." I stroked his damp cheek. "And I didn't help things. I can see now that Arianna was right. Paige could tell I wasn't sure. But we'll fix it. *I'll* fix it."

"You will?"

"Hell yeah, I will. *We* will, you'll see."

We would fix it. We had to. Because I had a hard time picturing any future that didn't have Paige and Riley in it.

Chapter 14

RILEY

It had been thirteen long days since I'd seen Paige. And despite my wishes, it was going to have to be one more.

"We're on in ten," said Clara, the floor manager, a serious-looking woman in her early thirties. She clutched a clipboard to a flat chest kept hidden beneath a bulky cardigan.

"Shit, shit, shit," I muttered as I tried Carter's number again. Where the hell was he? We'd planned to meet in Miami later tonight to surprise Paige and, hopefully, convince her to give our trio another chance.

Instead, the promoters of *Amber's Fall* had insisted that I, Amber, and Holden do an interview today on *The Jimmy Adams Show*, the hottest show in late-night TV. Apparently, there'd been a last-minute cancellation, and the show's producers were squeezing us in on the condition that all three of us appear. When I'd tried to desist, I'd been told in no uncertain terms that I'd be sued for breach of contract if I didn't show up at the studio in New York City at the appointed time.

This was a huge coup for the movie, but my love life hung in the balance. Why couldn't anyone understand that? The urge to throw it all away, say fuck it to the junket, fuck it to the movie, fuck it to my new book, and focus on fixing my relationship with Paige and Carter was so strong. Too strong. Maybe Carter was right. Maybe I did tend to lose myself in my relationships.

Writing defined me. I had to remember that.

All that had happened three hours ago, and since then, I'd tried calling Carter at least a hundred times. As I was about to hang up yet again, a breathless Carter came on the line. "Riley?"

"Yeah, it's me. Listen, I don't have much time. I got roped into doing *The Jimmy Adams Show*, and I'm on the air in ten minutes."

"*The Jimmy Adams Show*? That's awesome, Rye."

My chest tightened. Carter wouldn't think it was so wonderful if he knew that Amber and Holden were here too. I should tell Carter, admit the truth, but I couldn't deal with the fallout at ten minutes to airtime. Not that I expected Carter to be jealous. Then again, I'd never expected Paige to run off like she had.

"There's going to be a viewing party later that I have to attend as well. Anyway, I won't be able to get out to Miami tonight like we'd planned."

"Okay. So I'll call and see if I can rebook my ticket and change our hotel reservations."

"No, no. You should still go tonight."

"Without you?" Carter sounded confused. "Why would I do that?"

"I was thinking that Paige might be more willing to listen if it's just you." I glanced toward the floor manager. She signed five minutes to me with her fingers. I filled my lungs with air and blew out slowly. I hadn't been this nervous about an interview since I'd been grilled about the inappropriateness of my relationship with Amber by the college disciplinary board right before they fired my ass. "Anyway, she might feel less like we're ambushing her. And... you're better at talking to people than I am."

Carter chuckled. "Wow, you must really be on edge about doing the show to be saying that."

"I'm serious."

"Okay. I'll fly out as planned and see if I can talk to Paige."

"I'll call you when I get to town."

"Riley?"

"Yeah?"

"You're going to be great. And you know what else?"

"What?"

"I love you."

My chest filled with warmth and tears pricked my eyes. Christ, what I wouldn't give to feel the reassuring pressure of Carter's hand on my neck right now.

Yeah, and have him meet Amber and Holden. That would be fun.

My stomach churned and I shoved the thought away. I didn't want my past mistakes to taint what Carter and I shared, and hopefully, what Paige would share with us. Because we couldn't lose her. We wouldn't.

"I love you too, babe. And more importantly, I trust you with everything."

"I won't let you down, Rye. I will fix this. I promise."

I shook out my shoulders as Clara waved frantically at me. "Shit. I've got to go. Don't do anything I wouldn't do," I joked.

"Hot damn, then I guess all options are on the table."

Carter's deep rumbling laugh rolled over me. "You got it. Later, man."

Here goes nothing.

Pocketing my cell phone, after making sure to set it to vibrate, I followed Clara out of the green room, down the long corridors, and stopped behind the curtain shielding the entrance to the stage.

Was I going to be able to go out there and be civil when I still itched to slam my fist into Holden's handsome face? The last time we'd all met, it had turned into a giant screamfest. No doubt the producers were banking on a repeat performance. It would be super bad for my reputation, but it would be great for ticket sales. Everyone loved a scandal.

Clara counted down, silently mouthing, "Five, four, three, two, one."

I had vaguely heard the announcer saying my name when Clara shoved me through the opening in the curtain. The crowd cheered, making me feel like a rock star.

I wouldn't lie. I loved the attention showered on me by the audience. Still, I'd trade it to be with Carter and Paige in Miami. Too bad contracts didn't give two shits about love.

Waving to the audience, I turned to the host, Jimmy, who welcomed me with a handshake and bro hug. And then, all too soon, Amber was standing right in front of me, and she looked even more beautiful than before. Her long chestnut hair shone in the bright stage lights, and she wore a very tight, very short dress in a shade of pink that accentuated the delicateness of her skin.

She smiled at me and held out her hand. I steeled myself against the impact that her touch had always had on me. Pressing a light kiss to her cheek, I took her fingers in mine. The scent she wore tickled my nose, making me retreat quickly before I sneezed all over her.

Taking stock of my reactions, I didn't sense any tingling or tightening. No increased pulse. No heart slamming against my chest. In fact, the only impact she was having on me was a desire to get away from the potency of her perfume.

I held my hand out to Holden and prepared for the old anger to grab me, that feeling of betrayal, of the knife sliding between my ribs.

All I felt was the quick squeeze of Holden's fingers around my own, and then it was over.

After we'd taken our seats, I waited for the questions, which would likely focus more on the salacious details of our past relationship, the arguments and the ultimate failure, than on the movie we were actually promoting. Having all three of us here at once would be too much temptation for our host to ignore.

"So," Jimmy started. "How long has it been since the last time you were all together like this?"

Amber tittered and put her clenched fist between her breasts in a way I used to find so damn sexy. Now it seemed childish. Fake. But that wasn't a fair assessment. Was I allowing my resentment to color my perception of her?

Since neither Amber nor Holden answered the question, I decided I'd make the first move. "Not since a certain rather disastrous evening at Catch LA." Looking at the audience, I grinned and widened my eyes. On cue, the audience reacted with the laughter I'd expected.

The photos of our horrendous breakup had been plastered all over social media and grocery store checkout counter rags. Hell, they'd even made it onto CNN.

When I looked back at our host, whose expression showed his extreme pleasure that I had gone there, I accepted that this was what I had to do. I had to face my past, exorcise it even, and what better way than to do it in front of a national audience and my two former lovers? Because yeah, I *was* Riley fucking Kendrick.

Out of the corner of my eye, I saw Holden take Amber's hand and rest it on his thigh. It was a tender gesture that only a few months ago would have slayed me. Today, I felt nothing. Not even when her large diamond engagement ring twinkled in the bright stage lights.

"How long ago was that?" Jimmy asked, looking at Amber.

"Oh, I don't know. How long ago was it, honey?" she asked Holden.

Doing an admirable job of not looking at me, Holden took a moment as he seemed to count back. "Ah… It was around Thanksgiving. So what is that? Nine months?"

"Let me get this right," Jimmy said. "You've all been working on the same movie, yet you haven't even laid eyes on each other in all that time?"

"Well." Amber shot me a glance. "Riley was just a consultant on the movie, so most of what he did was by phone or email I guess."

Holden's jaw tightened and for the first time since the beginning of the interview, he faced me. "You left town right after, moved to the East Coast, right?"

As I met and held Holden's green stare, a sense of serenity swept over me. Compared to Carter, Holden was an immature kid. As for Amber, she wasn't half the woman Paige was. Maybe someday she would be, but right now, she and Holden were two kids caught up in the whirlwind of life in the spotlight. I had been there, so I knew what I was talking about. What had started out as a never-ending party with sexy, glamorous people determined to have the time of their lives soon became a cold and empty existence. No one cared about anyone. Loyalty was just a word.

Being rejected by Amber and Holden had been a harsh removal of the rose-tinted glasses I'd been wearing since stepping off the plane at LAX. The glamor had become tawdry. The people plastic. The emotions flat. That's when I'd known that I didn't belong there anymore.

My time with Carter and Paige had taught me I didn't need the world's attention. I only needed the attention of the two people I loved with all my heart. I loved who I was with them. I loved who they were with me. They made me a better person, and I liked to think I did the same for them.

Amber and Holden? Like a taste of maple-flavored syrup, they'd left me craving the real thing.

And I was damn certain I'd found the real thing with Carter and Paige.

I smiled at Holden and Amber, our host, and then the audience. "Hollywood, Los Angeles, they no longer held any appeal for me, so I went back home to Vermont."

Amber wrinkled her nose. "I could never live in such a small, boring place again."

"Jeezum Crow, honey," I said. "Vermont thanks you."

Amber smiled, then frowned, as though realizing that what I'd said wasn't the compliment she'd been anticipating.

The band played the standard rimshot, *ba dum tsh*, and the audience roared. Someone shouted, "Burn!"

Feeling like a shit for my cattiness, I continued. "A bright star like you needs to be in Los Angeles."

"Thank you, Riley," she said. "Don't you miss all the action, even a little?"

I shook my head. "Not at all."

"I can't even imagine going back there." She mock shuddered. "Everyone is so dull."

Jimmy winked. "Except the studly sociology professors."

"Yes," she said, flashing a quick look at me. "Except them."

I laughed, amazed by how little I felt toward her. I didn't dislike her. On the contrary, I could now think back to the early days of our relationship and be grateful for what we'd had. "You gave me my voice, Amber. I'll never forget that."

"Speaking of which, *Amber's Fall* releases in four days. Any plans?"

Holden kissed Amber's hand. "We'll be at Grauman's Chinese Theater for the premiere."

"I can't wait for everyone to see the movie. I'm sure you're all going to love it," Amber added.

"What about you, Riley? Will you be at Grauman's?"

The producers had, of course, wanted me there, but with my agent's help, we'd convinced the movie studio that I'd done my share with the week-long junket.

"I'm not exactly sure where I'll be on that day," I hedged. With some luck and a whole lot of groveling, I hoped to be in Miami tucked in bed with the two loves of my life.

"Interesting," Jimmy joked, rubbing his palms together. "Would that have anything to do with the people you were seen with at LOOP Nightclub in London?"

I smiled enigmatically.

A section of the audience began to chant, "Love is love."

Feeling more accepted than I had since first realizing I was bisexual, I tossed my head back and laughed. "Yes, it is."

"So this is serious?" Jimmy asked.

I rested my chin on my steepled fingers for a moment, considering my answer. How much should I reveal? I hadn't run this by either Carter or Paige. On the other hand, if I wanted things to work out with them, I had to be honest. I needed the world to know that to me, both my lovers were equal. Even though I'd been with Carter longer, Paige was in no way a third. She was an integral part of our relationship. I just hoped she'd see it that way.

"Carter and I have been together for about four months. We are rock solid. He's my life. We met Paige last month, and things clicked between us. In a short time, she's become our everything."

"So why aren't they here with you?" Amber asked, her tone more gentle, more honest, than I'd heard it in years.

I opened my arms to encompass the television set, the lights, the cameras, the audience. "This life isn't easy and it's not for everyone, and being outed by the London paparazzi was not at all on Paige's agenda."

"So she's debating which she wants more: her privacy, or you and Carter?" Jimmy asked.

"Yep."

"Think you'll be able to convince her?" Jimmy asked.

I smirked. "I can be quite persuasive."

Holden snorted, smiling for the first time. "Damn right. You fucking turned me bi."

"You, my friend"—I clapped his shoulder—"just needed the right man to bring out your fierce side."

I sat back as the audience hooted with laughter. What a difference a few hours made. I'd been dreading this interview, dreading seeing Amber and Holden again, fully expecting all the old feelings to rise up and make me miserable. Instead, I was at peace for the first time since the breakup. Truly at peace. All the anger and recriminations, the fears and disappointment were gone. Evaporated like so much water on a hot sidewalk.

The illusion had finally shattered.

Hollywood had been a mirage fueled by sex, drugs, and money. What

I had with Paige and Carter? That was real. Now, we needed Paige to understand that Carter and I were strong without her. But with her, we were complete.

CARTER

Would Paige even speak to me? Taking a deep breath of the sultry Miami air, I knocked on her door. A quick call to Arianna when I'd touched down had given me Paige's address, and I'd hailed a cab before I could talk myself into waiting until morning. Yes, it was late. So late, Riley's interview on *The Jimmy Adams Show* was close to airtime.

"Who is it?" Paige called through the door, her voice cautious.

Duh, of course. She wasn't used to social calls this late at night.

"It's me, Carter."

"Carter?" Her voice rose uncertainly and I heard the door locks disengaging, then the door swung open.

"Hey, beautiful." My heart slammed in my chest. Thank God she hadn't told me to get lost. And Jesus, she looked amazing. Her hair was pulled up in a messy ponytail, and there wasn't a speck of makeup on her face. She didn't need it.

"What are you doing here?" she asked.

"We need to talk."

"There's a thing known as the phone."

She hadn't made a move to let me in. Fuck. I scrubbed a hand through my hair. "We need to speak in person. So there can be no misunderstandings. No doubts."

"Can't you just… let this go?" She sounded so alone, so small. And she looked so lost.

Something inside me snapped. She, like Riley, didn't get it. Didn't get how amazing she was. How special.

"No, I can't let this go. I'm not giving up on you. On us."

She smiled tightly. "Did Riley send you?"

"I'm here because *I* damn well want to be here." I took a breath, trying to slow my pounding heart, to purge the anger from my voice. "I fucked up, Paige. I didn't tell you how I felt. I couldn't see past my insecurity about you, about how Riley felt about you. I was jealous."

"Of me?" She seemed startled, putting a hand on the notch at the base of her throat. "Why?"

"Riley's been crazy about you since he met you. It took him *months* to admit that he loved me. You? You stole his heart in less than three weeks."

She shook her head. "He *thinks* he loves me."

A mosquito buzzed in my ear, and when it landed on my neck, I slapped at it. I leaned against the doorjamb. "Do you think we can have the rest of this conversation inside? Where I won't be eaten alive?"

She nodded. "Yes. Sorry. I'm a little… flustered." She motioned me inside. "Are you thirsty?"

"Some ice water would be great."

The TV was on, *The Jimmy Adams Show* on low volume. She must have been planning to watch the interview. I wheeled my carry-on into the entryway and closed the door.

I took a seat on the sofa while she busied herself in the kitchen. She came back with a glass of water for me and a cup of tea for herself. The air-conditioning made the room pleasantly cool, and the water tasted great, the ice clinking in the glass as I nearly drained it, trying to think of what to say, how to convince her that Riley really loved her.

That *I* really loved her.

That we belonged together.

That we'd never be happy apart.

I opened my mouth to speak, but stopped when Jimmy announced his next guests—Amber, Holden, and Riley. Huh. Riley hadn't mentioned that Amber and Holden would be there. My fingers tightened on the glass, already slick with condensation, and I carefully set it on the table. "Could you turn the volume up?" I asked.

Paige had taken a seat beside me on the couch, but she'd put at least a foot of space between us. Not that I expected any different. In fact, I'd expected her to sit on the armchair, entirely out of reach.

So maybe things weren't as dire as I'd thought.

But a lot was riding on what happened onscreen. Why hadn't Riley told me?

Did he still have feelings for Amber? For Holden? Or had he guessed that I'd be upset and hadn't wanted to deal with it?

Because I was definitely not calm. I glanced at Paige, who'd pulled her knees up to her chest, her eyes glued to the screen, her bottom lip caught between her teeth.

Yeah, she wasn't all that calm either.

Amber and Holden came out first, the two of them glowing and gorgeous, the rock on Amber's finger catching the stage lighting and sparkling. And then Riley came out from the opposite side of the stage, looking a bit off-balance, but then he brightened at the roar from the audience, the girls screaming his name almost as loudly as they'd screamed Holden's.

Yeah, Riley was a fucking literary rock star. His dark hair gleamed in the light, his cheeks a little flushed, his eyes bright as he kissed Amber's cheek and shook Holden's hand. I studied Riley's body language, surprised to see him so at ease. He had tensed up a bit when he'd touched them, then he seemed to relax, sprawling back in the chair and giving Jimmy a wide smile, a smile that only grew wider when Jimmy alluded to the infamous breakup that had been in all the gossip rags for weeks.

Riley didn't miss a fucking beat. He took the bait and ran with it, not giving Jimmy the satisfaction of tripping him up, not even blinking when the audience howled. That smile only grew wider. What the fuck?

I looked at Paige, and she raised both eyebrows, clearly as thrown as I was.

Riley seemed utterly serene. Unruffled. At fucking ease, next to the two people who'd sliced his heart in two and then stomped on it.

Now they were discussing how dull Amber thought Vermont was. And Riley... Riley actually got off a good burn on Amber, then seemed to think better of it. He was even *thanking* Amber for giving him his voice.

Apparently Jimmy wasn't entirely happy that the interview was going so smoothly, because he brought up the night at LOOP Nightclub in London.

The night that had cost me my job. And possibly cost Riley and me our relationship with Paige. She tensed beside me, sucking in a breath.

Jimmy had just asked Riley about "the people" who'd been seen with him that night, and the audience started chanting "Love is love."

Riley smiled again, soaking up the cheers, and then he laughed. He looked so damn happy.

"So this is serious?" Jimmy asked.

Paige and I both leaned forward.

"Carter and I have been together for about four months. We are rock solid. He is my life. We met Paige last month, and things clicked between us. In a short time, she's become our everything."

Paige let out a little gasp, and I reached out and touched her leg. She didn't take my hand, but she didn't shy away either, letting my hand rest on her knee.

"So why aren't they here with you?" Amber asked.

Riley opened his arms, gesturing to the lights, the set, the audience. "This life isn't easy, and it's not for everyone, and being outed by the London paparazzi was not at all on Paige's agenda."

"So she's debating what she wants more: her privacy, or you and Carter?" Jimmy asked.

"Yep."

"Think you'll be able to convince her?" Jimmy asked.

"I can be quite persuasive."

Holden snorted. "Damn right. You *bleep*ing turned me bi."

Riley clapped the guy on the shoulder. "You, my friend, just needed the right man to bring out your fierce side."

That brought the house down, the audience dissolving into cheers and laughter, and the show cut to commercial.

Paige muted the TV and finally touched my hand, giving it a little squeeze before releasing it, then she turned to face me, and I withdrew my hand to my own lap.

"That did not go how I thought it would," Paige said.

"Me either."

"He looks… happy."

I shook my head. "He looks like he's over Amber and Holden. Like he's moved on." I touched Paige's wrist. "That's because of us."

Paige sighed. "I don't know. Amber is such a knockout. I didn't look that good at her age. I've *never* looked that good. How could Riley possibly want me after that?"

She really had no idea. Not a fucking clue. And that only made me love her more. I scooted over to Paige and hauled her onto my lap, my cock springing to attention when her hip pressed against it. "You don't get it, beautiful. You are goddamn amazing." I brushed a few stray hairs off her flushed cheeks, then drew her face to mine. "And you drive me crazy." I pressed my lips to hers, then pulled back, cupping her cheeks in my hands. "I love you, Paige. I should've said it back in London. I guess I needed Arianna to call me on my bullshit first."

"Ari? You spoke to her?"

"More like she dropped some truth on us. Especially me."

I stroked my thumbs along Paige's cheekbones, her hazel eyes locked on mine, her body trembling in my arms. "You mean it?" she finally asked.

"I do. I love you. As much as I love Riley. You balance us out. You make me laugh. You make me happy. And I can't imagine giving that up."

Her eyes welled with tears. "Jesus, Carter. I don't know what to say."

Tell me you love me. That's all you have to do.

But she didn't quite believe yet. Tears slid down her cheeks, and I kissed them away, licking the salt from my lips. "We have all the time in the world, Paige. There's no pressure for you to say or do anything you don't want to."

I kissed her lips again, and she kissed me back this time, her mouth opening beneath mine, a sigh of satisfaction leaving her and making my cock swell painfully against her hip.

I pulled back, breathing hard. "I want you, beautiful." I shifted my hips, letting my cock rub against her, so she couldn't mistake what I was saying.

"Should we do this?" she whispered.

"Riley and I have had sex before and after we met you. This isn't any different. And he knows I came to see you."

"You don't think he'll be upset?"

I kissed the tip of her nose. "He told me once that for this to work, we all need to develop relationships with each other. We all need to bond as pairs, in addition to being together, or there will always be some distance. And that distance can breed insecurity. And jealousy."

Paige nodded. "That makes sense." She leaned forward and slipped her arms around my neck. "So I get to have my wicked way with you?"

I smiled. "I thought you'd never ask."

She kissed me again so sweetly, her breasts crushed against my chest, her luscious hips and ass rubbing against my straining cock.

So she hadn't said she loved me. Or Riley. Yet.

But she was thinking about the future, a future with the two of us. And that was good enough for now.

I let her control the kiss, let her set the pace, and kept my need to possess her in check. Tonight was all about Paige. About showing her how much she was loved.

I hadn't slept with a woman on my own, no Riley in the picture, since my divorce two years ago. The blow job Paige had given me in the maze didn't really count, since that had been a one-way interaction. Tonight was about the both of us. Two people, showing their love for each other.

Paige slipped her hands inside my button-down, her fingers grazing my collarbones as she kissed me. I unbuttoned my shirt to the waist, pulling it loose from my jeans, baring myself for her pleasure.

She smiled at me and kissed one of my nipples, tweaking the other with her delicate fingers.

Jesus, she was gorgeous. So soft and yielding in my arms, her skin like silk as I kissed down her neck, eating up her moans like they were my last meal.

Riley was right; I hadn't let myself really bond with her yet, not in the way I should have, largely because sex for us had always been about the trio, never only the two of us. Somehow I'd managed to keep Paige at a slight remove, even as she'd burrowed under my skin and into my heart.

But now that I was here, now that she was moaning for me alone, responding to my touch, looking into my eyes, smiling and letting down her hair for me, and only me, something had changed, was changing.

She's mine.

And I'm hers.

Her hands fell to my belt buckle, and I put my own over them. "Not so fast," I murmured. "Let me make you feel good, Paige."

I hooked my thumbs in the waistband of her yoga pants and started to tug them over her hips.

She placed her hands over mine. "You know, it's been a hot day, and I feel like my shower was a long time ago."

I grinned. "And I've been flying. Got a bathtub big enough for two?"

She shrugged. "I think you'll take up most of it."

"Well, then, you'll have to sit on my lap."

"You'd like that, wouldn't you?" she asked, her fingers caressing the bulge in my jeans.

"You already know the answer."

She rose, and I followed her into a good-sized bathroom. She leaned over to start the tub and pour in some bath beads, and I stepped behind her, grinding my swollen cock against her perfect ass. She pressed back into me, and I pulled off her pants and underwear, leaving her in a loose T-shirt, which she quickly shed, to reveal no bra underneath. Her nipples pebbled under my gaze, and I quickly shed the rest of my clothes.

"You'd better get in first," she said.

I stepped into the hot, frothy water, the contrast in temperature making me hiss with pleasure. I sat down and offered her a hand to steady her as she stepped in, careful to avoid trampling my balls.

I spread my knees, and she nestled between them, settling back against my chest. I folded my arms around her and kissed her neck. My cock was pressing against the top of her ass crack, and I had the crazy urge to touch her there, to take her there, but I wasn't sure how she'd react.

Best to take it slow, take it easy, until she indicated she was willing to try it.

I ran a thumb along the seam of her ass, and she shivered, but she didn't flinch away. I did it again, and she looked at me over her shoulder. "I haven't ever..." She started, then let her voice trail off.

"And you don't have to unless you want to."

I kissed her shoulder, and she met my lips with her own. "I've thought about it, and I think it's something I might like to try." She reddened. "Taking both of you, at the same time."

Fuck. My cock twitched. Yeah, I'd thought about it too. Riley and I had shared women that way, but doing it with Paige would be something else.

Something special.

"I want that too." I kissed her temple and put an arm across her body below her breasts and pulled her snugly against me. "But tonight, it's just us."

She stilled, then put an arm over mine. "I'm glad you came."

Some bit of tension in my chest finally uncoiled. "I am too." I kissed her shoulder, nipping at her skin. "I was jealous of you. That's why I couldn't say that I loved you before. I couldn't even *see* it."

She shifted in my arms so she could look at me, her brow crinkling adorably. "I still can't believe you were jealous of me."

"Believe it. It took Riley months to tell me he loved me, and it happened only after he'd left—run away, really, though he doesn't see it that way." I swallowed down the lump that still threatened to close off my throat, even now. "And in only a few weeks, he was telling you he loved you. I'd seen it all over his face well before then, I'd heard it in his voice when he talked about you. I tried not to be jealous, but I failed."

"Oh Carter." She cupped my cheek and kissed me on the mouth. "You don't get it, do you?"

"Get what?"

"Being on a trip together, it's a million times more intense than dating someone like you'd normally do. You're together almost 24/7, and you have all these new experiences, and you have all the time in the world to talk and hang out together. Each day is like months and months of dates all rolled into one."

She was right; it explained how rapidly my feelings for her had developed, and if I was able to fall for her so quickly, and with Riley around to boot, how must it have been for just the two of them?

Probably a lot like the times I'd spent alone with Paige on the trip—intense and intimate, the moments of laughter, sharing confidences, distilled and concentrated, the effect so much more potent than that of a typical encounter.

Because we hadn't had to deal with the real world, with our normal lives, with paying bills, with fulfilling obligations to others. We'd been in a fantasy that was nevertheless real. We'd seen each other with our masks ripped away, with the ordinary constraints of life set aside.

We'd *seen* each other.

"That makes sense; it explains why I feel so strongly about you. Why I love you already. Why I want you in my life. In our lives."

She held my eyes, her breathing a bit faster than normal. Then she reached out and ran a wet thumb across my bottom lip. "I love you too, Carter. I was afraid to let myself even think it. About either of you. Because then I'd have to risk losing you by telling you about Emma."

"I get it."

"But does Riley? And I have to wonder how much I hurt him by not telling him I loved him." Her eyes closed, and tears welled out around her lashes. "He's been so patient. He's sent me the sweetest texts. And I haven't replied to any of them. I couldn't."

I stroked her cheek. "It's okay. He's okay."

She opened her eyes and looked at me. "But he isn't here."

"Only because of the interview. We'd planned to come down together, and this came up last minute, and the movie producers wouldn't let him turn it down. But"—I leaned forward and kissed her—"I'm glad it worked out this way. You and I needed to talk."

She nodded and kissed me back. "And we need to finish what we started on the couch."

I let a grin spread across my face. "I love how you think."

We drained the tub and rinsed off in the shower. I was barely able to keep my hands off her long enough for us to make it to the bed, where I pushed her back onto the mattress and spread her legs. Settling between them, my hands holding her inner thighs apart, I gazed at her glistening pussy. She squirmed under my hold. "Just do it," she whispered.

I chuckled and ran a finger along her slit, opening her up, grazing over her clit, making her moan and stiffen. "You're beautiful, Paige."

She put an arm across her face. "Stop staring."

I stuck two fingers in my mouth, wetting them, then started stroking her, making her gasp. "You *are* beautiful. Whether you believe it or not. And if my words don't convince you, my cock should. It's dying to get inside you."

She sighed, but said nothing. I leaned forward, blowing gently on her pussy, before sucking her clit into my mouth, swirling my tongue around the rapidly swelling nub.

"Jesus," she groaned, her hands fisting the sheets, her hips arching to meet me.

I took my time, building her pleasure slowly, stoking it carefully, until she was panting and begging me, each soft "please" like a lightning bolt to my cock.

She was going to wreck me, and I didn't care. The only thing that mattered was that she loved me. She'd finally said it; she'd finally let me in.

And I was more than ready to do the same.

PAIGE

I couldn't stop writhing, couldn't stop begging Carter to let me come, to stop this sweet, sweet torture he was inflicting on me with every sweep of his tongue, every plunge of his fingers inside me.

I'd thought Riley was amazing at oral, and he was, but Carter—Carter was *patient*. He took his time, didn't push me high and fast. And now I was flying so high I wasn't sure I'd ever come down, even when he finally, finally, let me tumble over the edge, the pleasure rippling through my body in an intense wave that left me blissful and tingling. I shuddered and cried out, my thighs clasping his head, my fingers in his hair. "Oh

Jesus, oh Jesus, oh Jesus," I chanted.

When I finally let him go, he kissed my inner thigh and climbed up over me, his rock hard cock pressing into me. He rubbed the head of it against my still-swollen clit, setting off a series of aftershocks that made me press my hand against his chest. "Stop for a minute. I beg you," I panted.

"No rest for the wicked," he whispered in my ear, and I opened my lids.

The slight crow's feet around his eyes, the twinkle in his gaze, the curving of his sinful mouth filled my chest with warmth. "I love you, Carter. I really, truly do."

He pretended to buff his nails on his bare chest. "That good, huh?"

I laughed and swatted at his arm. "Yeah, it was that good, and you know it." I sobered and stroked his cheek. "But that has nothing to do with how I feel."

"Like the world just got a whole lot more wonderful?"

"Yeah. Like that." I reached down and wrapped my palm around him, stroking him gently. He thrust into my grip and moaned, his eyes closing. "Roll onto your back," I whispered. "Let me take care of you."

He did as I asked, and I started kissing his face and neck, taking my time, licking and nipping him along the way to my destination.

God, he was gorgeous, all sculpted perfection, the hard planes of his chest and the ridges and valleys of his abs rippling beneath my touch.

His cock bobbed in the air, a drop of pre-cum slicking the tip. I licked it up before taking him in my mouth, enjoying his moan of pleasure as I swirled my tongue over the head.

I thought of the time he'd "punished" me in the garden maze. I'd been excited and turned on by the possibility of being caught, by the erotic charge of submitting to a powerful man I'd barely known at the time. My lover's lover.

But now—now I wanted to please Carter, to make him come so hard he saw stars. To show him how much he mattered to me.

Because he did. I loved Riley; I'd known it for what seemed like a long time. But Carter was different. If Riley had charged into my life and battered down my defenses, Carter had taken the opposite approach—politely knocking on the door and waiting for an invitation. He wasn't in a hurry like Riley; he wasn't as demanding.

Carter was kind and giving, someone who looked before he leapt, someone who would catch me if I fell. Not that Riley wouldn't try. But he might not understand *how* to help.

Carter would, or he'd know how to ask.

In all the excitement that seemed to trail in Riley's wake, it was easy to overlook Carter, easy to take him for granted.

But that was not at all what he deserved.

I descended on his cock, hardening my lips into a tight ring that made Carter groan as I sucked his length into my mouth. He was longer than Riley, and there was no way I could take all of him. But I was going to do my best.

"God, Paige, whatever you're doing with your mouth, keep doing it."

I swirled my tongue around him as I moved up and down, my hand joining in at the base to try to cover his entire shaft.

"Jesus," he gasped when I quickly bobbed over the head several times, that tight ring formed by my lips giving him plenty of sensation.

He thrust up slightly and met me, almost making me gag. He must be close.

I sped up my efforts, but he stopped me. "I want to come inside you," he said.

"You sure?"

He nodded. "I want to look in your eyes, beautiful."

I grabbed a condom out of the top drawer in the nightstand.

Carter reached for it. I shook my head. "I'm taking care of you, remember? Lie back and let me do all the work."

He crossed his arms behind his head. "Okay then. You tell me what you want me to do."

"Not a damn thing," I said as I rolled the condom over him.

I rose up to straddle him, rubbing my slick heat over his cock, making us both groan, before I positioned him at my entrance and slowly descended onto him, inch by inch.

I felt so full. He reached for my hips, his large hands warm on my skin. I raised myself up, then slid back down, twisting my hips along the way, the novel sensation making me cry out. I rose and fell, rose and fell, gradually increasing the speed, the delicious friction inside me increasing by the second.

"You feel so damn good," he said. "But beautiful, you're going too slow."

"Still?" I panted, rocking myself back and up, my hips circling him, his cock hitting me in places that made me cry out in bliss.

"Yeah," he murmured, his hands tightening on my waist. He pulled me up, then slammed me back down as he rose to meet me, his eyes locked on mine.

The increase in speed and pressure cranked the pleasure up, until I felt like I was going to explode. And then I did, clenching hard around him and sending him over the edge too.

He hammered into me a few more times, then relaxed back against the mattress, his breathing labored. "Fuck." He stretched out like a well-satisfied lion. "That was amazing."

"We ought to do this more often."

"We will." I lay down beside him, and he gathered me close, pressing a kiss to my temple. I curled into his side, then flung a leg possessively over him.

He was mine; I was his. And I wasn't letting him go.

And tomorrow, I hoped I could make things right with Riley as well. Because the three of us? We were meant to be.

Chapter 15

RILEY

Maybe I should have called Carter first before barging over to Paige's apartment. I had no idea how things had gone down between them last night. For all I knew, she'd slam the door in my face.

Ball cap tugged low over a pair of shades, I handed the cab driver a couple twenties and stepped out onto the sidewalk. In front of me was a modest apartment complex made up of a series of three-story buildings linked together by exterior stairwells. I scanned the numbers on the buildings, quickly spotted Paige's, and climbed the stairs to the third floor.

I had my hand in the air about to knock, when the door opened to reveal a pretty blonde girl, short and a little rotund. Her eyes sparkled as brightly as her smile.

"Oh my God," she squealed, slapping her hands over her mouth. "I saw you in the parking lot. And… oh… I can't believe it!"

I grinned, loving how expressive Paige's daughter was. I set my roller suitcase on the landing and leaned against the wall. "You know who I am?"

"Of course. Doesn't everyone?"

"I know you too. You're Emma."

Hands on her hips, Emma frowned at me. "Why do you know me?"

"I'm… uh…" I stopped.

Grow some balls, Kendrick.

I cleared my throat and tried again. "I'm your mom's boyfriend."

Emma shook her head, sending her long curls whipping around her face. "No. My mom's boyfriend is in the kitchen."

"Carter's here?"

Emma's eyes widened and she cradled her hands against her chest. "Oh, Mom, you're in trouble," she called out loudly. "Your *other* boyfriend is here."

Roaring with laughter, I hung onto the doorframe. Paige was going to kill me. "It's okay, Emma. I'm not mad."

She scrunched her face up. "You're not?"

"Nope. I think Carter's a really great guy."

Emma whispered loudly, "And he's cute."

"Yes, he is."

"You're pretty cute too," she added, grinning.

"Am I now?"

"I like your hat."

Well, there went my ego. Shot down by an eighteen-year-old. Guess it wouldn't be the first time. I bit back a smile. "Want to try it on?"

"Can I?"

"Sure." I placed it on her head, then handed her my sunglasses. "Want these too?"

"Mm-hmm!" She snatched the glasses from my hand and hurriedly put them on. The result was cute as hell. "Can I take a picture? Mom got me a phone with a camera."

I went down on one knee beside her and smiled as she snapped a selfie. "You won't put that on the Internet, right?"

"No way. Mom said that's a big no-no."

Thank you, Paige. At least the paparazzi wouldn't be knocking down the door today.

Emma grabbed my hand. "Come on!"

Barely managing to latch onto the handle of my suitcase and shut the door to the apartment, I was dragged into the kitchen. It was an idyllic scene, like something out of a sappy rom-com. The sun spilling into the small space bathed Paige and Carter in a warm golden glow as they sat at a small round table eating breakfast. In their bathrobes.

"Well, isn't this cozy," I said.

I'd meant it as a joke, but Paige's reaction showed she'd taken it quite differently. Nerves or guilt? Hopping to her feet, she tightened the belt on her robe. She then adjusted the lapels, then her hair, but didn't make a move toward me. Seeing her so jumpy made my chest constrict. I just hoped nerves were all it was, and that she didn't have bad news for me. Hoping for the best, but prepared for the worst, I left my suitcase next to the counter and walked farther into the kitchen.

Paige gave me a small, awkward wave. "Hi, Riley."

I swallowed, then bent to kiss her cheek. "Hello, Paige. It's good to see you."

Emma tugged on my sleeve. "You gonna kiss Carter too?" she asked, her tone teasing. "You said he was cute."

My eyes went to the man I hadn't seen in over a week. Carter looked good. Really good. Relaxed and happy.

Carter had obviously spent the night here. He'd probably had sex with Paige. God knows I would have. So why was Paige so anxious? Had they decided they were better off without me? A knot formed in the pit of my stomach. Was my worst nightmare coming true… again?

All loose-limbed, Carter stood and sauntered over toward me. A corner of his mouth kicked up. "You told Emma I was cute?"

Seeing the softening in Carter's features and the hint of humor in his voice, I smiled back, the knot in my gut loosening a bit. "I did. Whatcha gonna to do about it, big man?"

"This." Carter grabbed the front of my shirt and pulled me against his chest. Our lips crashed together in a kiss that left me breathless and needing more.

Carter still wanted me. But did Paige?

When Carter stepped back, I heard Emma's giggling, but before I could respond to it, Paige stepped between me and Carter. She tapped her finger on my lips and drew it down in a line over my chin, along my neck, and into the opening of my shirt before twisting it playfully in my chest hairs. "I've got to say, Riley, I'm a little jealous."

"Of me?" Carter's kiss had been scorching.

"No, of Carter."

Oh. Holding onto my shirt with one hand, she grabbed my neck with the other and pulled me down. I took her into my arms and kissed her soundly, letting her know exactly how much I'd missed her and how much I wanted to be in her life. When she tightened her hold on the back of my shirt and dug her fingers into my hair, my heart fluttered, and I prayed I was reading the situation correctly. Because if I was wrong, I was in for a world of hurt.

"OMG!" Emma exclaimed. "I'm calling Aunt Ari." Then she ran out of the room.

Carter rested his arm lightly around Paige's shoulders. They looked so good together. She glanced up at him, her eyes soft and thankful. I could totally understand the look. Lord knew having Carter hold you like that, all warm and strong, was one of the best feelings in the world, right up there with being fucked by him. I wished I were standing between the two of them. I'd had enough of being the odd man out.

As though reading my thoughts, Paige took my hand, then Carter's. "Let's go into the living room."

I settled onto the couch, Carter beside me. When Paige sat on Carter's lap, I again felt a pang of jealousy. Of course, it made sense she would be more comfortable with Carter right now. They'd had a chance to talk it out, whereas I hadn't seen or heard from Paige in fourteen days. Fourteen long days.

Paige took hold of my hand again. "Are you really okay with this?"

"I've already told you that I'm happy you have a kid. More than happy, really. Emma is a riot."

"And she clearly likes you," Carter added.

My heart warmed. I liked Emma too. "I understand the difficulties with her situation, Paige. I might not be a dad or a special-ed teacher, but I think Emma and I will get along great."

"Probably because in terms of maturity, you and Emma are the same age," Carter teased.

Careful not to hit Paige, I punched Carter's arm. "Fuck off. You're jealous because she likes me more than she likes you."

"Nah, she just wants your hat." Carter grinned.

I grinned back, the tension in my chest easing.

Only Paige wasn't smiling. I brushed my fingers along her cheek. "Talk to me."

Keeping her eyes on her fingers, where she played with her belt, Paige shrugged. "What about this?" She looked up and indicated her and Carter's robes and all that they entailed.

Ah… she was worried about having slept with Carter. That one was easy to answer. "I'm thrilled actually."

She snorted out a laugh. "I find that hard to believe."

"It's true. Unless…" My gut twisted again. "Unless the two of you being together means you don't want me."

Paige and Carter exchanged a look I couldn't read. She nodded and returned her attention to me. "Tell us how the interview went."

Carter nudged my shoulder. "It looked like you were having a good time with Amber and Holden."

"It's show business, and that's all it ever was. I know that now." I shifted on the couch and took one of their hands in each of mine. "The whole time I was sitting there, answering questions with Amber and Holden about our time together, all I could think about was how badly I wanted to be here, with both of you."

I looked away, afraid to show them how much I cared, how vulnerable I felt. Either one could hurt me with just a word. "As soon as the viewing party was over, I boarded the first red-eye to Miami."

Tears streaming down her cheeks, Paige threw herself into my arms. "I love you, Riley. So much. And I'm really sorry for not believing you in London."

Relief washed over me. "I love you too, sweetheart." I held her face in my hands and kissed her wet cheeks. "Taking all this on, me, my past, and my fame, it's a lot to ask. You needed time, and that's okay."

Carter circled his arms around Paige and me, then kissed each of us. "I love you both."

We kissed him back, and Paige cried some more. "I love you too, Carter. Oh God, I'm a mess." She laughed and dried her cheeks moments before Emma came barreling into the living room.

"Aunt Ari wants to take me to lunch. Can I go? Please, please, please!"

"Yes," we all answered at once, laughing.

I buried my face in Paige's hair. "I really do like Aunt Ari."

Carter grinned. "She's got the best ideas."

Paige jumped to her feet. "I should get dressed before Ari arrives."

"Mind if I grab a shower?" I asked.

"Hot damn!" Carter said, jumping to his feet. He extended a hand and pulled me up, then pointed down the hall. "Bathroom's the last door on the left."

I patted his cheek and struck a sassy pose. "Well, aren't you an eager beaver."

"You have no idea." Carter turned me around and smacked me on the ass. "Now go."

Clicking my heels smartly, I saluted. "Yes, sir."

Carter growled. "Don't you fucking tease me."

"Language, boys," Paige called from her room.

Carter shook his head in mock exasperation. "What the heck have I gotten myself into?"

"Heaven?" I asked.

We grinned at each other. "Fucking A."

"Boys!"

CARTER

I had to believe we were doing the right thing. For all of us, including Emma.

Still in my bathrobe, I leaned against the wall and watched silently as Paige saw Emma and Ari out the door. "Thank you, Ari. See you later, Emma. I love you."

Emma turned to wave over her shoulder as she followed Ari down the stairs leading to the parking lot. "Love you too, Mom. See you later, Riley.

You too, Carter."

Paige's daughter was a darling and surprisingly clear-spoken. Many of the students I'd had with Down syndrome, even those with the mosaic variant, hadn't been so verbal. It was a pleasure to hear her joy and to know she was already comfortable enough with me and Riley to tease us. Paige had done a fine job raising her, especially given she'd been mostly on her own. And that was something that was going to change. Going forward, Paige and Emma would have both me and Riley to depend on.

Once Emma was in the car, Paige closed the apartment door and leaned against it. Her hand on her stomach, she took several slow, tremulous breaths. I understood her nerves, because this was it. We were going to have sex again, although it was going to be more than that. We loved each other, all three of us. This time, we'd be making love, and none of us would ever be the same again.

Butterflies fluttered in my stomach as I looked at Paige, then Riley. We were about to embark on the journey of a lifetime, one that after my divorce, I'd never thought to try again, especially with a woman. Livia had burned me, betrayed me, wounded me deeply. And these two people standing before me had healed me. How was that even possible? Scarcely more than a month ago, I hadn't even known Paige, and I had thought for sure my relationship with Riley had self-destructed. Yet, here I was. Here we were.

Riley hooked a strand of hair behind Paige's ear. "Everything all right?"

"Just a little nervous," she admitted.

I joined them, and taking Paige's hand, I brought her between me and Riley where we held her closely. Using a finger under her chin, Riley forced her to look up. "We'll never do anything you don't want, whether that's in the bedroom or out of it. You're in control here, Paige."

Nodding, she stroked Riley's smooth cheek. "I've never touched you without a beard." She smiled, and I knew exactly why. Somehow, despite his twenty-eight years, Riley had skin as soft as a baby's. Even though I would never admit it out loud, I'd spent many a night running my fingers over Riley's face when the man had been sleeping too soundly to awaken from the touch. I'd dreamed of being able to do that whenever I wanted. Miraculously, my dream was coming true.

"Do you like it? I can grow the beard back. The producer thought it would be better to look more like the Riley in the movie for the interviews."

"About that," Paige said, making my stomach clench. I'd thought she had accepted Riley's explanation regarding his feelings for Amber and Holden earlier that morning.

"I wanted to tell you how touched I was with your honesty during the interview. What you said, well… it meant a lot," she finished.

Relief flowed down my spine. I slid my hand up to Riley's nape, loving the sound of his sharp inhale. Yes, I knew the effect I had on him when I did that. It thrilled and amazed me each time Riley submitted to me so freely. It made me love him even more. Which wasn't to say I didn't enjoy returning the favor, because God knew I did. And I wasn't ashamed for Paige to see it. In fact, I hoped she did. And soon.

"I really do love you," Riley said with a smirk as he tightened his embrace around Paige's shoulders. "Even if it seems a little fast to you."

"I know." She lifted herself up onto her toes and placed a gentle kiss on his mouth. My cock twitched and began to fill. Was it strange that I loved seeing my lovers kiss? That it turned me on? That I wasn't jealous? That their joy made me happy? If so, then fuck it. I'd be strange.

"I guess it's true what they say." I moved my hand up Paige's back to roll her hair around my fist. Standing there with both my lovers in my arms, I felt on top of the world. "When it's right, you don't need months and years to figure it out. You know right away."

"Indeed." Riley smirked, and his beautiful brown eyes danced. He reached behind Paige's legs and back, scooping her up into his arms.

She squealed with delight. "Oh my God. You'll pull a muscle."

Riley snorted. "I may not be as built as Carter, but I can carry my woman into the bedroom."

"*Our* woman," I shouted as I raced ahead into the bedroom, shucked my bathrobe, and stretched out on Paige's bed.

"Our woman," Riley echoed. Seconds later, he deposited Paige beside me on the mattress. His eyes landed on the teddy bear on her dresser. "You kept it," he said to Paige, joy in his voice.

"Of course I did. *You* gave it to me."

"That means you didn't give up on me. Or us."

"I guess a part of me was hoping it wasn't over."

I cut in. "Now I feel bad that I didn't give you a gift too."

She stared at me, her full lips curving into a lascivious smile. "You're a gift all by yourself. You look like Sunday brunch laid out like that." As she spoke, she traced a finger up my leg. Her heated gaze and her touch moving impossibly closer to my cock made me shiver. "All muscles, tan, and that cat-who-got-the-cream grin."

"Hey," Riley said. "Am I not a gift too?"

Paige and I looked at him, then at each other. "I don't think your swollen ego needs any more stroking," I said.

"Speaking of swollen…" Riley groaned, his eyes dropping below my waist. "I want to lick you all over."

My cock, rock solid against my abs, bounced in invitation. "Be my guest," I ground out, my voice strangled by desire.

"I'll take the top," Paige said, and without a word, Riley hopped onto the foot of the bed. His gaze locked on mine, he raised one of my feet and began to suck on my toes, one at a time from the smallest to the largest.

I melted into the mattress. My back arched and a moan ripped from my chest. "Oh Christ."

Beside me, Paige made a mewling sound. Her thighs pressed against each other and I smelled the distinct scent of her arousal. I cracked open an eye. "Strip, beautiful," I ordered her.

With trembling fingers, she pulled off her T-shirt, revealing her gorgeous, full breasts, which swung freely when she bent over to remove her pants. But being braless wasn't the only surprise Paige had for us. "Fuck me," I muttered, looking at Riley.

His eyes met mine.

"Commando," we said in unison. Paige might not know how that affected me, but Riley certainly did. Jeez, I'd be in for quite the ride with these two.

Naked at last, Paige placed a knee on the bed and crawled up to kneel at my side. She leaned over me, and oh-so slowly brought her mouth closer to mine, hovering above it for an excruciatingly long moment, before finally pressing, touching. I sighed out my pleasure at her taste, the warmth of her firm lips tugging on mine just as Riley pulled on my toes, swirling his tongue around and between them. Fuck. If they didn't slow down, I was going to come in minutes.

Paige's small hands moved lightly over my chest. Her fingers traced my ribs, my abs. She kissed along my jaw, nibbling and biting her way down my neck, tasting my tendons and collarbone. I squirmed under her ministrations, dying for someone to touch my cock. My hands ran up and down her spine, and occasionally, I eased a finger between her ass cheeks, trying to spur her along a downward path. But that wasn't to be. Although I made her shiver, she persisted. Her pink tongue pointed out of her mouth, and with a mischievous glance at my face, she flicked it against my nipple. When it peaked, she bit down gently, then alternated between the two.

In no time at all, I couldn't take it anymore. "Come here," I called to her, my voice thick. Grasping her hips, I turned her and pulled her over me so she straddled my head. And there they were, those sweet bits of flesh that could drive me to my knees.

Taking hold of her ass, I raised my head, ready to play, but again, she had other plans. My breath stuttered in my chest as her warm, wet tongue speared my navel, swirling around, then dipping into it. Jesus. And then Riley's head disappeared and my cock was engulfed in the cavern of his hot mouth. "Oh fuck, Rye," I whimpered. Yes, I whimpered. And who could blame me? Riley was a cock-sucking superstar who knew exactly how and when to put his talents to good use.

Inches from my nose, temptation beckoned. The scent of Paige's glistening pussy tickled my senses as a fresh wave of arousal hit her. Unwilling to resist any longer, I parted her lips and swiped my tongue over her clit.

"Oh, oh. Wow!" she cried, pressing herself against my hands. Licking and sucking her outer lips, I zeroed in on her entrance and penetrated her with my tongue, filling her as deeply as I could. Her tangy taste exploded on my tongue, causing me to thrust my hips.

Riley pulled back, sucking hard as he went. His hand gripped the base of my cock. Paige raised her head from where she'd been nibbling and licking my belly. What were they doing? "Fuck, don't stop," I begged.

Jerking me once, Riley winked at me. "We're just getting started, babe."

Once again, the head of my cock was encased by firm lips and a warm mouth. This time it was Paige's. She ran her tongue around the ridged edge, dipped it into my slit. I bucked against her and cried out, "Oh, Jesus. Yes."

Riley dug one hand into Paige's hair, directing her gently while his other hand gripped my cock and followed Paige's movements as she bobbed up and down. It felt like my entire shaft was buried deep in her mouth, her throat. Fuck, the two of them working in concert, the incredible sensations they were creating, were making me crazy.

Before I could humiliate myself by being a selfish pig, I once again raised my head to return to Paige the pleasure she was giving me. I'd take care of Riley later. For now, though, I concentrated on the delicious treat before me. Sucking her clit into my mouth, I flicked it with the tip of my tongue, varying the rhythm and pressure. Her increasingly loud moans and the rocking of her hips told me all I needed to know.

As I was about to insert a finger into her pussy, she released my cock. She looked at Riley, then back at me over her shoulder. "Not like this." I stilled and took my mouth off her. Even as shudders wracked her body, she swung her leg over me to sit by my hip. "I want you inside me." Her lips pursed. She closed her eyes briefly, then opened them again, with more determination shining from those gorgeous hazel orbs. "Both of you."

Riley patted my thigh. "Hop on. When Carter's done, I'll take you."

"No," she said. "You misunderstood me. I want you, both of you"—she swung her head from Riley to me—"at the same time."

Riley looked at me, raising his brow. I knew what he was asking. Whenever we'd shared a woman, we'd quickly negotiated who would take her how. A questioning look was all it had taken.

But this time the arched brow and the cocky tilt to Riley's lips set me on fire. And the opportunity to tease him was too good to pass up. "Riley should take the back, since he… uh…"

Riley's grin fell and his eyes narrowed. "Watch it, fucker."

Paige's gaze darted between us. "Is there a problem?"

"No," Riley said quickly, rubbing his hand along her arm. "Carter's just being a dick."

I smirked. "Not my fault Little Carter is a bit bigger than Little Riley."

"Oh!" Paige's eyebrows popped and her hand went to her mouth as she caught on to the teasing.

"It's fucking proportional, all right?" Riley muttered.

I blew him a kiss. "It's so damn hot when my Riley is all riled up." I sat up and pulled him to me, crushing his mouth in a wild kiss. It felt like ages instead of only days since we'd been together. Truth was, I couldn't live without him… or Paige for that matter. Not anymore. And even if I could, I didn't want to.

This right here, the three of us, connected, in love, making love, this was what I wanted. Now and forever.

PAIGE

Could I truly be enough for Riley and Carter? They were everything I'd ever wanted, but didn't think I'd ever have. Nothing in my life had come close to what I experienced sexually and emotionally when I was with them. I loved seeing my men like this, razzing each other, laughing and roughhousing. Their teasing was sexy, and something I'd never been a part of before.

Sex with Dylan had been full of hormonal angst and intense attempts to "do it right." My orgasm had never been a guarantee, nor had it been something my ex strove to help me achieve. I'd had a little better luck with a couple of the men I'd dated later on.

But Riley and Carter took me to another freakin' dimension.

Riley climbed off the bed and reached into his suitcase, extracting a box of condoms and some lubricant. He pulled on Carter's legs, tugging him closer to the end of the bed, and handed him a condom. "Suit up, Gigantasaurus Rex."

Carter beamed, and despite my ever-increasing nerves, I laughed. Life with these two was going to be so much fun.

Still on his back, Carter rolled the condom over his shaft. When Riley motioned for me to open my hand, I did, and he squeezed some lubricant onto my palm and pointed to Carter. "Slick him up, and when you're ready, climb on board."

I choked out a laugh. "So romantic." I tried to appear calm on the outside, but inside, my heart was hammering in my chest. Could I go through with this? I'd had their fingers in my bottom, though they were far smaller than their... Eyeing Carter's erection, I shivered, imagining how it would feel to have him inside me there. Would it hurt? Riley had seemed to enjoy it when Carter had taken him.

Reaching out, I gripped Carter's shaft, relishing the heft of it in my palm. Slowly, I eased my hand up and down the silky length, massaging the engorged head each time I reached the top.

After wiping my hands on the sheets, I swung a leg over Carter's waist and leaned forward, positioning myself so his erection slid between my folds. He groaned and placed his hands on my breasts, pinching my nipples between his fingers. My belly tensed as renewed arousal pooled at the apex of my thighs.

When Carter bent his knees and drew his legs farther apart, I thought it was to give himself more leverage to thrust against me. That was until I heard the deep guttural groan that rumbled from his chest. A flush raced up his neck and reddened his cheeks, and with glazed eyes, he watched Riley over my shoulder.

"God, Rye. Fucking move," he complained.

I whipped my head around and sucked in a breath. Riley stood at the foot of the bed, his erection half buried in Carter's bottom. One of Carter's legs rested on Riley's shoulder, while the other, Riley held away from his body with a hand on Carter's muscled thigh. The man was splayed open, bared to Riley's view... and now mine.

Riley's gaze met mine and locked.

He looked gorgeous and powerful as he penetrated Carter more fully with a swing of his hips. His shaft disappeared with each forward movement, Carter's hole gripping it tightly. Desire speared through me, setting my flesh on fire. My own bottom clenched with a deep-seated need to be filled.

When an involuntary moan escaped my lips, Riley reached between my legs to grip Carter's shaft. "Take him in, sweetheart. Let Carter feel what I felt last time we were all together."

Shifting to face Carter, who had stopped playing with my breasts, I lifted my hips up and lowered myself over his thick erection. My muscles stretched with each additional inch, and there were many, until he was fully inside me.

"Oh, God," I said, reaching for Carter. Heat radiated from my core as I flushed and trembled, overwhelmed by the depth of his penetration.

Carter pulled me down until I was resting on his chest. "You feel so damn good, Paige," he whispered. Capturing my lips in a searing kiss, he explored every surface of my mouth with his tongue in an erotic dance that left me breathless.

Hands parting my butt cheeks startled me out of the kiss. Carter smiled. "Relax. Let Riley get you ready."

My belly quivered with fear and, yes, with anticipation too. "Hold me?" I asked Carter.

"Always."

When a finger slipped inside my bottom, I hissed and Carter kissed me again. It was slow, sweet, and incredibly tender. My heart ached with love for him. And pretty soon, my vision blurred with tears.

Carter pulled back and searched my face. He must have found what he was looking for, because he slid his arms down my back to grip my bottom. With one cheek in each hand, he squeezed and ground against me, even as a second finger entered me.

Our movements began to take on a rhythm, one echoed in Carter's groans. Peeking over my shoulder, I saw that Riley was still inside Carter. "You're surprisingly coordinated," I said, biting back a moan as he pushed a third finger into me.

He grinned. "It gets even better."

Riley gently moved his fingers in and out, shivers tearing through me at the decadent sensations his touch aroused. I could barely concentrate. Still, there was something I needed to understand. "I thought you were a bottom."

"I'm many things."

"But always..." Carter's words were interrupted by a grunt as Riley gave a sharp thrust. "...in command. Bottoming isn't about being submissive. As you've no doubt noticed, Riley's the dominant partner, regardless of what position he takes."

Carter's assertion took me back to the erroneous conclusions I'd made that day at the spa. I'd assumed, because of his size and because he'd been the one to "pitch" as it were, that Carter was the dominant partner. Boy, had I gotten things twisted around.

"You got it, babe." Riley smoothed his free hand down Carter's raised leg and lightly squeezed his sac.

Carter's reaction was explosive. His back arched despite my weight pressing him into the mattress. "Stop. Oh, God. Stop. You're gonna make me come."

Relenting, Riley gripped the base of Carter's shaft and held it tightly. His knuckles pressed against my clitoris in a way I was certain was no accident. I pushed down on his hand and moaned at the additional pressure. It felt heavenly.

"Please, Riley," I begged. "I need you now."

Riley pulled out of Carter, who grumbled his dissatisfaction as he lowered his feet to the bed. Grinning, Riley gave a little tug to Carter's sac, eliciting another groan from him. Then he tore off the condom to quickly replace it with a fresh one, which he generously slathered with lubricant.

Holding my shoulders, Carter turned me around. "Ready?" he asked, concern evident in his eyes.

I lowered myself to fully rest against his chest and brought my lips next to his ear. "Will it hurt?" I whispered.

"A little at first. Breathe through it and try to keep your ass as relaxed as possible."

With one hand at my back and the other around my waist, Carter cradled me against him. His lips touched my neck where he nibbled the spot under my ear that drove me mad.

At the same time, I began to feel an intense pressure in my bottom.

"Breathe," Carter reminded me.

I struggled to obey him and directed my focus on his jaw. On his ear. I bit and licked, lavishing him with my love.

There was a sharp pain, and then relief, followed by the most curious sliding sensation, and then I felt the warmth of Riley's flesh against my bottom and back. "Is this it?" I asked between gasps.

"Now is when the fun starts," Riley said into my ear. His cheek brushed my earlobe, and I could tell he was smiling.

"How do you feel?" Carter asked.

Biting my lip, I took a moment to evaluate my body. Both men were completely buried inside me. It was extraordinary really. I'd never felt so full before. So close to anyone else. "Like I'm going to explode if one of you doesn't start moving," I said as the sensations became too much. My urgent tone had them both chuckling. Not at all the response I was hoping for.

Riley held me tightly as he withdrew from me almost completely, then sank into me again. There was that odd gliding, then the feeling of being full to bursting.

"Your turn," Riley said to Carter.

Inhaling deeply, Carter first withdrew, then pressed on my lower back as he pushed back up into me. My breath cut off sharply when the head of his erection rubbed against something deep inside me. The pleasure arrowing through my body was stronger, more intense than usual.

Wide-eyed, I raised my head and looked at Carter. "Oh wow."

Riley lightly slapped my bottom. "And that's just the start, sweetheart."

"There's more?"

"Oh yeah." Carter's eyes sparkled. "Hold on."

Not wanting to disappoint, I clutched his shoulders and forced myself to stay loose, ready for anything my two lovers did to me.

The wait was short. Riley pulled out while Carter pushed in, and then they reversed directions. I could feel them moving inside me, bringing life to nerve-endings in places I didn't know existed.

"Oh! Oh!" I cried out as mind-numbing bliss consumed me. Although my eyes were open, I couldn't see anything. My entire existence was centered on my body and the delicious feelings flooding me.

A finger circled my clitoris, then pressed against it. And before I knew it, I was flying. Worlds collided. Colors exploded. My body contracted around the two shafts filling me so utterly, so completely.

Carter let out a deep grunt, and Riley's warmth covered my back. His hands left my hips and locked onto Carter's biceps. He pushed into me again. His warm breath feathered my shoulder as he moaned, the sound triggering another delicious aftershock that left me a quivering mess.

Carter's arms reached around Riley's back, and with me sandwiched between the two men, they kissed. Their shafts, separated only by the thinnest of barriers, connected within me and pulsed as Carter and Riley orgasmed. I was one with them, surrounded and filled by them. My heart swelled and tears flooded my eyes.

I wasn't alone anymore. I was theirs. Carter, Riley, and I were a team, a trio, a triad. We shared an invisible bond, one stronger than I'd ever thought possible.

Reaching back, I cupped Riley's nape with one hand and gripped Carter's hair with the other. "You two are the best thing to ever happen to me. I'm so lucky to have you in my life." A lump formed in my throat, and I sniffed back more tears. "I know long-distance relationships are hard, but... could we please give it a try?"

Riley chuckled and lightly kissed my shoulder. Carter slid his hands up and down my sides. "We're not leaving," Riley said.

"You're not?"

"Nope." Carter grinned. "You're stuck with us."

"Oh my God."

"Will you have us?" Riley asked, and I hated the hesitation and uncertainty in his voice.

"Of course! How could you think otherwise?" Although I asked the question, I knew the answer. I'd caused his lack of confidence by leaving him and Carter in London. Even if it took years to make up for it, I'd try. I never wanted either of them to doubt my love or my commitment to our relationship. Never again.

Riley rocked his hips, making both me and Carter moan. "Just checking," he said, sounding amused. Very gently, he pulled out of me and tossed the used condom into the trash can beside the nightstand.

Carter rolled over and slowly disengaged. He brushed a few strands of hair off my face. "Are you okay?"

God, I loved how caring he was. Thoughtful, kind, and gentle. Whether with me or Riley, and there was no doubt in my mind he'd be the same with Emma, Carter was ever the caretaker.

I smiled at him and Riley, who lay down on my other side. “Never better,” I said, never having meant anything more.

Chapter 16

RILEY

After holing up in Paige's apartment for a week, I was chomping at the bit to get outside, go places, do things. The paparazzi hadn't located me yet, but it was only a matter of time, and I really didn't want to put Paige or Carter through that nightmare again. But I couldn't stay in Paige's apartment forever either.

My phone rang, and seeing the number, I scrambled to answer. The day after my arrival in Miami, I had contacted a real estate agent who had a reputation for working with celebrities and of being above reproach in protecting and maintaining her clients' privacy.

"Mr. Kendrick," the agent said. "This is Barbara Longwood. I found something I think will be perfect for you and your unique… uh… situation."

"Great," I said, trying to hold back my enthusiasm and impart at least a modicum of professionalism. "Tell me about it."

"It's a four-bedroom, four-bath, two-story penthouse, with formal dining room, private deck and hot tub. There's also a gym and a swimming pool in the building, as well as twenty-four-hour security at the entrance." I heard the clicking of a keyboard, and then Barbara added, "I've just sent you the details. Take a look at the photos and let me know what you think."

I navigated to my inbox and opened the email from Barbara. I clicked on the link and thumbed through the photos. It was perfect. Somehow, Barbara had found a place that met all of my numerous requirements and then some. "When can I see it?"

"That's where things get complicated. The owner is leaving the country on business in a couple days and will be away for several months. He'd be relieved to sell before then, so if you were to make a good offer right now, it would be almost a sure thing."

I'd seen the address on the listing and it was nearby. "I can be there in thirty minutes."

"With your partners?"

I swallowed against the tightness in my throat at the complete lack of judgment in Barbara's voice. I knew what I was getting into. I knew it wouldn't always be easy. But people like her gave me hope. "Yes. Of course."

"Wonderful."

I ended the call and left the bedroom to find the two loves of my life. "Paige, Carter, let's go. I've got a surprise for you."

Paige poked her head out of the kitchen. "What? Where?"

Her wide-eyed owl expression made me laugh. "Come with me and you'll see."

"What's going on?" Carter asked, sitting up on the couch and rubbing the sleep from his eyes.

He looked so adorable, I had to kiss him. "When did you become such a sleepyhead?"

"Since I started living with the two of you," Carter pretend-grumbled. "Even the Energizer Bunny couldn't keep up."

Paige joined us and circled her arms around both our necks. "It seems Riley has a surprise for us."

"Oh?" Carter's brow arched.

"And I'm not telling, no matter what you do."

"Not even if we—" Carter lunged forward and tickled my waist with both hands, while Paige set upon my armpits and thighs.

"Oh God, oh God," I cried. Laughing, I turned and twisted, trying desperately to get away from their hands, those four weapons of torture. When I tripped and fell to the floor, they straddled my body, pinning me down.

"Spill," Carter said in his most commanding voice.

"No!"

Paige slid her small hand along my thigh to cup my cock and balls. She squeezed gently. "Tell us."

"Never."

"Squeeze harder," Carter ordered. The sparkle in his blue eyes belied the grim tone of his voice.

Chuckling, Paige firmed her hold, but shook her head. "No, I can't do it. I like what he's got there too much to do it harm."

I sighed dramatically. "Thank fuck."

"Fine," Carter pouted. "Should I kiss your boo-boo, you big baby?"

"Yes, yes you should." My cock hardened at the mere thought of Carter's gorgeous mouth stretched around my shaft. "But..." I exhaled sharply, trying to wrap my brain around the fact that I was about to turn down sex. What had happened to me? When had I become so fucking mature? "We can't right now." Nudging Carter off me, I rose and held my hand out to help Paige to her feet, then Carter. "We have somewhere to be."

Twenty minutes later, we entered Admiral Place. "Good afternoon, sir," a man in a guard's uniform greeted us.

"Hi," I said. "Here to meet Mrs. Longwood."

The guard checked the list and nodded, before walking over to the elevator. He pressed the button. When the doors opened, he slid a card through the reader on the number pad inside and pressed PH2. "Have a good visit," he said, stepping back.

The chrome and glass elevator with light gold walls and black carpeting shouted money, something Paige was clearly noticing as well. Her brow furrowed. "Where are we, Riley?"

"You'll see."

Not satisfied with my response, she turned to Carter, who simply shrugged and pulled her against his chest. "Just go with it. Riley's surprises are usually good."

Her gaze flicked to me. "I guess I need to get used to not always being the one making decisions."

"No," I said. "You'll be making the decisions. We will. Together."

She pressed her hand to my cheek. "I like the sound of that."

Carter patted her ass with one hand and mine with the other. "I like the things we do together."

Paige giggled and stepped away, while I pushed my ass harder against Carter's hand. When Carter lightly shoved me away, I crossed my arms and glared. "You shouldn't start what you can't finish."

"Who says—"

The elevator pinged and the doors opened.

I straightened my shirt and ushered Paige and Carter into Penthouse Number Two, the building's top-floor condo.

"Oh." Paige's hand went to her chest as she slowly turned in a circle, taking in the marbled entrance. "This is beautiful."

Barbara appeared at the end of the hallway. "Mr. Kendrick, please come in. All of you."

I shook Barbara's hand, then prepared to make the introductions, my stomach flipping. "Mrs. Longwood, this is my boyfriend, Carter Templeton, and our girlfriend, Paige Sutherland."

The words fell from my lips, a bumbling mixture of pride and joy, and trepidation. It was the first time I'd said the words, the first time I'd introduced Carter and Paige as my boyfriend and girlfriend at the same time.

A flush stained Paige's cheeks. She held out her hand. "It's a pleasure to meet you, Barbara."

After Carter shook hands with her as well, Barbara beamed. "I can tell you'll all be so happy here."

Paige's brows popped up. "Here?" She turned to look at me.

"Let's have a look around." I placed my hand at the small of her back and motioned Carter forward.

The entire duration of the tour, I barely managed to keep myself in check. The penthouse was exactly what we needed. There'd be space for a private gym and an office, and even a room for Emma so she could stay with us whenever she wanted. Then there was the oversized balcony with its view of Miami and the Atlantic Ocean. I could already imagine long romantic evenings of making love in the dying sunlight.

When we made our way back to the living room, Barbara clutched her hands. "So? It's wonderful, isn't it?"

Paige bit her lip and Carter shoved his hands into his pockets. My heart hammered. "Thank you, Mrs. Longwood. May we have a few minutes, please?"

"Of course," she said. "I'll wait for you in the lobby." She slipped out and quietly closed the door to the penthouse behind her.

"What's going on, Riley?" Carter asked.

I wrapped my arms around myself. Christ. I felt like a teenager lying to my parents about going to a party. Which was foolish. I had nothing to hide. No reason to be scared or ashamed. Unless… they weren't at the same point as I was in our common path.

Paige blinked rapidly and turned away. She opened her arms. "Are you planning to buy this place, Riley?"

"Yes."

"Oh, okay." She took another step away, then stopped and shook her head. "No. It's not okay." She spun around to face me. "So that's it? The experiment's over, just like that?"

"No… what?" All words and thoughts fled my brain under the impact of Paige's words and Carter's glower.

"What the fuck, Riley? You're planning to move out and you didn't even think to discuss it with us first?"

"So much for making decisions together," Paige added, stepping up to Carter's side.

I plunged my fingers into my hair. Fuck! How had they gotten the wrong impression? "That's not it at all. Okay, I do want to move out, but

I want *all* of us to move out, or rather, to move in. Here. Together."

"You want to live here?" Paige smirked. "I won't make enough money in my entire life to be able to afford my share."

"Neither will I," Carter grumbled. "Especially now that I'm freshly unemployed."

"I know, I know," I pleaded. "I love Paige's apartment. The problem is... well..." Shit. No matter how I said it, I'd sound like a pompous ass. "Look, I'm famous, okay? The paparazzi and the fans haven't found me yet, but that's only because I haven't left Paige's place all week. I can't live like that long-term."

Carter cupped Paige's shoulders and his gaze met mine over her head. "I get that, especially now that the movie is out and it's a hit." He slowly scanned what we could see of the penthouse. "It's beautiful for sure." He closed his eyes. "But..."

Paige stared at me. "We can't afford it."

"But *I* can."

"So what?" Paige huffed out. "Are we going to be a kept man and woman? Do you have any idea how that will look?"

I stepped closer and ran my hands down her arms. When she stiffened under my touch, my heart cracked. "What's the alternative?" I asked softly. "Celebrity, or even being involved with one, has a price, and this is it. I need the security this place offers. *We* need it." I searched their faces, blinking back the burning in my eyes. "I hope that price isn't too high for you, both of you."

Carter's hand landed on my shoulder, warm and heavy. Comforting. "I get it, Rye. We'll have to find ways for Paige and me to feel like this is our place too."

"Yes, of course. I want this to be *our* home. Not just mine. Look, I'd live anywhere as long as you were both there. But it wouldn't be safe. The last thing I want is for either of you, or Emma, to be in danger because of me."

"Emma?" Paige asked.

"Yes. I thought the room down the hall from the master would be perfect for her... I know she lives in the group home, but she could stay with us on holidays, vacations, and weekends, or whenever she wants."

Emotions welled in Paige's eyes. "Emma figured into your decision?"

I took her hand in mine. "Of course. Your daughter is a part of you, so she's a part of me too. Of us, our family. She'd be welcome here as often as you want. That room would be hers and hers alone."

Paige threw her arms around my neck. "You are the perfect man, you know that?"

"Nah," I said, returning her embrace. "I'm far from it."

"Hey." Carter surrounded us with his arms. "I think I should be jealous."

I snorted. "You're not?"

"No, because I agree. We're perfect together."

"Come here," I said, my voice gruff. We shared a three-way kiss, sealing the deal, and my heart soared. Never before had I been so happy, so sure of the future. And it was due to these two people: my muses, my lovers, my everything. "What do you say we go sign on the dotted line?"

"We?" Carter asked and Paige echoed.

I nodded. "*Our* home. It's my gift to both of you."

"Oh God. I didn't think I could love you so much." Paige wrapped her arms around my waist.

Carter grinned. "I didn't think I could love you more."

Paige groaned. "This competitive thing is going to take some getting used to."

"Oh, I don't know," I teased. "It sure comes in handy in bed."

"Is sex all you men think about?" she asked with fake exasperation.

Carter and I locked eyes. "Yep," we said, tumbling her down to the floor.

The penthouse needed christening, and we were just the triad to do it.

CONTINUE THE ADVENTURE!

Hello, Vanessa here! Want to be part of our VIP Readers list and get all the behind-the-scenes scoop about what *really* happens at Total Indulgence? Want to be part of our ARC team? Sign up at www.totalindulgencetours.com.

If Facebook is more your style, join our Total Indulgence VIP Readers' Lounge!

www.facebook.com/groups/
totalindulgencevipreaderslounge

We hope you enjoyed "coming" along on our Jolly Old England Romance Writers' Retreat trip, where we saw the sights of England and Scotland and the insides of many bedrooms, courtesy of my boss Paige and the always hunky Riley and Carter. RAWR!

If you loved our little romp, please give us a thumbs-up review. We're not on Yelp yet, but we are on Amazon and Goodreads!

Oh, I have the best news! You remember the band, King's Cross, that played at the Cavern Club? Well, we've planned an adventure for them, and it's in Tahiti. Six hot guys in small bathing suits—I'm sooo there!

Keep reading for a special preview of *Her Two Men in Tahiti*!

A SPECIAL PREVIEW OF *HER TWO MEN IN TAHITI* (TOTAL INDULGENCE, BOOK 2)

Three hearts face the music…

They've haunted my dreams since the last time we hooked up. Two hot British rock stars who spent a week devoting themselves to my pleasure. I never thought I'd see them again. Yet here we are in Tahiti, trying to keep their band, King's Cross, from fracturing. But how can I help, when I'm at the heart of their problems?

SKY

I left them to save them, but I nearly destroyed myself in the process. Can my heart survive doing it all over again?

ROD

I had them, for one brief week before it all fell apart. Now she's gone, and he's rejected me one too many times. How can I be around him every day, when he reminds me of everything I've lost?

DEV

I had a glimpse of happiness, but it came in the form of all I knew to be wrong. I was raised to deny what my heart so desperately wants. How much longer can I go on this way?

Warning: Contains an abundance of creative British swear words, oiled-up men wrestling on the beach, wild monkey sex in a tree house, and the worst of intentions leading to the ultimate in satisfaction.

SKY

I awoke slowly to the heaven I'd been in for the past week: smack dab between two hot rock stars: Rod "Hot Rod" Taylor and Dev Stone of King's Cross. *British* rock stars, no less. For some reason, they'd taken a "fancy" to my American accent while we were working together and invited me to take a wild "holiday" together. Me, Sklyar River, struggling life coach and team building facilitator.

I didn't know what I was doing here, other than having the best sex of my life. Rod and Dev were intense and fun and wild—well, Rod more so than Dev. Rod had initiated our little threesome, and Dev and I had eagerly joined in.

Dev was on my left and Rod on my right, both of them nestled against me, Dev's short black hair in disarray, his golden brown skin so dark against mine. Last night he'd said he was never letting me go, and Rod had echoed the sentiment.

Me. They wanted *me*. Two rock stars, who could have anyone.

I told them I had to think about it. But I was done thinking; I was all in. As crazy as it was, I loved them, and I would do whatever it took to be with them, including giving up my business in San Francisco.

Rod stirred against me, his right hand still cupping my breast, the one with the little freckle near the nipple. He'd named it Beatrice—the freckle, that is. I'd asked him why and he'd shrugged. "It just looks like a Beatrice."

That was Rod for you—kind of silly under his ultra-glam rock star exterior. He was the kind of guy Adam Lambert took styling cues from. Spiky brown hair with blond streaks, guyliner galore. And oh, could he fill out a pair of leather pants. His thick, hard cock pressed into my hip, Dev's in the same state on my other side. Should I wake them up for round one of today's escapades?

I started sliding a hand along Rod's hip, then stopped myself. My bladder was squealing, and if I'd learned anything about Rod and Dev, it was that once we got started, it would be quite a while before we'd stop. Better zip into the bathroom and freshen up, then initiate the festivities.

I carefully crept out of the hotel room bed and into the bathroom. Might as well brush my teeth and shower while I was there.

When I was done, I tried to run a brush through my tangle of dark brown curls, but it was pretty hopeless—I needed some deep conditioning to sort out this snarl. And they'd just mess it up anyway, one or the other of them winding it around his fist and pulling just hard enough to make me wet and achy. A wave of heat ran through me at the memory of last night—Dev in my mouth, Rod buried in my pussy, me writhing between them.

How had I gotten so lucky?

I walked back into the bedroom and stopped short. Dev was spooning Rod, his cock pressed against Rod's firm ass. Interesting. Rod was openly bisexual—"anything sexual" as he put it—but Dev was adamantly straight, or so he'd said. Was there something more between them, something I wasn't supposed to see?

Rod rolled over so he and Dev were face to face, and Dev nuzzled into the crook of Rod's neck and threw a leg over his hip. What the hell?

They looked hot together, and I certainly didn't object to the idea of the two of them being together sexually. But… if they werc, where did that leave me?

The two of them had grown up together. They'd known each other for almost twenty years. They were as close as two people could be and not be married—though in a way they were, because of the band.

Why were they hiding this from me? Didn't they trust me?

Apparently, I was good enough to fuck, but not worthy of being in their confidence.

Dev exhaled loudly, then he murmured, "I love you."

Rod's eyes snapped open. "I never thought I'd hear you say it." He smiled and closed his eyes, tightening his arms around Dev, and my stomach dropped to the floor.

Now I understood why Rod had instigated our threesome. He'd wanted me to be the sexual bridge between him and his straight best friend. He'd used me to get what he really wanted. And now he—they—didn't need me.

My eyes started to burn, but damn it, I wasn't going to cry. They didn't deserve my tears, and they didn't deserve my heart.

I quietly dressed and packed my things, the two of them holding each other in their sleep. A lump in my throat, I snuck out and shut the door, already calling for a ride.

I wiped the damn tears away while I arranged for my taxi.

This was the last time I was going to follow my stupid, foolish heart. It never looked before it leapt.

But I should have known better. Two guys, one girl? It had been too good to be true.

Six Months Later

Rod

I wandered into the photographer's studio a quarter hour late and proper shit-faced. Nigel Standen, the bloke we'd hired to manage King's Cross, gave me the stink eye. But what did the lazy sod expect? The only way I would make it through this fucking nightmare of a photoshoot was to arrive anything but sober.

The photographer, a lush blonde bird with an impressive rack, introduced herself as Zoe while eyeing me up and down. My attire was rock star chic, grungy holed jeans and a leather jacket worn over a ripped and stretched out T-shirt. It was all I'd had time to throw on after an angry call from Nigel pulled me out of the warm arms of Trisha and Tristan.

"Just crawled out of a gutter, mate?" Zoe asked.

"No, just crawled out of bed."

"I suppose it'll have to do," she said, wrinkling her nose. "Let's get started."

My bandmates grunted their hellos while she herded us together in front of a mockup of our new album cover. "A little closer now, please," Zoe instructed.

I ground my teeth and swung a loose arm around Damon Mercury, the newest member of King's Cross, a Yank guitarist we'd recruited at the label's urging to give the band a harder sound. On his other side, flanked by Mick, Jules, and Chet, stood Devkinandan Prakesh, aka Dev Stone, the love of my life, former best mate, eternal enemy, and constant knife in my back.

Damon took a whiff of me. "Dude, you smell like sex. Just how many people were you with last night?"

"Twins. And it was this morning."

"Female?"

I grinned. "One of each."

He held up his fist for me to bump. "Dude. You're my hero."

"All right then," Zoe said, after shooting photos from various angles. "Shirts off."

Dev tossed the photographer a shy smile, then tugged his shirt over his head. I barely managed to bite back a groan, and my mouth went dry at the sight of all that smooth copper skin. His muscles flexed and relaxed, rippling under the glow of the photographer's lights. Zoe's eyes brightened, and Dev hammed it up for her, striking poses like some sort of bodybuilder, the fucking wanker.

Not so long ago, all that flesh, those toned muscles, and so much more had been on display for me. Within my grasp. But when I'd dared to take what was so readily offered, Dev had thrown a strop.

Didn't the tosser understand what he'd done to me? How his rejection had flayed my skin and left me bare. Exposed. Destroyed.

He'd pushed me away. Shamed me.

But never again.

"Rod?"

The photographer frowned at me.

"What?" I snapped.

"Your shirt."

I looked around and saw I was the only one still fully dressed. With a grumble, I removed my jacket and tossed my T-shirt into the corner. It landed on top of Dev's. Fucking Christ. Was that as close as I'd get to him now? How pathetic was I that such a small thing had my cock stirring?

Zoe looked us over and positioned Dev and me in the center, with the other blokes around us. As the lead singer, I was the face of King's Cross, and Dev was the lead guitarist—but fuck, he wasn't anymore. He'd stepped back to rhythm guitar and let Damon take his place. Another thing I was pissed about. He'd probably done it just to get away from me. Dev wrote the music and I wrote the lyrics. That was how it had always been.

We were best mates. Emphasis on "were."

These days, Dev didn't talk to me. We hadn't written the songs we needed for the tour we were kicking off in just a month, not to mention the album we hadn't yet recorded. Nigel was running out of excuses for the delays.

And everyone blamed me.

But was it my fault? I'd always been honest about who I was. My sexuality was out there for everyone to see. And Dev had been my friend throughout it all. Until…

A noise drew my attention. Dev's breath caught in his throat, a sound like the one he made when he came. My eyes shot to his face only to see him transfixed by Zoe. She placed her hand on his shoulder to guide him into position. A flush rose up his chest, then darkened his neck and face.

When she smiled at him, his chest puffed out.

"Zoe," he asked in his sexy-as-fuck East Indian accent. "Are you a fan of the band?"

"Of course." She chuckled. "Who isn't?"

"Who's your favorite?" Damon asked, holding up his arm and flexing his bicep, which made his tattoos seem to come alive.

Her eyes lingered on Dev before she focused on Damon. "Maybe you're my favorite. That's some right proper ink," she said as she moved around us.

Yeah, right. Her favorite was Dev. A blind man could see it. And as much as I wished it right now, I wasn't blind. Dev wanted her too.

And I wanted everyone to shut up and fuck off. We needed to finish this torture session yesterday. My muscles were shaking, maybe from keeping the position too long, or maybe it was the fucking agonies. What I wouldn't give for a couple dexies right about now.

"Rod, give us a smile," Zoe said.

A corner of my lip rose, and she started to laugh. "That's a snarl, love. Try again."

Nigel lifted his heft off the chair he'd been sitting in and grabbed my chin. "Are you high?"

"Not nearly high enough."

Dev sighed and the sound wrapped around my heart. It was suddenly difficult to breathe. We'd always promised each other we wouldn't let the rock star life take over, but that had been *before*. Now I couldn't make it through a day without indulging in one mind-altering substance or another. And on days like today, where I had to see *him*, it was all I could do not to drown.

Nigel shook his head in thinly veiled disgust and returned to his seat like the gormless worm he was. Having given up on me, Zoe turned to Dev and cupped his jaw. Her thumb touched his bottom lip. His gaze shot to me.

I glared back.

He cleared his throat and looked away. But it was no use. I could feel his heat, smell his arousal, and the urge to scream, fight, or fuck took me over.

I couldn't do this.

I couldn't be this close to Dev and not touch him.

I couldn't stand to see him every day and know that he'd never be mine.

Tearing my eyes from his profile, I stepped away from the group. Slowly at first, but as the distance mounted, so did my speed. I snatched my shirt off Dev's, grabbed my jacket, and stormed out of the room, ignoring the calls of my bandmates, of the photographer, and mostly, of Dev.

A hand gripped my arm and spun me around. I stared at it, the dark on my light.

"You can't leave," Dev said, his stormy eyes the color of a muddy lake bottom.

Once again, I tore my gaze away. I couldn't do this if I looked at him, and I had to do this, before it all killed me.

"I quit," I said softly.

Dev's breath caught, and his fingers tightened on my wrist. "You can't."

Anger rose inside me, a boiling cauldron. I ripped my wrist out of his grasp. "I just did."

"Rod, no. Come on, mate. Don't be a prat. King's Cross is your life."

No, Dev. You're *my life.*

"You'll be fine without me."

Flags of crimson marked Dev's dark cheekbones. "Rod, for fuck's sake. Don't throw everything away just because—"

I lowered my voice so only he would hear. "Because my supposed best mate keeps stringing me along, pulling me closer with one hand, and pushing me away with the other? Yeah." I wasn't worried about myself. I was pansexual and proud of it. But it wasn't my place to out Dev to the world. Hell, he wasn't even out to himself.

"I can't give you what you want." His voice broke and he turned his head away from me.

I closed my eyes. "And I can't stand the sight of you."

I spun on my heel and left the studio, deaf to everything except the sound of my heart cracking.

END OF SPECIAL PREVIEW

ABOUT DANA DELAMAR

Dana Delamar is the author of erotic romance, LGBTQ romance, and the "Blood and Honor" romantic suspense series, which is set in Italy among the Calabrian Mafia. Her first book, *Revenge*, received 4 stars from *RT Book Reviews*, was a Top Pick at The Romance Reviews, and was a double-finalist for Best First Book and Best Romantic Suspense in the 2013 Booksellers Best Awards.

Her second book, *Retribution*, received 4 stars from *RT Book Reviews* and was a semi-finalist in the Kindle Book Review's 2013 Best Indie Book Awards. Her book *Malavita* was a quarter-finalist in the 2014 Amazon Breakthrough Novel Awards, and her book *Redemption* was a finalist in the 2014 Maggie Awards and a semi-finalist in the Kindle Book Review's 2014 Best Kindle Book Awards.

Dana is also an editor with over thirty years of editing experience in both fiction and nonfiction and has worked with everyone from newbie writers to experienced pros. The books she's edited have won numerous awards and critical acclaim, including two Top Picks from *RT Book Reviews*.

www.danadelamar.com

ABOUT KRISTINE CAYNE

Kristine Cayne is the author of erotic romance, LGBTQ romance, and romantic suspense. Her books have won numerous awards and acclaim. Her first book, *Deadly Obsession*, was an *RT Book Reviews* Top Pick and won Best Romance in the 2012 eFestival of Words Best of the Independent eBook Awards. Her second book, *Deadly Addiction*, won two awards at the 2014 eFestival of Words and 1st place in the INDIE Awards, Romantic Suspense Category (a division of Chanticleer Book Reviews Blue Ribbon Writing Contests).

Her book *Under His Command* won Best BDSM Romance at the 2012 Sizzling Awards and was a finalist in the 2013 eFestival of Words and 2013 RONE (Reward of Novel Excellence) Awards, and her book *Everything Bared* was a finalist in the Erotic category of the I Heart Indie awards.

www.kristinecayne.com

ALSO BY DANA DELAMAR AND KRISTINE CAYNE

BY DANA DELAMAR

Blood and Honor: A Mafia Romance Series

Malavita (Prequel)
Revenge (Book One)
Retribution (Book Two)
Redemption (Book Three)
Reckoning (Book Four)

BY KRISTINE CAYNE

Six-Alarm Sexy Series: A Firefighter Erotic Romance Series

Aftershocks (Prequel)
Under His Command (Book One)
Everything Bared (Book Two)
Handle with Care (Book Three)
Lover on Top (Book Four)
Baby, Be Mine (Book Five)
Stripped Down (Book Six – coming soon)

Seattle Fire Series
(Six-Alarm Sexy Spin-off)

In His Arms (Book One – coming June 2018)

Men of Boyzville: A Gay Romance Series
(Six-Alarm Sexy Spin-off)

Going All In (Book One)
Wrangling the Cowboy (Book Two – coming soon)

Deadly Vices: A Romantic Suspense Series

Deadly Obsession (Book One)
Deadly Addiction (Book Two)
Deadly Betrayal (Book Three)

Other Works

Guns 'N' Tulips
Un-Valentine's Day
Origins: Men of M.E.R. in *Shadows in the Mist*

Made in the USA
Columbia, SC
04 June 2018